REIGN OF TERROR

BY RAINIMATOR

MORTIMER

Published in 2022 by Mortimer Children's
An Imprint of Welbeck Children's Limited,
part of Welbeck Publishing Group.
Based in London and Sydney.
www.welbeckpublishing.com

First published by Carlton Books in 2019

ISBN: 978 1 83935 189 1

Printed in Dongguan, China
1 3 5 7 9 10 8 6 4 2

Creator: Rain Olaguer
Script: Rain Olaguer and Eddie Robson
Special Consultant: Beau Chance
Design: Jacob Da'Costa, WildPixel and RockJaw Creative
Editorial Manager: Joff Brown
Design Managers: Emily Clarke, Matt Drew and Sam James
Production: Melanie Robertson

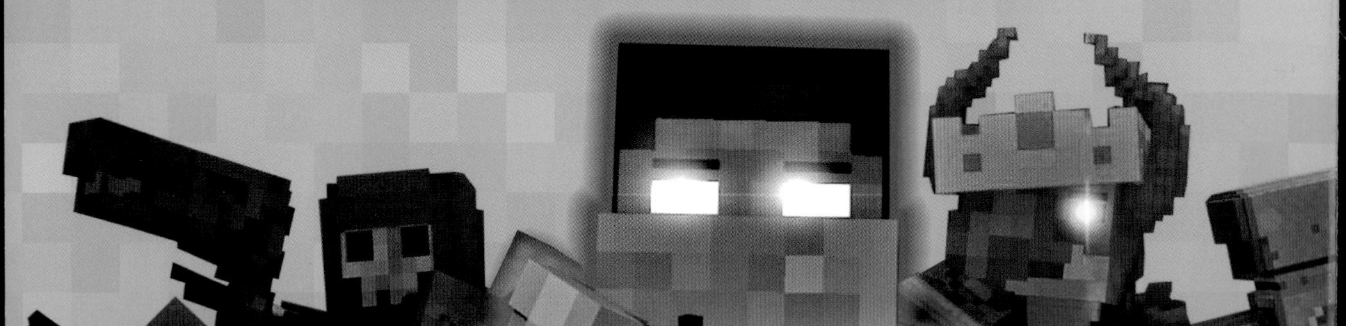

REIGN OF TERROR

BY RAINIMATOR

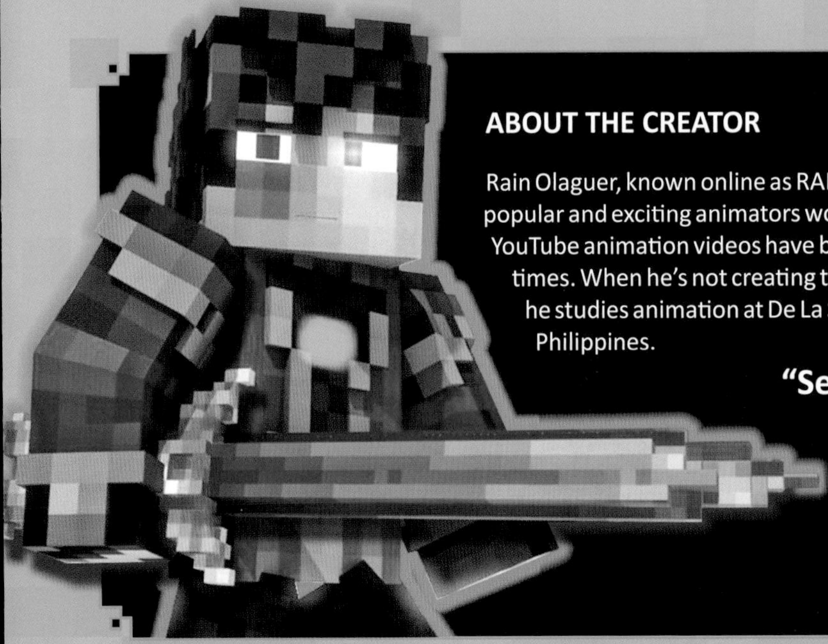

ABOUT THE CREATOR

Rain Olaguer, known online as RAINIMATOR, is one of the most popular and exciting animators working today. His amazing YouTube animation videos have been viewed over 125 million times. When he's not creating the latest chapter in his epic saga, he studies animation at De La Salle College of St. Benilde in the Philippines.

"Seeing the stories I've written come to life is my passion."

MORTIMER

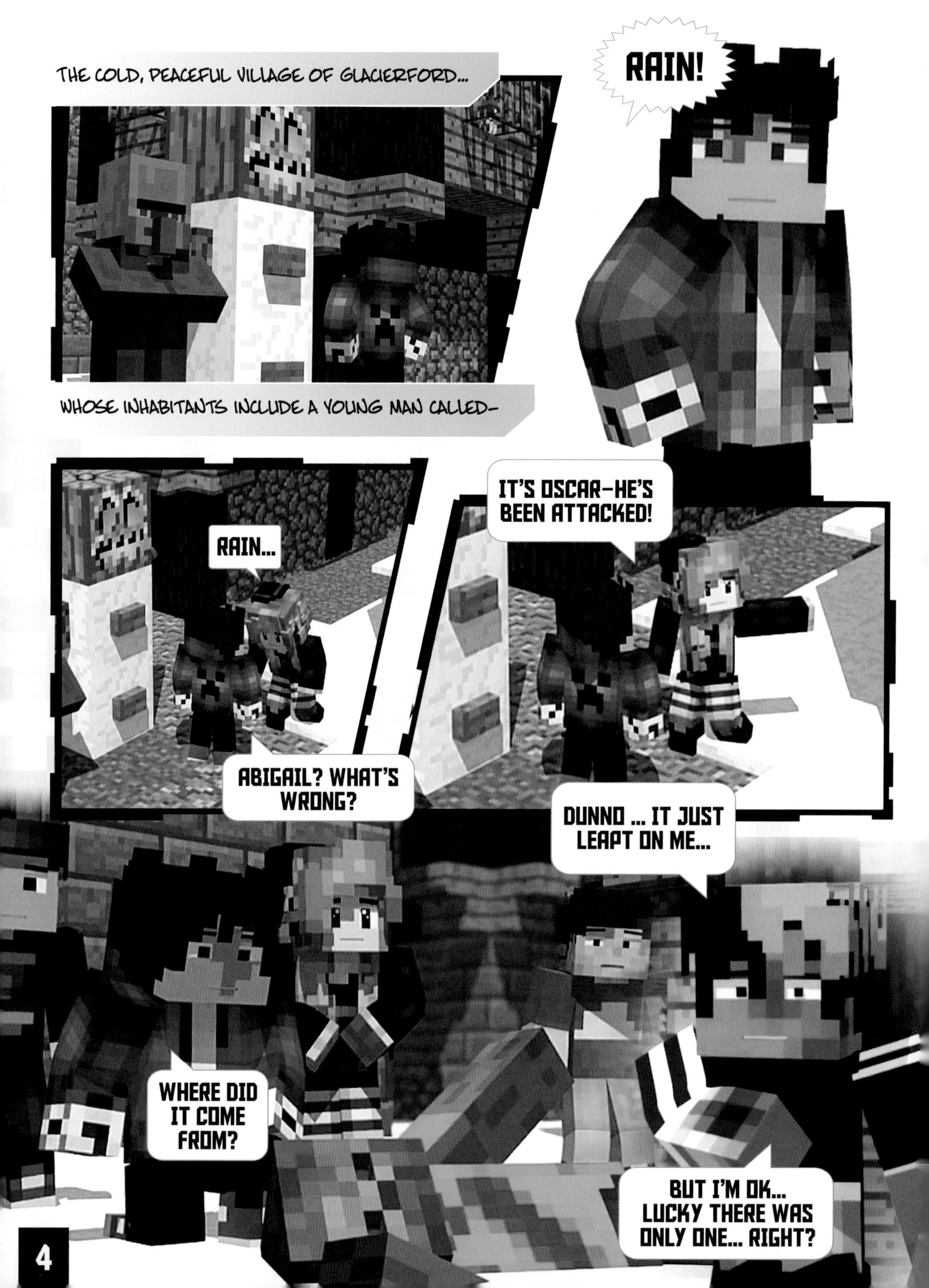
THE COLD, PEACEFUL VILLAGE OF GLACIERFORD...
WHOSE INHABITANTS INCLUDE A YOUNG MAN CALLED-
RAIN!
RAIN...
ABIGAIL? WHAT'S WRONG?
IT'S OSCAR-HE'S BEEN ATTACKED!
DUNNO ... IT JUST LEAPT ON ME...
WHERE DID IT COME FROM?
BUT I'M OK... LUCKY THERE WAS ONLY ONE... RIGHT?

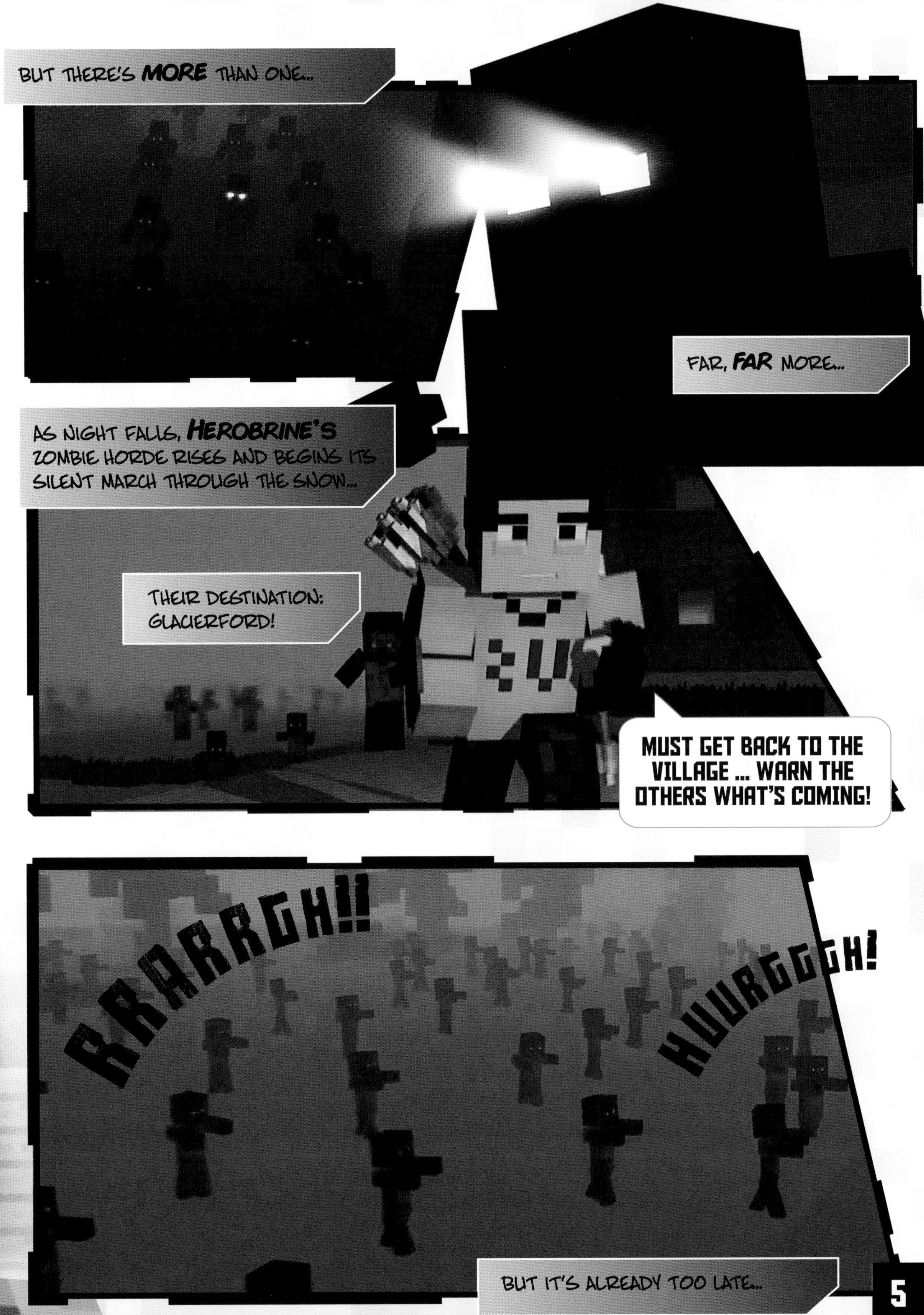
BUT THERE'S MORE THAN ONE...
FAR, FAR MORE...
AS NIGHT FALLS, HEROBRINE'S ZOMBIE HORDE RISES AND BEGINS ITS SILENT MARCH THROUGH THE SNOW...
THEIR DESTINATION: GLACIERFORD!
MUST GET BACK TO THE VILLAGE ... WARN THE OTHERS WHAT'S COMING!
RRRARRGH!!
HUURGGGH!
BUT IT'S ALREADY TOO LATE...

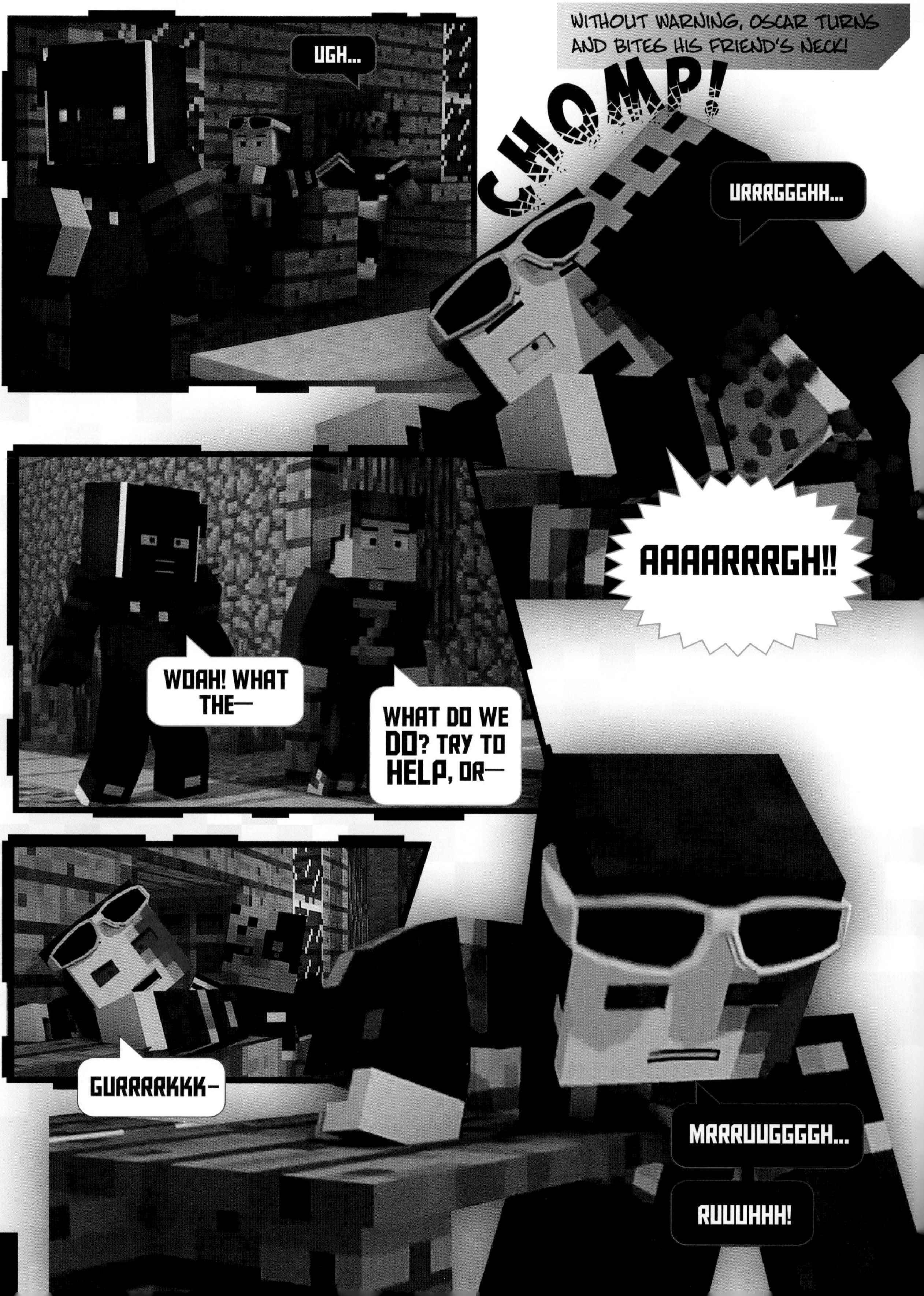

UGH...
WITHOUT WARNING, OSCAR TURNS AND BITES HIS FRIEND'S NECK!
CHOMP!
URRRGGGHH...
AAAARRRGH!!
WOAH! WHAT THE—
WHAT DO WE DO? TRY TO HELP, OR—
GURRRRKKK-
MRRRUUGGGGH...
RUUUHHH!

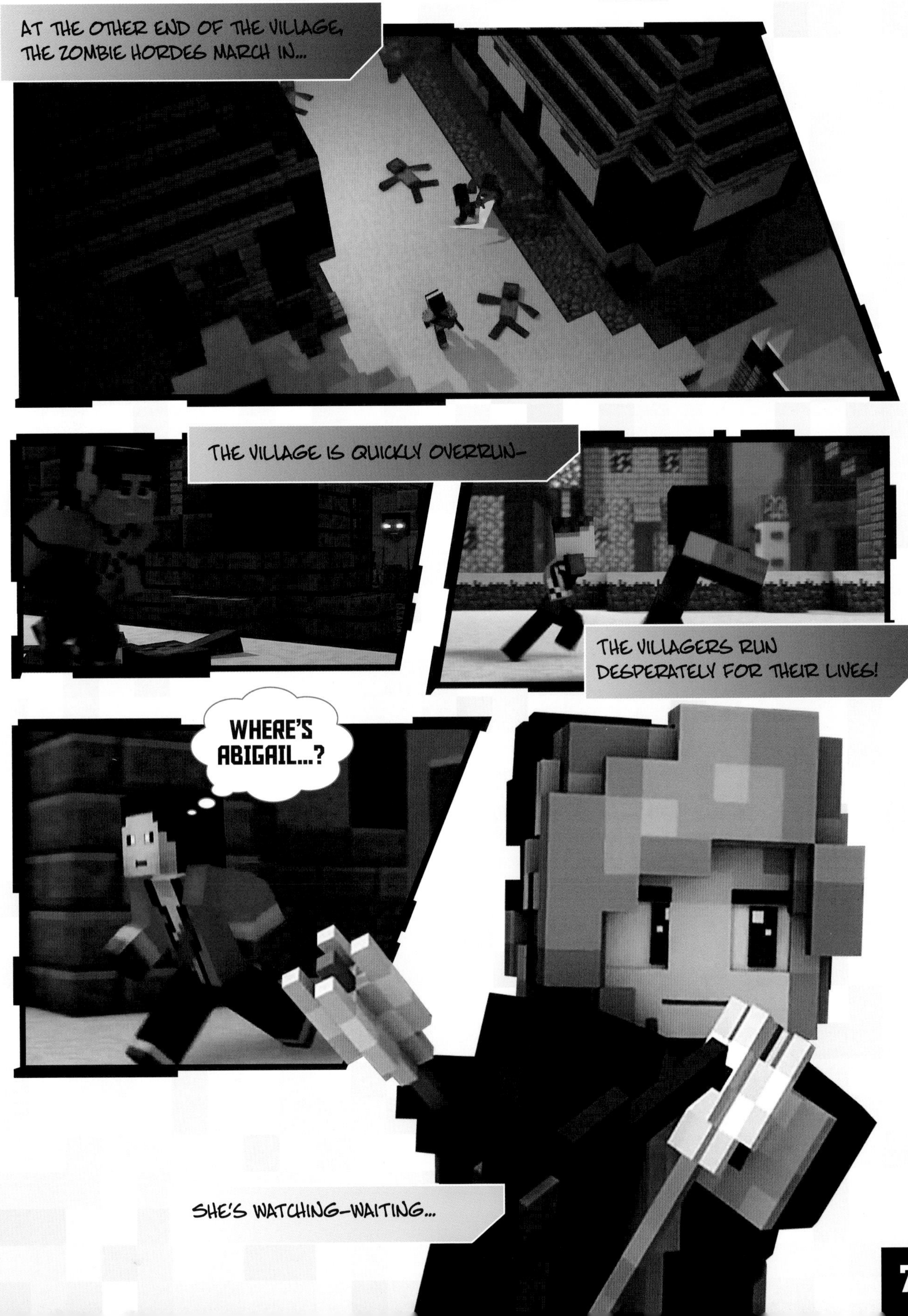

AT THE OTHER END OF THE VILLAGE, THE ZOMBIE HORDES MARCH IN...
THE VILLAGE IS QUICKLY OVERRUN-
THE VILLAGERS RUN DESPERATELY FOR THEIR LIVES!
WHERE'S ABIGAIL...?
SHE'S WATCHING-WAITING...

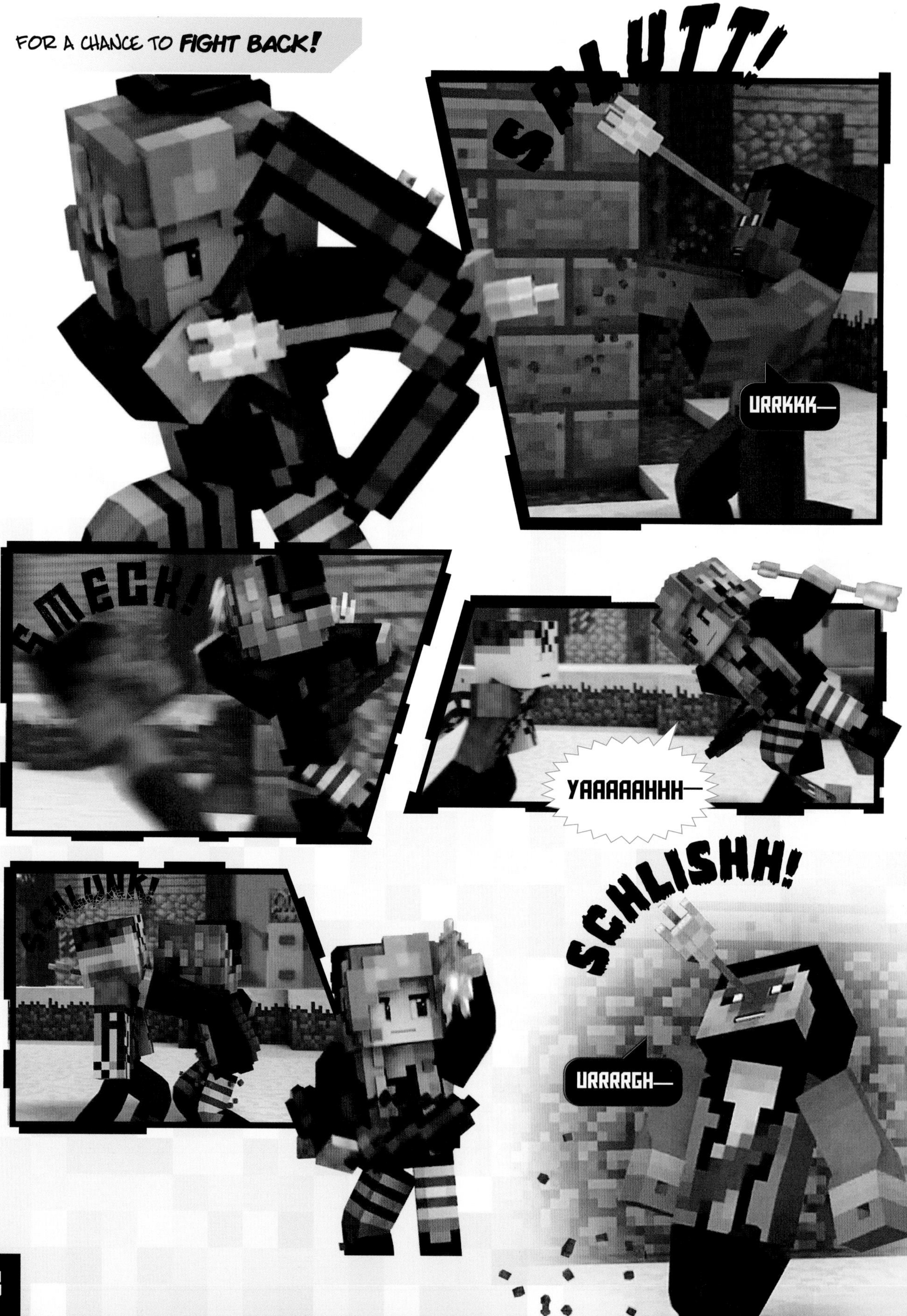
FOR A CHANCE TO FIGHT BACK!
SPLUTT!
URRKKK—
SMECK!
YAAAAAHHH—
SCHLUNK!
SCHLISHH!
URRRRGH—

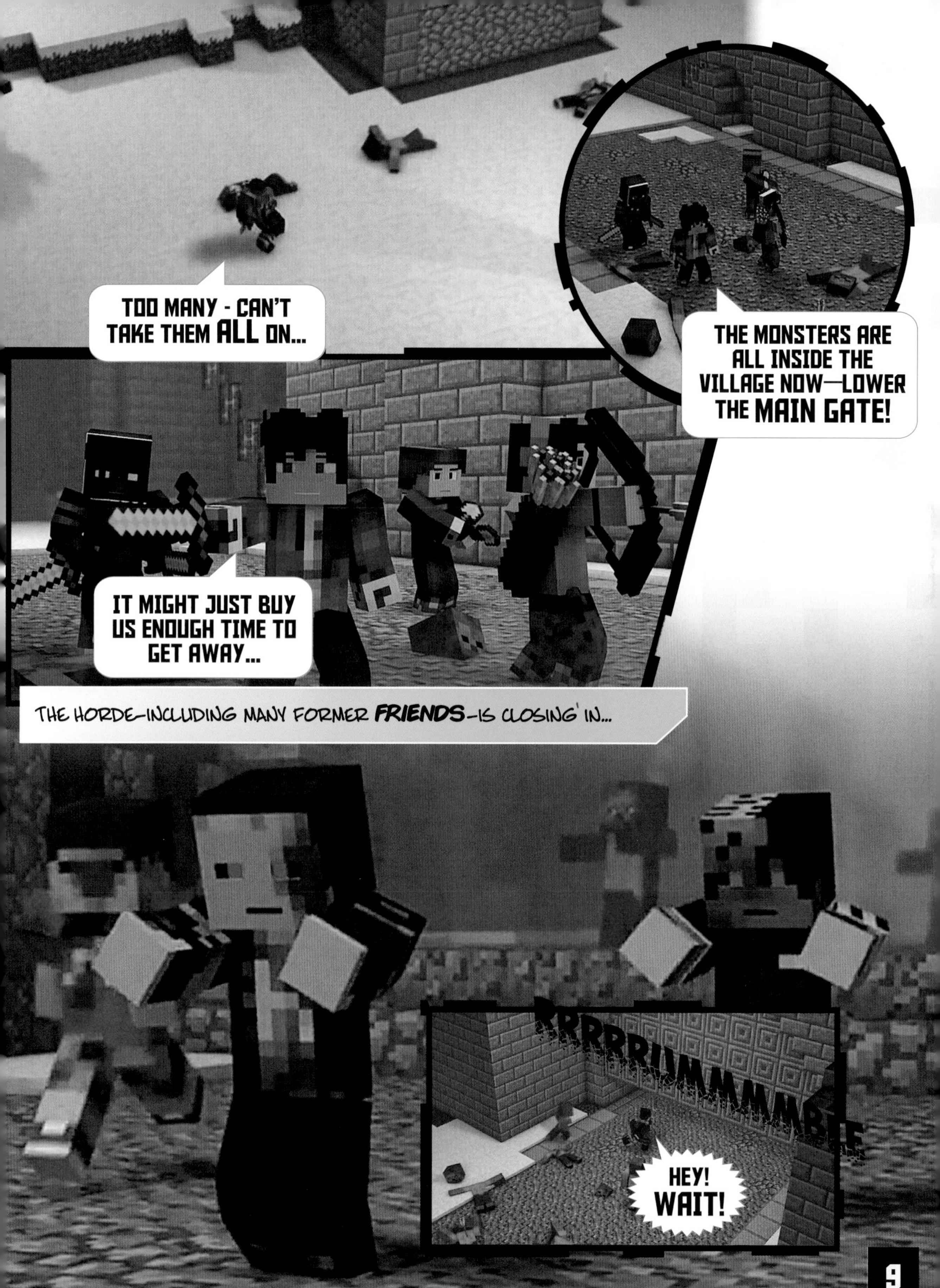
TOO MANY - CAN'T TAKE THEM ALL ON...
THE MONSTERS ARE ALL INSIDE THE VILLAGE NOW—LOWER THE MAIN GATE!
IT MIGHT JUST BUY US ENOUGH TIME TO GET AWAY...
THE HORDE—INCLUDING MANY FORMER FRIENDS—IS CLOSING IN...
RRRRRRUMMMMMMBLE
HEY! WAIT!

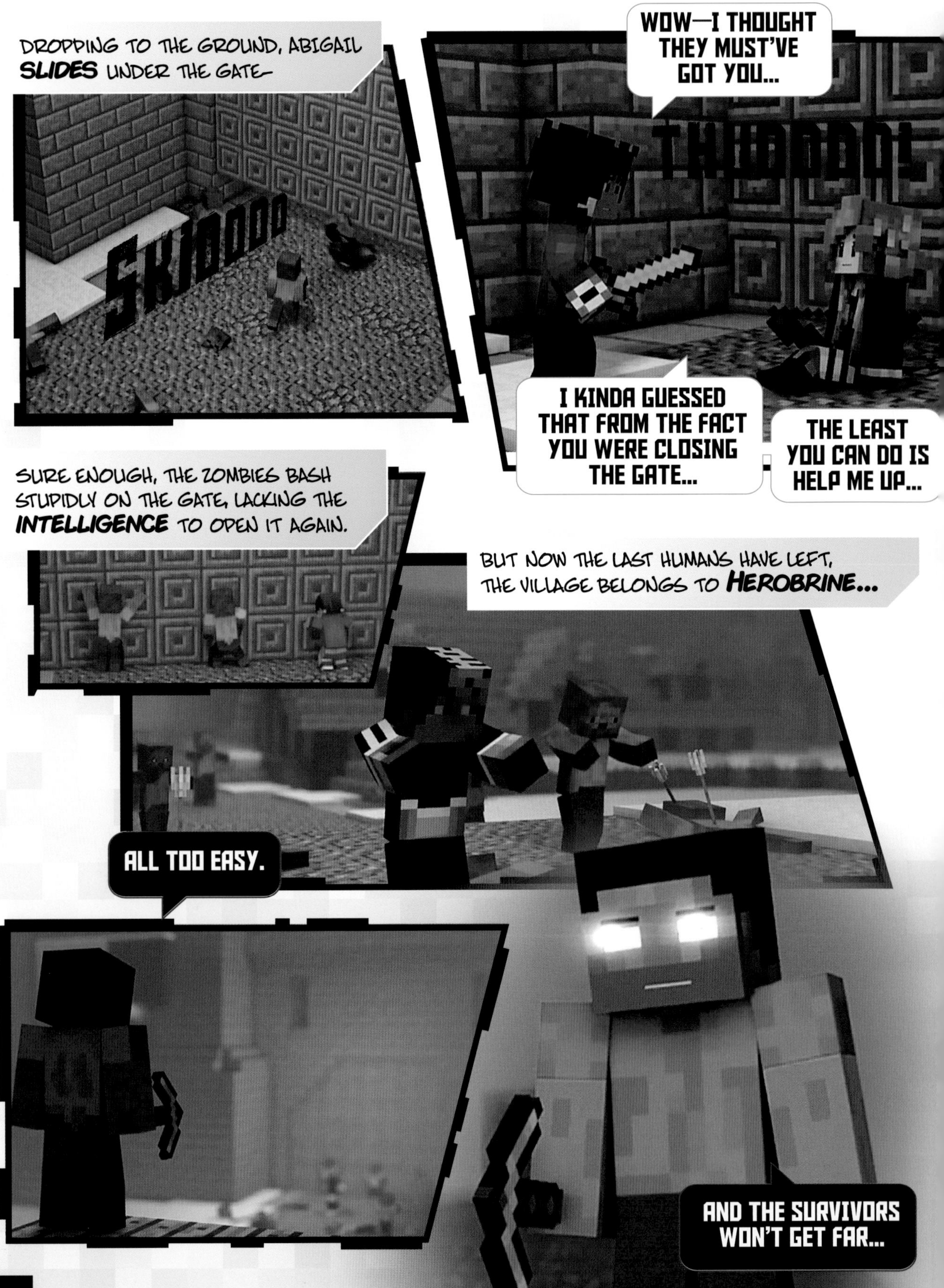

DROPPING TO THE GROUND, ABIGAIL **SLIDES** UNDER THE GATE–
SKIDDDD
WOW—I THOUGHT THEY MUST'VE GOT YOU...
THUDDDD!
I KINDA GUESSED THAT FROM THE FACT YOU WERE CLOSING THE GATE...
THE LEAST YOU CAN DO IS HELP ME UP...
SURE ENOUGH, THE ZOMBIES BASH STUPIDLY ON THE GATE, LACKING THE **INTELLIGENCE** TO OPEN IT AGAIN.
BUT NOW THE LAST HUMANS HAVE LEFT, THE VILLAGE BELONGS TO **HEROBRINE...**
ALL TOO EASY.
AND THE SURVIVORS WON'T GET FAR...

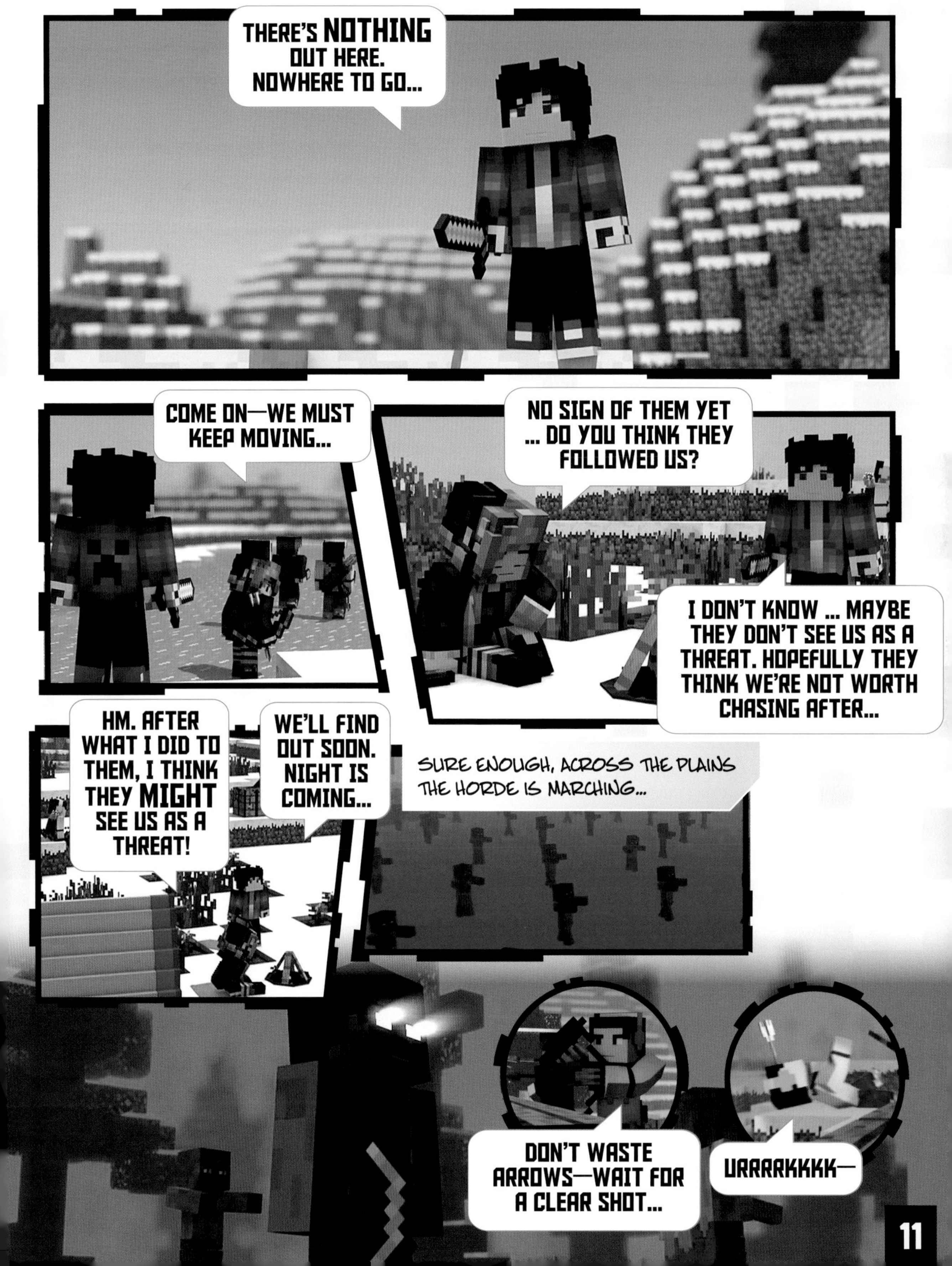

THERE'S NOTHING OUT HERE. NOWHERE TO GO...
COME ON—WE MUST KEEP MOVING...
NO SIGN OF THEM YET ... DO YOU THINK THEY FOLLOWED US?
I DON'T KNOW ... MAYBE THEY DON'T SEE US AS A THREAT. HOPEFULLY THEY THINK WE'RE NOT WORTH CHASING AFTER...
HM. AFTER WHAT I DID TO THEM, I THINK THEY MIGHT SEE US AS A THREAT!
WE'LL FIND OUT SOON. NIGHT IS COMING...
SURE ENOUGH, ACROSS THE PLAINS THE HORDE IS MARCHING...
DON'T WASTE ARROWS—WAIT FOR A CLEAR SHOT...
URRRRKKKK—

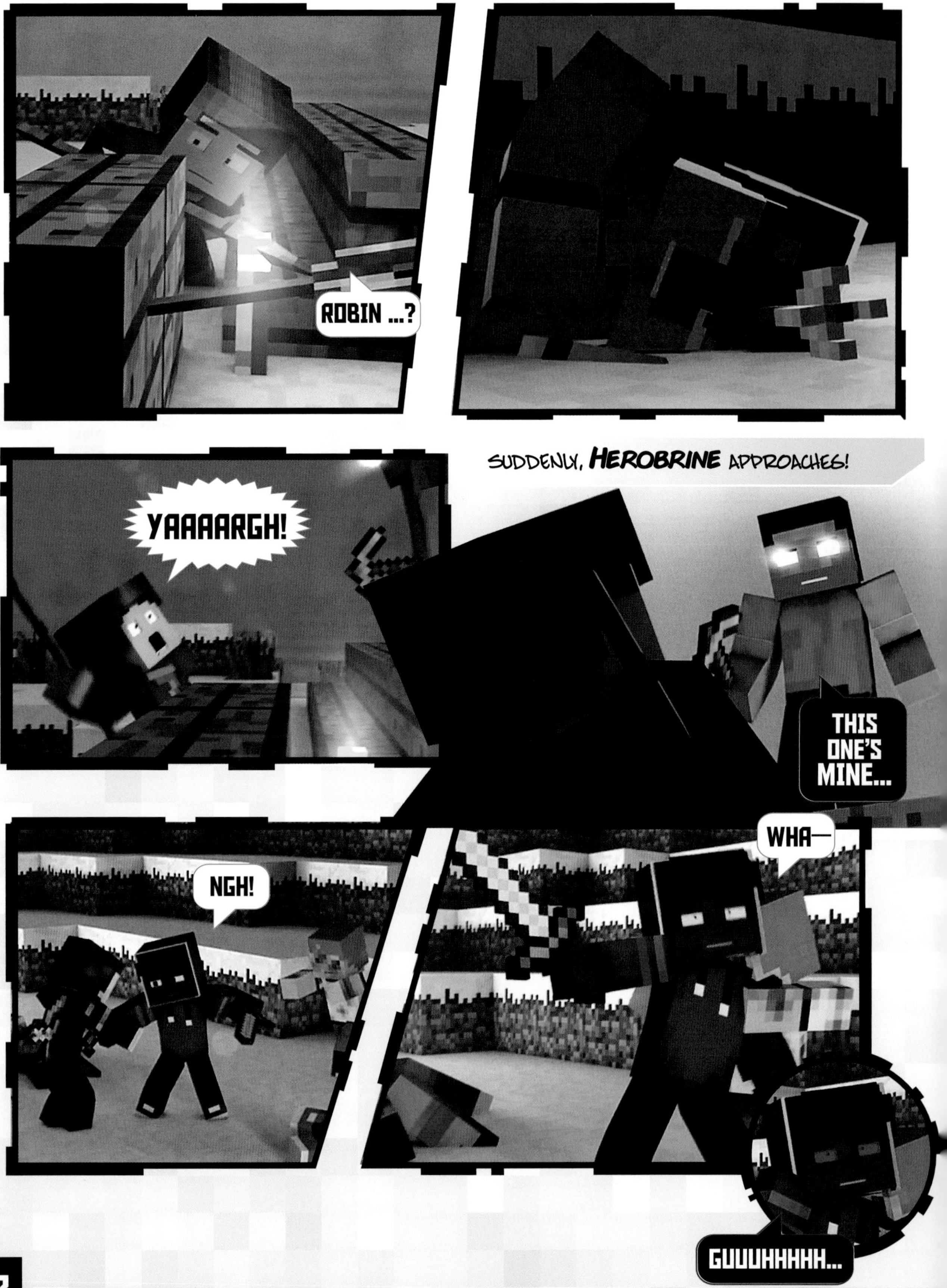
ROBIN ...?
YAAAARGH!
SUDDENLY, HEROBRINE APPROACHES!
THIS ONE'S MINE...
NGH!
WHA—
GUUUHHHHH...

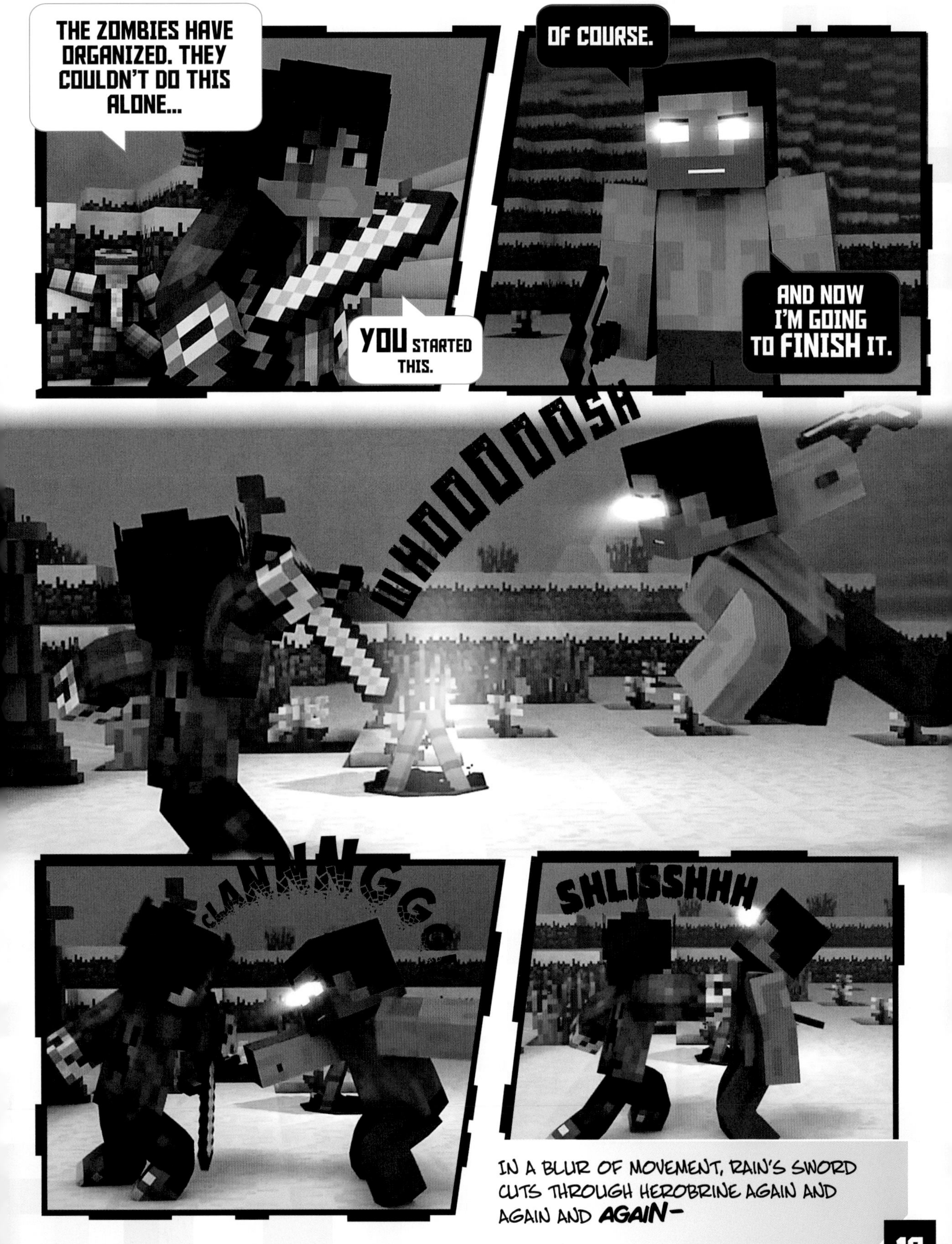
THE ZOMBIES HAVE ORGANIZED. THEY COULDN'T DO THIS ALONE...
YOU STARTED THIS.
OF COURSE.
AND NOW I'M GOING TO FINISH IT.
WHOOOOOOSH
CLANNNNGG
SHLISSHHH
IN A BLUR OF MOVEMENT, RAIN'S SWORD CUTS THROUGH HEROBRINE AGAIN AND AGAIN AND AGAIN–

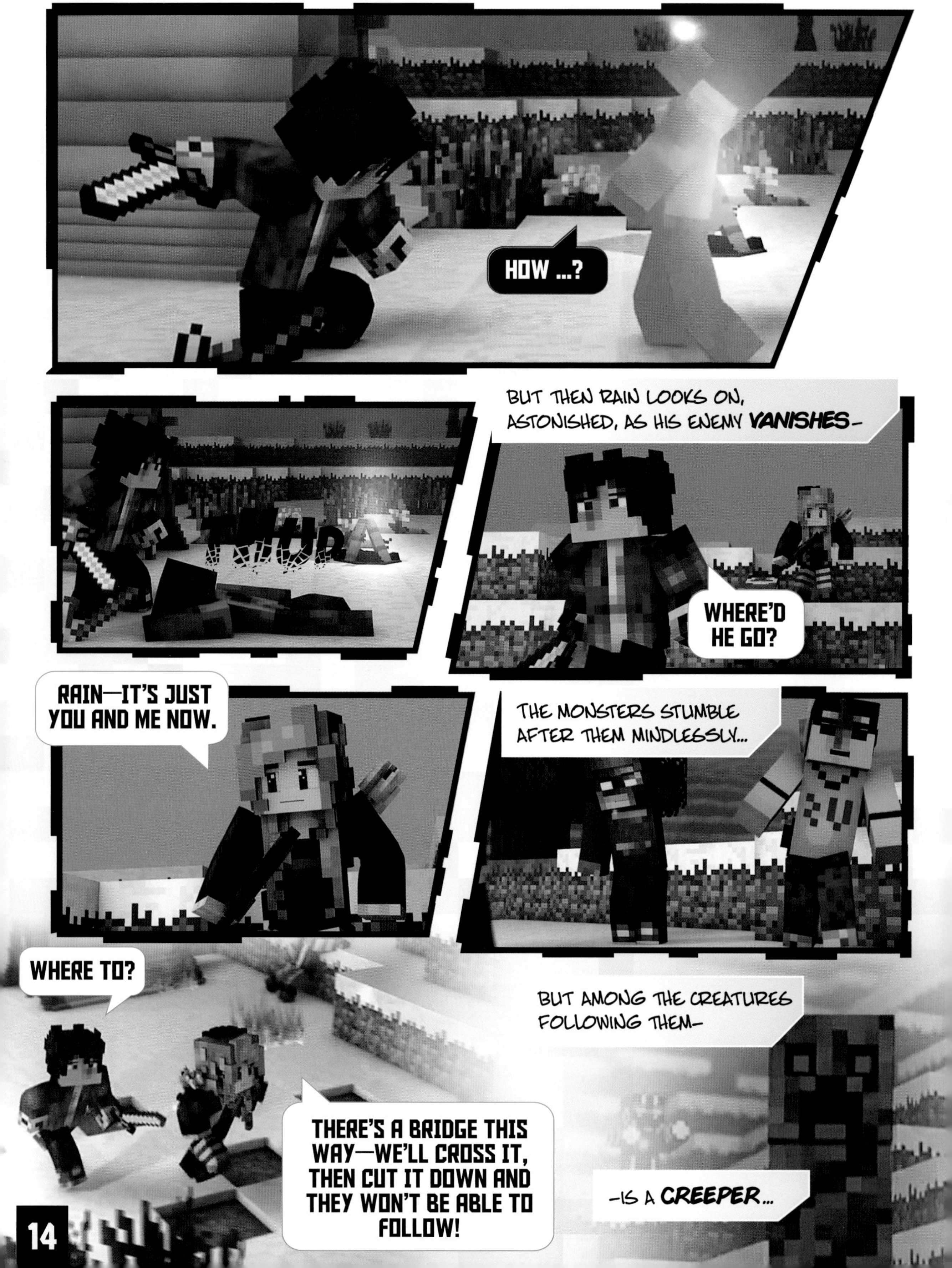
HOW ...?
THUD
BUT THEN RAIN LOOKS ON, ASTONISHED, AS HIS ENEMY **VANISHES**–
WHERE'D HE GO?
RAIN—IT'S JUST YOU AND ME NOW.
THE MONSTERS STUMBLE AFTER THEM MINDLESSLY...
WHERE TO?
THERE'S A BRIDGE THIS WAY—WE'LL CROSS IT, THEN CUT IT DOWN AND THEY WON'T BE ABLE TO FOLLOW!
BUT AMONG THE CREATURES FOLLOWING THEM–
–IS A **CREEPER**...

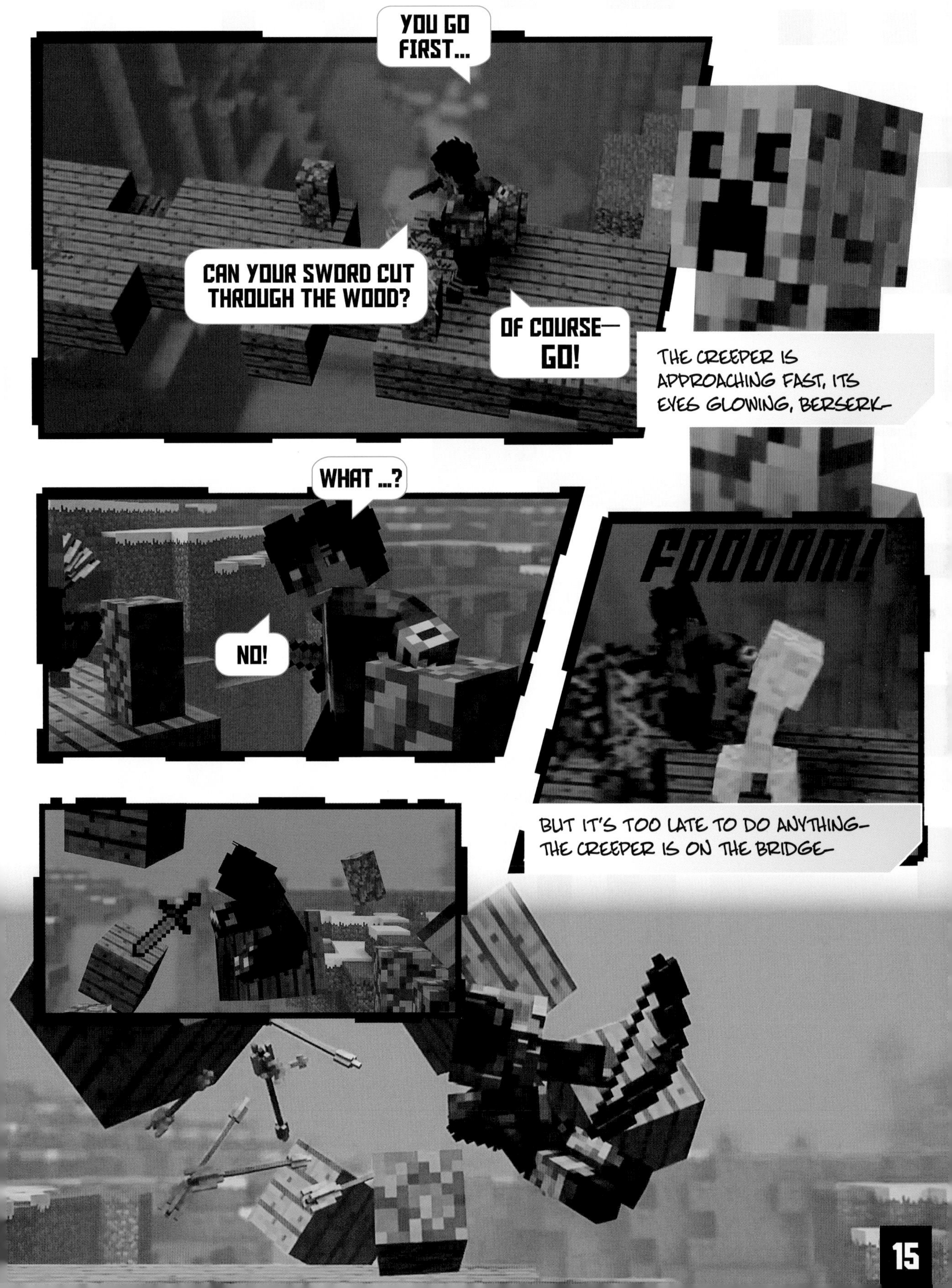

YOU GO FIRST...
CAN YOUR SWORD CUT THROUGH THE WOOD?
OF COURSE— GO!
THE CREEPER IS APPROACHING FAST, ITS EYES GLOWING, BERSERK–
WHAT ...?
NO!
FOOOOM!
BUT IT'S TOO LATE TO DO ANYTHING– THE CREEPER IS ON THE BRIDGE–

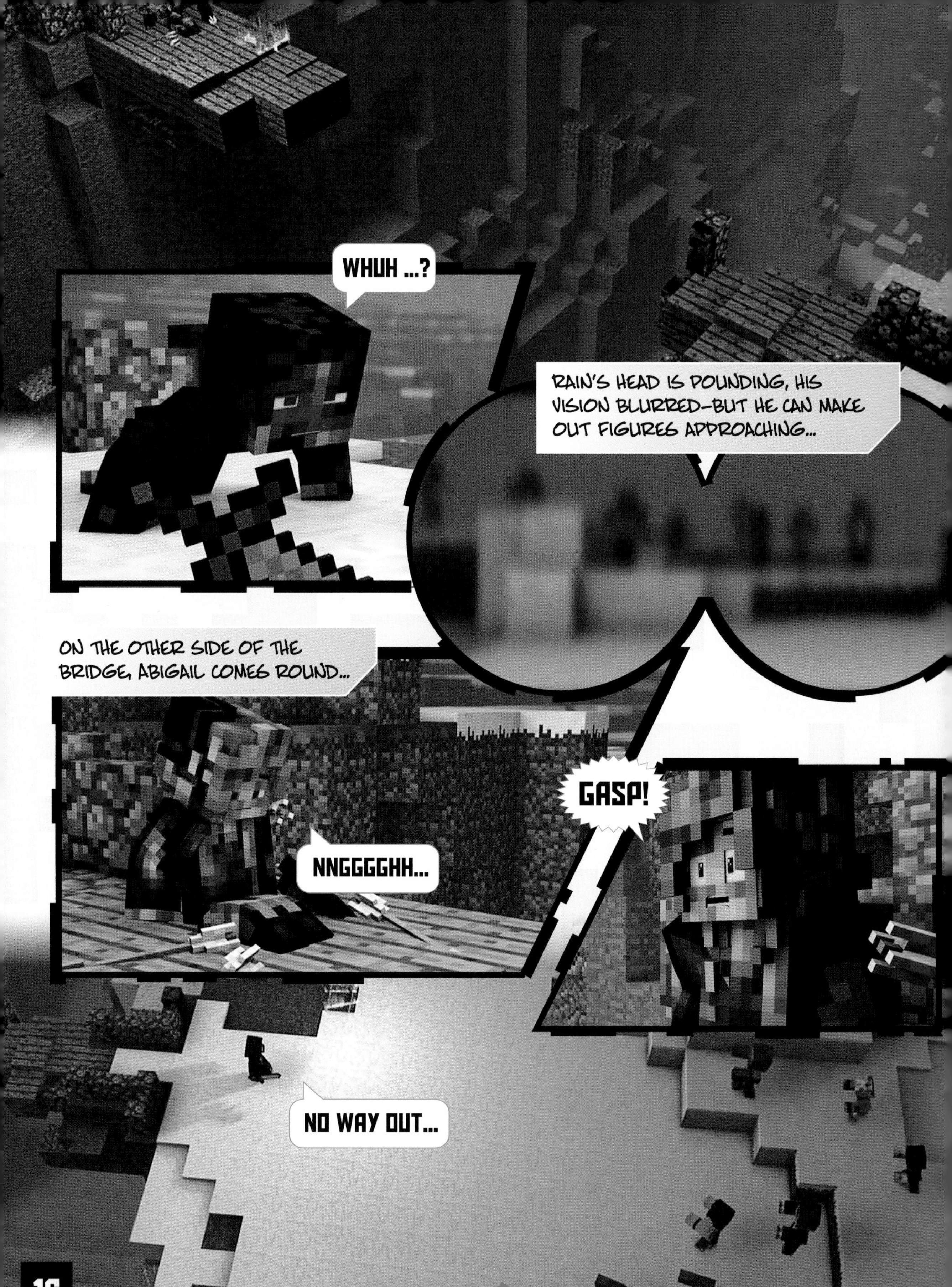
WHUH ...?
RAIN'S HEAD IS POUNDING, HIS VISION BLURRED—BUT HE CAN MAKE OUT FIGURES APPROACHING...
ON THE OTHER SIDE OF THE BRIDGE, ABIGAIL COMES ROUND...
NNGGGGHH...
GASP!
NO WAY OUT...

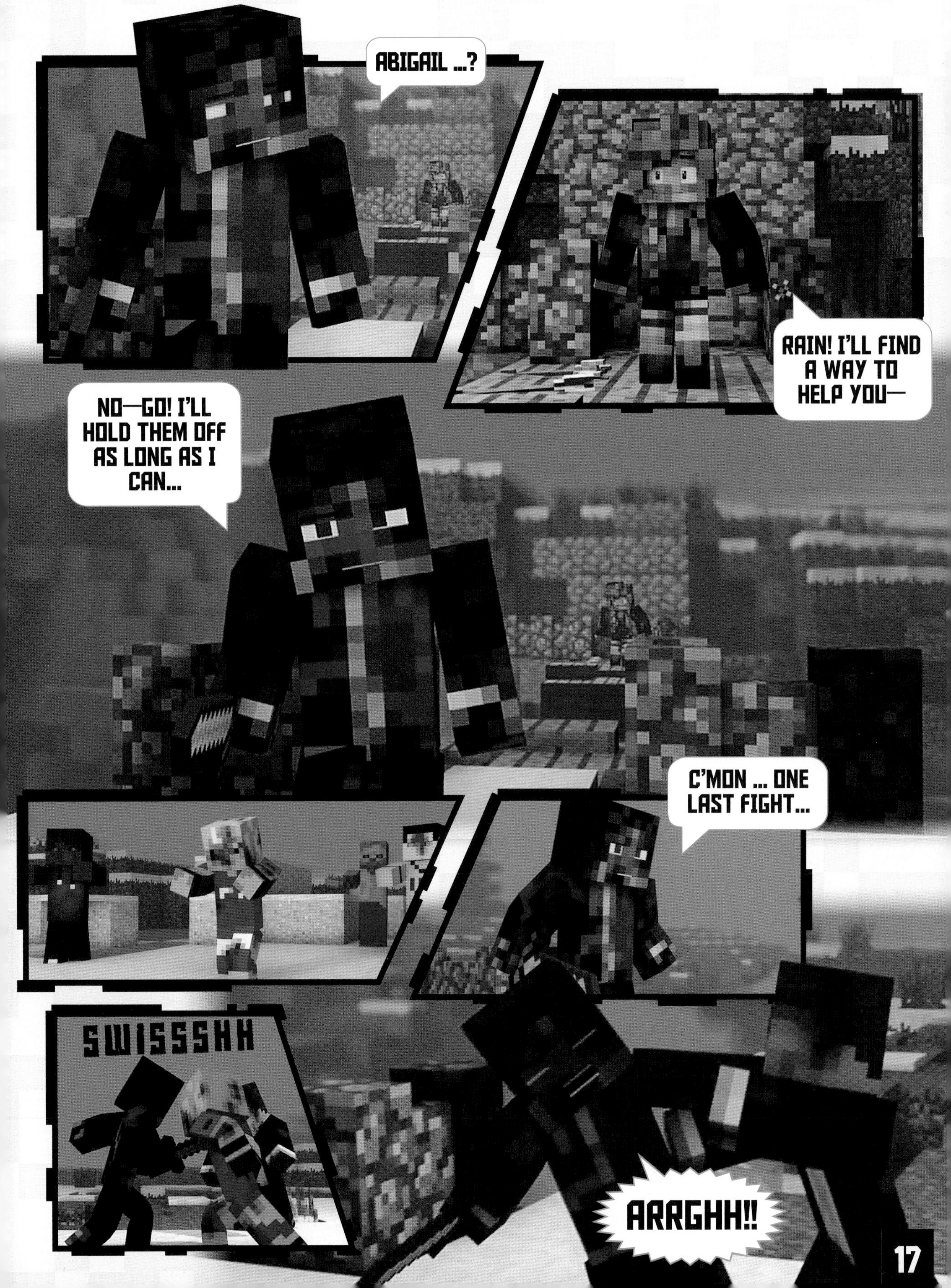
ABIGAIL ...?
RAIN! I'LL FIND A WAY TO HELP YOU—
NO—GO! I'LL HOLD THEM OFF AS LONG AS I CAN...
C'MON ... ONE LAST FIGHT...
SWISSSHH
ARRGHH!!

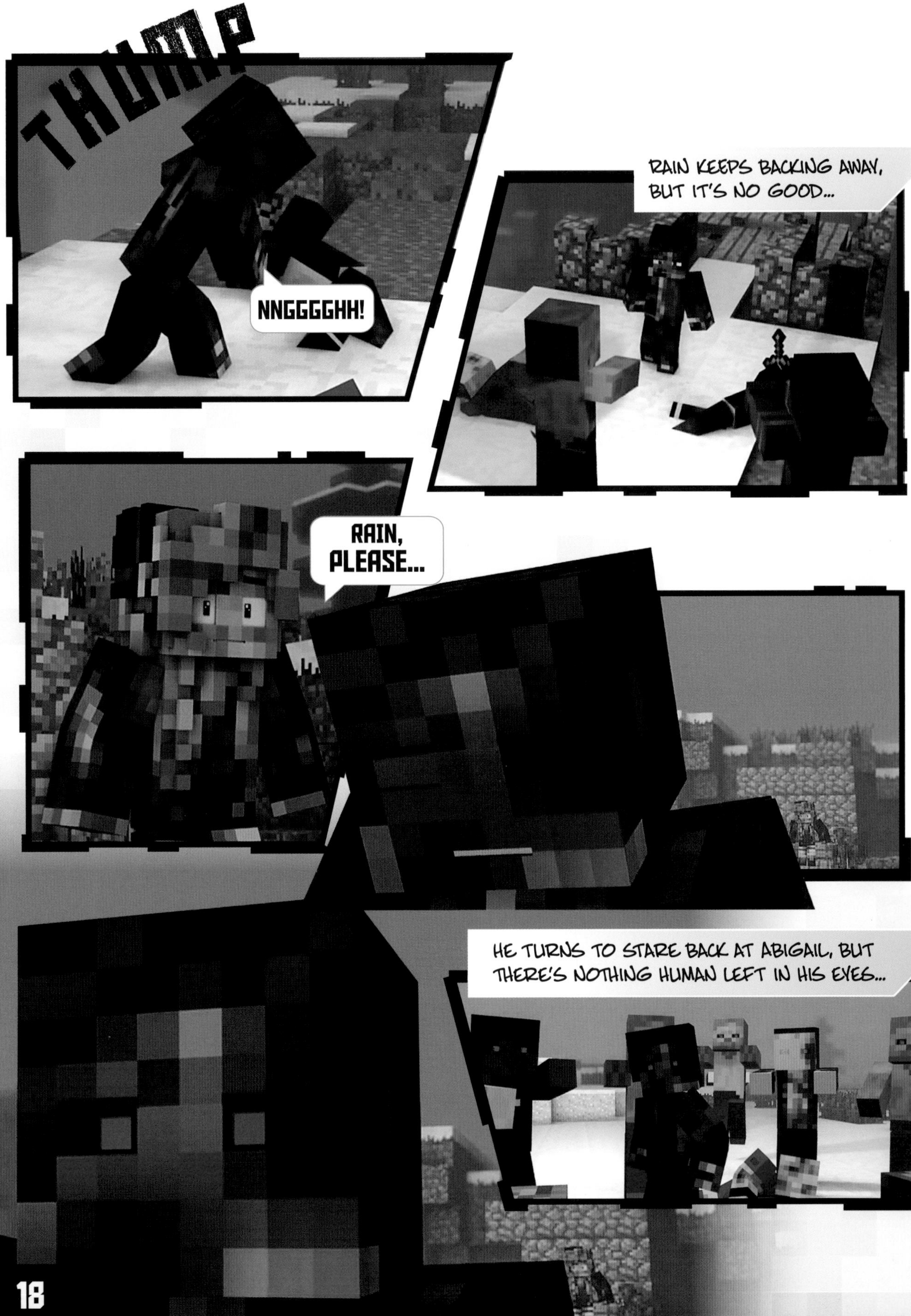
THUMP
NNGGGGHH!
RAIN KEEPS BACKING AWAY, BUT IT'S NO GOOD...
RAIN, PLEASE...
HE TURNS TO STARE BACK AT ABIGAIL, BUT THERE'S NOTHING HUMAN LEFT IN HIS EYES...

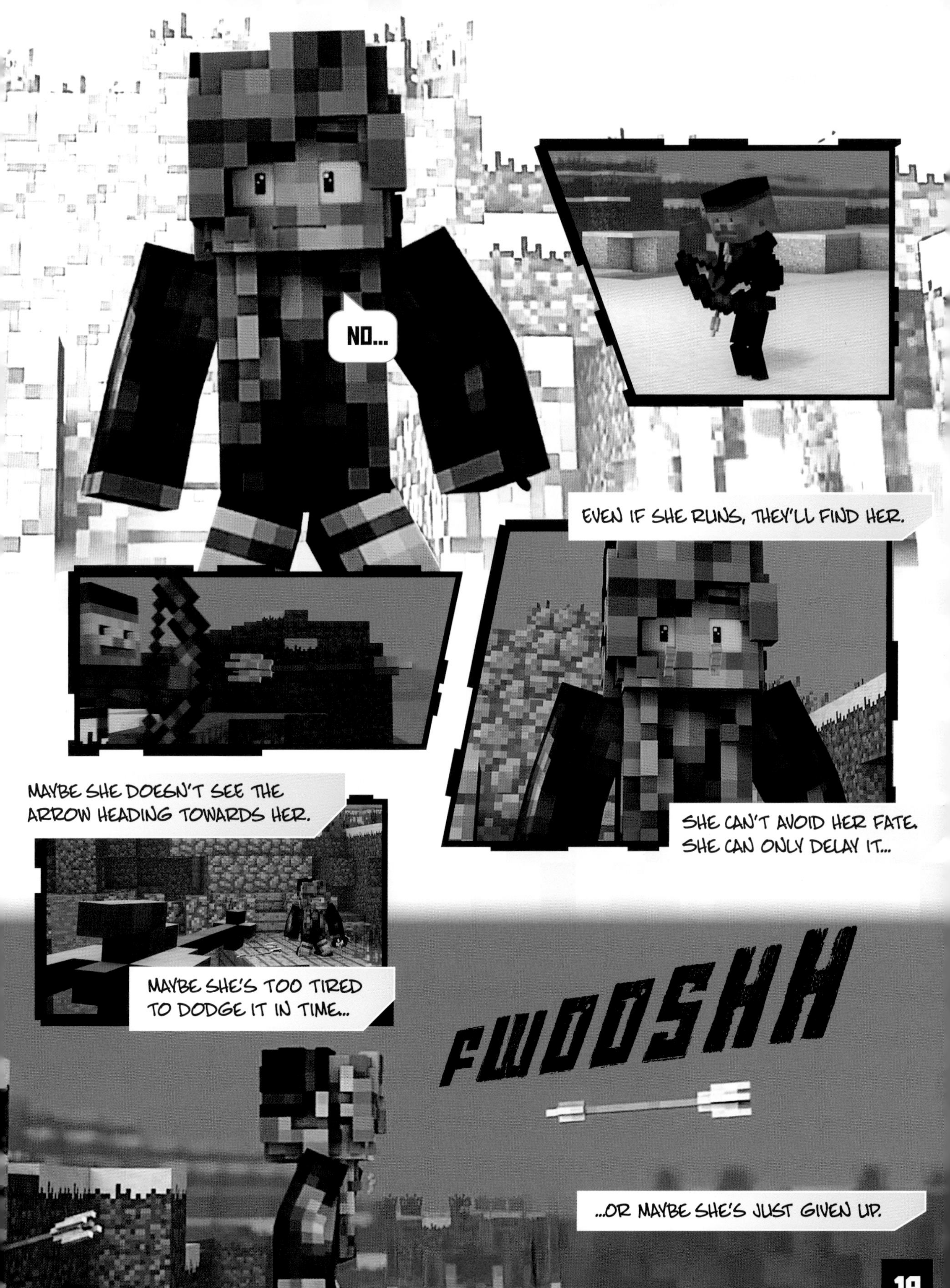
NO...
EVEN IF SHE RUNS, THEY'LL FIND HER.
SHE CAN'T AVOID HER FATE. SHE CAN ONLY DELAY IT...
MAYBE SHE DOESN'T SEE THE ARROW HEADING TOWARDS HER.
MAYBE SHE'S TOO TIRED TO DODGE IT IN TIME...
FWOOSHH
...OR MAYBE SHE'S JUST GIVEN UP.

THE ZOMBIFIED RAIN SHUFFLES BLINDLY INTO THE RAVINE...

GRUUUGGGHHH...

...AND LIES AT THE BOTTOM, BARELY ALIVE.

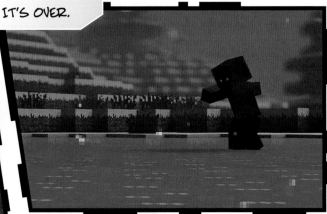

IT'S OVER.

OR IS IT ...?

GALLOMP
GALLOMP
GALLOMP
GALLOMP
GALLOMP
GALLOMP

BLAM
BLAM
BLAM
BLAM

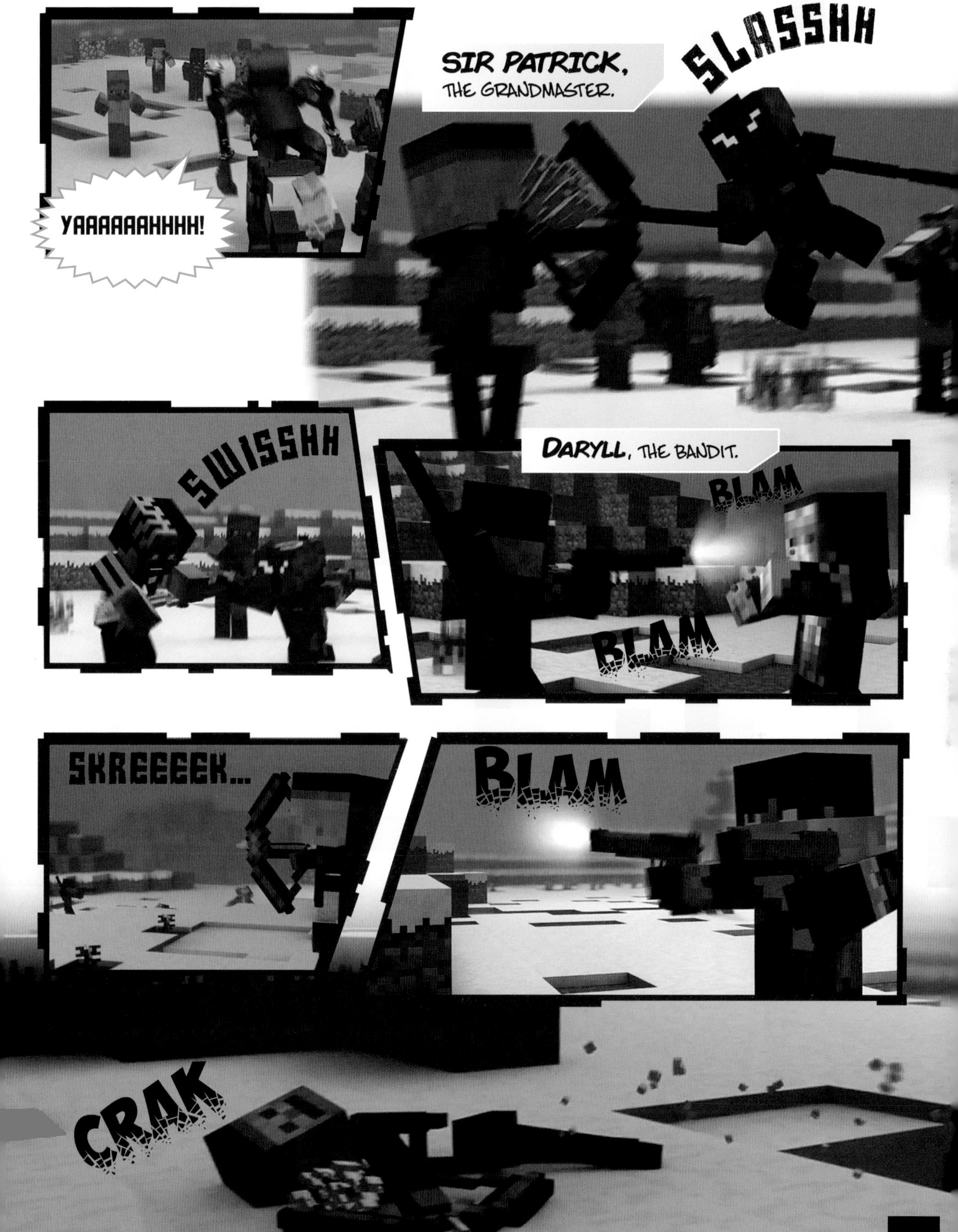

YAAAAAAHHHH!
SIR PATRICK,
THE GRANDMASTER.
SLASSHH
SWISSHH
DARYLL, THE BANDIT.
BLAM
BLAM
SKREEEEK...
BLAM
CRAK

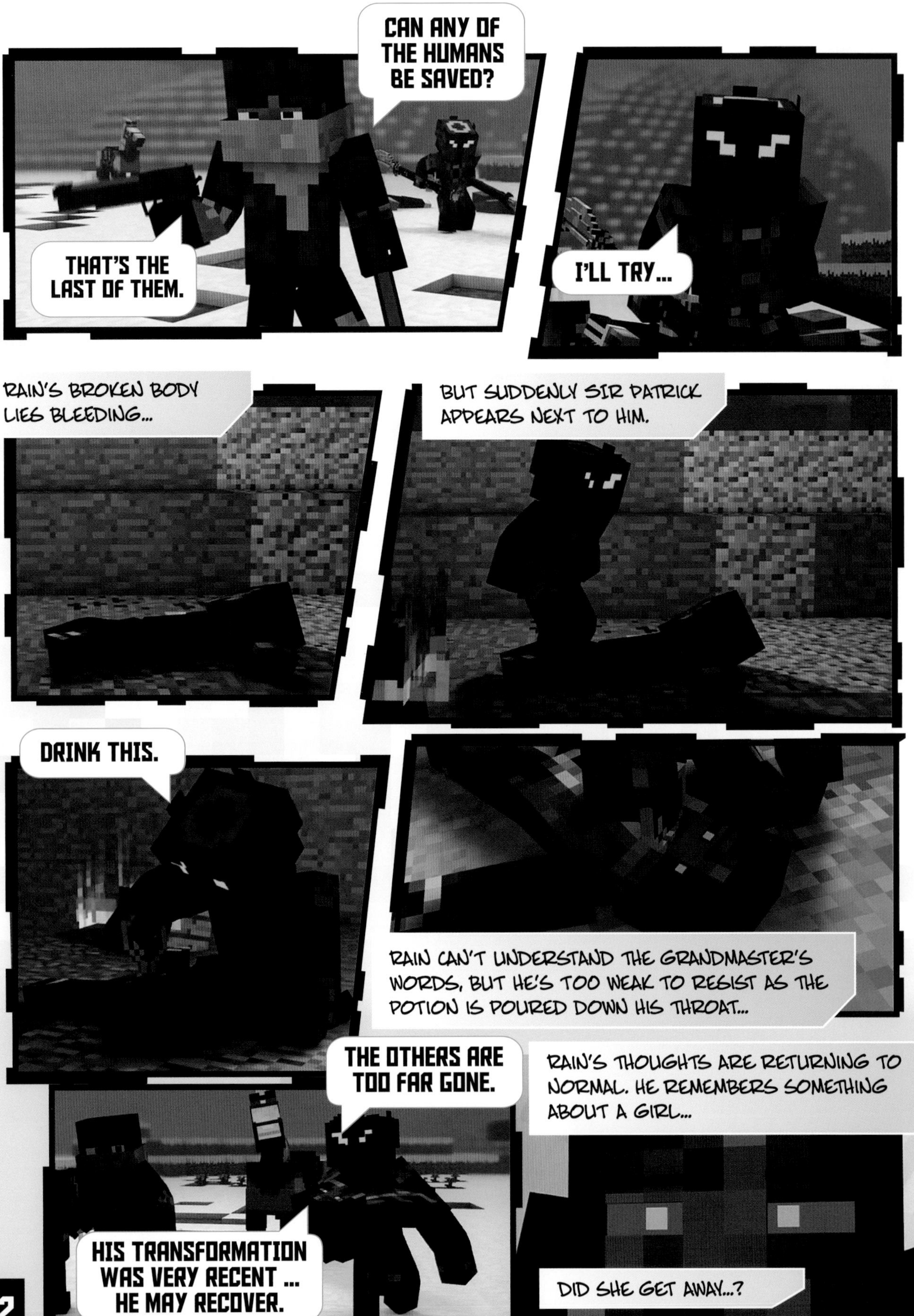
CAN ANY OF THE HUMANS BE SAVED?
THAT'S THE LAST OF THEM.
I'LL TRY...
RAIN'S BROKEN BODY LIES BLEEDING...
BUT SUDDENLY SIR PATRICK APPEARS NEXT TO HIM.
DRINK THIS.
RAIN CAN'T UNDERSTAND THE GRANDMASTER'S WORDS, BUT HE'S TOO WEAK TO RESIST AS THE POTION IS POURED DOWN HIS THROAT...
THE OTHERS ARE TOO FAR GONE.
HIS TRANSFORMATION WAS VERY RECENT ... HE MAY RECOVER.
RAIN'S THOUGHTS ARE RETURNING TO NORMAL. HE REMEMBERS SOMETHING ABOUT A GIRL...
DID SHE GET AWAY...?

RAIN'S MEMORIES OF THE JOURNEY ARE HAZY.

HE SLEEPS THROUGH SOME OF IT...

WE NEED TO GO FASTER, BUT I'M AFRAID TOO MUCH MOVEMENT WILL WORSEN HIS INJURIES.

THEN THE HORSE'S STEP WILL JOLT HIM PAINFULLY.

WE MUST HOPE LADY **AZURA** CAN DO SOMETHING FOR HIM WHEN WE REACH THE FORTRESS...

FORTRESS? RAIN HAS HEARD OF THE FORTRESS, SEEN IT FROM A DISTANCE...

BUT HE'S NEVER BEEN INSIDE...

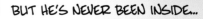

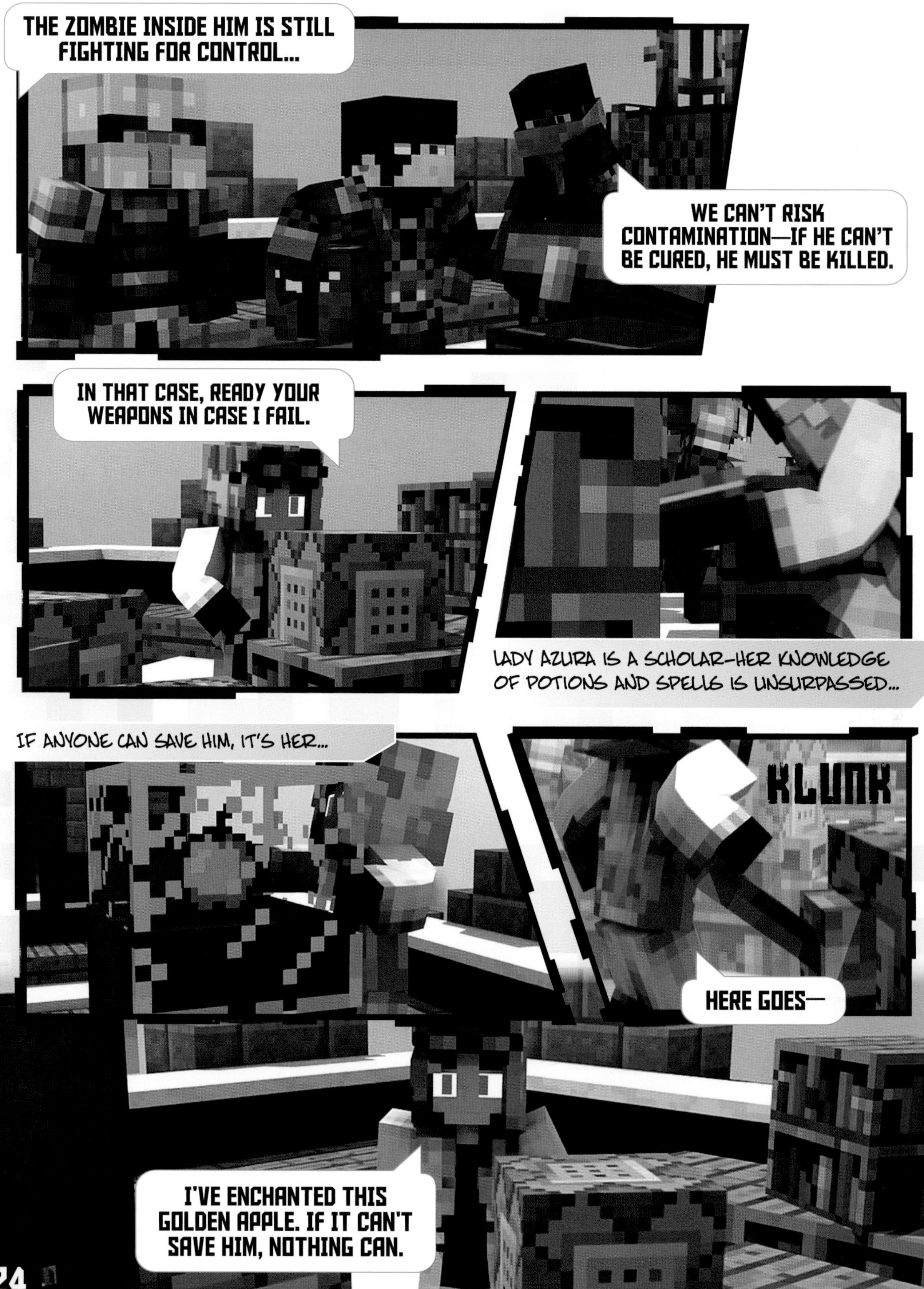
THE ZOMBIE INSIDE HIM IS STILL FIGHTING FOR CONTROL...
WE CAN'T RISK CONTAMINATION—IF HE CAN'T BE CURED, HE MUST BE KILLED.
IN THAT CASE, READY YOUR WEAPONS IN CASE I FAIL.
LADY AZURA IS A SCHOLAR—HER KNOWLEDGE OF POTIONS AND SPELLS IS UNSURPASSED...
IF ANYONE CAN SAVE HIM, IT'S HER...
KLUNK
HERE GOES—
I'VE ENCHANTED THIS GOLDEN APPLE. IF IT CAN'T SAVE HIM, NOTHING CAN.

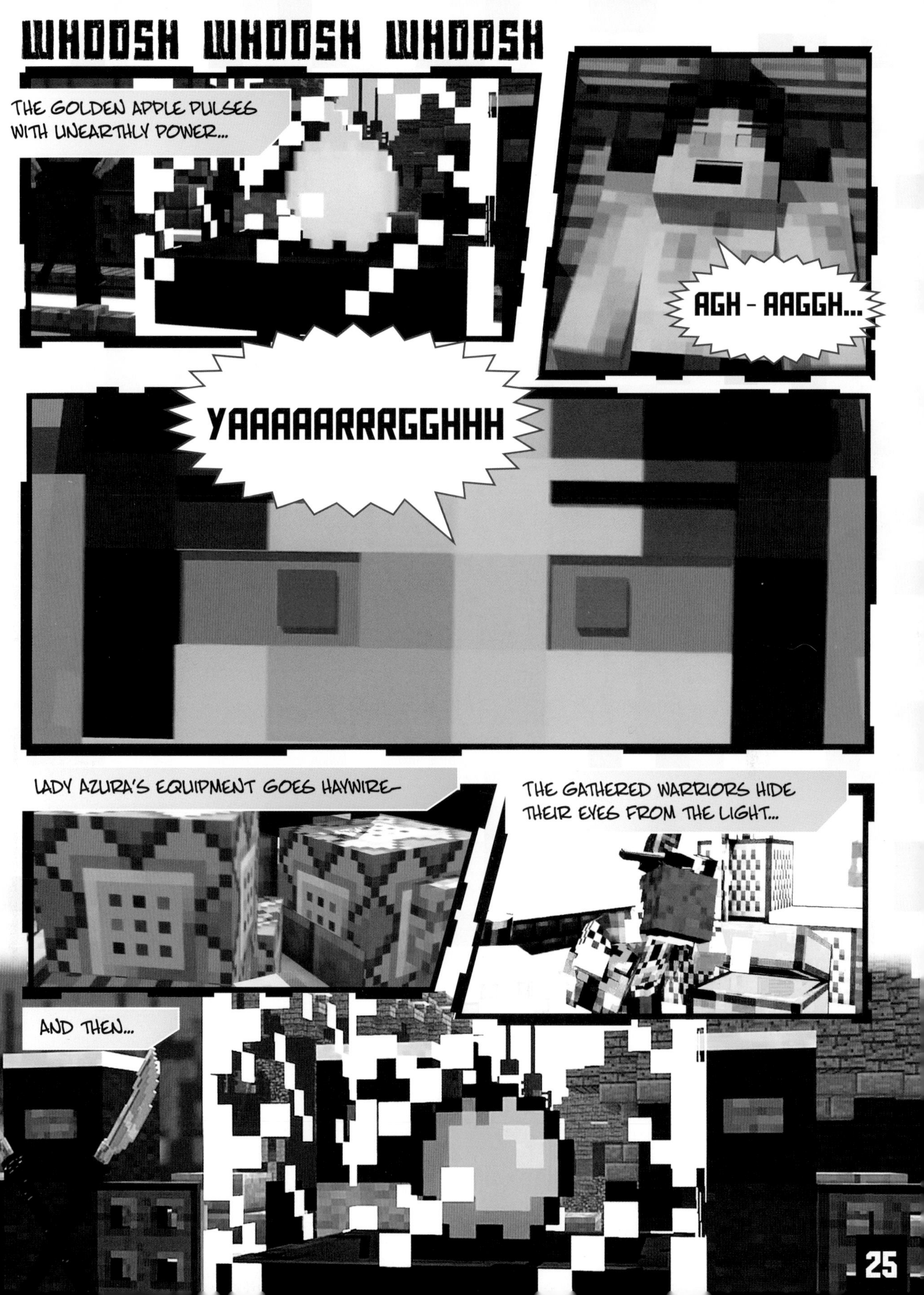
WHOOSH WHOOSH WHOOSH
THE GOLDEN APPLE PULSES WITH UNEARTHLY POWER...
AGH - AAGGH...
YAAAAARRRGGHHH
LADY AZURA'S EQUIPMENT GOES HAYWIRE–
THE GATHERED WARRIORS HIDE THEIR EYES FROM THE LIGHT...
AND THEN...

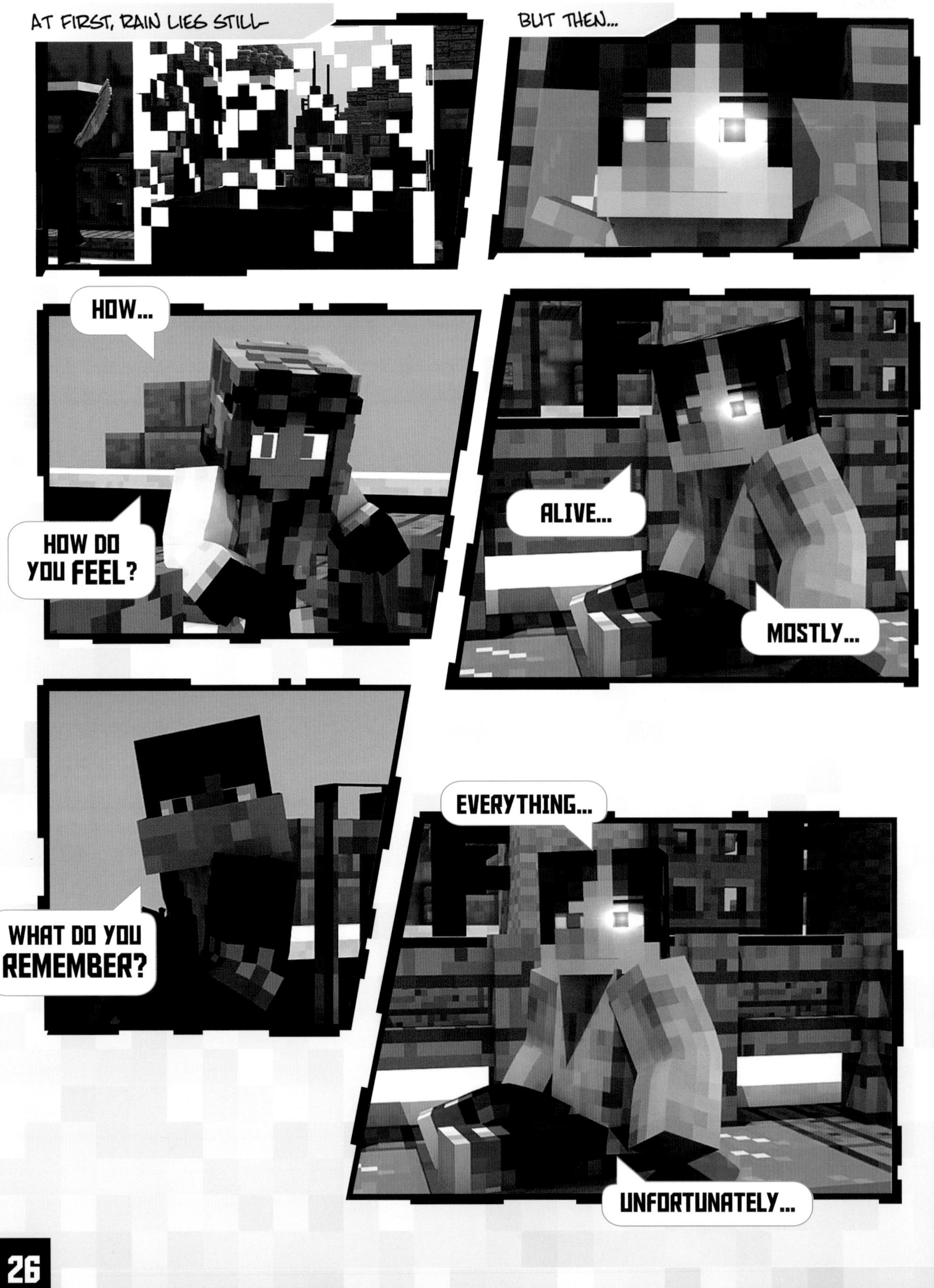
AT FIRST, RAIN LIES STILL-
BUT THEN...
HOW...
HOW DO YOU FEEL?
ALIVE...
MOSTLY...
WHAT DO YOU REMEMBER?
EVERYTHING...
UNFORTUNATELY...

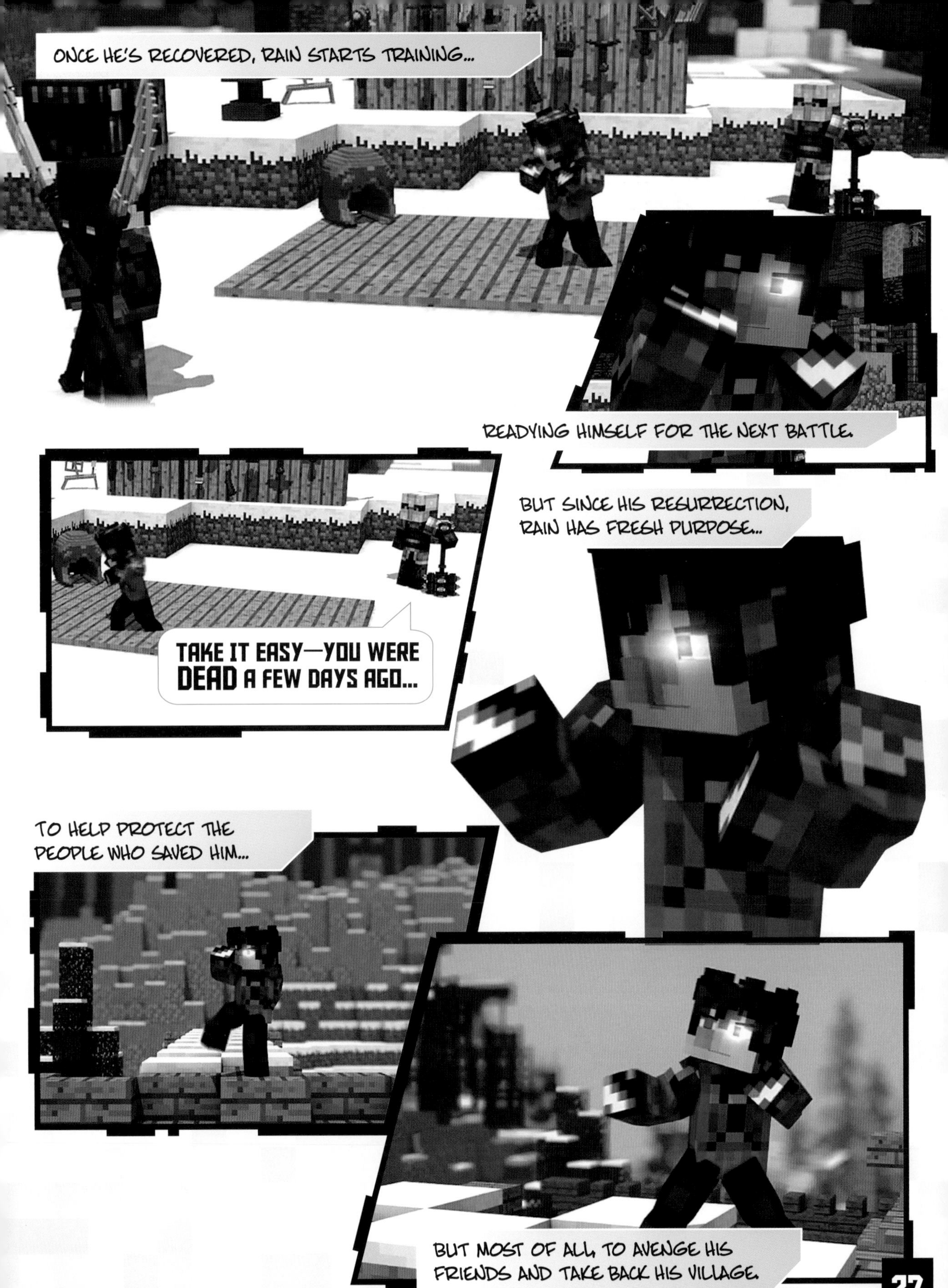
ONCE HE'S RECOVERED, RAIN STARTS TRAINING...
READYING HIMSELF FOR THE NEXT BATTLE.
TAKE IT EASY—YOU WERE DEAD A FEW DAYS AGO...
BUT SINCE HIS RESURRECTION, RAIN HAS FRESH PURPOSE...
TO HELP PROTECT THE PEOPLE WHO SAVED HIM...
BUT MOST OF ALL, TO AVENGE HIS FRIENDS AND TAKE BACK HIS VILLAGE.

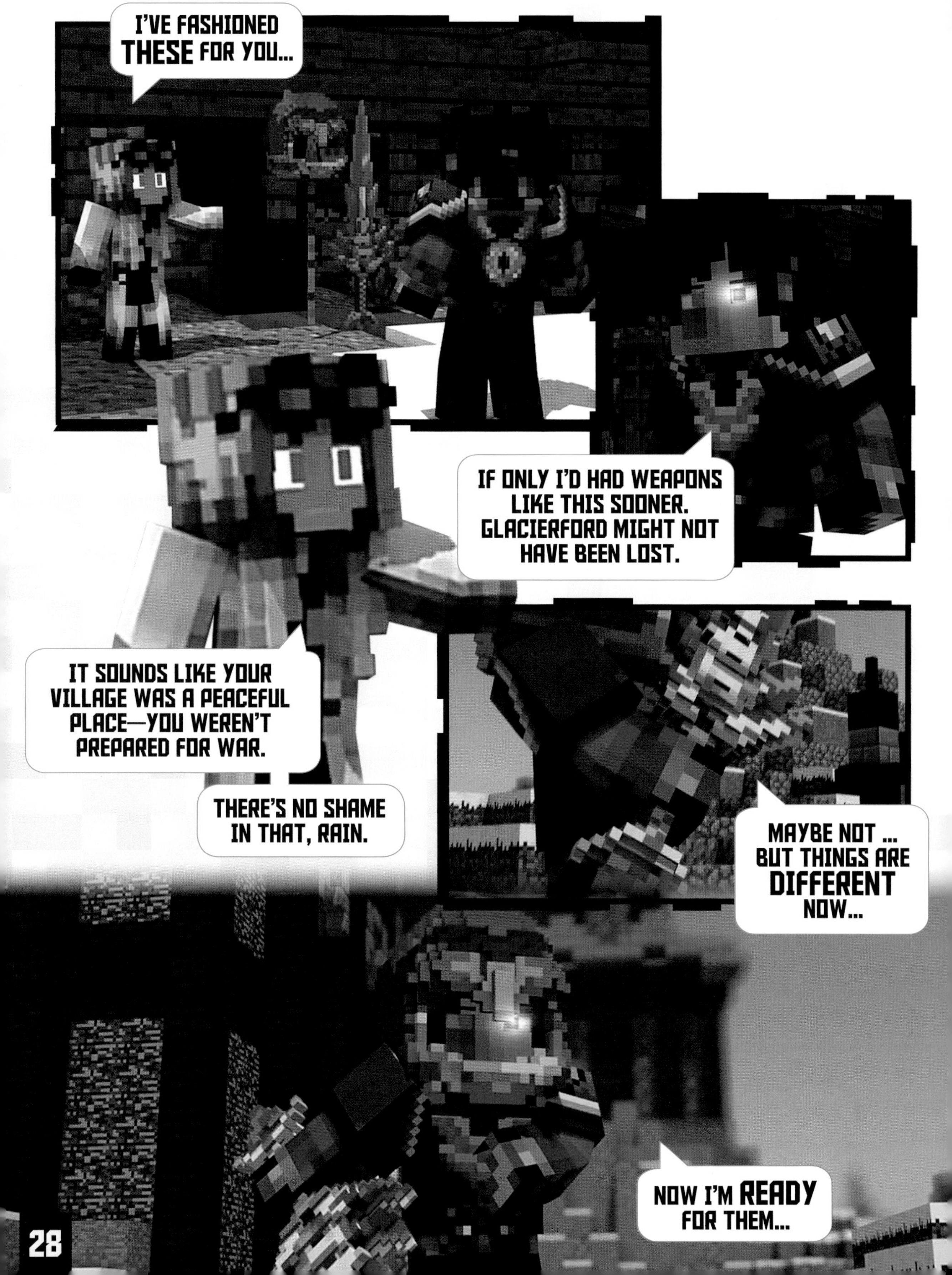
I'VE FASHIONED THESE FOR YOU...
IF ONLY I'D HAD WEAPONS LIKE THIS SOONER. GLACIERFORD MIGHT NOT HAVE BEEN LOST.
IT SOUNDS LIKE YOUR VILLAGE WAS A PEACEFUL PLACE—YOU WEREN'T PREPARED FOR WAR.
THERE'S NO SHAME IN THAT, RAIN.
MAYBE NOT ... BUT THINGS ARE DIFFERENT NOW...
NOW I'M READY FOR THEM...

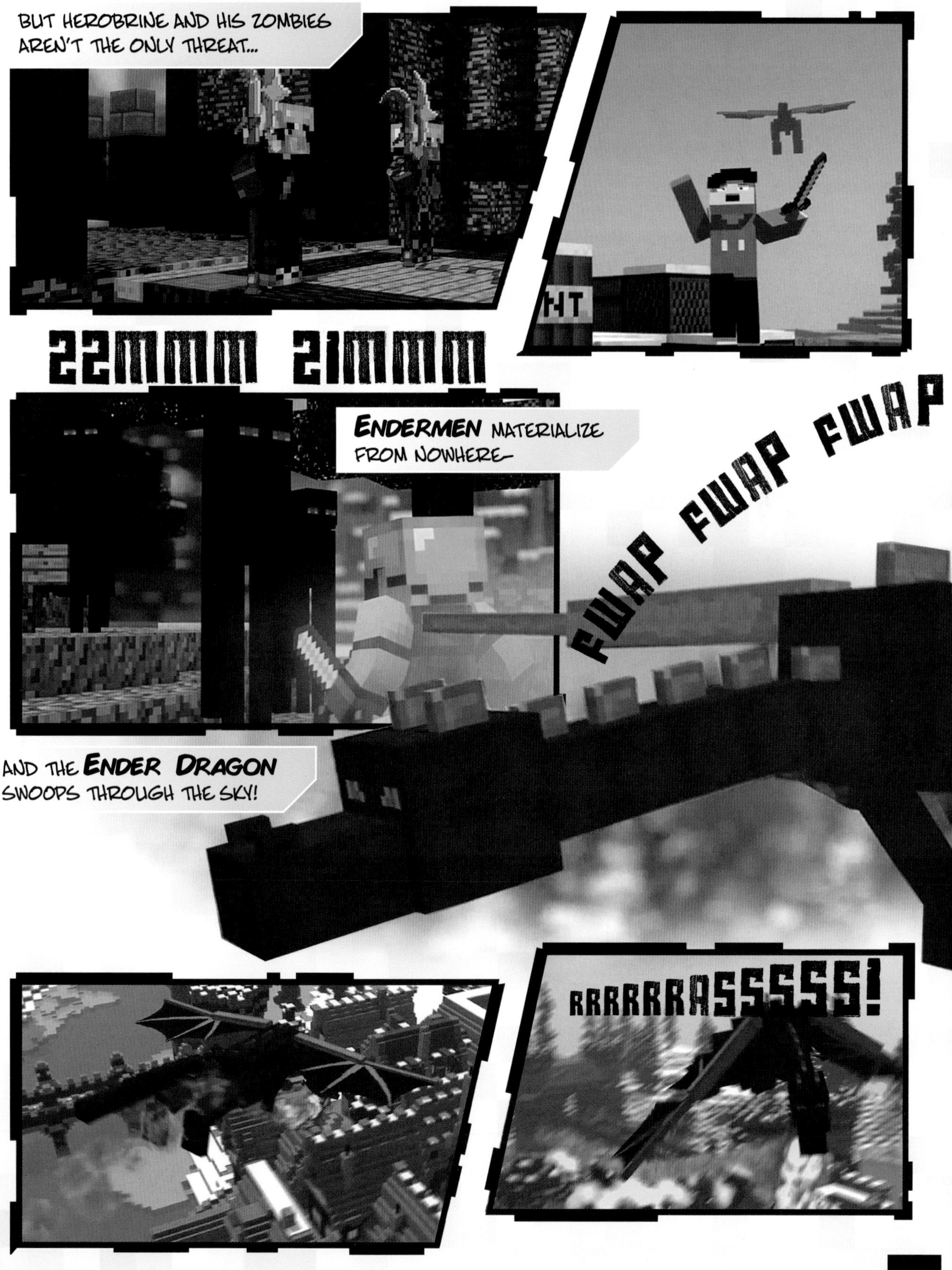

BUT HEROBRINE AND HIS ZOMBIES AREN'T THE ONLY THREAT...
22MMM 21MMM
ENDERMEN MATERIALIZE FROM NOWHERE–
FWAP FWAP FWAP
AND THE ENDER DRAGON SWOOPS THROUGH THE SKY!
RRRRRRASSSSS!

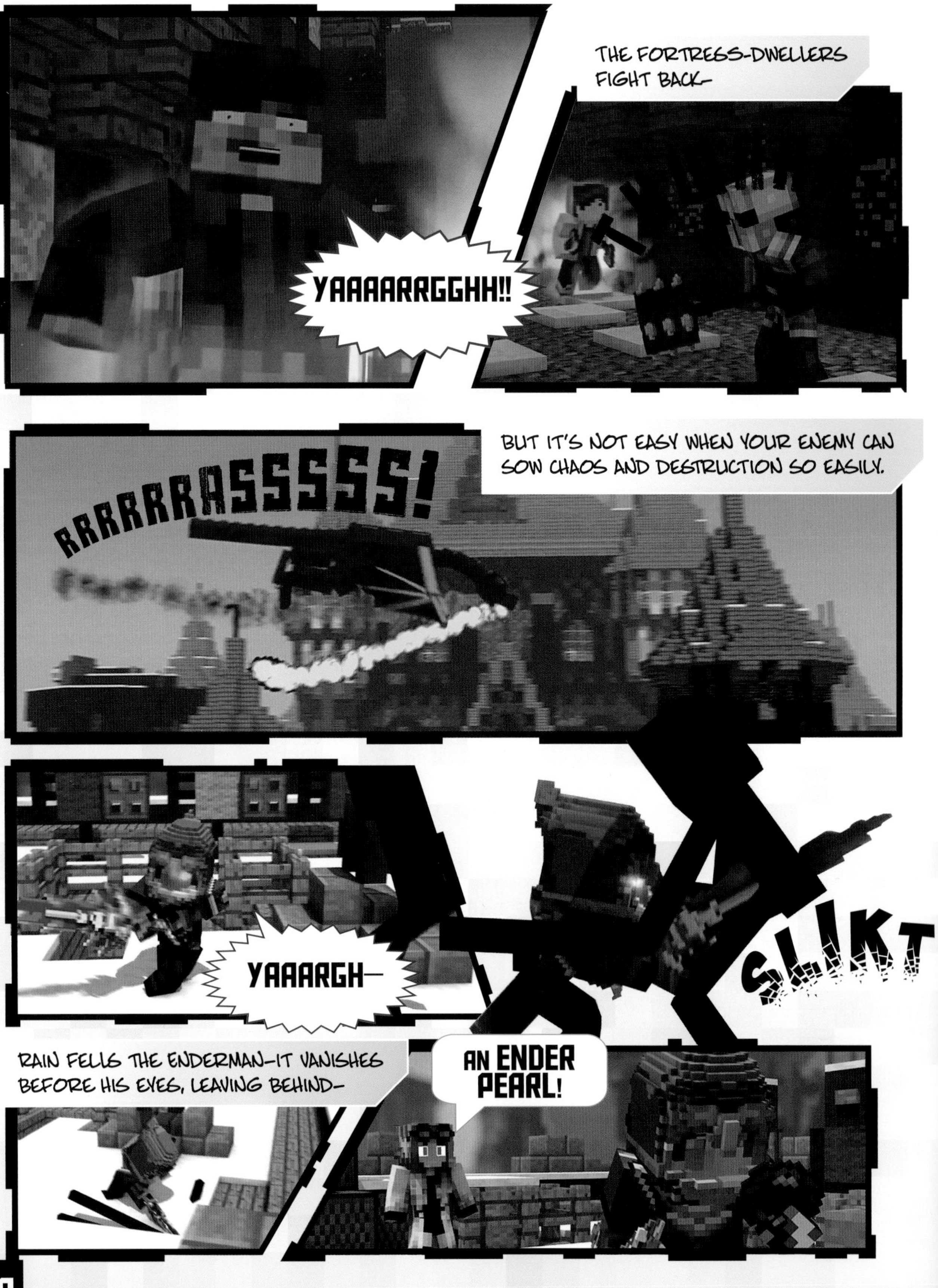

THE FORTRESS-DWELLERS FIGHT BACK-
YAAAARRGGHH!!
BUT IT'S NOT EASY WHEN YOUR ENEMY CAN SOW CHAOS AND DESTRUCTION SO EASILY.
RRRRRRASSSSSS!
YAAARGH—
SLIKT
RAIN FELLS THE ENDERMAN–IT VANISHES BEFORE HIS EYES, LEAVING BEHIND-
AN ENDER PEARL!

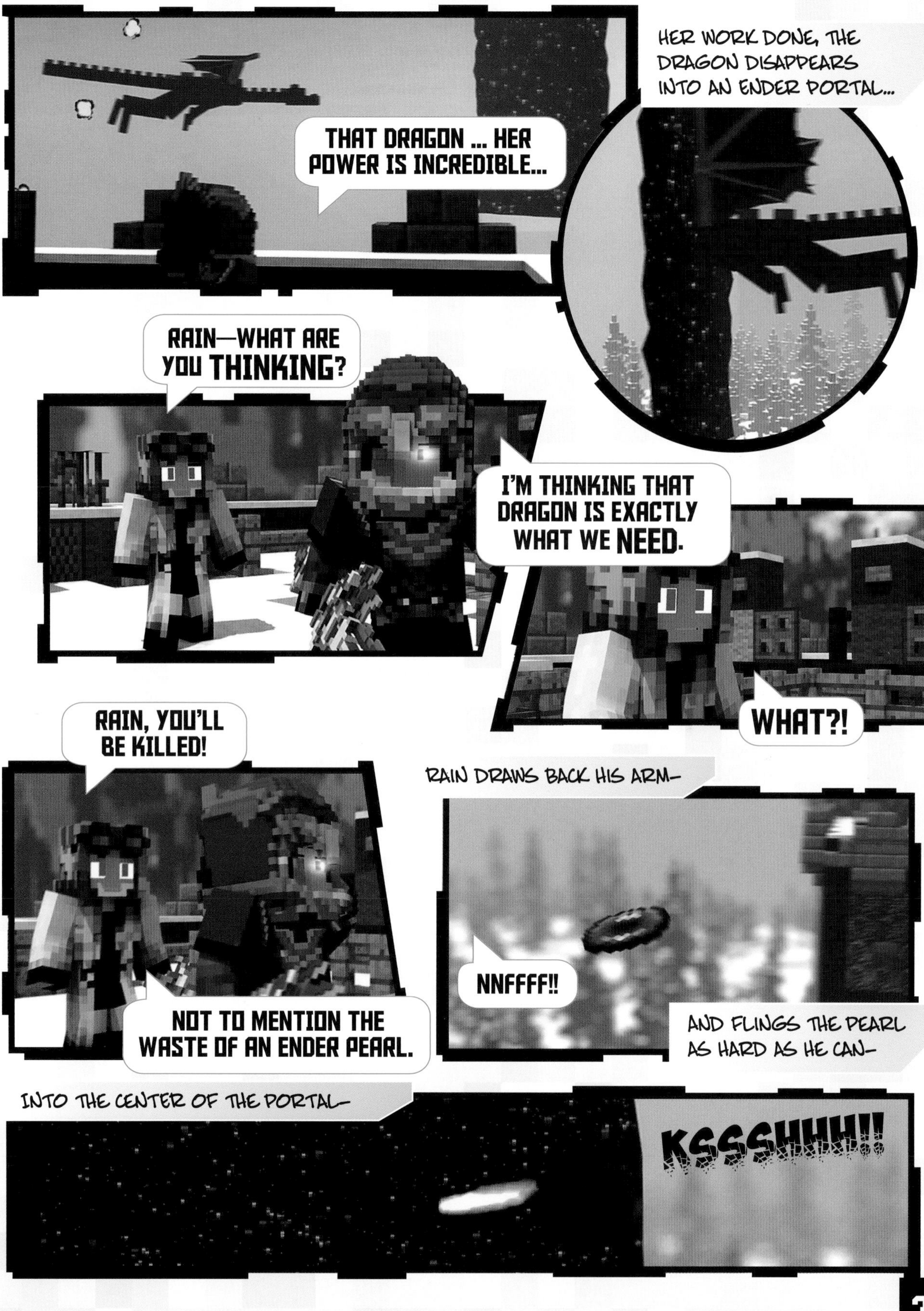
HER WORK DONE, THE DRAGON DISAPPEARS INTO AN ENDER PORTAL...
THAT DRAGON ... HER POWER IS INCREDIBLE...
RAIN—WHAT ARE YOU THINKING?
I'M THINKING THAT DRAGON IS EXACTLY WHAT WE NEED.
WHAT?!
RAIN, YOU'LL BE KILLED!
NOT TO MENTION THE WASTE OF AN ENDER PEARL.
RAIN DRAWS BACK HIS ARM—
NNFFFF!!
AND FLINGS THE PEARL AS HARD AS HE CAN—
INTO THE CENTER OF THE PORTAL—
KSSSHHH!!

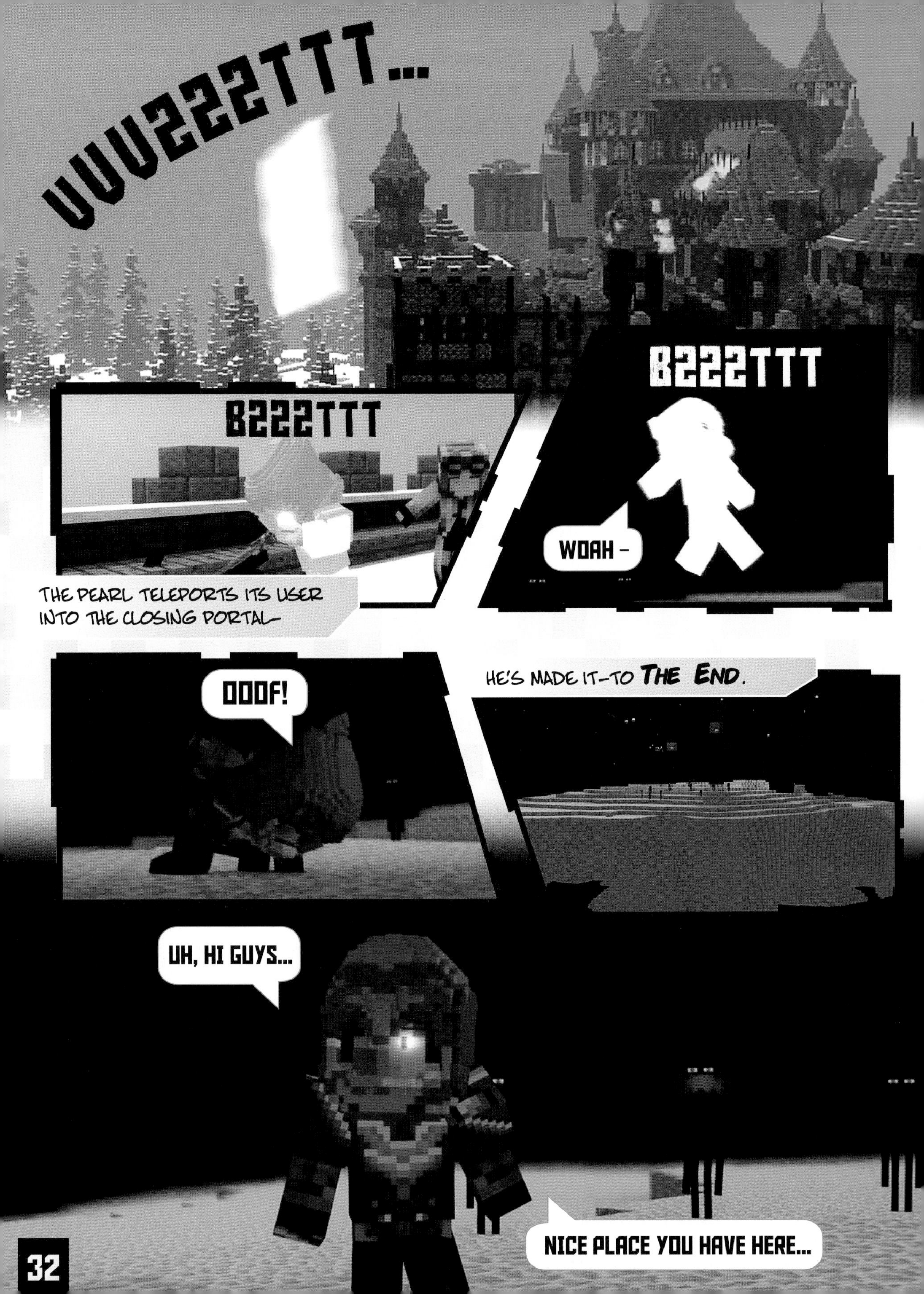
VVVZZZTTT...
BZZZTTT
THE PEARL TELEPORTS ITS USER INTO THE CLOSING PORTAL–
BZZZTTT
WOAH –
OOOF!
HE'S MADE IT–TO THE END.
UH, HI GUYS...
NICE PLACE YOU HAVE HERE...

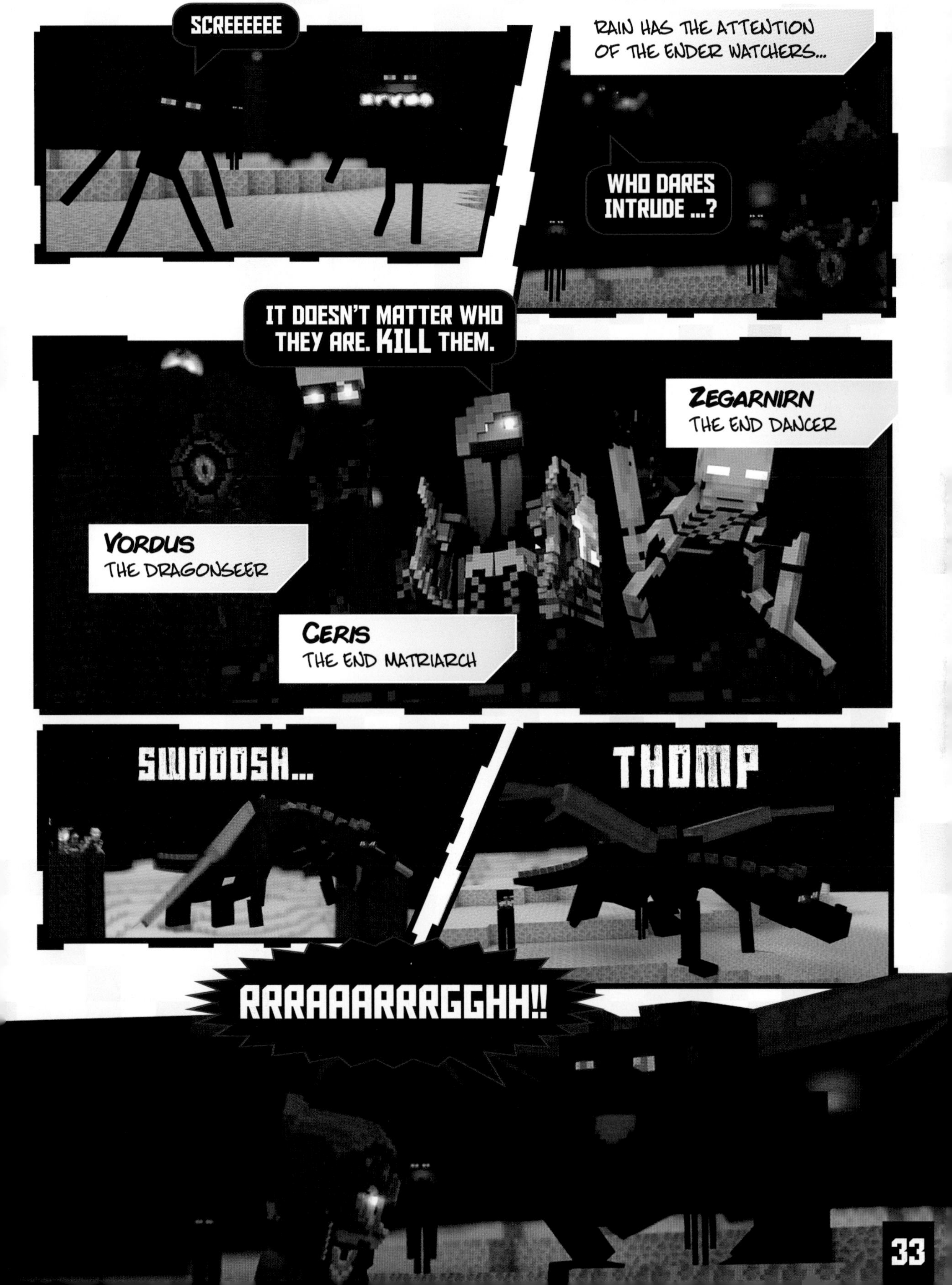
SCREEEEEE
RAIN HAS THE ATTENTION OF THE ENDER WATCHERS...
WHO DARES INTRUDE ...?
IT DOESN'T MATTER WHO THEY ARE. KILL THEM.
ZEGARNIRN
THE END DANCER
VORDUS
THE DRAGONSEER
CERIS
THE END MATRIARCH
SWOOOSH...
THOMP
RRRAAAARRRGGHH!!

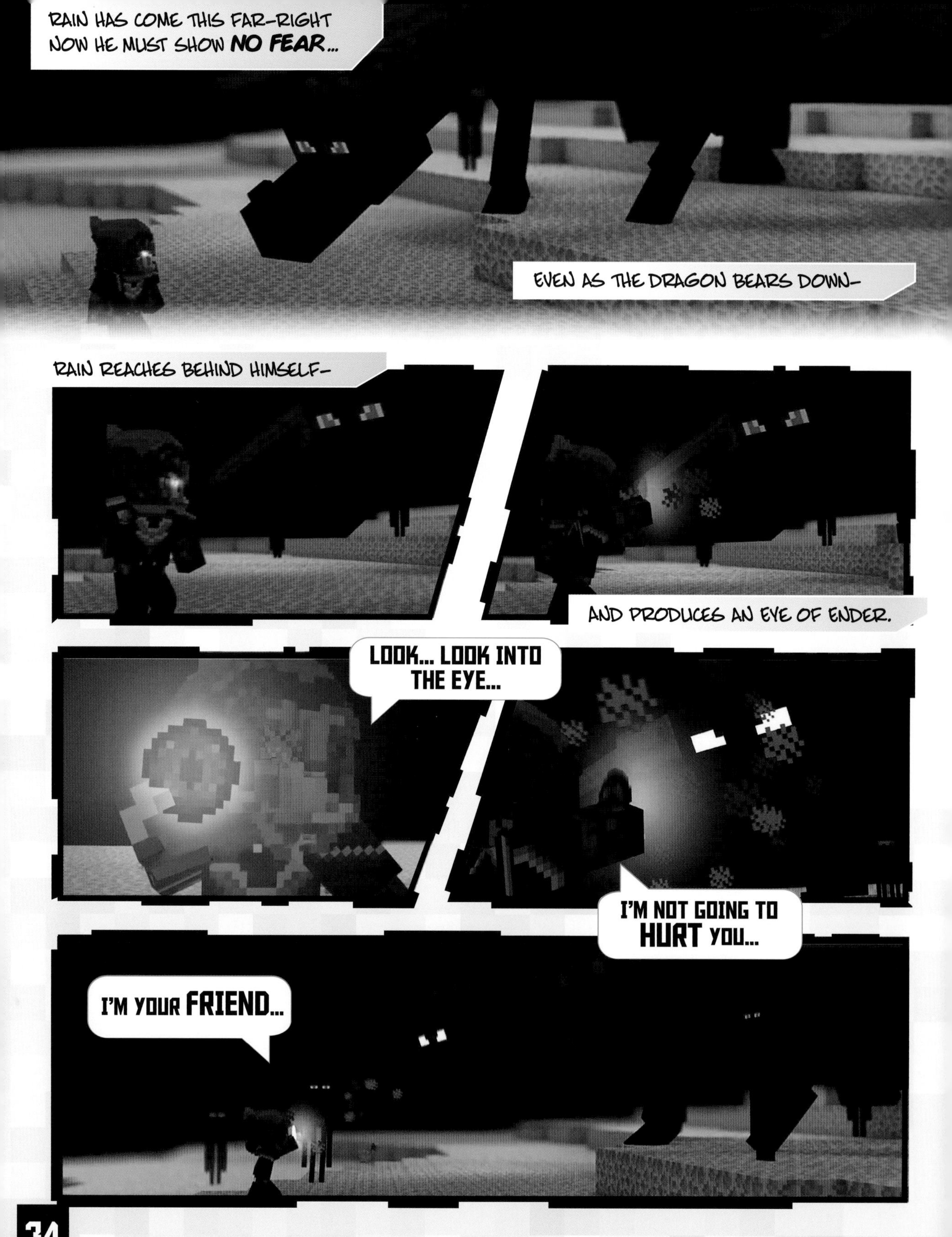
RAIN HAS COME THIS FAR–RIGHT NOW HE MUST SHOW NO FEAR...
EVEN AS THE DRAGON BEARS DOWN–
RAIN REACHES BEHIND HIMSELF–
AND PRODUCES AN EYE OF ENDER.
LOOK... LOOK INTO THE EYE...
I'M NOT GOING TO HURT YOU...
I'M YOUR FRIEND...

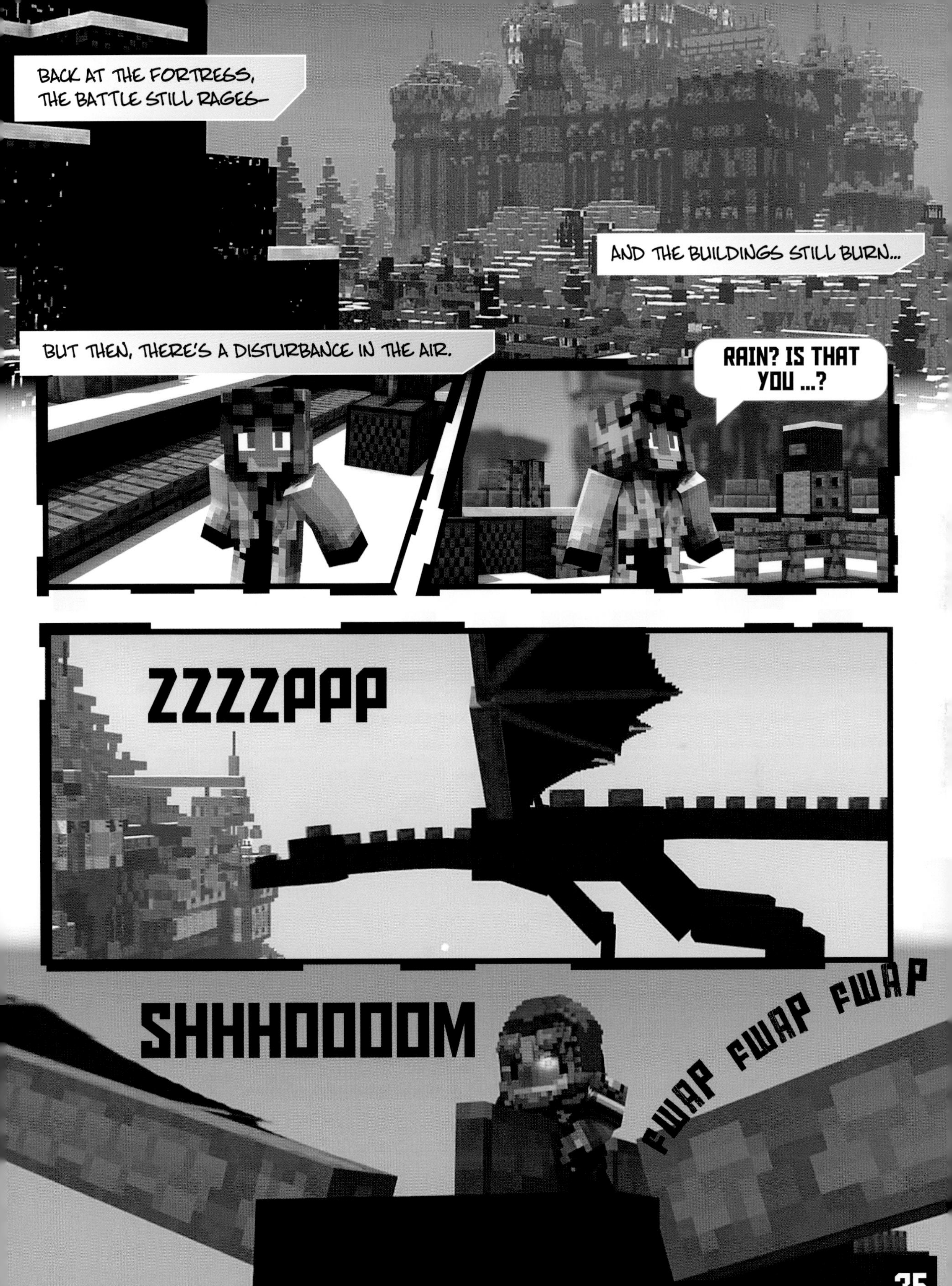
BACK AT THE FORTRESS, THE BATTLE STILL RAGES–
AND THE BUILDINGS STILL BURN...
BUT THEN, THERE'S A DISTURBANCE IN THE AIR.
RAIN? IS THAT YOU ...?
ZZZZPPP
SHHOOOOM
FWAP FWAP FWAP

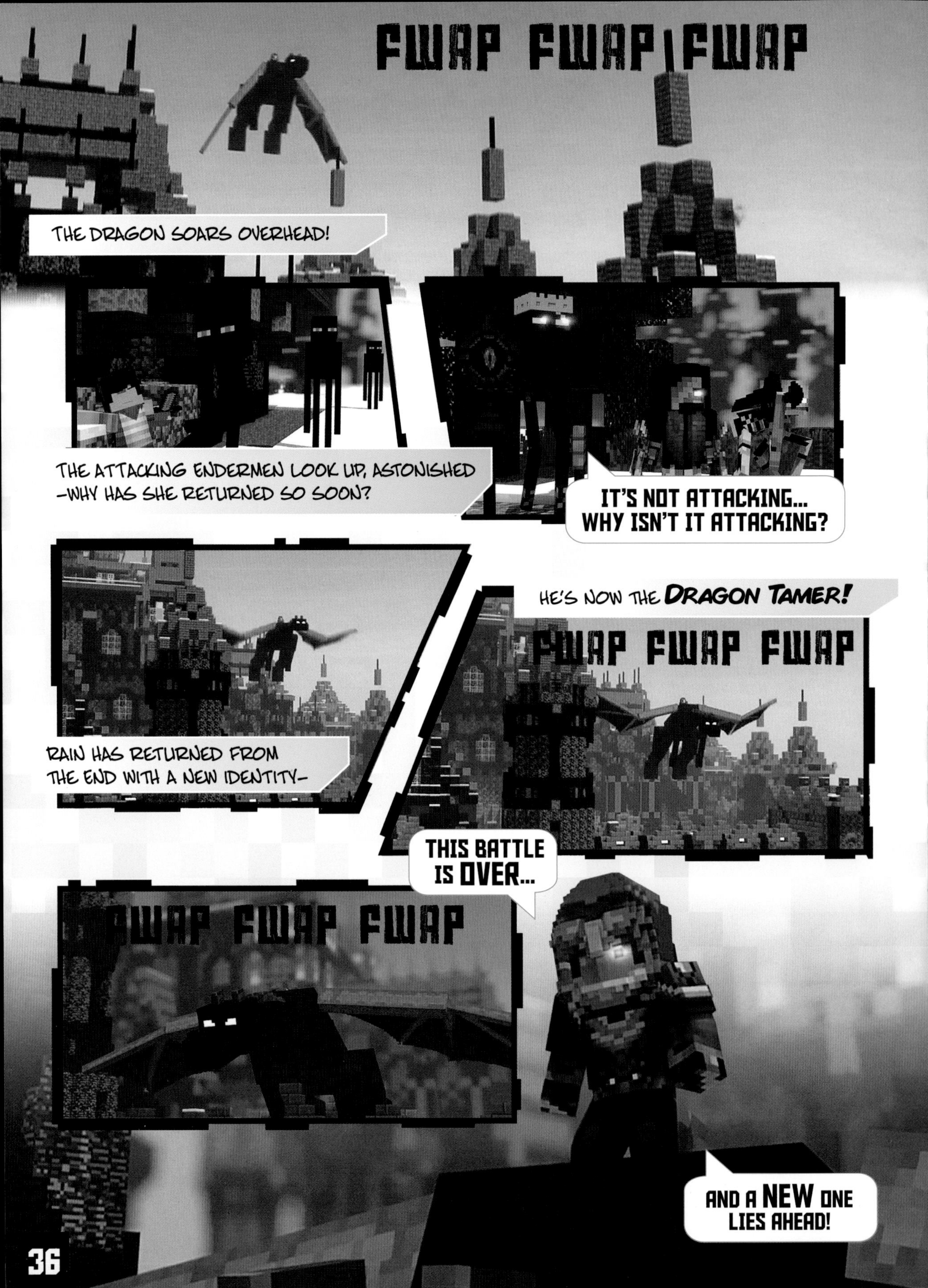
FWAP FWAP FWAP
THE DRAGON SOARS OVERHEAD!
THE ATTACKING ENDERMEN LOOK UP, ASTONISHED -WHY HAS SHE RETURNED SO SOON?
IT'S NOT ATTACKING... WHY ISN'T IT ATTACKING?
RAIN HAS RETURNED FROM THE END WITH A NEW IDENTITY-
HE'S NOW THE DRAGON TAMER!
FWAP FWAP FWAP
THIS BATTLE IS OVER...
WAP FWAP FWAP
AND A NEW ONE LIES AHEAD!

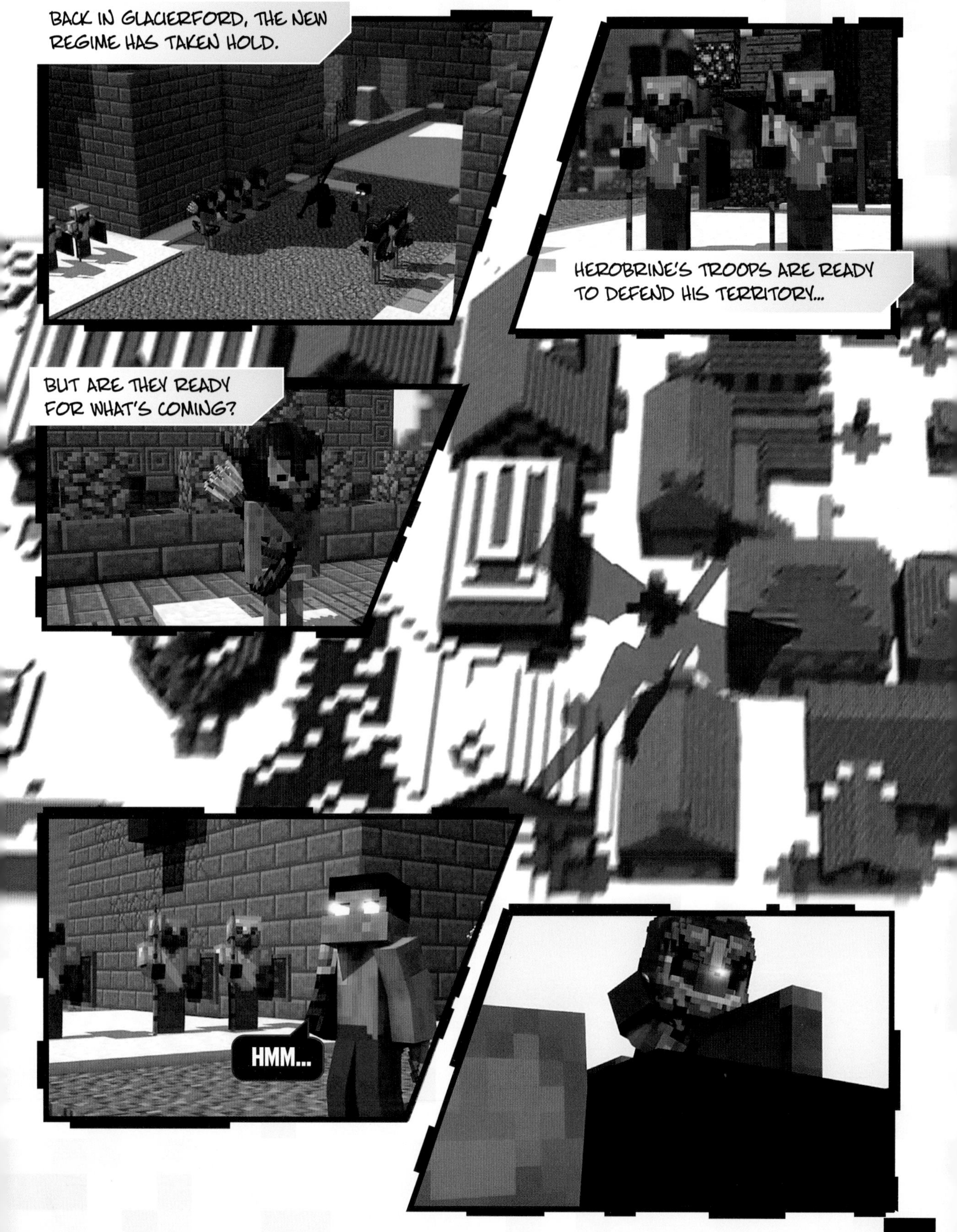
BACK IN GLACIERFORD, THE NEW REGIME HAS TAKEN HOLD.
HEROBRINE'S TROOPS ARE READY TO DEFEND HIS TERRITORY...
BUT ARE THEY READY FOR WHAT'S COMING?
HMM...

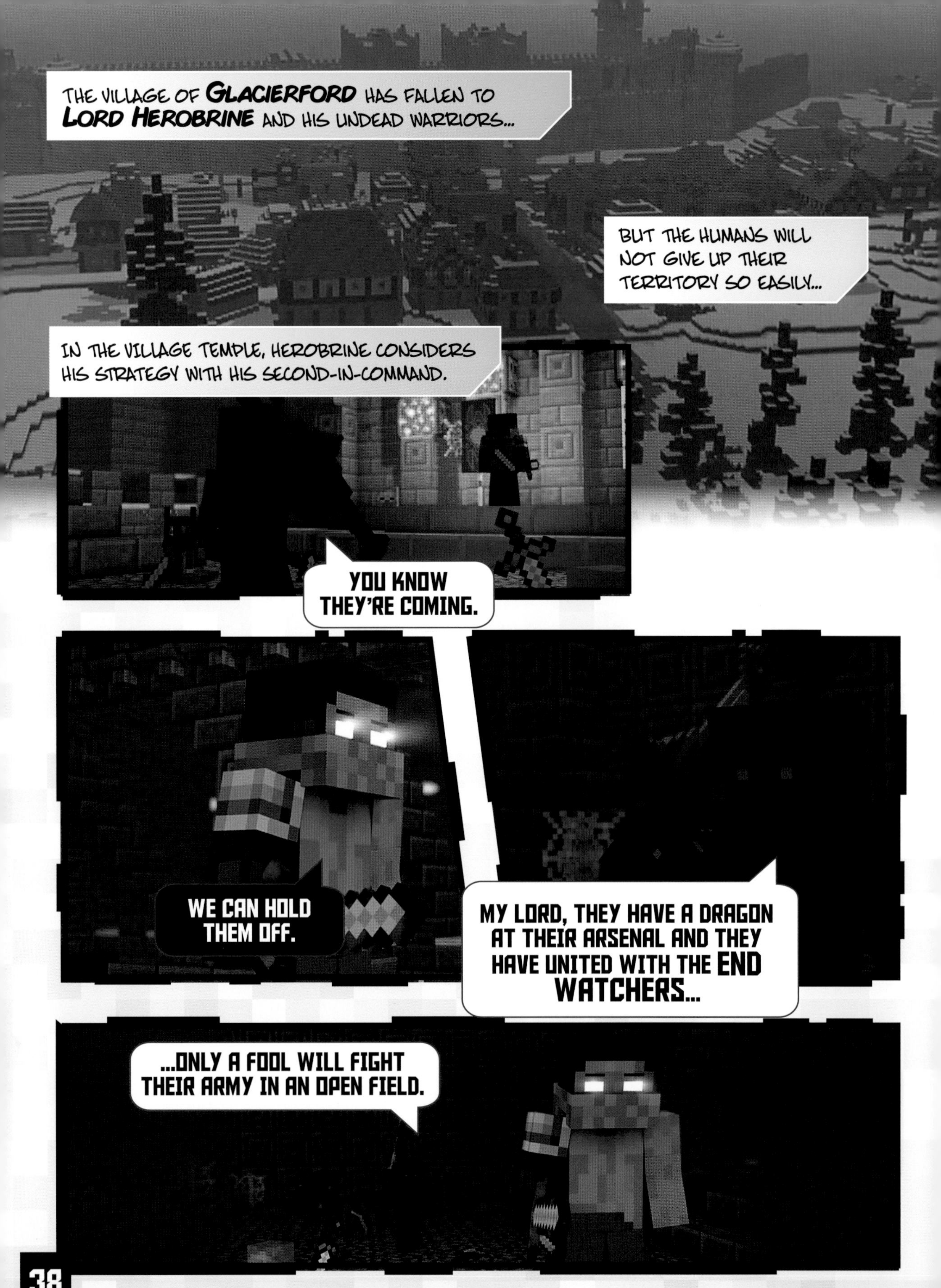

THE VILLAGE OF GLACIERFORD HAS FALLEN TO LORD HEROBRINE AND HIS UNDEAD WARRIORS...
BUT THE HUMANS WILL NOT GIVE UP THEIR TERRITORY SO EASILY...
IN THE VILLAGE TEMPLE, HEROBRINE CONSIDERS HIS STRATEGY WITH HIS SECOND-IN-COMMAND.
YOU KNOW THEY'RE COMING.
WE CAN HOLD THEM OFF.
MY LORD, THEY HAVE A DRAGON AT THEIR ARSENAL AND THEY HAVE UNITED WITH THE END WATCHERS...
...ONLY A FOOL WILL FIGHT THEIR ARMY IN AN OPEN FIELD.

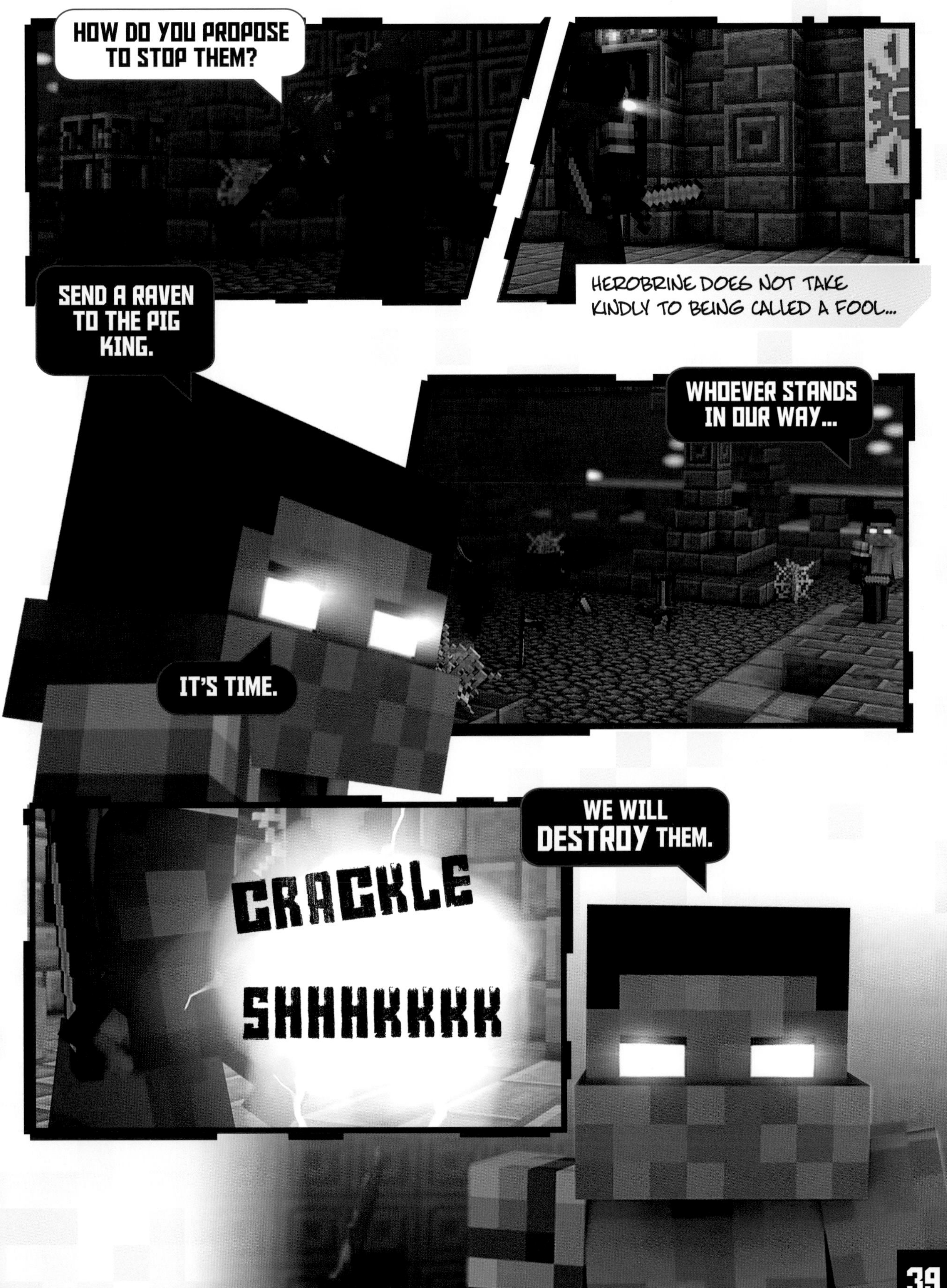
HOW DO YOU PROPOSE TO STOP THEM?
HEROBRINE DOES NOT TAKE KINDLY TO BEING CALLED A FOOL...
SEND A RAVEN TO THE PIG KING.
WHOEVER STANDS IN OUR WAY...
IT'S TIME.
WE WILL DESTROY THEM.
CRACKLE
SHHHKKKK

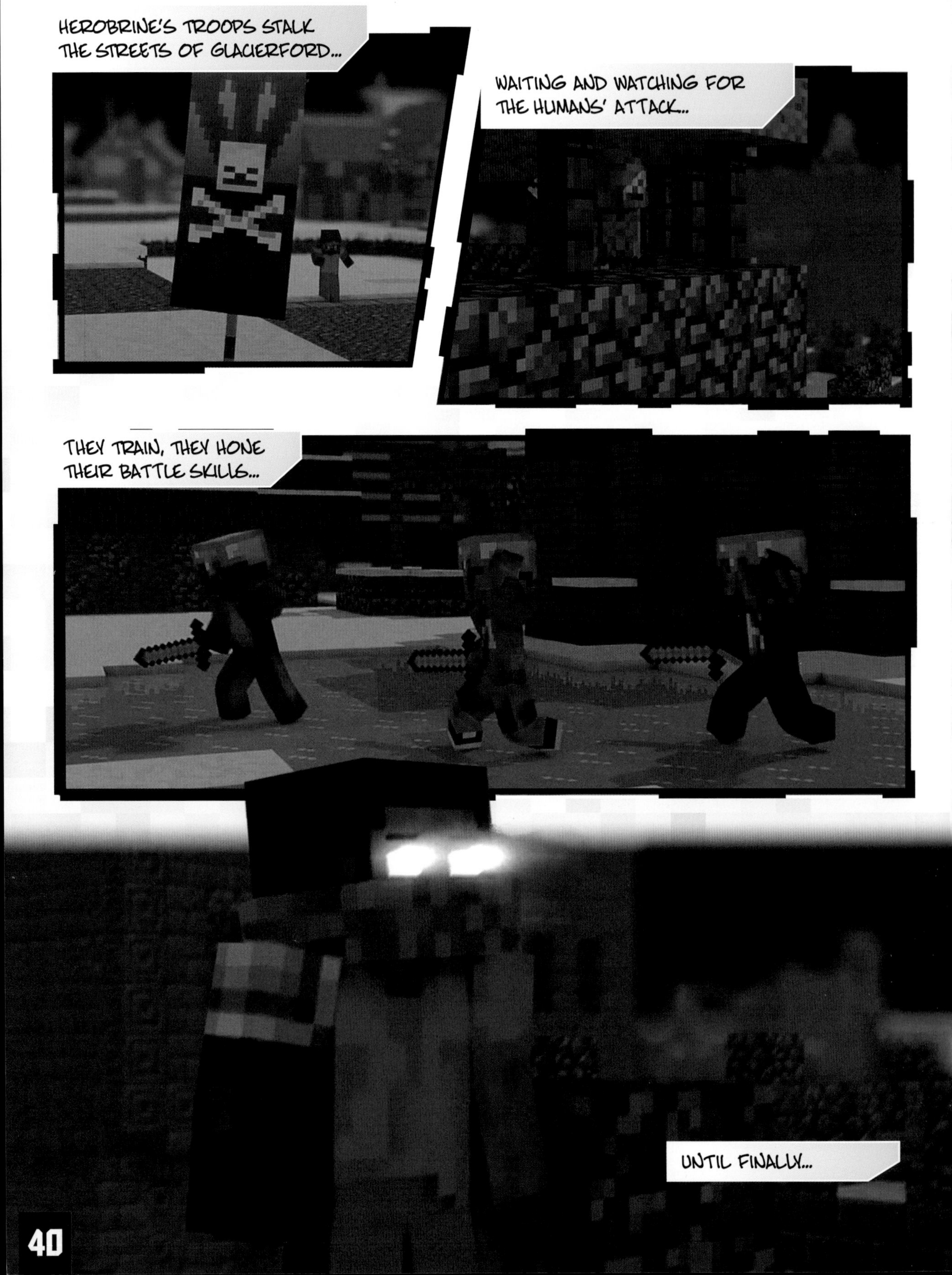
HEROBRINE'S TROOPS STALK THE STREETS OF GLACIERFORD...
WAITING AND WATCHING FOR THE HUMANS' ATTACK...
THEY TRAIN, THEY HONE THEIR BATTLE SKILLS...
UNTIL FINALLY...

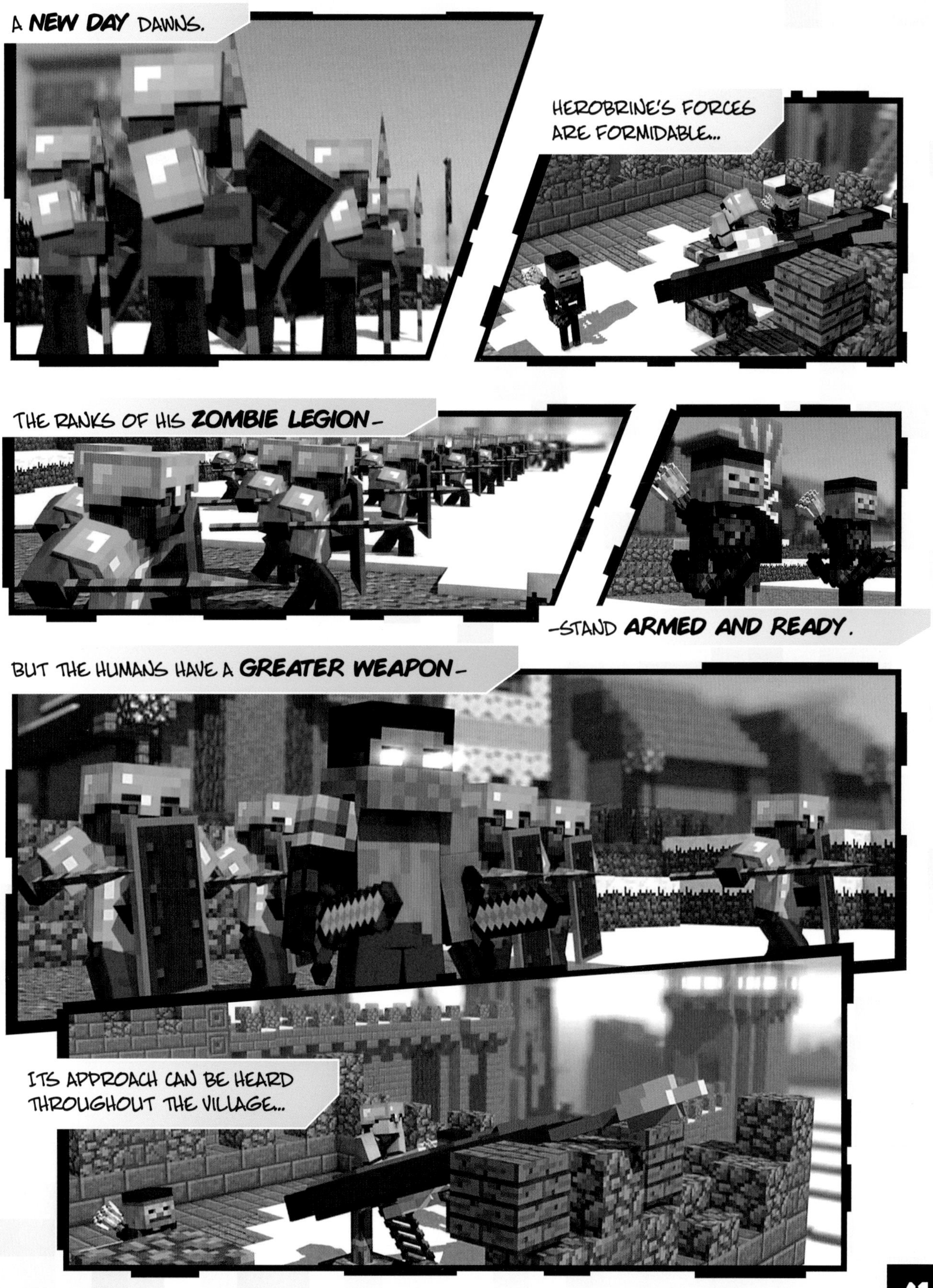
A NEW DAY DAWNS.
HEROBRINE'S FORCES ARE FORMIDABLE...
THE RANKS OF HIS ZOMBIE LEGION-
-STAND ARMED AND READY.
BUT THE HUMANS HAVE A GREATER WEAPON-
ITS APPROACH CAN BE HEARD THROUGHOUT THE VILLAGE...

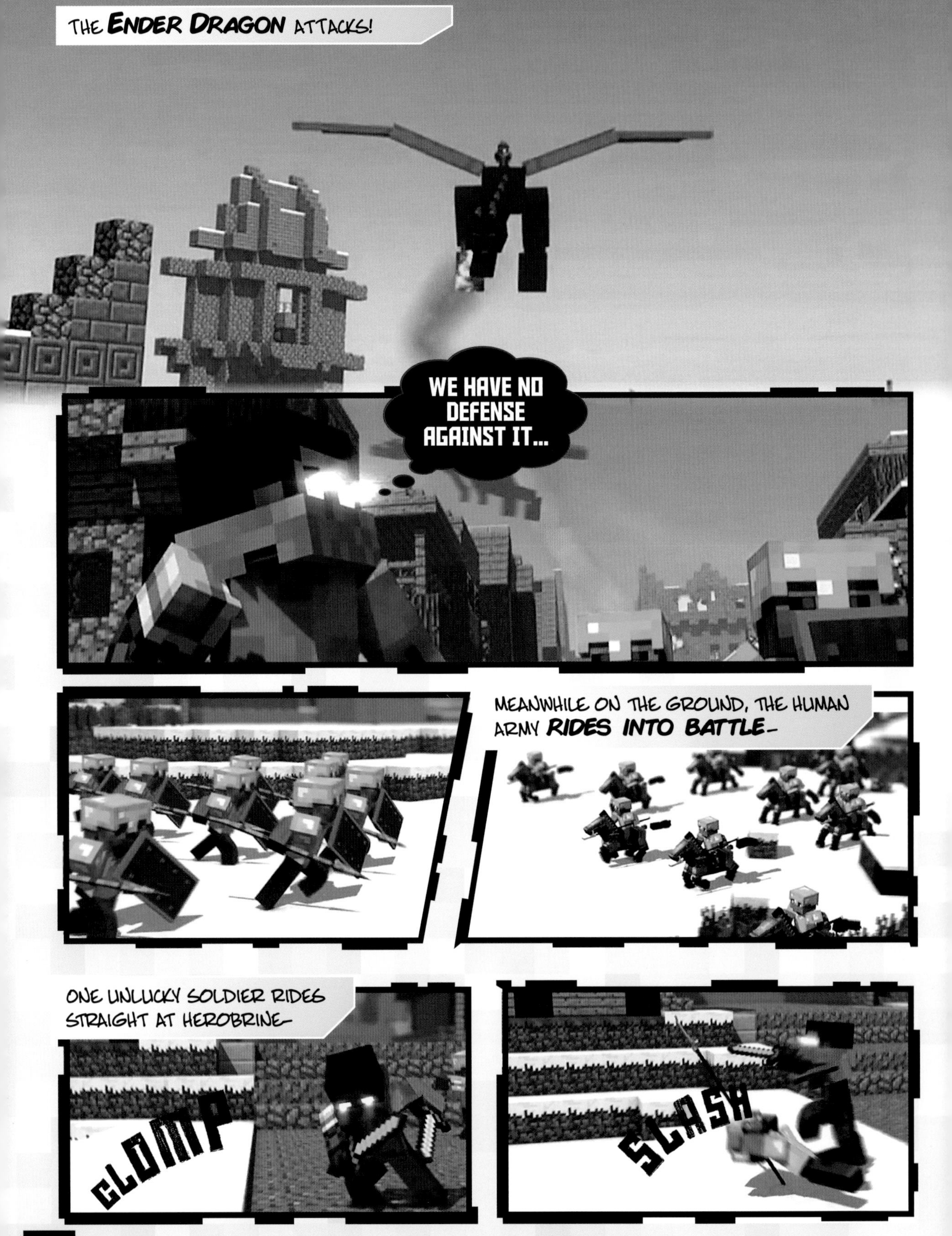
THE ENDER DRAGON ATTACKS!
WE HAVE NO DEFENSE AGAINST IT...
MEANWHILE ON THE GROUND, THE HUMAN ARMY RIDES INTO BATTLE-
ONE UNLUCKY SOLDIER RIDES STRAIGHT AT HEROBRINE-
CLOMP
SLASH

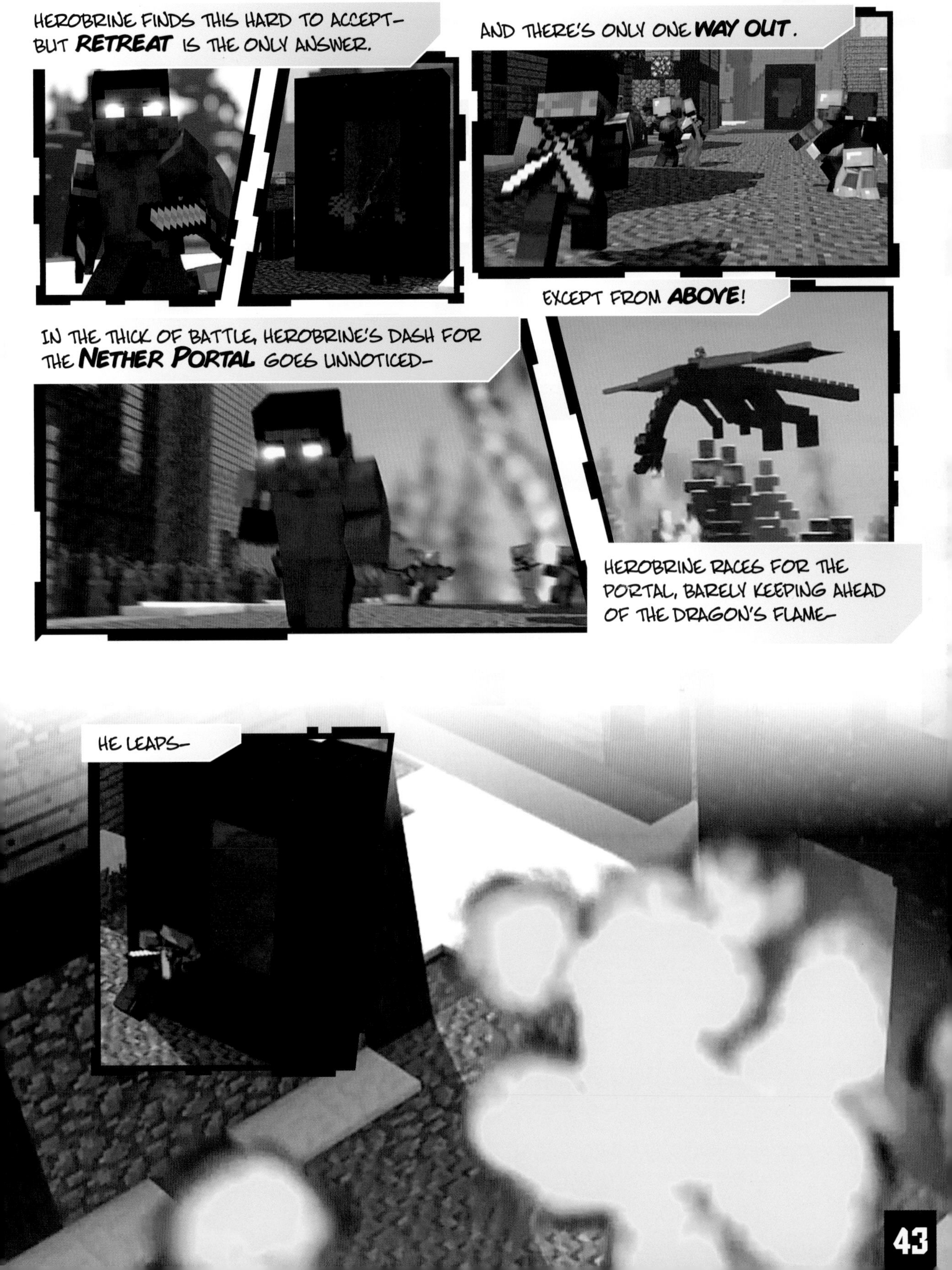
HEROBRINE FINDS THIS HARD TO ACCEPT- BUT RETREAT IS THE ONLY ANSWER.
AND THERE'S ONLY ONE WAY OUT.
IN THE THICK OF BATTLE, HEROBRINE'S DASH FOR THE NETHER PORTAL GOES UNNOTICED-
EXCEPT FROM ABOVE!
HEROBRINE RACES FOR THE PORTAL, BARELY KEEPING AHEAD OF THE DRAGON'S FLAME-
HE LEAPS-

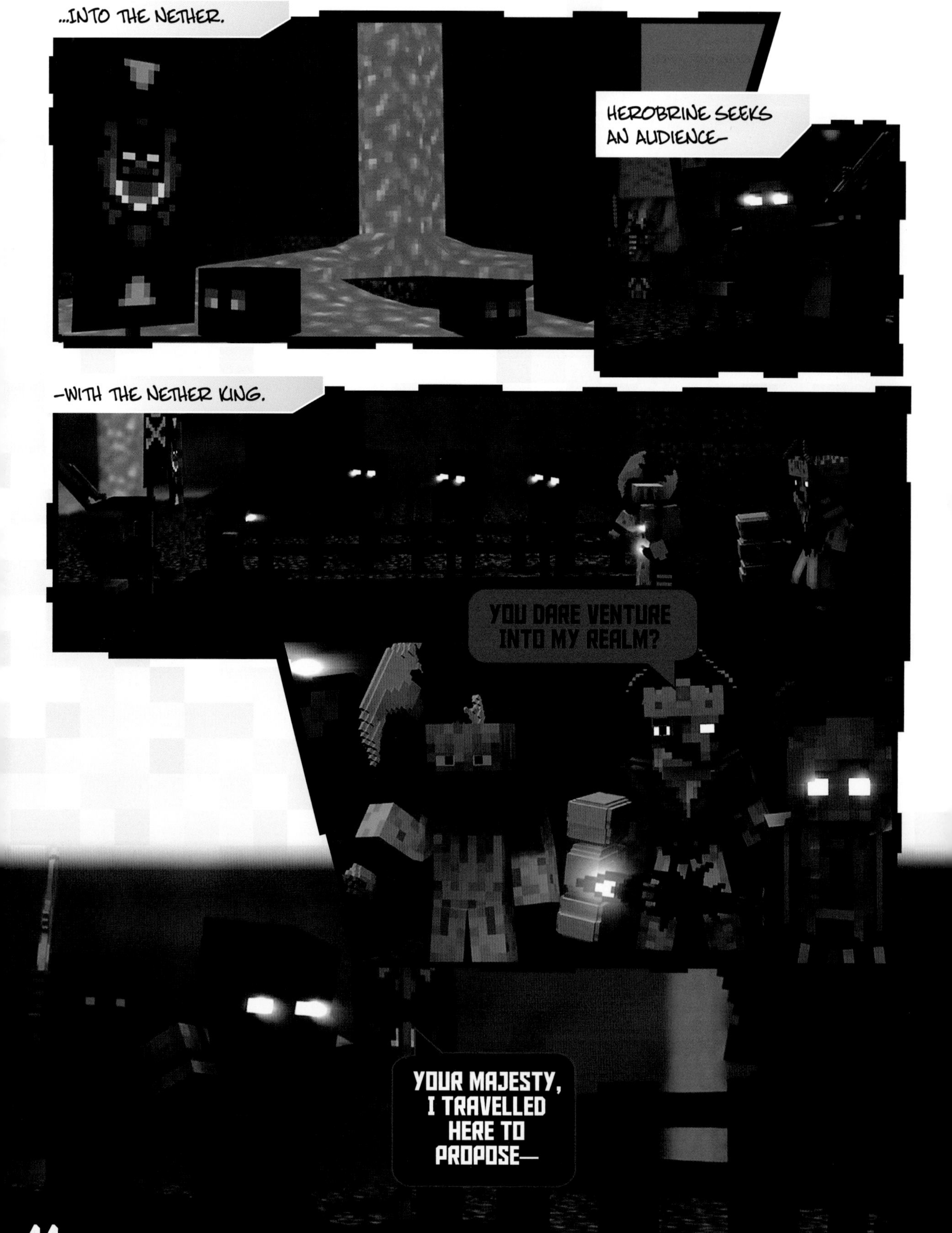
...INTO THE NETHER.
HEROBRINE SEEKS AN AUDIENCE–
–WITH THE NETHER KING.
YOU DARE VENTURE INTO MY REALM?
YOUR MAJESTY, I TRAVELLED HERE TO PROPOSE—

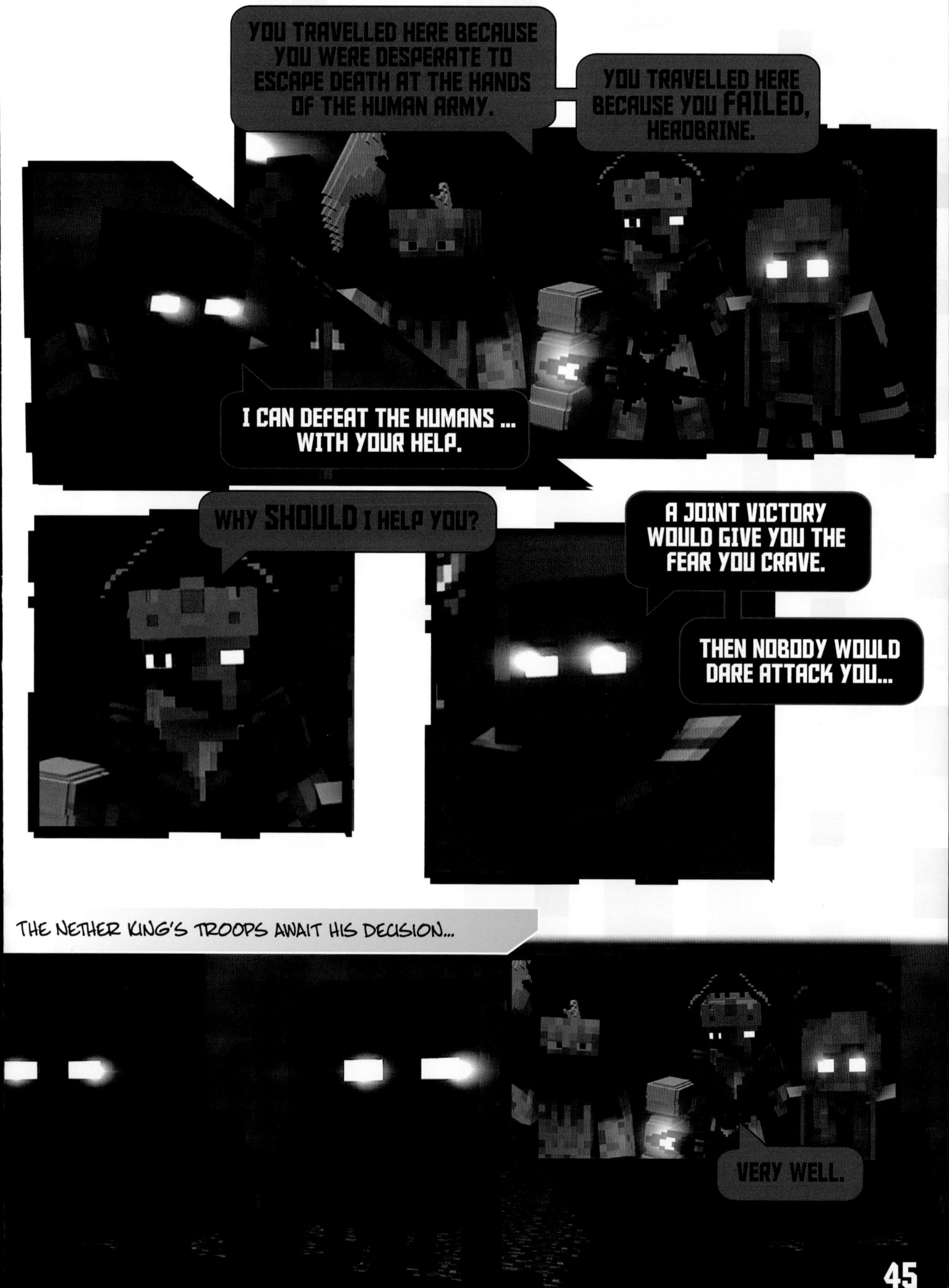

YOU TRAVELLED HERE BECAUSE YOU WERE DESPERATE TO ESCAPE DEATH AT THE HANDS OF THE HUMAN ARMY.
YOU TRAVELLED HERE BECAUSE YOU FAILED, HEROBRINE.
I CAN DEFEAT THE HUMANS ... WITH YOUR HELP.
WHY SHOULD I HELP YOU?
A JOINT VICTORY WOULD GIVE YOU THE FEAR YOU CRAVE.
THEN NOBODY WOULD DARE ATTACK YOU...
THE NETHER KING'S TROOPS AWAIT HIS DECISION...
VERY WELL.

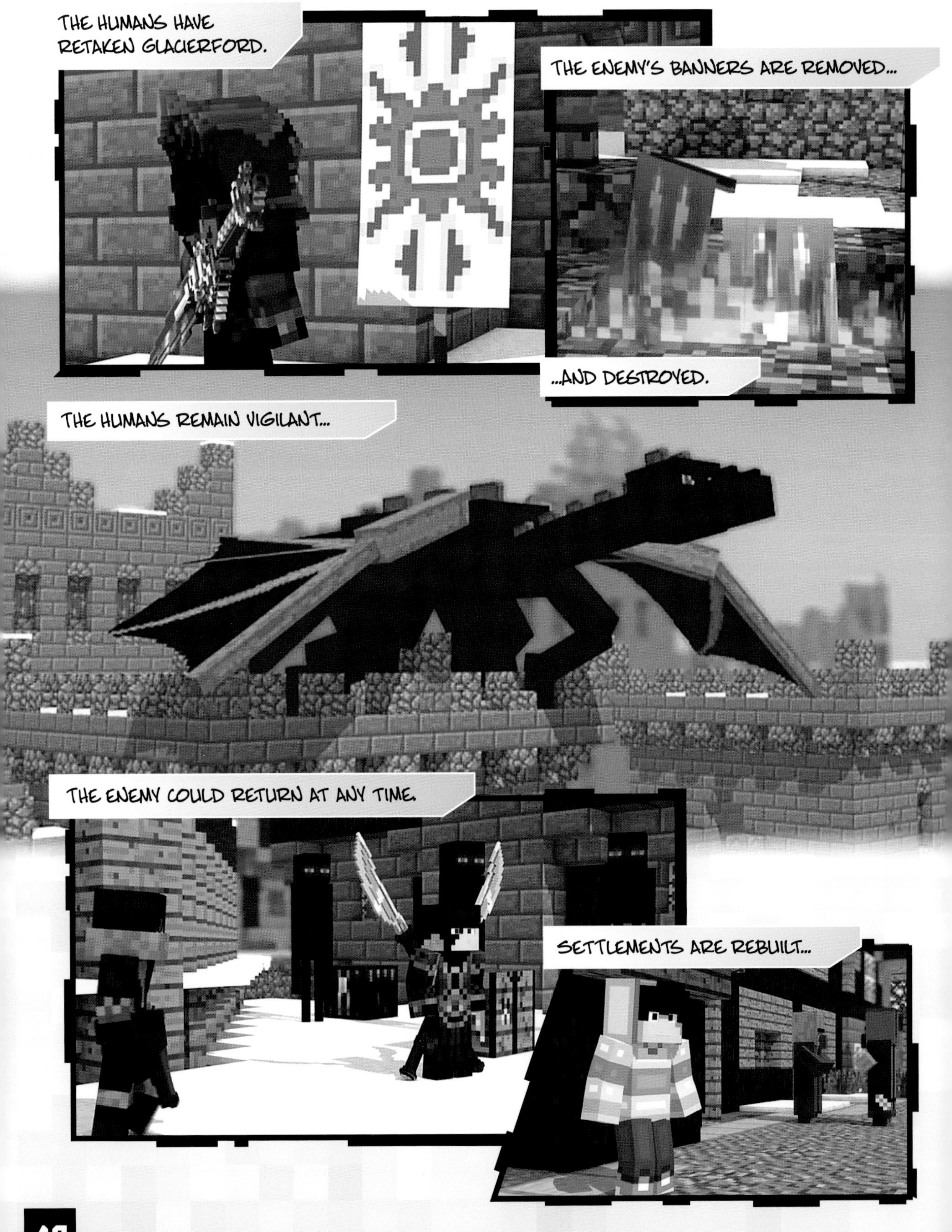
THE HUMANS HAVE RETAKEN GLACIERFORD.
THE ENEMY'S BANNERS ARE REMOVED...
...AND DESTROYED.
THE HUMANS REMAIN VIGILANT...
THE ENEMY COULD RETURN AT ANY TIME.
SETTLEMENTS ARE REBUILT...

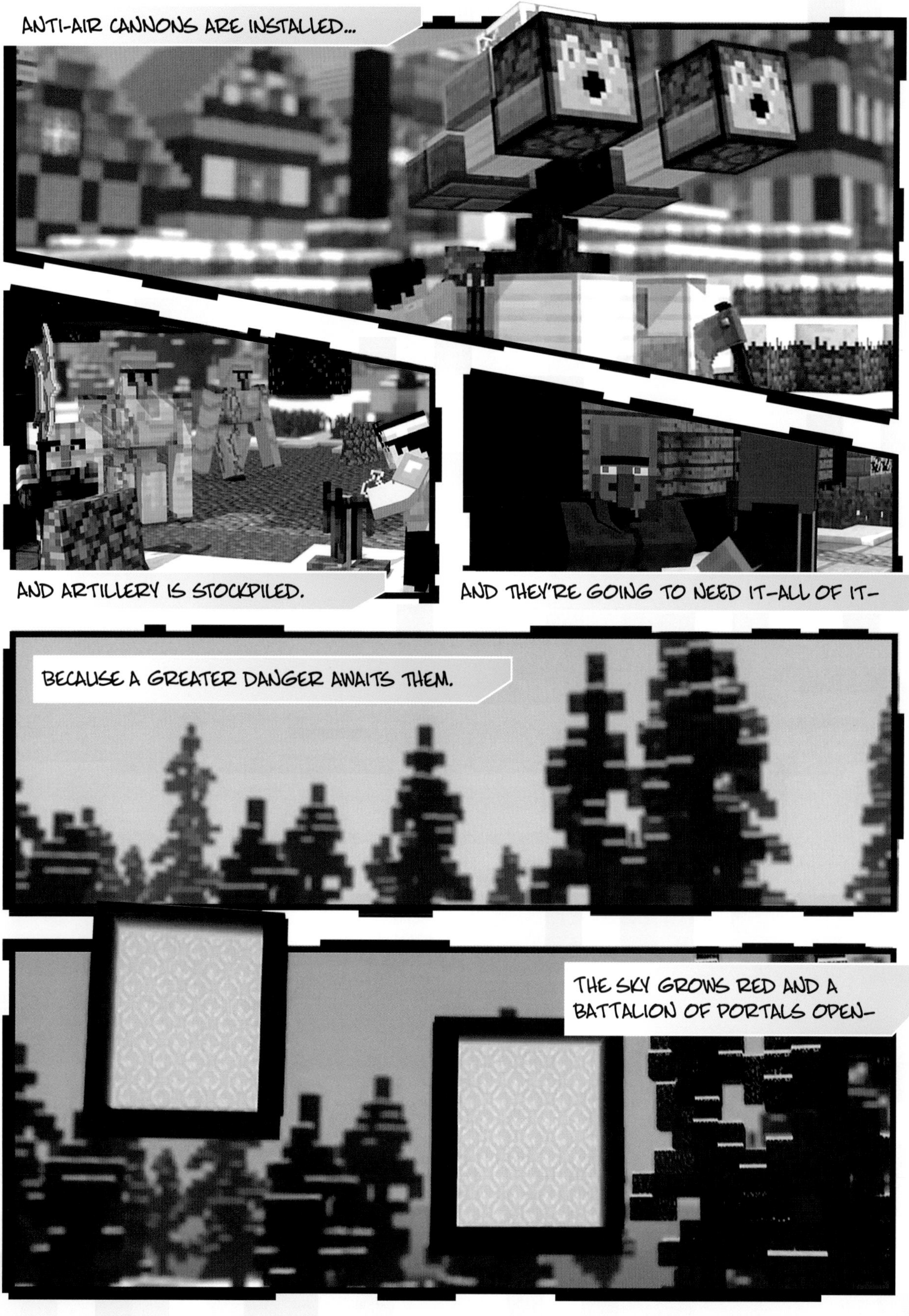
ANTI-AIR CANNONS ARE INSTALLED...
AND ARTILLERY IS STOCKPILED.
AND THEY'RE GOING TO NEED IT—ALL OF IT—
BECAUSE A GREATER DANGER AWAITS THEM.
THE SKY GROWS RED AND A BATTALION OF PORTALS OPEN—

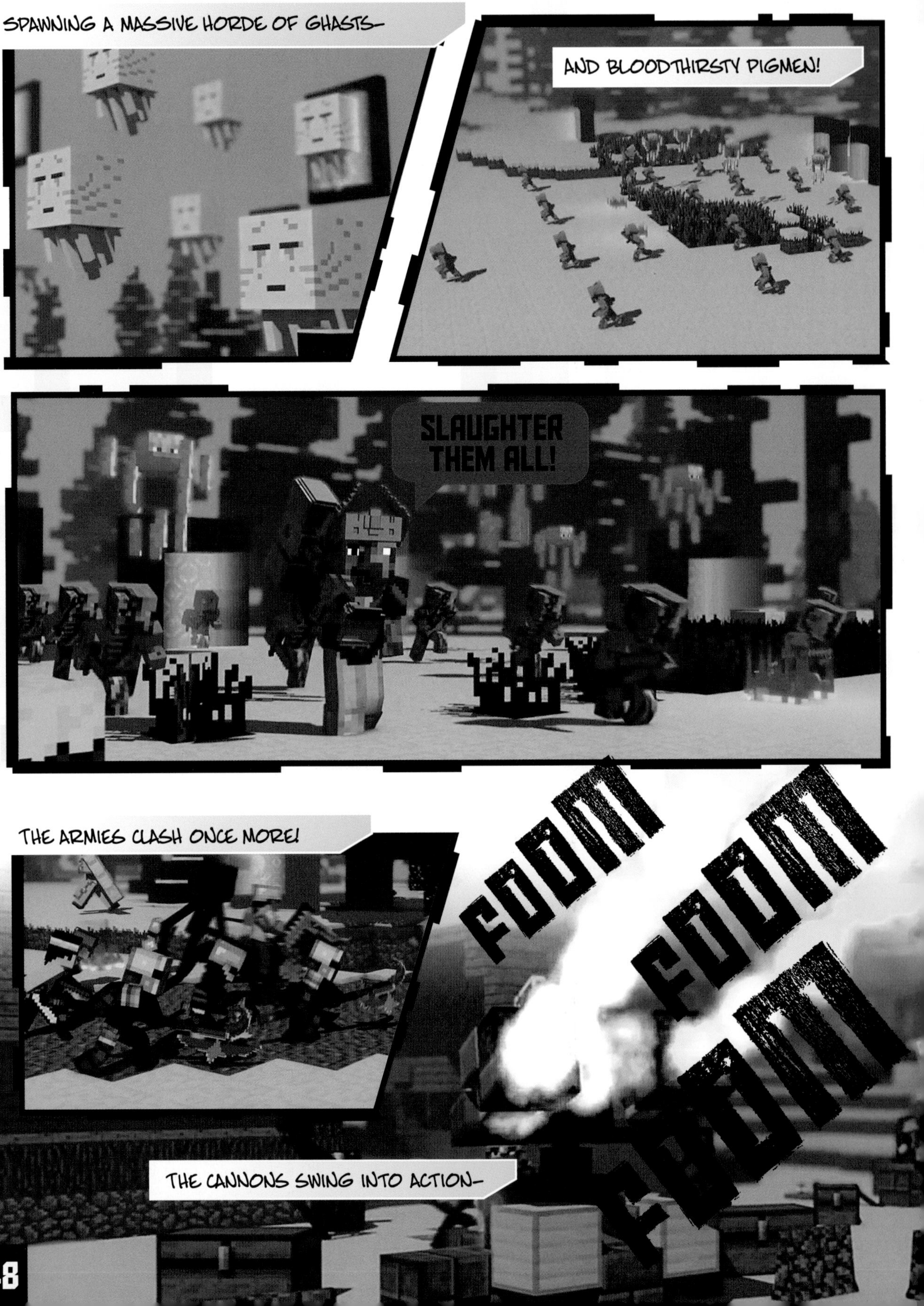

SPAWNING A MASSIVE HORDE OF GHASTS–
AND BLOODTHIRSTY PIGMEN!
SLAUGHTER THEM ALL!
THE ARMIES CLASH ONCE MORE!
FOOM
FOOM
FOOM
THE CANNONS SWING INTO ACTION–

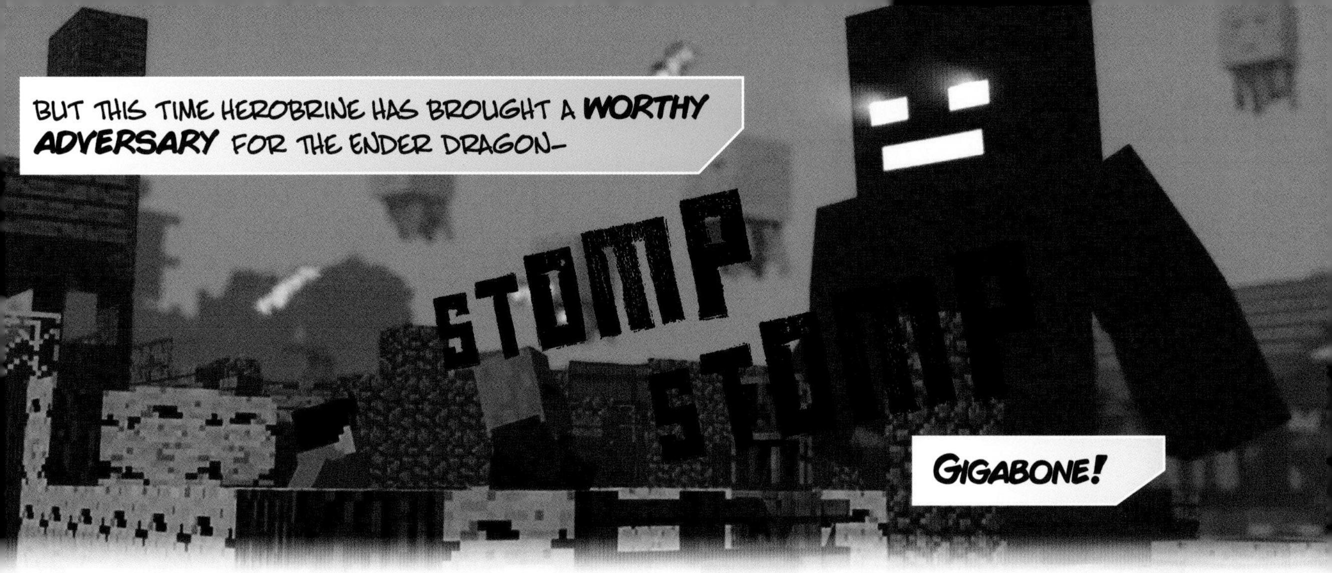
BUT THIS TIME HEROBRINE HAS BROUGHT A **WORTHY ADVERSARY** FOR THE ENDER DRAGON—
STOMP
STOMP
GIGABONE!

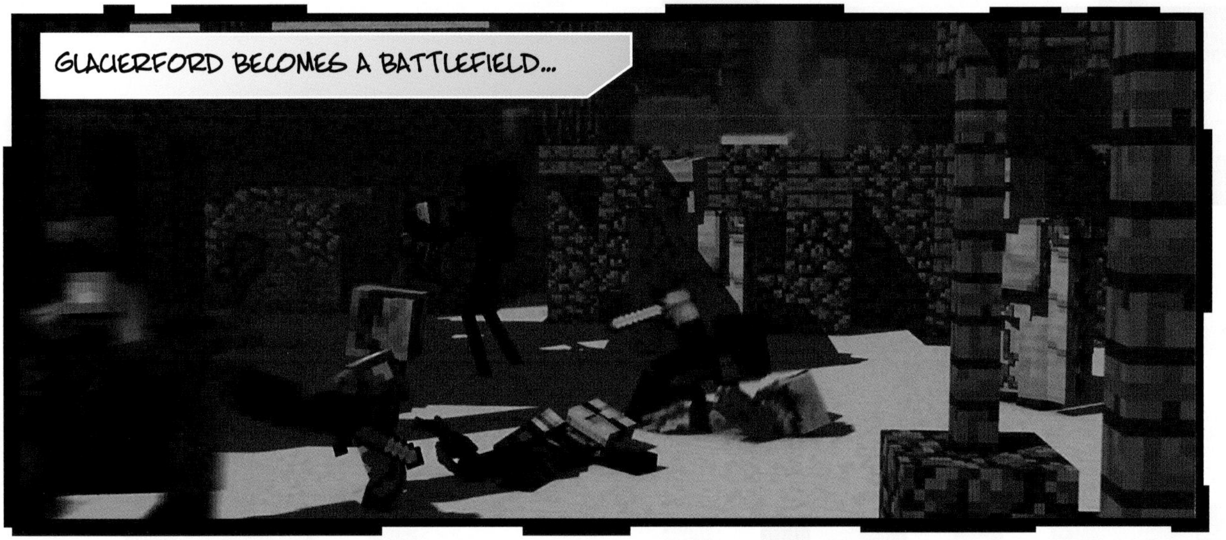
GLACIERFORD BECOMES A BATTLEFIELD...

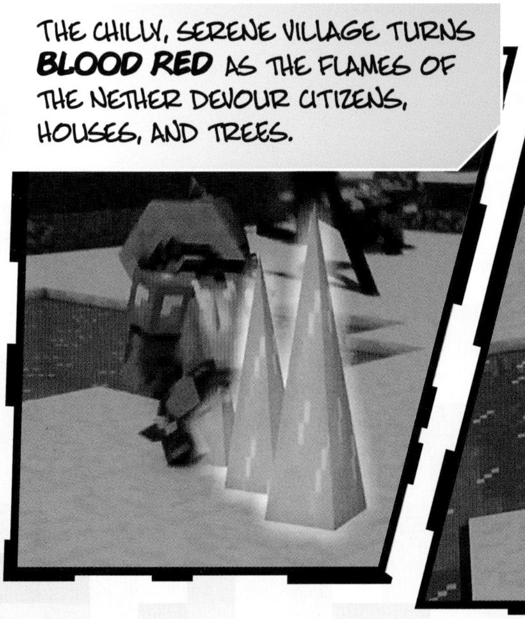
THE CHILLY, SERENE VILLAGE TURNS **BLOOD RED** AS THE FLAMES OF THE NETHER DEVOUR CITIZENS, HOUSES, AND TREES.

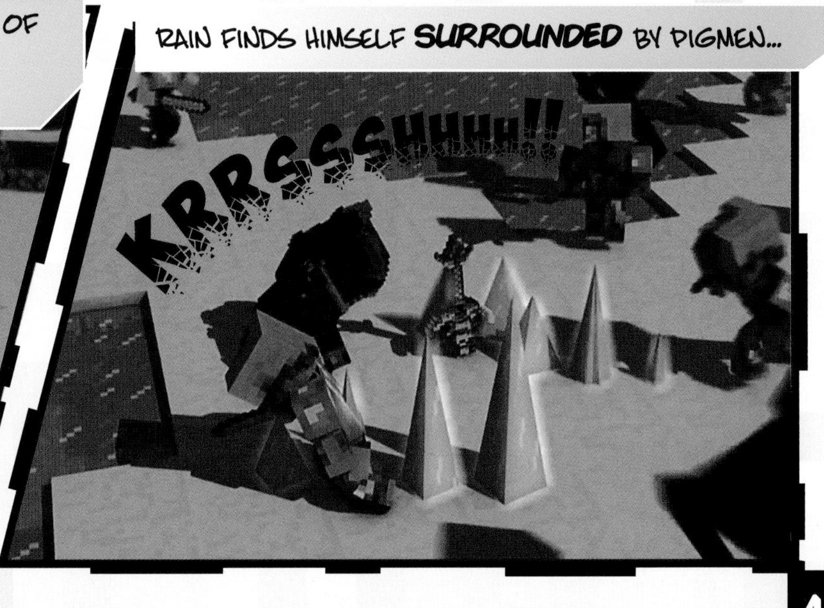
RAIN FINDS HIMSELF **SURROUNDED** BY PIGMEN...
KRRSSSHHHH!!

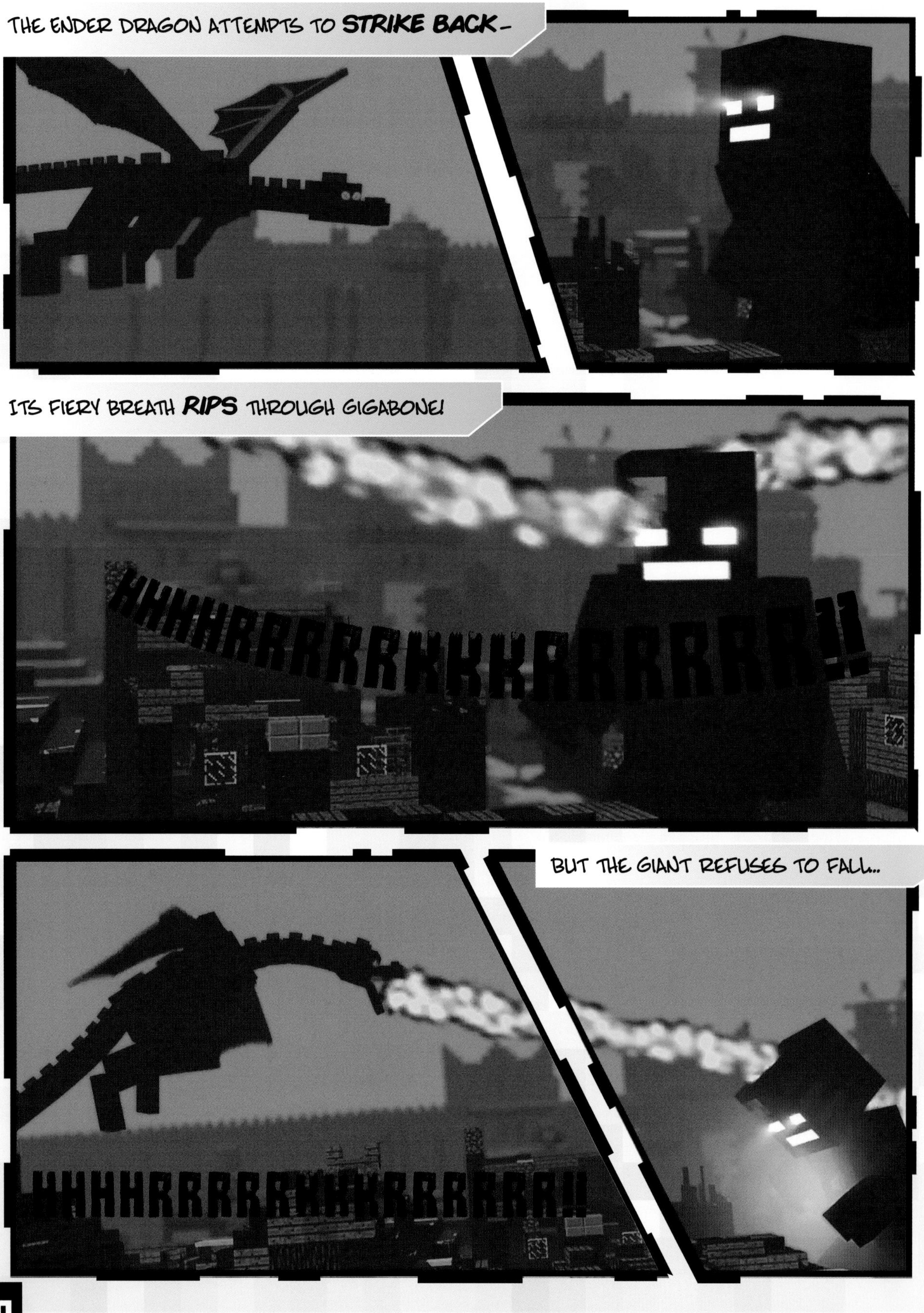
THE ENDER DRAGON ATTEMPTS TO **STRIKE BACK**-
ITS FIERY BREATH **RIPS** THROUGH GIGABONE!
HHHHRRRRRRKKKKRRRRRRRR!!
BUT THE GIANT REFUSES TO FALL...
HHHHRRRRRRKKKKRRRRRRRR!!

AS FIRE RAINS DOWN FROM THE SKY, THE VILLAGERS—AND RAIN—RUN FOR **COVER**...

BUT THEN HE LOOKS UP AND SEES A FAMILIAR FACE—

ABIGAIL. THE GIRL WITH WHOM HE FLED GLACIERFORD, WHO DIED WITH HIM IN THE ZOMBIE ATTACKS—

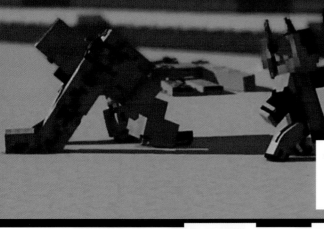

BUT WHILE HE HAS REGAINED HIS HUMANITY SINCE RISING FROM THE DEAD, SHE HAS CHANGED—**HORRIBLY** CHANGED—

SHE IS NOW THE **NETHER PRINCESS**.

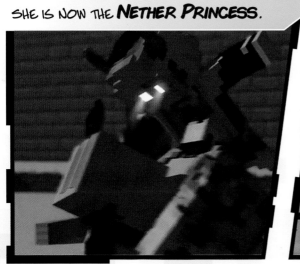

WHAT ... WHAT'S **HAPPENED** TO YOU?

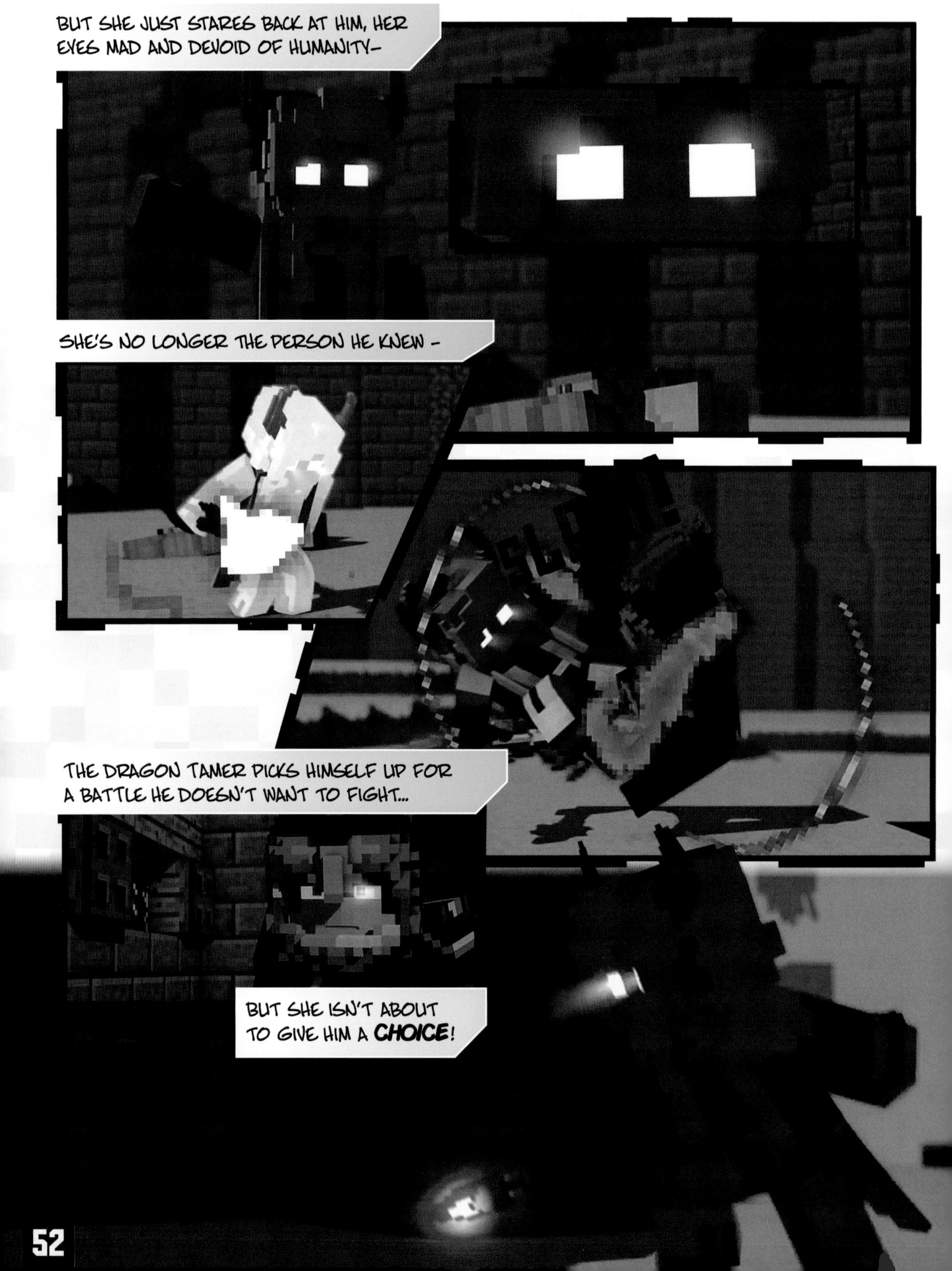

BUT SHE JUST STARES BACK AT HIM, HER EYES MAD AND DEVOID OF HUMANITY–
SHE'S NO LONGER THE PERSON HE KNEW –
THE DRAGON TAMER PICKS HIMSELF UP FOR A BATTLE HE DOESN'T WANT TO FIGHT...
BUT SHE ISN'T ABOUT TO GIVE HIM A CHOICE!

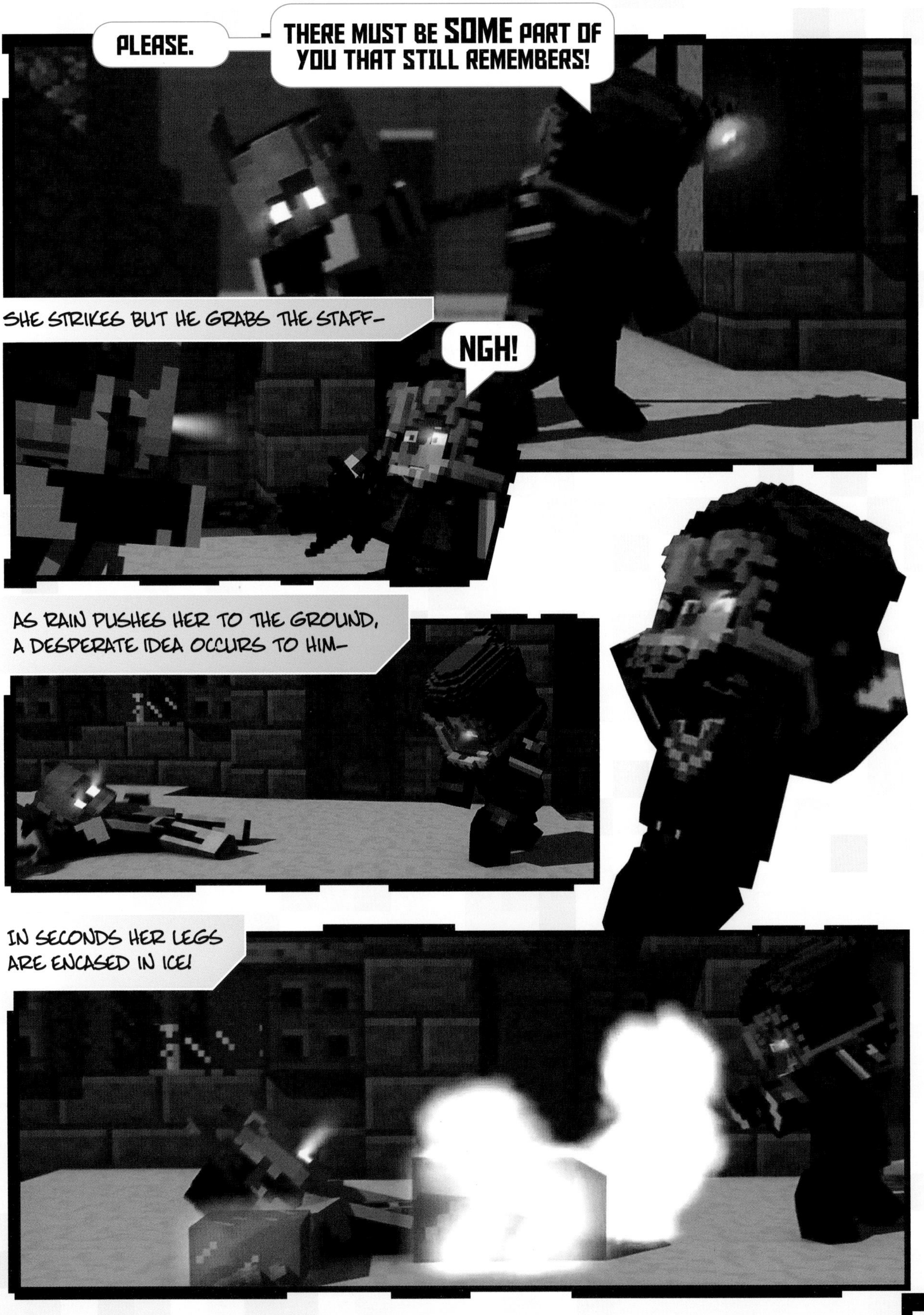
PLEASE.
THERE MUST BE SOME PART OF YOU THAT STILL REMEMBERS!
SHE STRIKES BUT HE GRABS THE STAFF–
NGH!
AS RAIN PUSHES HER TO THE GROUND, A DESPERATE IDEA OCCURS TO HIM–
IN SECONDS HER LEGS ARE ENCASED IN ICE!

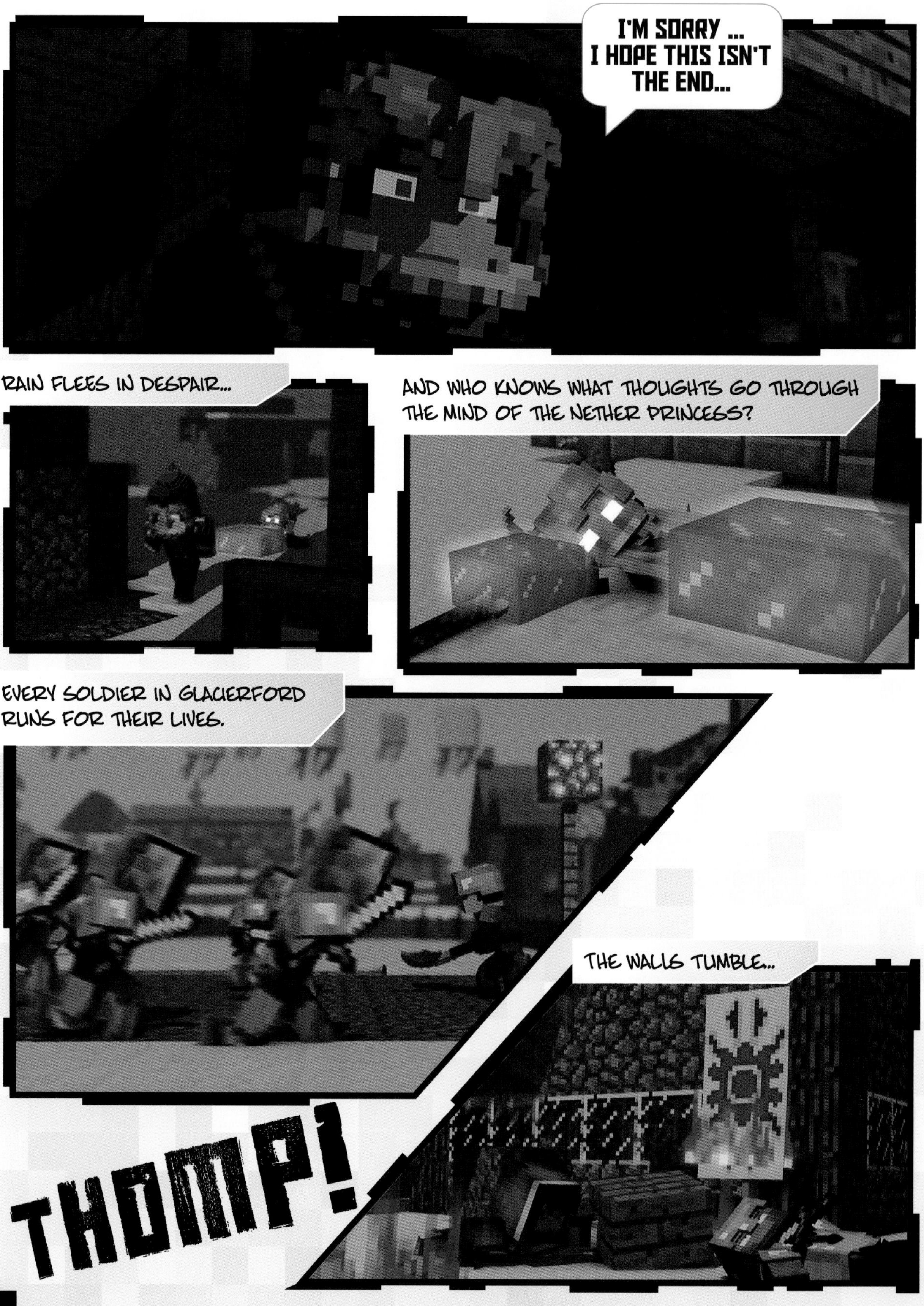
I'M SORRY ... I HOPE THIS ISN'T THE END...
RAIN FLEES IN DESPAIR...
AND WHO KNOWS WHAT THOUGHTS GO THROUGH THE MIND OF THE NETHER PRINCESS?
EVERY SOLDIER IN GLACIERFORD RUNS FOR THEIR LIVES.
THE WALLS TUMBLE...
THOMP!

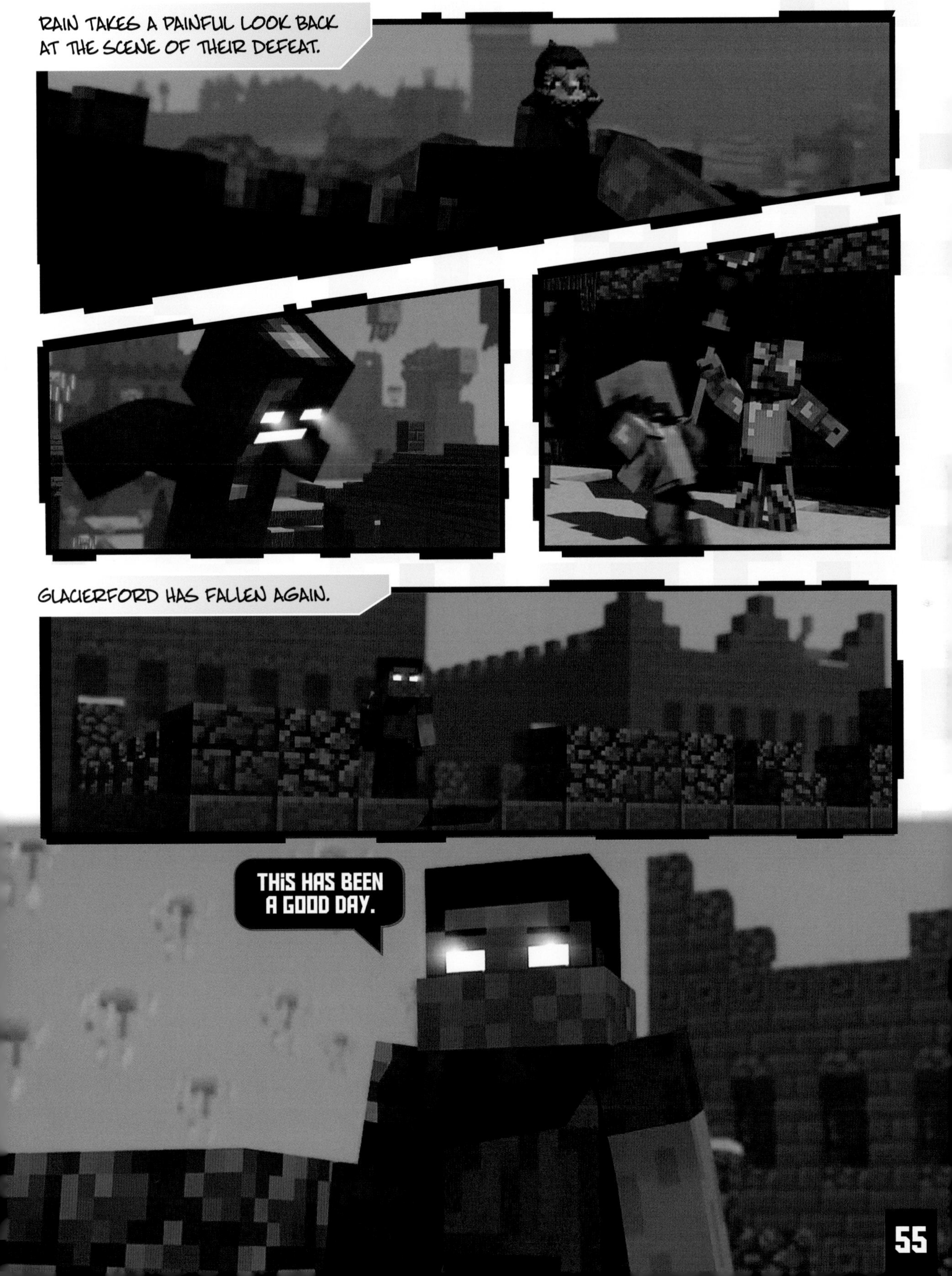
RAIN TAKES A PAINFUL LOOK BACK AT THE SCENE OF THEIR DEFEAT.
GLACIERFORD HAS FALLEN AGAIN.
THIS HAS BEEN A GOOD DAY.

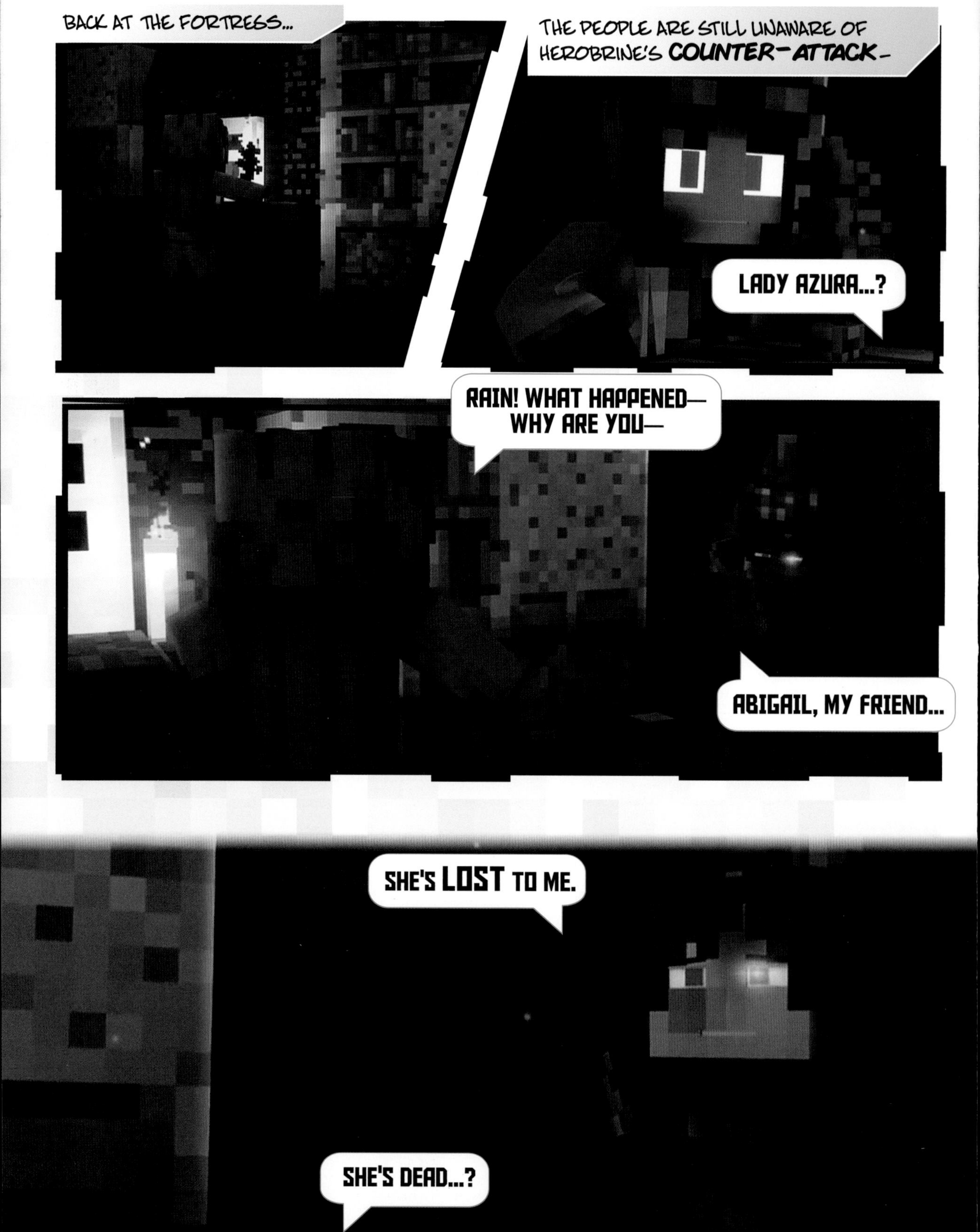
BACK AT THE FORTRESS...
THE PEOPLE ARE STILL UNAWARE OF HEROBRINE'S COUNTER-ATTACK-
LADY AZURA...?
RAIN! WHAT HAPPENED— WHY ARE YOU—
ABIGAIL, MY FRIEND...
SHE'S LOST TO ME.
SHE'S DEAD...?

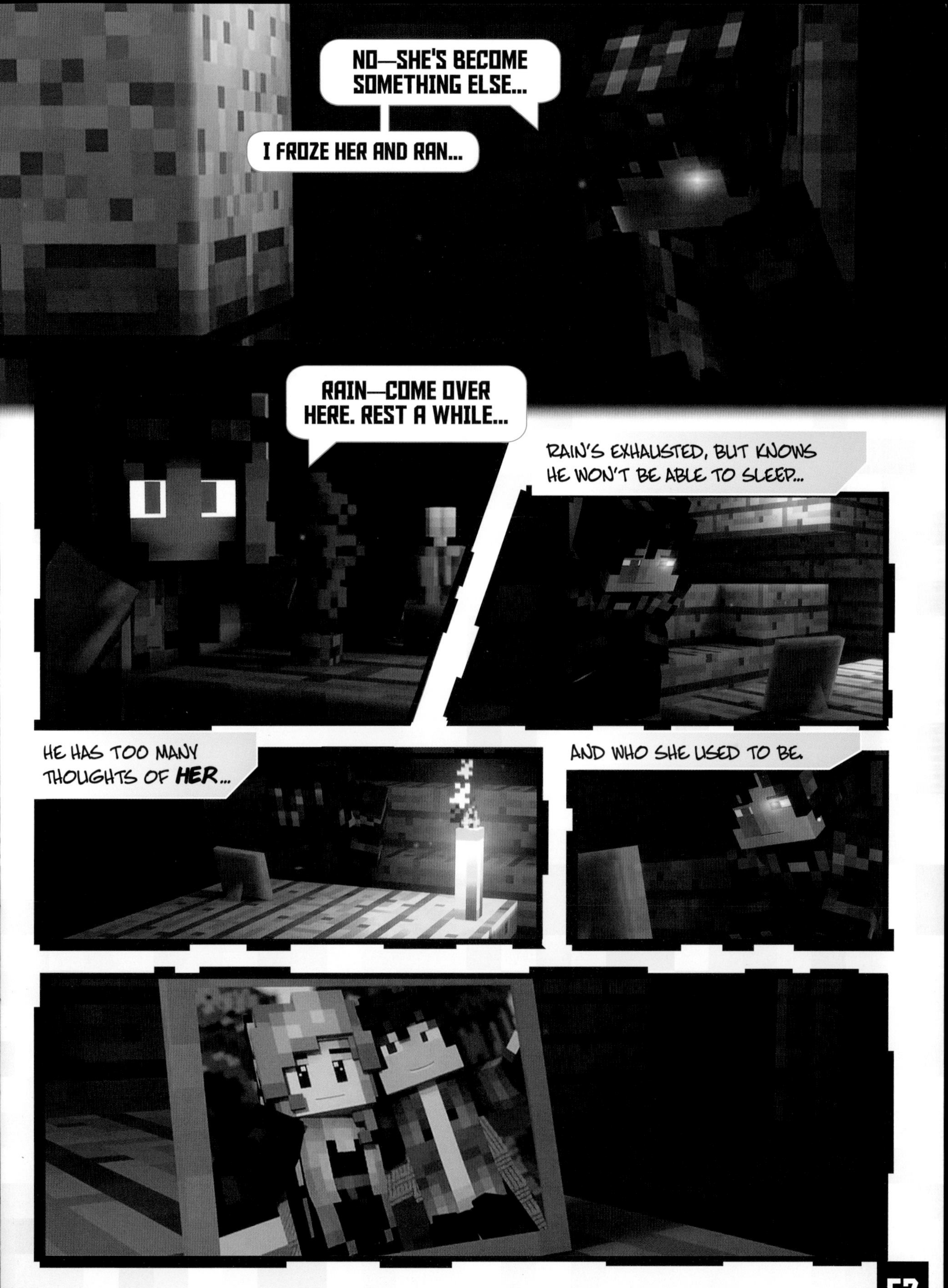
NO—SHE'S BECOME SOMETHING ELSE...
I FROZE HER AND RAN...
RAIN—COME OVER HERE. REST A WHILE...
RAIN'S EXHAUSTED, BUT KNOWS HE WON'T BE ABLE TO SLEEP...
HE HAS TOO MANY THOUGHTS OF HER...
AND WHO SHE USED TO BE.

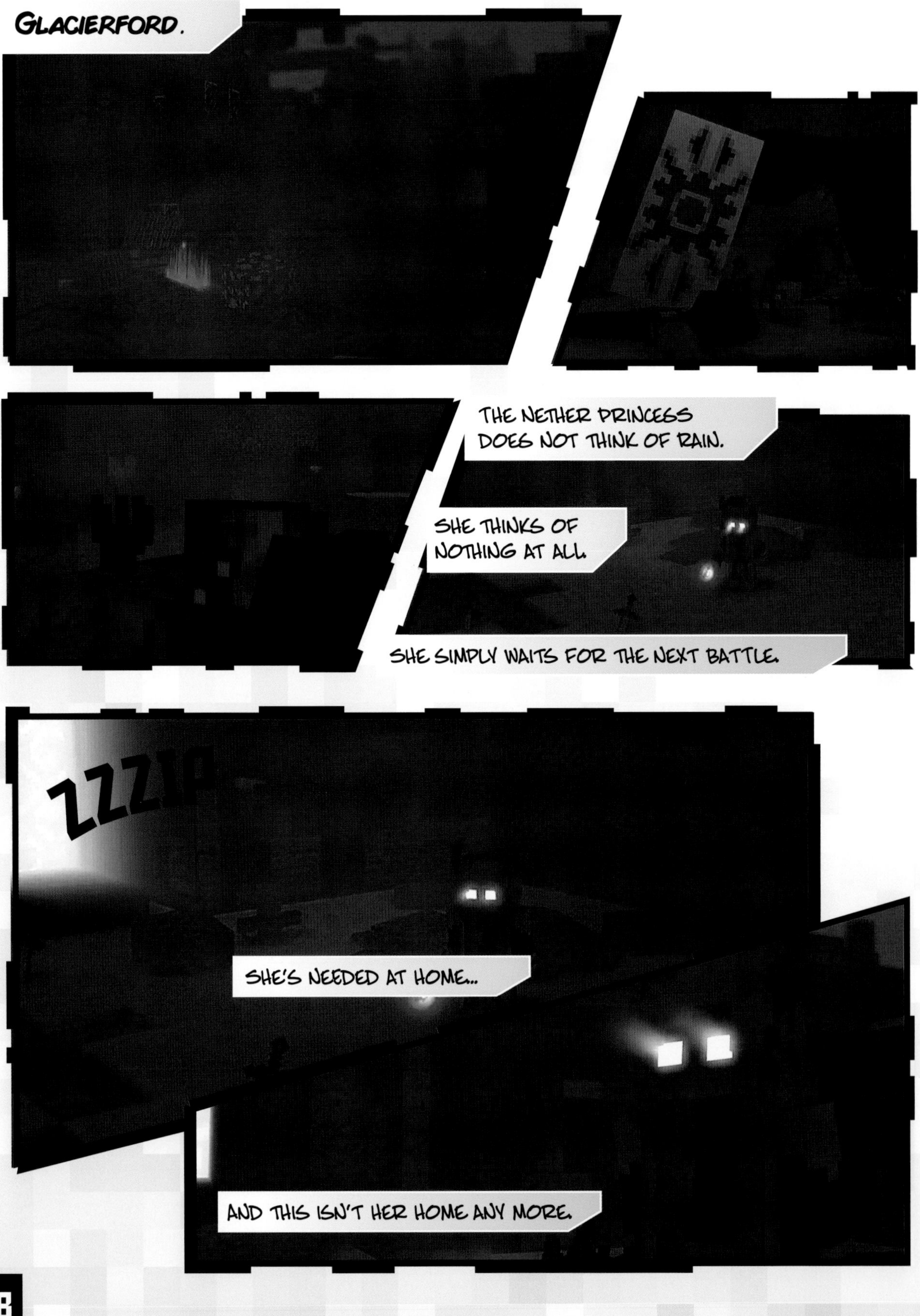
GLACIERFORD.
THE NETHER PRINCESS DOES NOT THINK OF RAIN.
SHE THINKS OF NOTHING AT ALL.
SHE SIMPLY WAITS FOR THE NEXT BATTLE.
ZZZIP
SHE'S NEEDED AT HOME...
AND THIS ISN'T HER HOME ANY MORE.

RAIN HAS SEARCHED FOR A WAY TO CHANGE HER BACK.

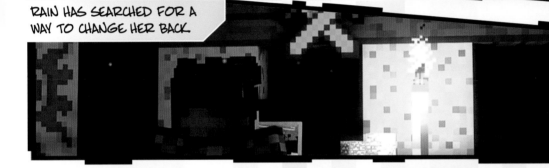

BUT THERE IS NONE.

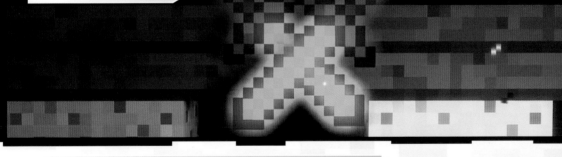

THE ONLY SOLUTION IS AT THE SHARP END OF A SWORD.

I MUST DO THIS...

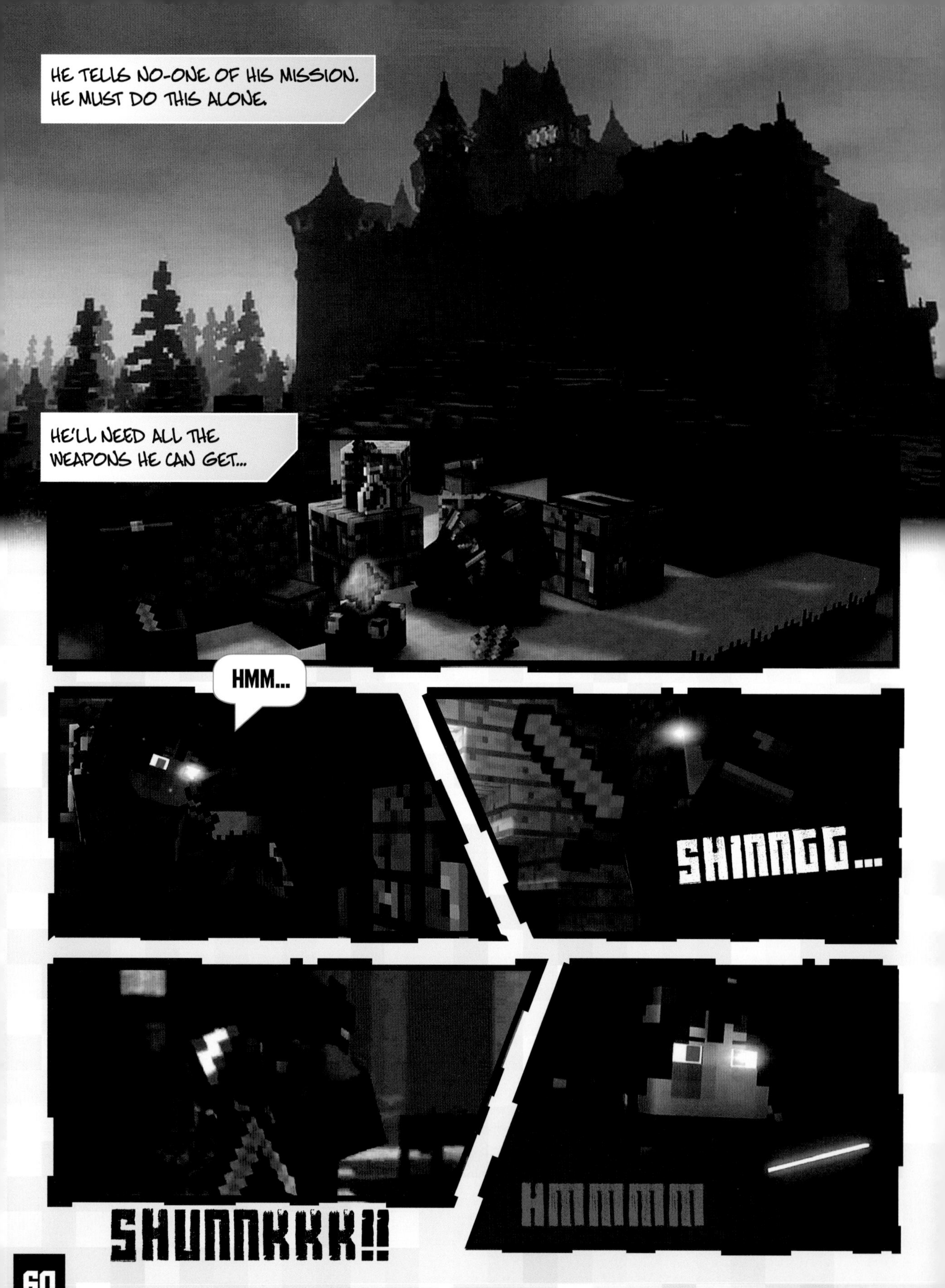
HE TELLS NO-ONE OF HIS MISSION. HE MUST DO THIS ALONE.
HE'LL NEED ALL THE WEAPONS HE CAN GET...
HMM...
SHINNGG...
SHUNNKKK!!
HMMMMM

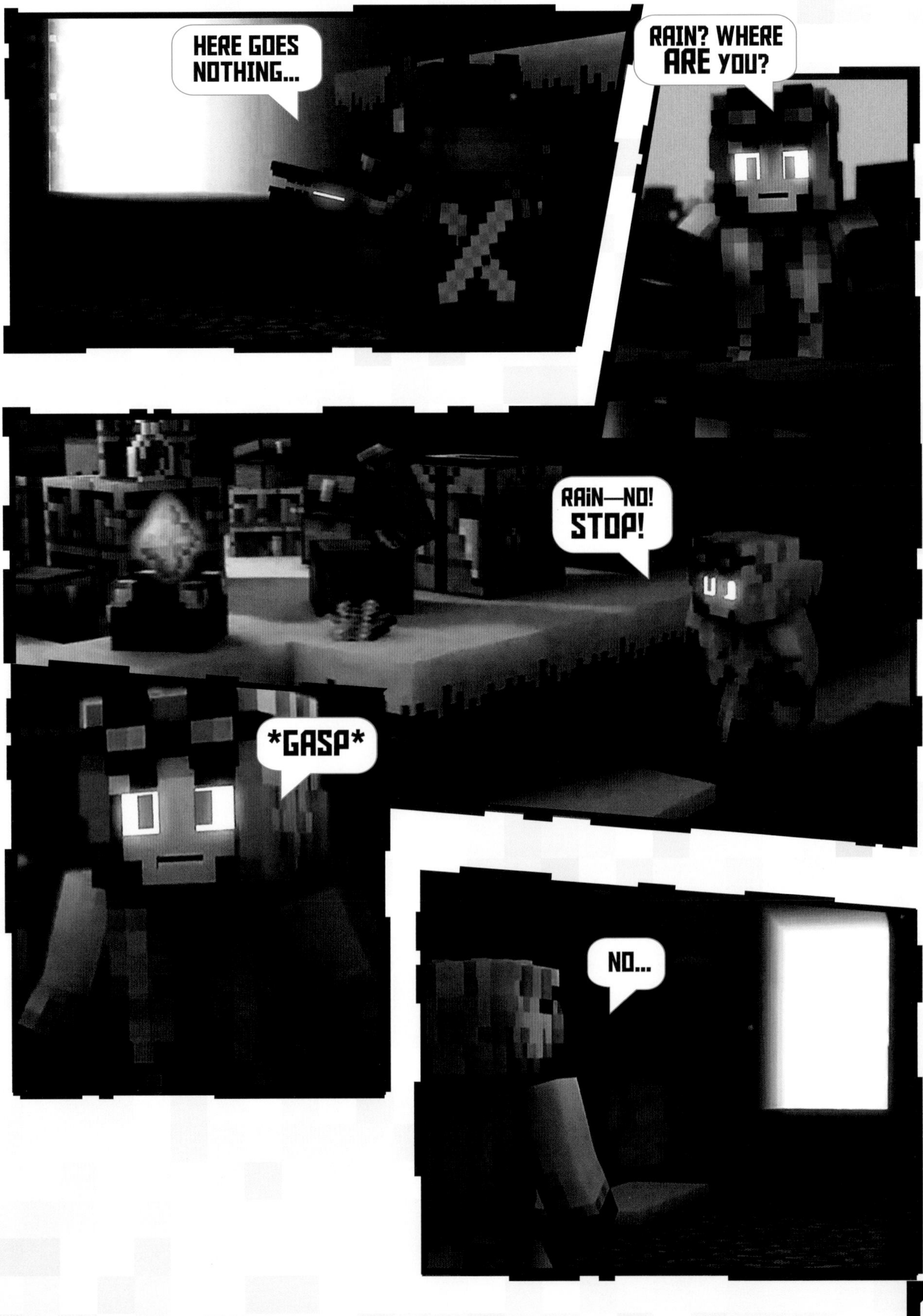
HERE GOES NOTHING...
RAIN? WHERE ARE YOU?
RAIN—NO! STOP!
GASP
NO...

MEANWHILE, THE NETHER WELCOMES A NEW ARRIVAL—

I'VE COME TO SEE THE **PRINCESS**.

YOU CAN LET ME PASS...

OR I CAN GO **THROUGH** YOU.

THE REACTION IS EXACTLY WHAT RAIN EXPECTS.

BUDDAPOWPOWPOWBUDDAPOW

YAAAAHHH!!

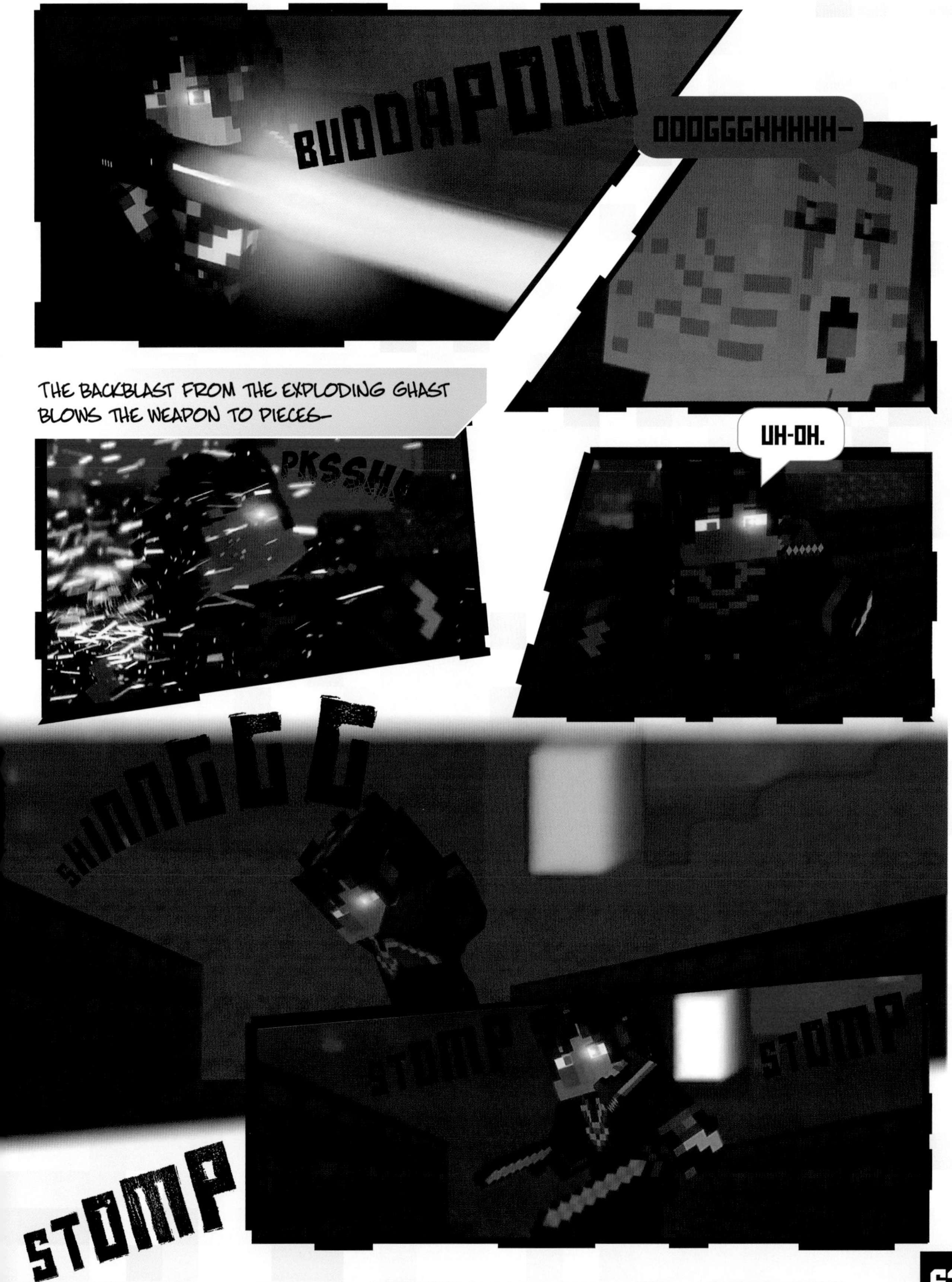
BUDDAPOW
OOOGGGHHHHH-
THE BACKBLAST FROM THE EXPLODING GHAST BLOWS THE WEAPON TO PIECES-
PKSSH
UH-OH.
SHINNGGG
STOMP
STOMP
STOMP

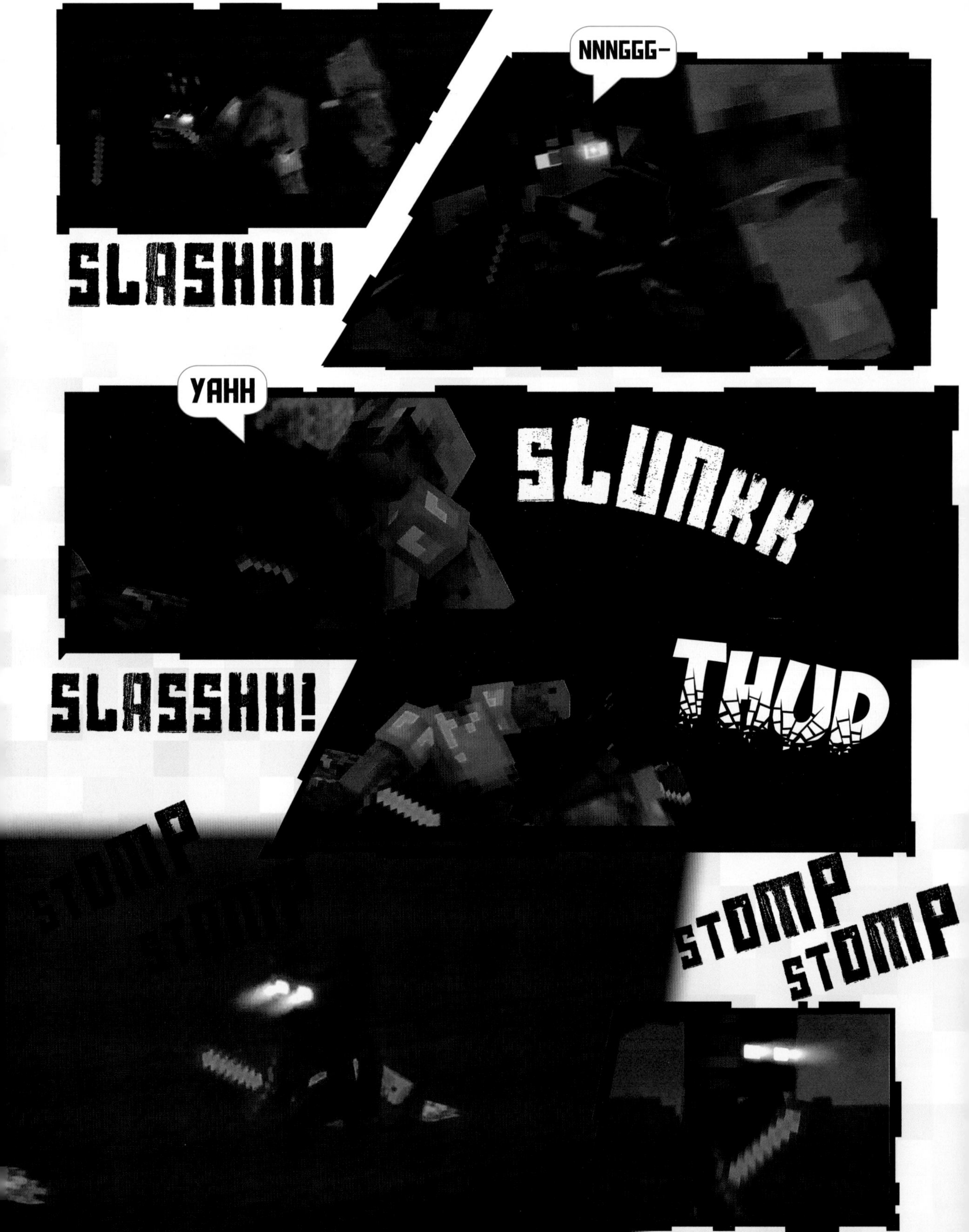
SLASHHH
NNNGGG–
YAHH
SLUNKK
SLASSHH!
THUD
STOMP
STOMP

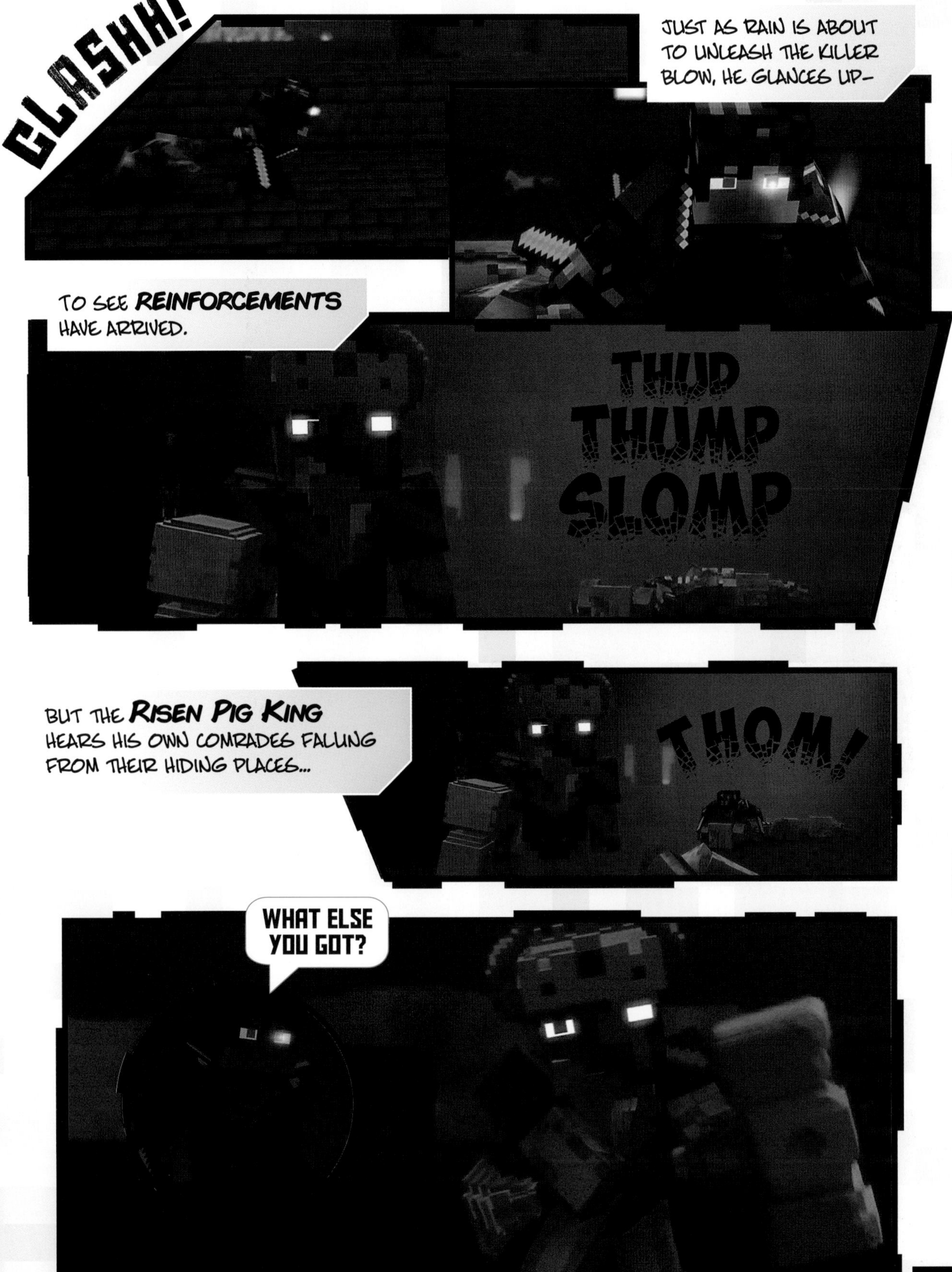
CLASHH!
JUST AS RAIN IS ABOUT TO UNLEASH THE KILLER BLOW, HE GLANCES UP-
TO SEE REINFORCEMENTS HAVE ARRIVED.
THUD
THUMP
SLOMP
BUT THE RISEN PIG KING HEARS HIS OWN COMRADES FALLING FROM THEIR HIDING PLACES...
THOM!
WHAT ELSE YOU GOT?

THEY RUSH AT EACH OTHER-
KRUNNCH!!
SMEK
OOOOOFF-
BATTERED AND BRUISED, RAIN GETS TO HIS FEET...
NNNGGHHH...
DOMP DOMP DOMP DOMP
RRRAAAAGHH-

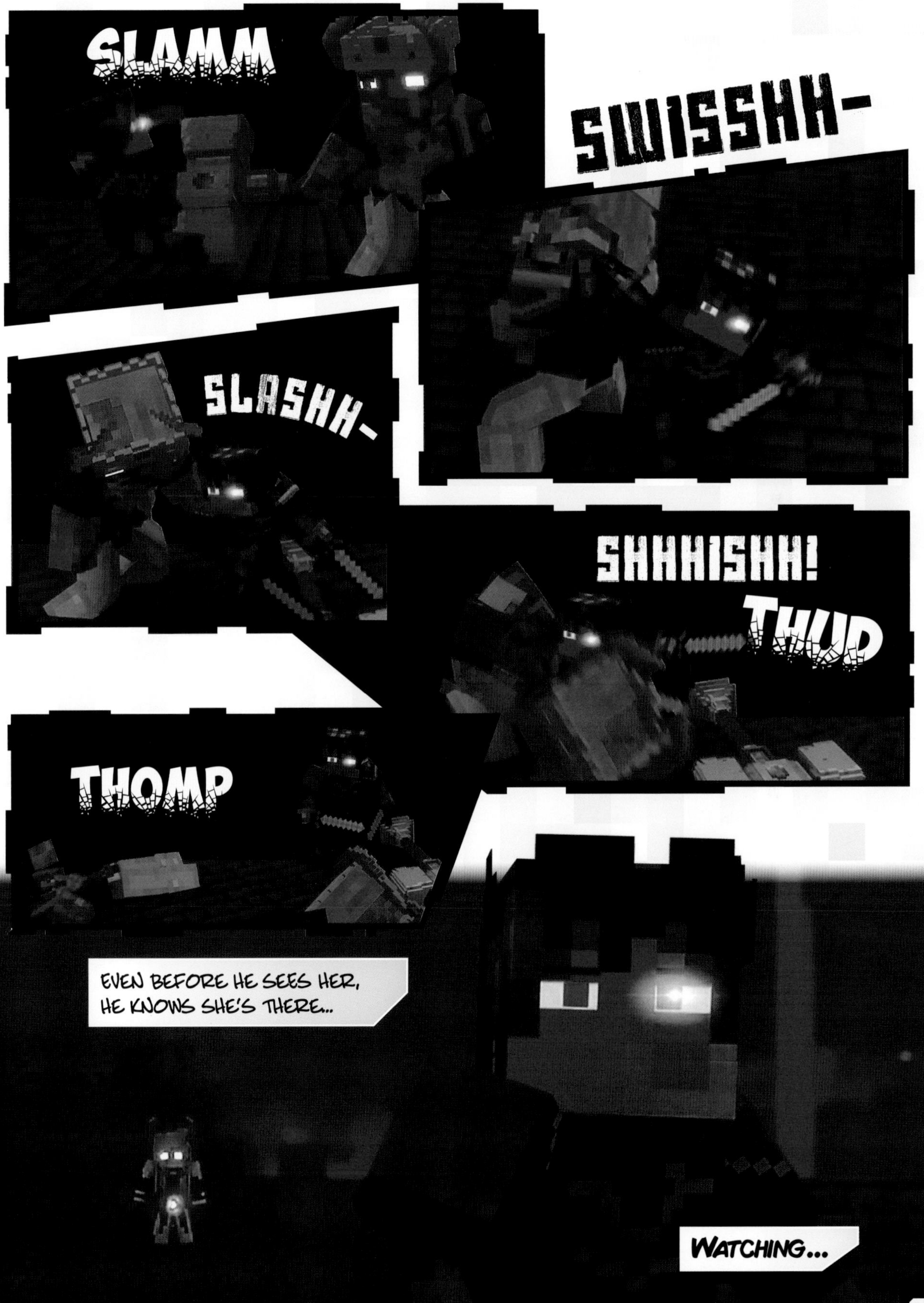

SLAMM
SWISSHH-
SLASHH-
SHHHISHH!
THUD
THOMP
EVEN BEFORE HE SEES HER, HE KNOWS SHE'S THERE...
WATCHING...

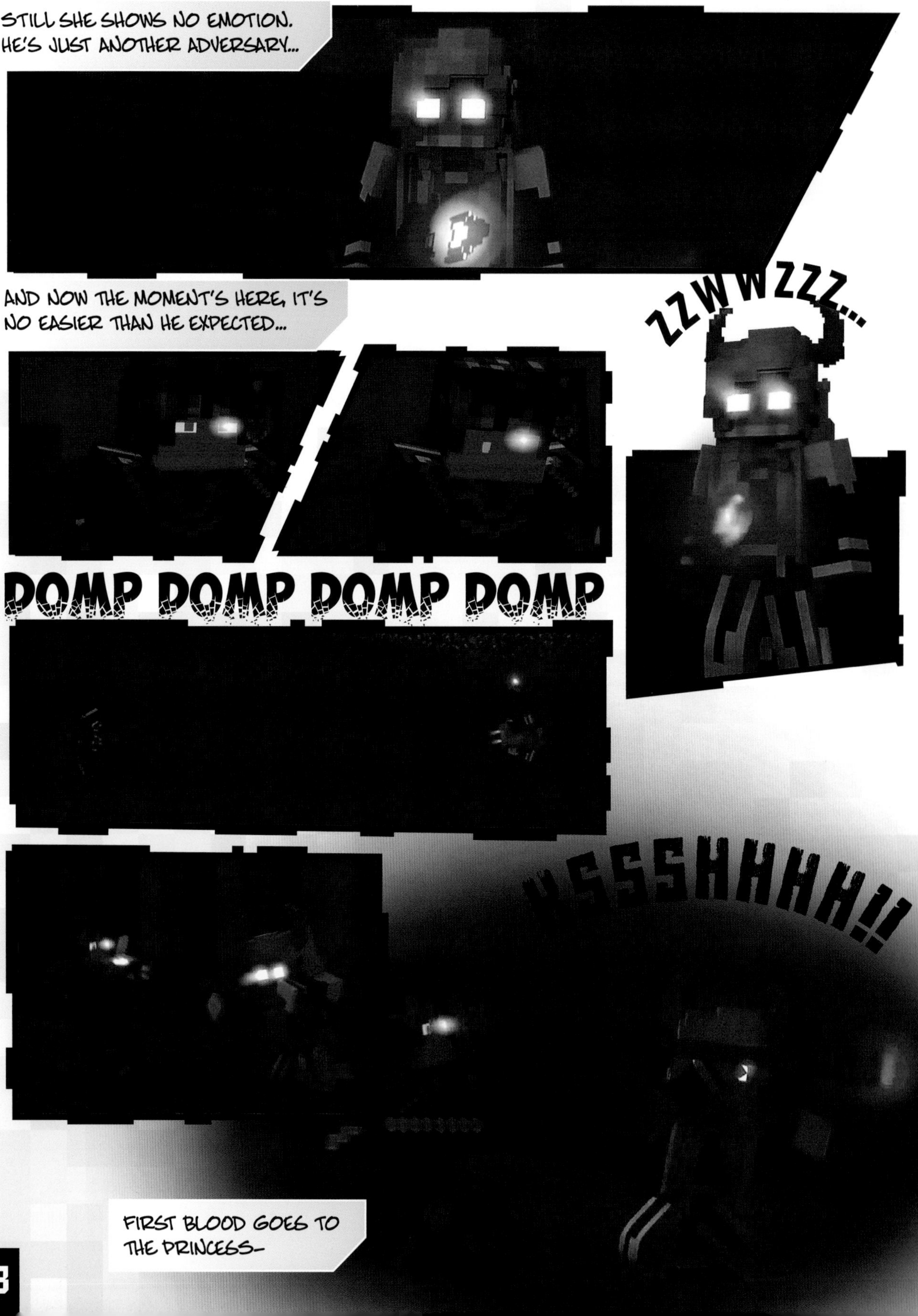

STILL SHE SHOWS NO EMOTION. HE'S JUST ANOTHER ADVERSARY...
AND NOW THE MOMENT'S HERE, IT'S NO EASIER THAN HE EXPECTED...
ZZWWZZZ...
DOMP DOMP DOMP DOMP
SSSHHHH!!
FIRST BLOOD GOES TO THE PRINCESS-

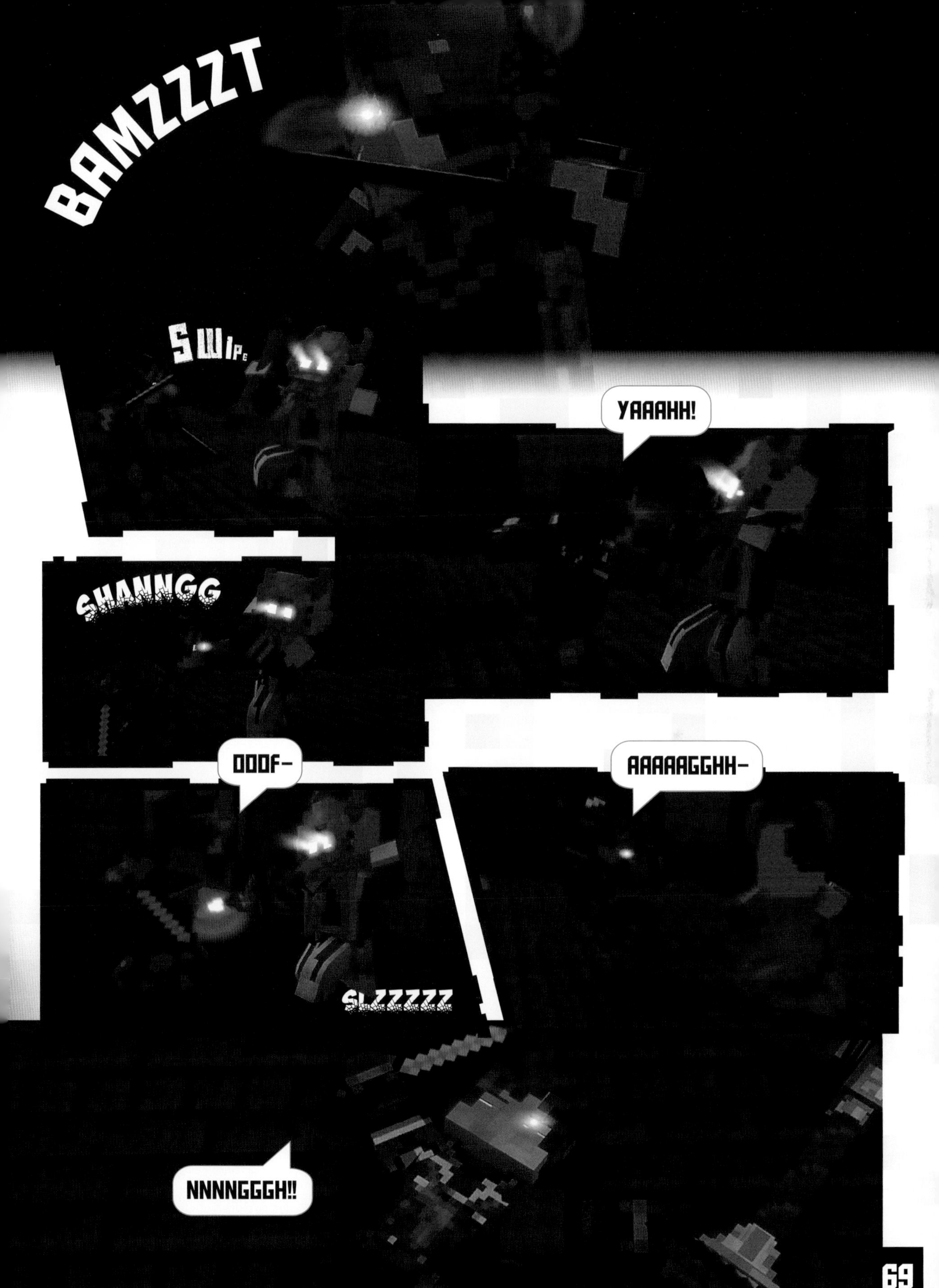
BAMZZZZT
SWIPE
YAAAHH!
SHANNGG
OOOF-
AAAAAGGHH-
SLZZZZZ
NNNNGGGH!!

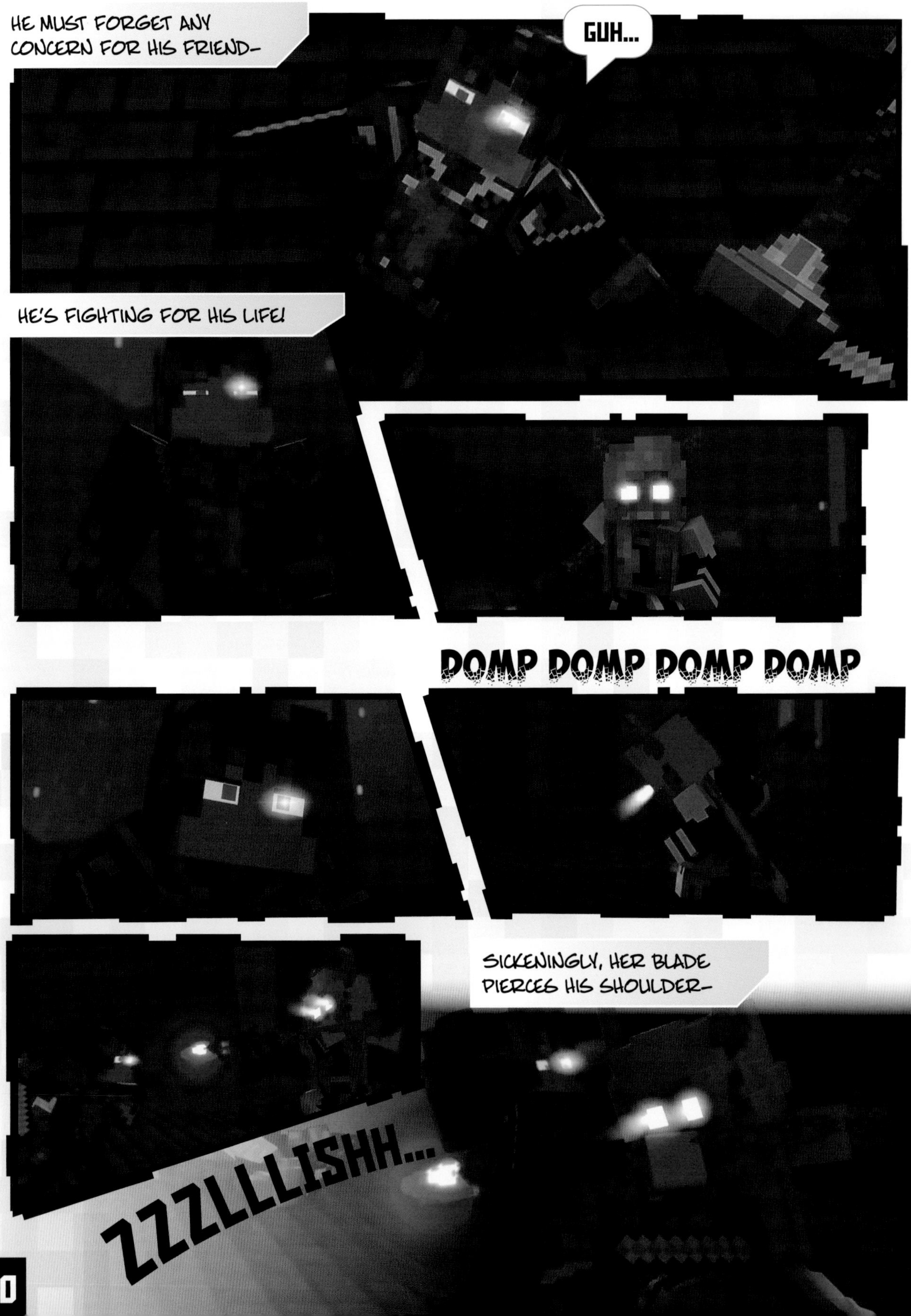
HE MUST FORGET ANY CONCERN FOR HIS FRIEND-
GUH...
HE'S FIGHTING FOR HIS LIFE!
DOMP DOMP DOMP DOMP
SICKENINGLY, HER BLADE PIERCES HIS SHOULDER-
ZZZLLLISHH...

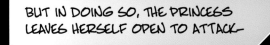

BUT IN DOING SO, THE PRINCESS LEAVES HERSELF OPEN TO ATTACK—

SHLUNK!

UHNNNN....

THUD

THE INJURED RAIN SLUMPS BESIDE HER AND WATCHES THE LIGHT GO OUT IN HER EYES...

THUMP

PERHAPS HOPING TO SEE **SOMETHING** HUMAN IN THERE...

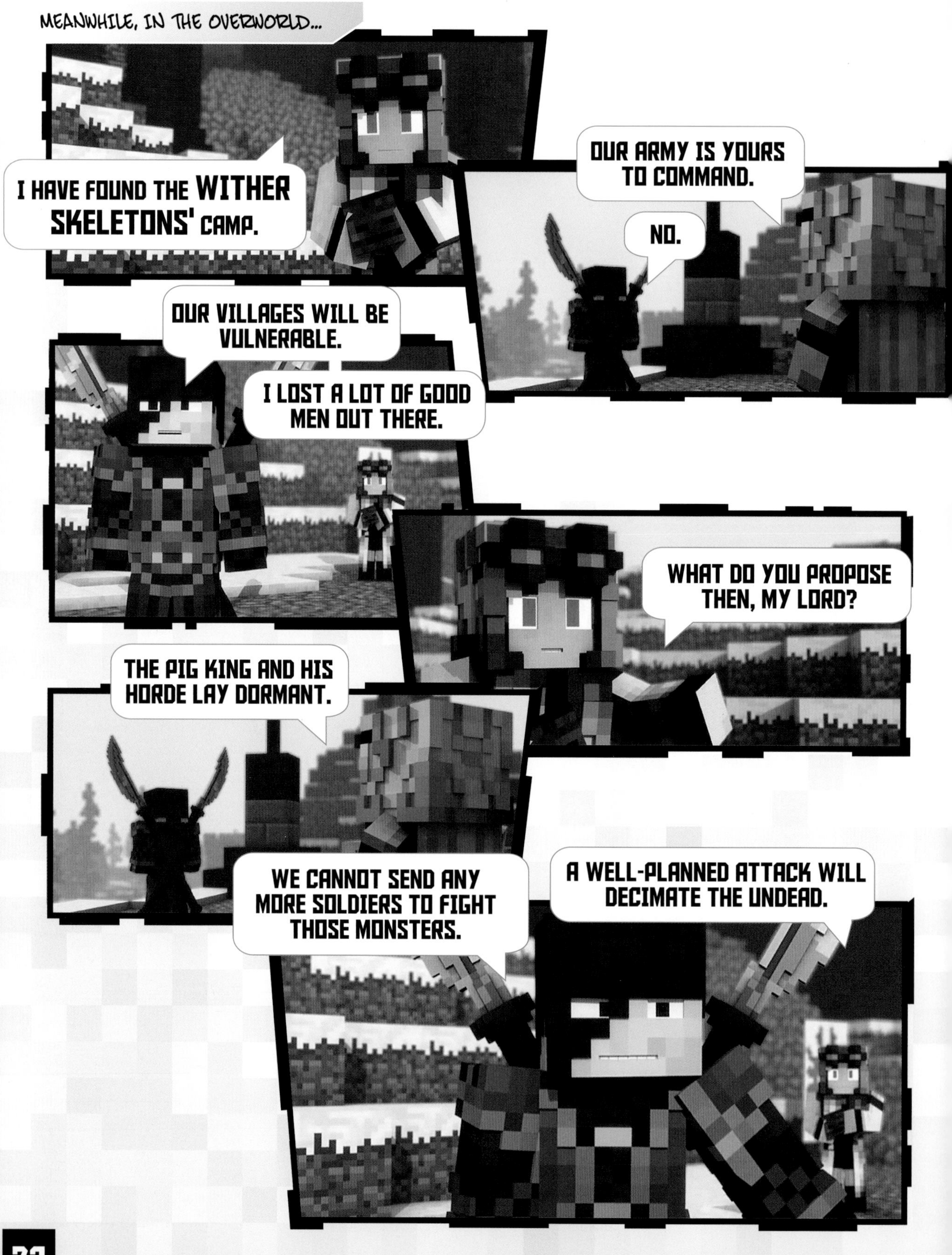
MEANWHILE, IN THE OVERWORLD...
I HAVE FOUND THE WITHER SKELETONS' CAMP.
OUR ARMY IS YOURS TO COMMAND.
NO.
OUR VILLAGES WILL BE VULNERABLE.
I LOST A LOT OF GOOD MEN OUT THERE.
WHAT DO YOU PROPOSE THEN, MY LORD?
THE PIG KING AND HIS HORDE LAY DORMANT.
WE CANNOT SEND ANY MORE SOLDIERS TO FIGHT THOSE MONSTERS.
A WELL-PLANNED ATTACK WILL DECIMATE THE UNDEAD.

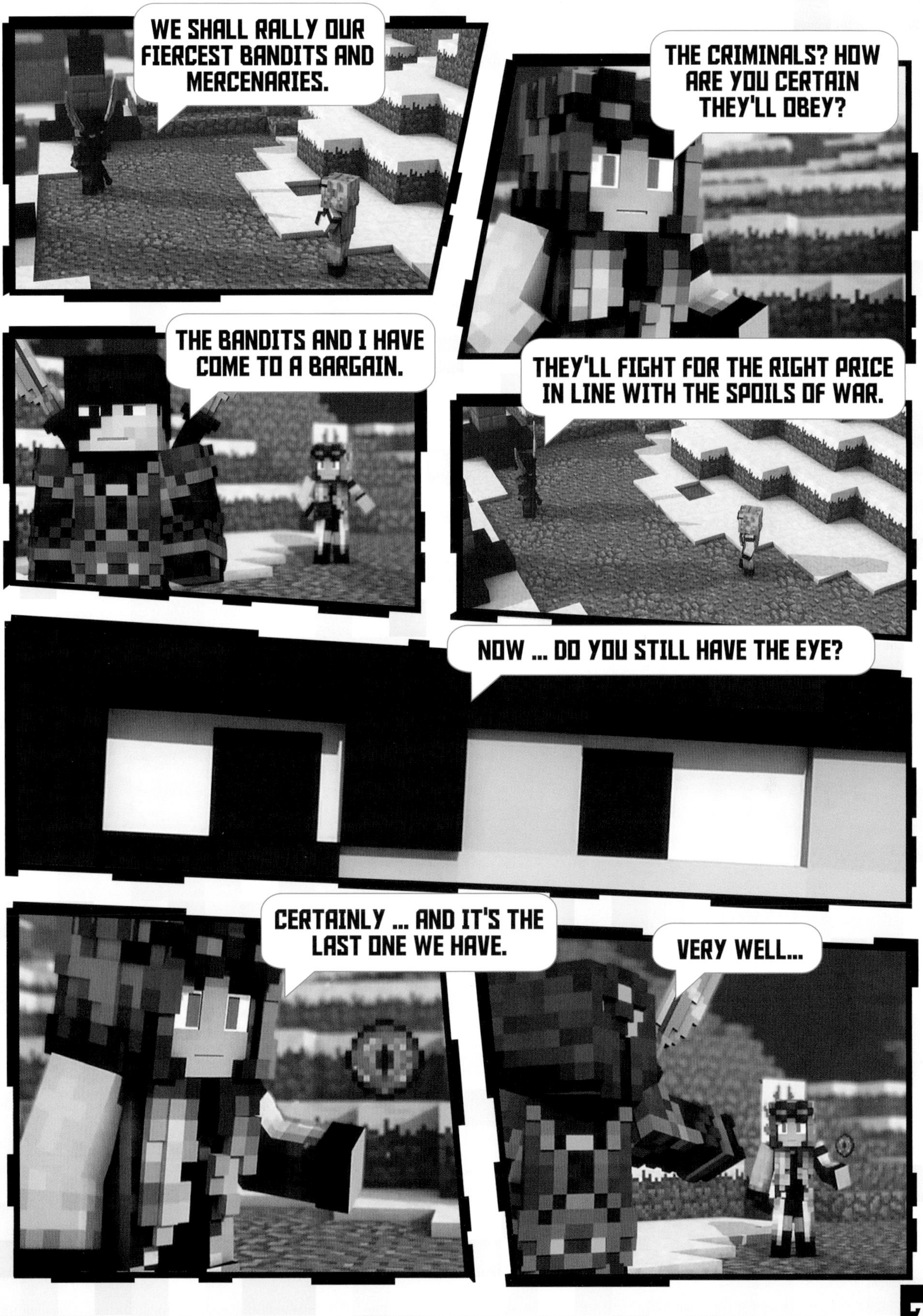
WE SHALL RALLY OUR FIERCEST BANDITS AND MERCENARIES.
THE CRIMINALS? HOW ARE YOU CERTAIN THEY'LL OBEY?
THE BANDITS AND I HAVE COME TO A BARGAIN.
THEY'LL FIGHT FOR THE RIGHT PRICE IN LINE WITH THE SPOILS OF WAR.
NOW ... DO YOU STILL HAVE THE EYE?
CERTAINLY ... AND IT'S THE LAST ONE WE HAVE.
VERY WELL...

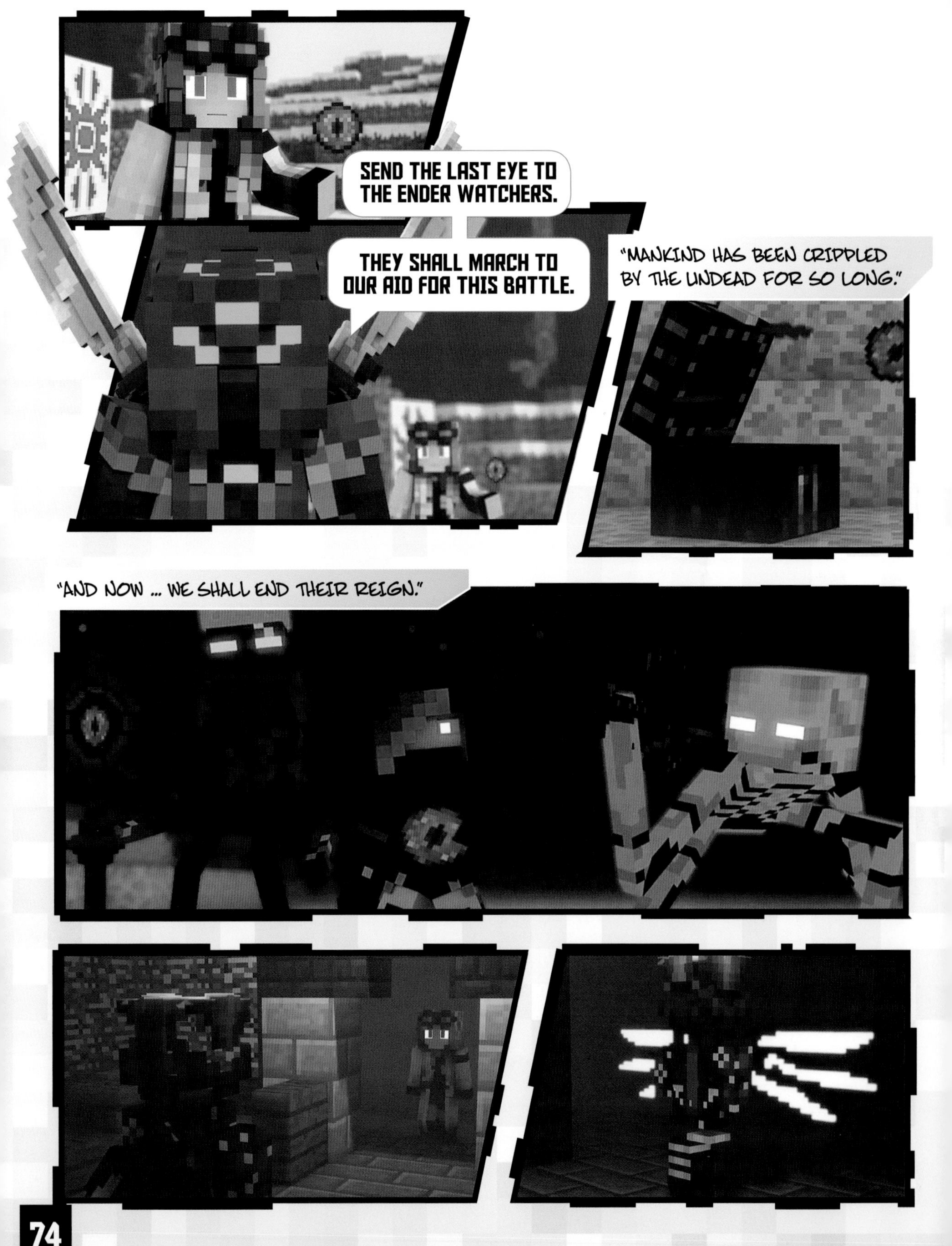
SEND THE LAST EYE TO THE ENDER WATCHERS.
THEY SHALL MARCH TO OUR AID FOR THIS BATTLE.
"MANKIND HAS BEEN CRIPPLED BY THE UNDEAD FOR SO LONG."
"AND NOW ... WE SHALL END THEIR REIGN."

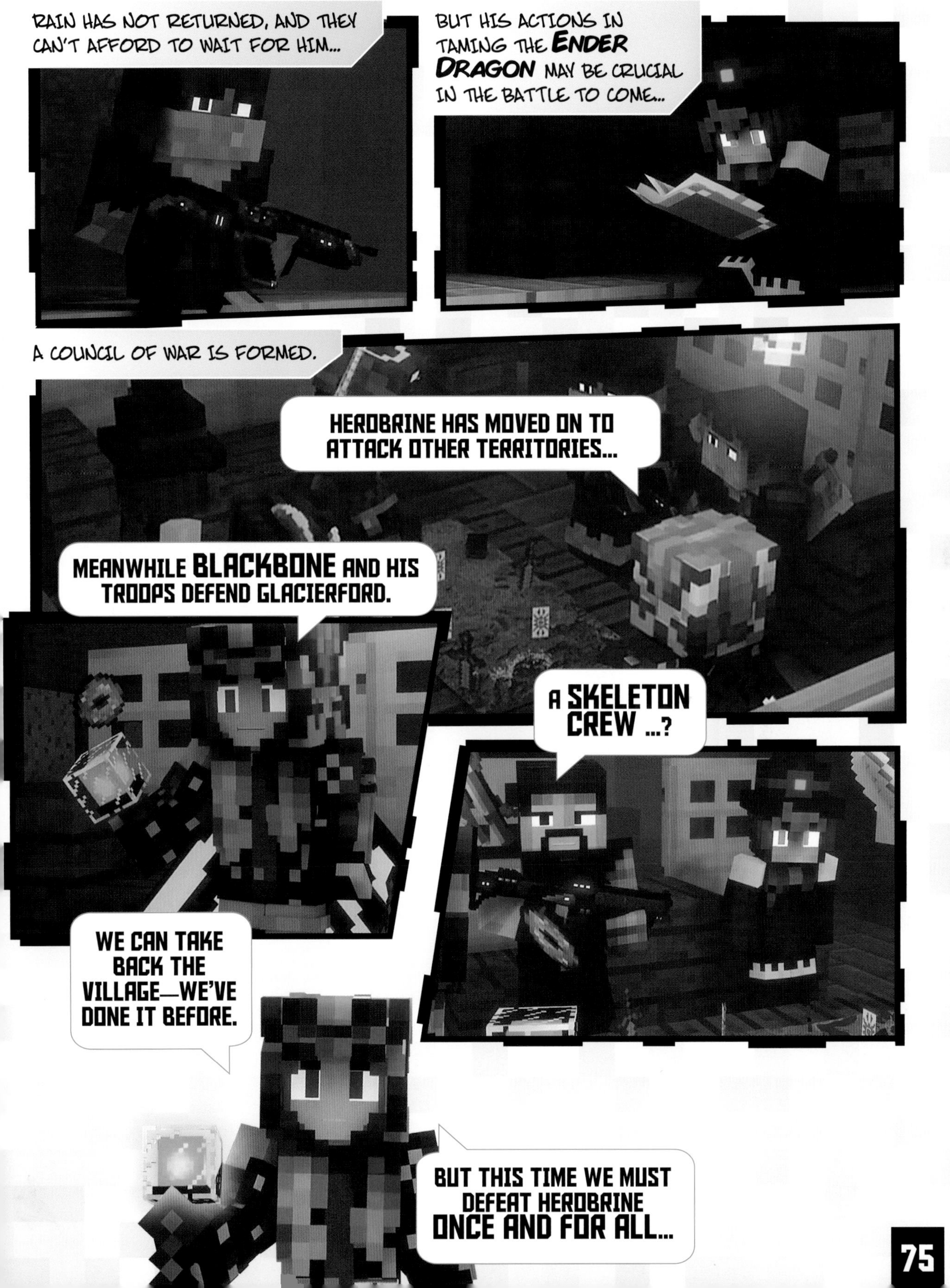
RAIN HAS NOT RETURNED, AND THEY CAN'T AFFORD TO WAIT FOR HIM...
BUT HIS ACTIONS IN TAMING THE ENDER DRAGON MAY BE CRUCIAL IN THE BATTLE TO COME...
A COUNCIL OF WAR IS FORMED.
HEROBRINE HAS MOVED ON TO ATTACK OTHER TERRITORIES...
MEANWHILE BLACKBONE AND HIS TROOPS DEFEND GLACIERFORD.
A SKELETON CREW ...?
WE CAN TAKE BACK THE VILLAGE—WE'VE DONE IT BEFORE.
BUT THIS TIME WE MUST DEFEAT HEROBRINE ONCE AND FOR ALL...

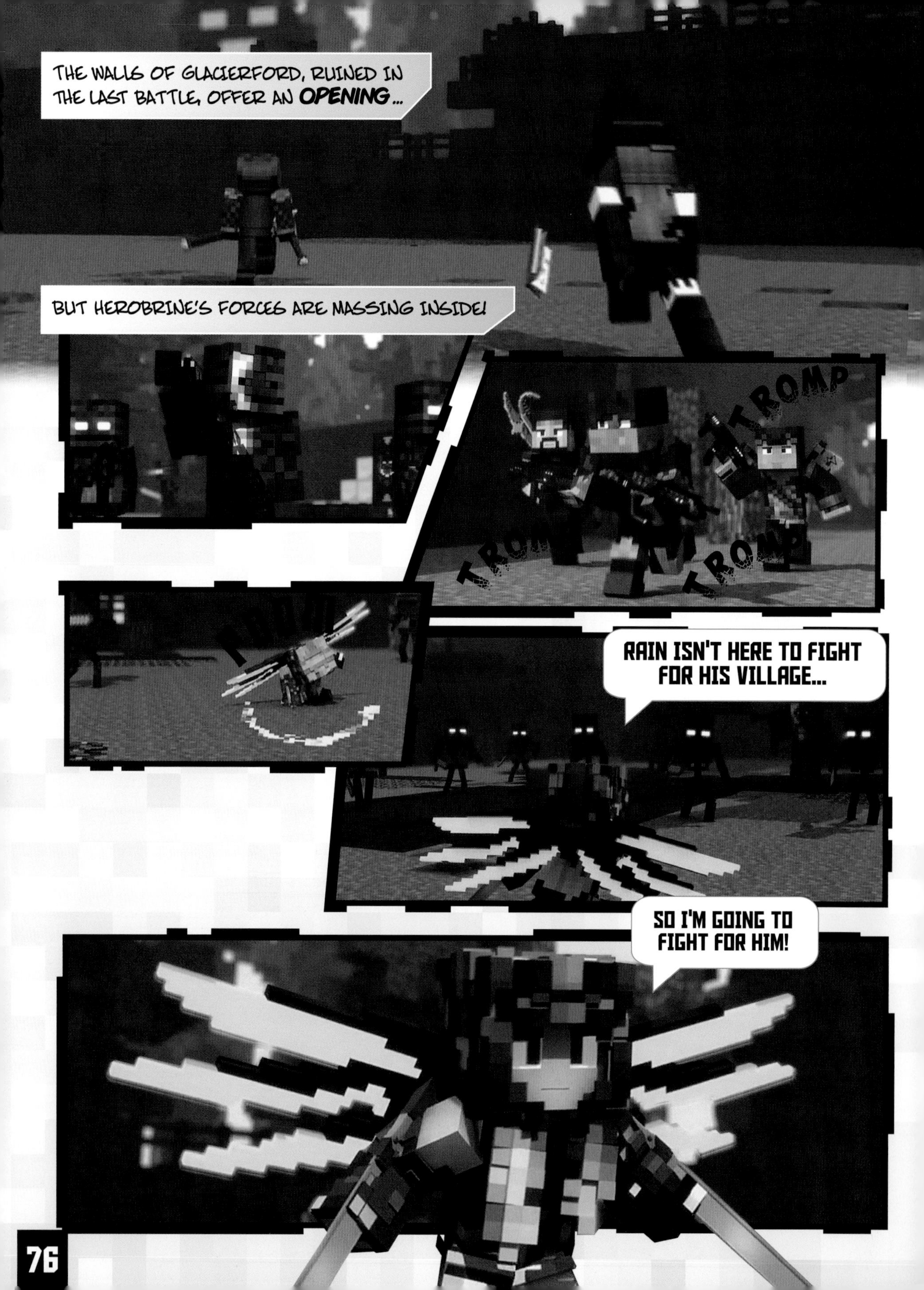
THE WALLS OF GLACIERFORD, RUINED IN THE LAST BATTLE, OFFER AN OPENING...
BUT HEROBRINE'S FORCES ARE MASSING INSIDE!
TROMP
TROMP
TROMP
TROMP
RAIN ISN'T HERE TO FIGHT FOR HIS VILLAGE...
SO I'M GOING TO FIGHT FOR HIM!

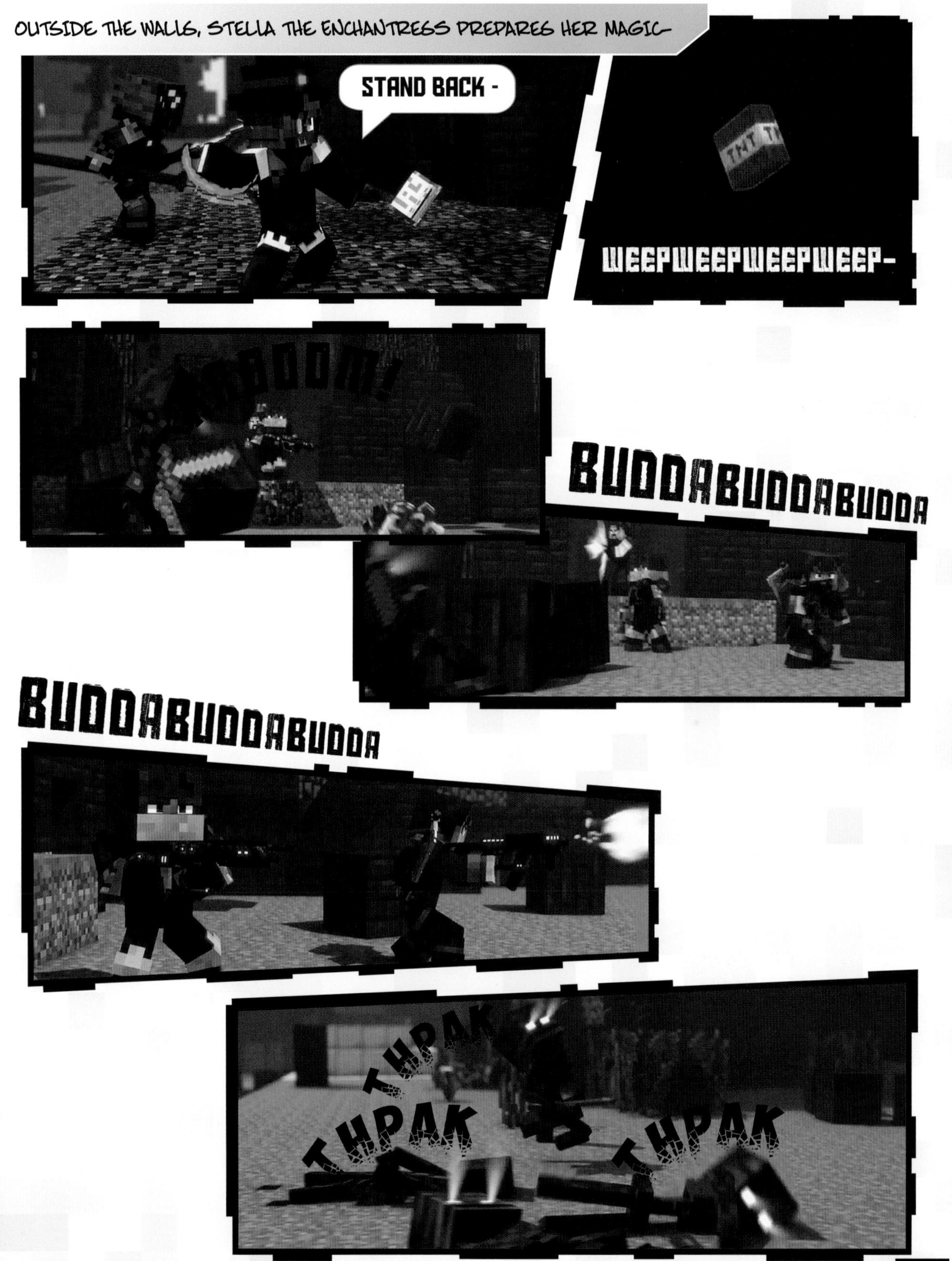
OUTSIDE THE WALLS, STELLA THE ENCHANTRESS PREPARES HER MAGIC-
STAND BACK -
WEEPWEEPWEEPWEEP-
BUDDABUDDABUDDA
BUDDABUDDABUDDA
THPAK
THPAK
THPAK

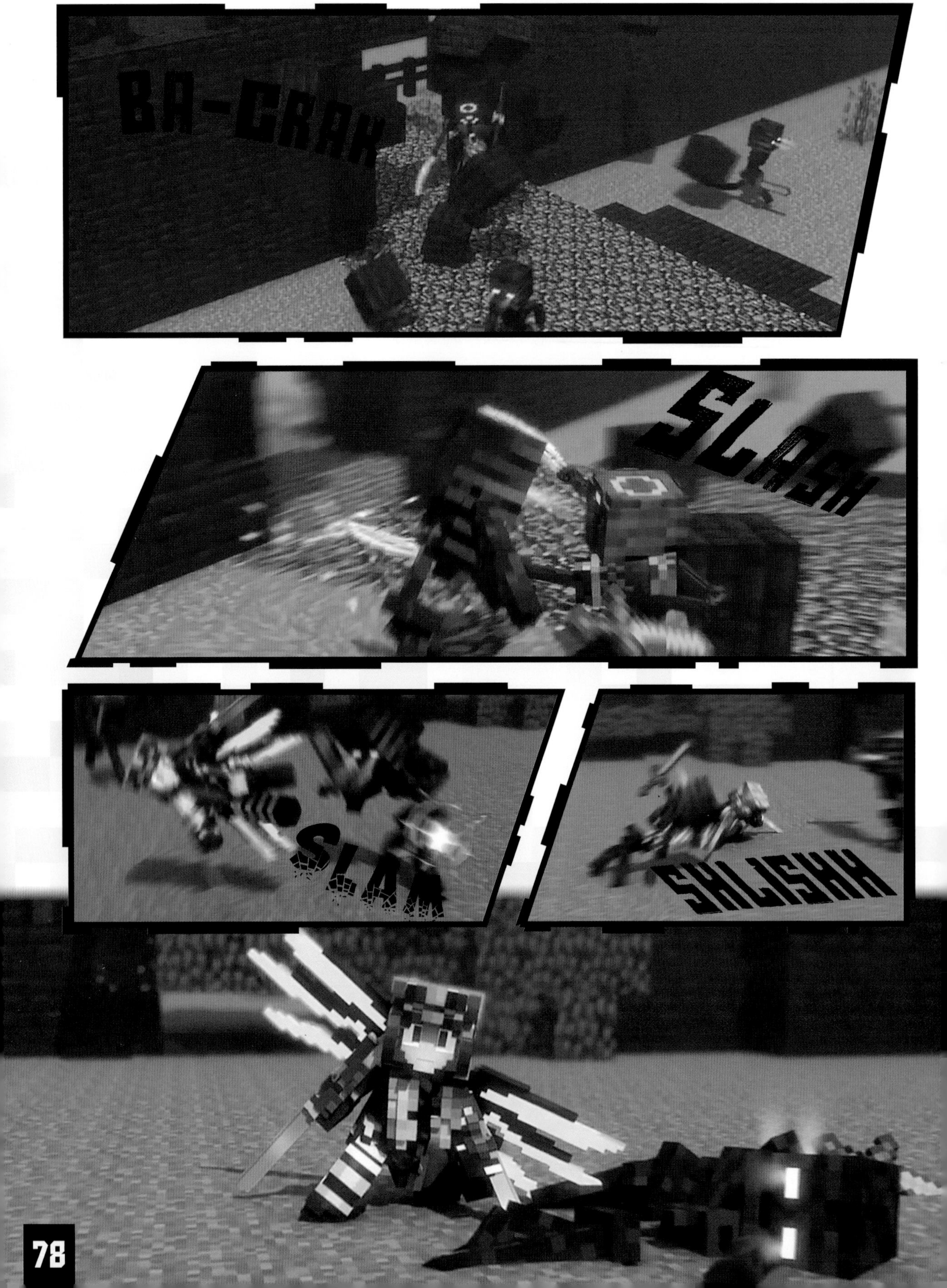
BA-GRAK
SLASH
SLAM
SHLISHH

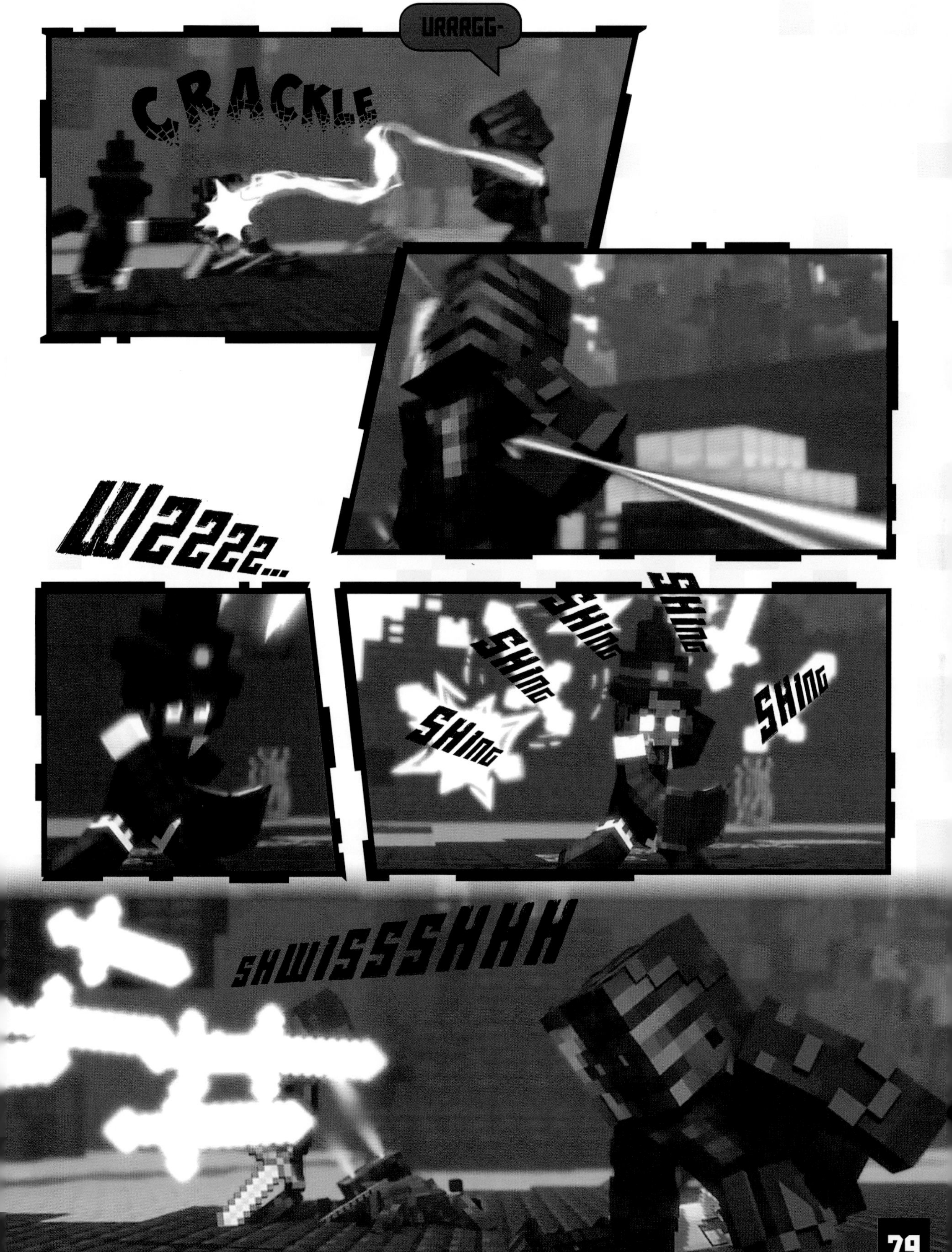
URRRGG-
CRACKLE
WZZZZ...
SHING
SHING
SHING
SHING
SHING
SHWISSSSHHH

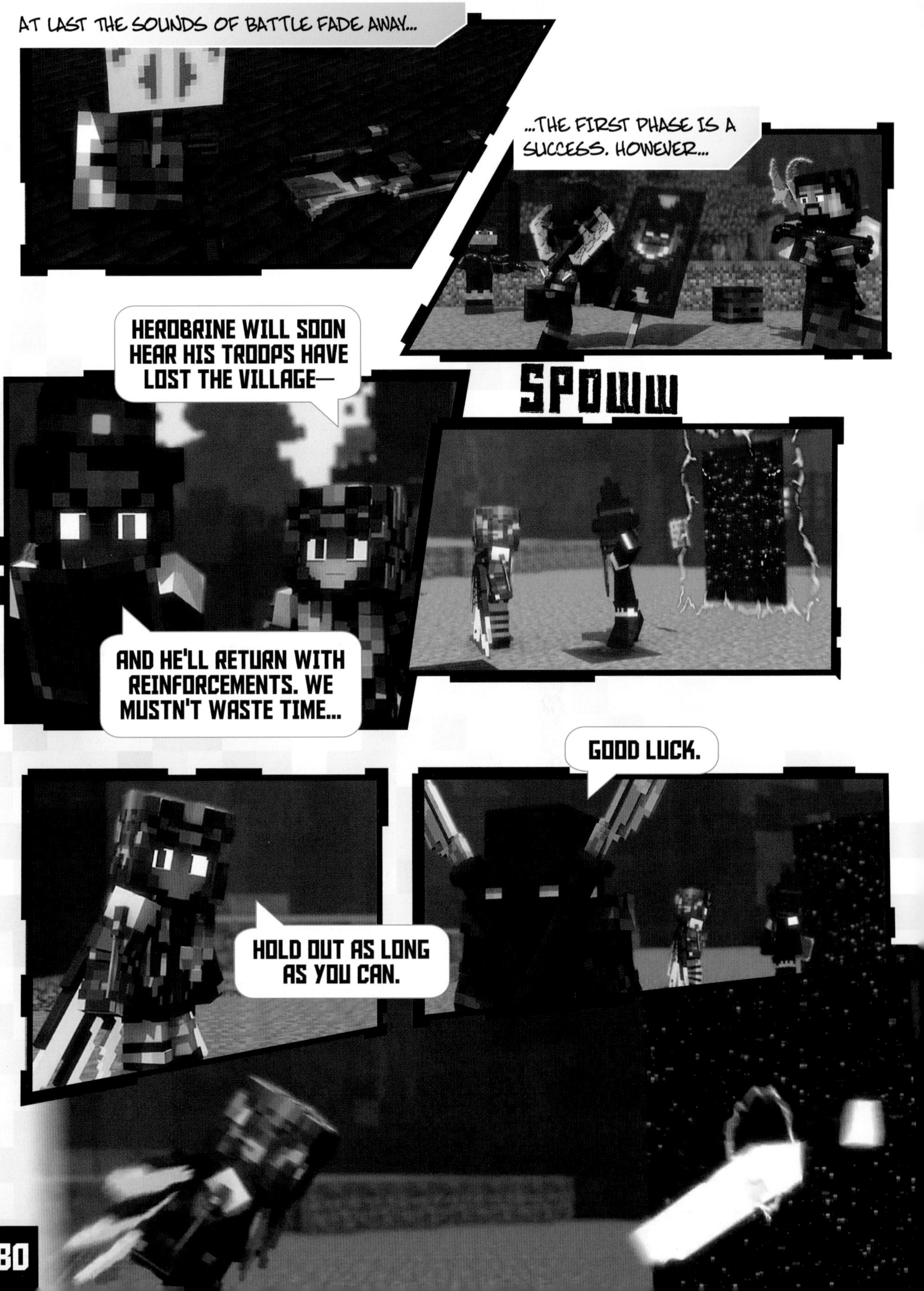

AT LAST THE SOUNDS OF BATTLE FADE AWAY...
...THE FIRST PHASE IS A SUCCESS. HOWEVER...
HEROBRINE WILL SOON HEAR HIS TROOPS HAVE LOST THE VILLAGE—
AND HE'LL RETURN WITH REINFORCEMENTS. WE MUSTN'T WASTE TIME...
SPOWW
GOOD LUCK.
HOLD OUT AS LONG AS YOU CAN.

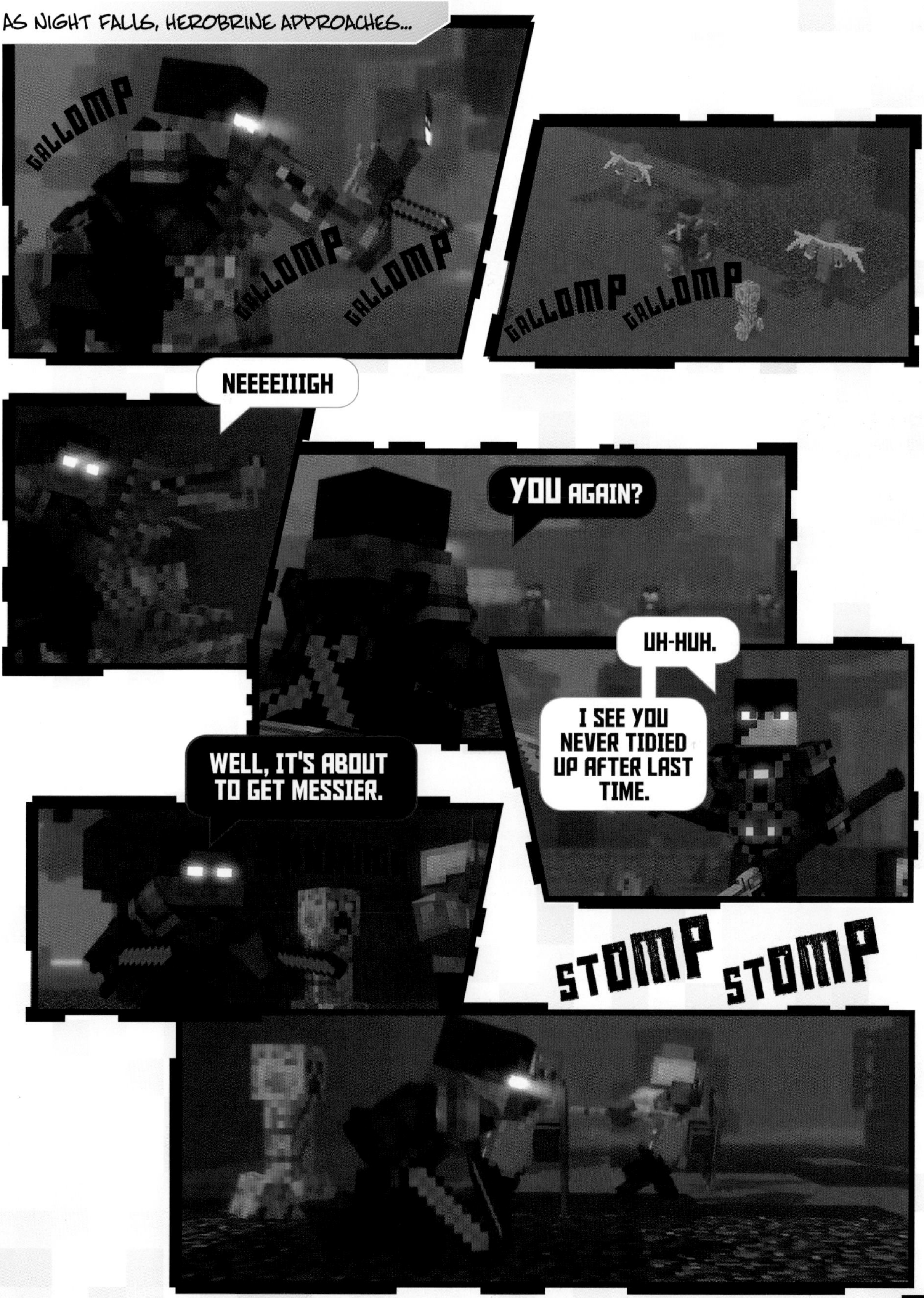
AS NIGHT FALLS, HEROBRINE APPROACHES...
GALLOMP
GALLOMP
GALLOMP
GALLOMP GALLOMP
NEEEEIIIGH
YOU AGAIN?
UH-HUH.
I SEE YOU NEVER TIDIED UP AFTER LAST TIME.
WELL, IT'S ABOUT TO GET MESSIER.
STOMP STOMP

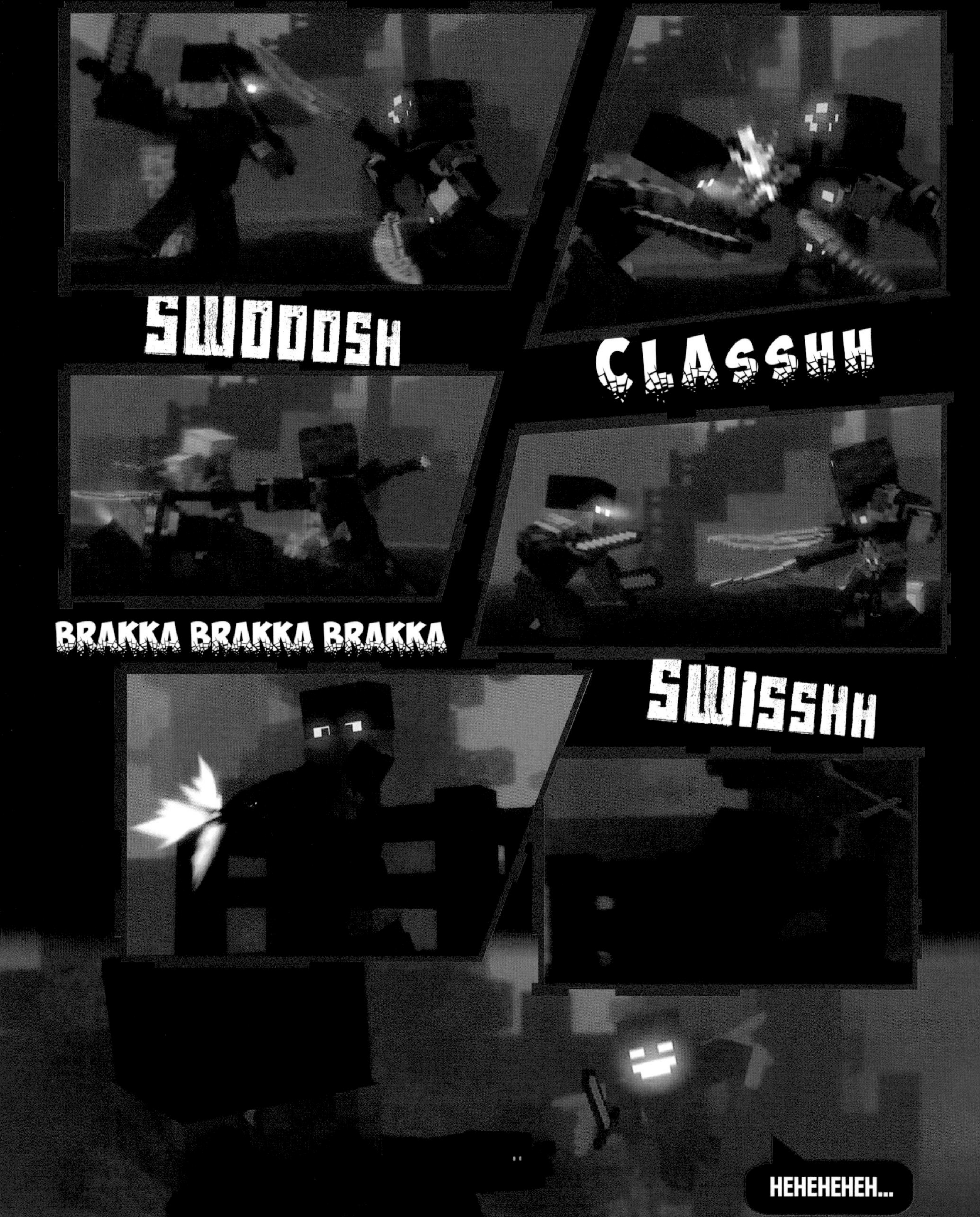
SWOOOSH
CLASSHH
BRAKKA BRAKKA BRAKKA
SWISSHH
HEHEHEHEH...

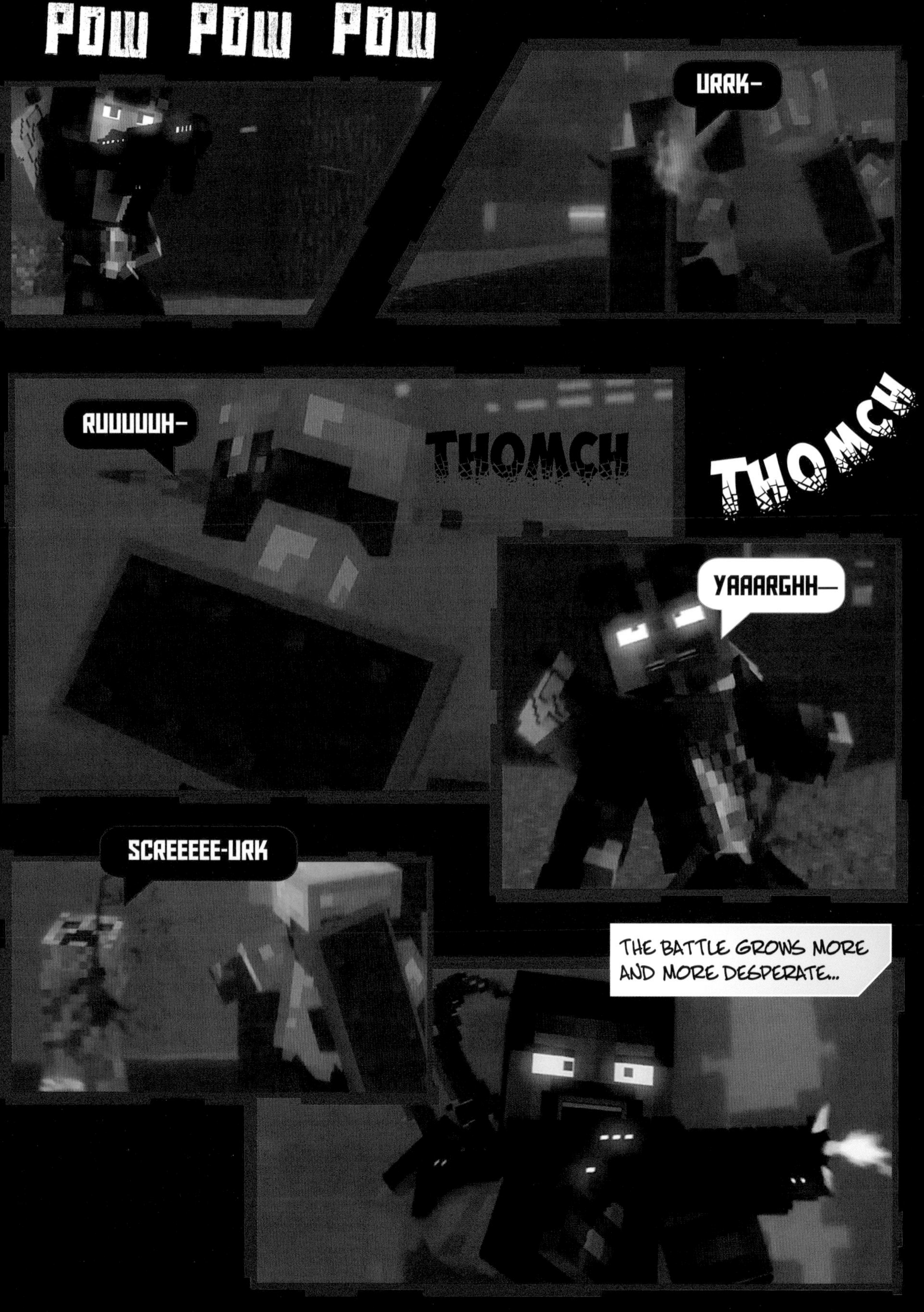
POW POW POW
URRK-
RUUUUUH-
THOMCH
THOMCH
YAAARGHH—
SCREEEEE-URK
THE BATTLE GROWS MORE AND MORE DESPERATE...

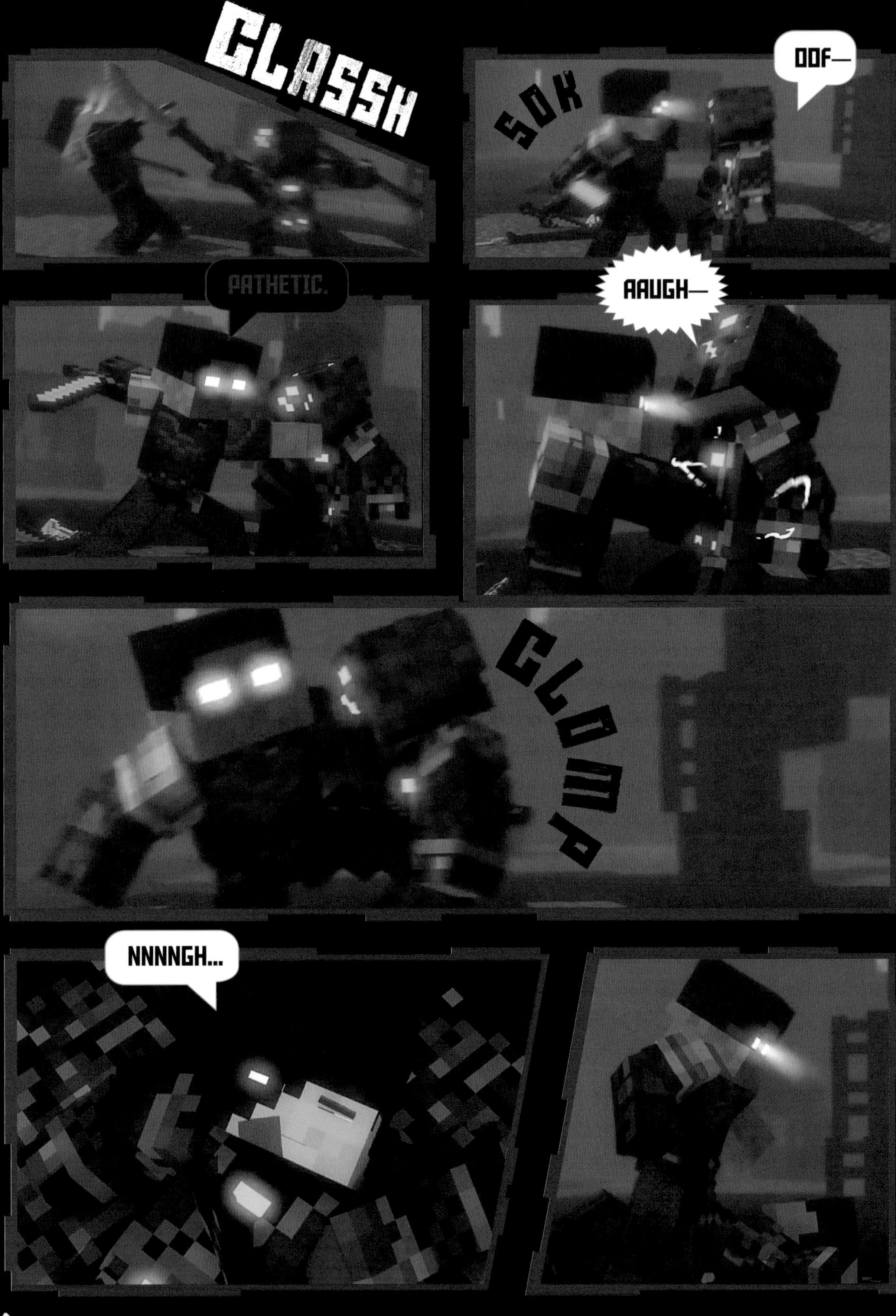
CLASSH
SOK
OOF—
PATHETIC.
AAUGH—
CLOMP
NNNNGH...

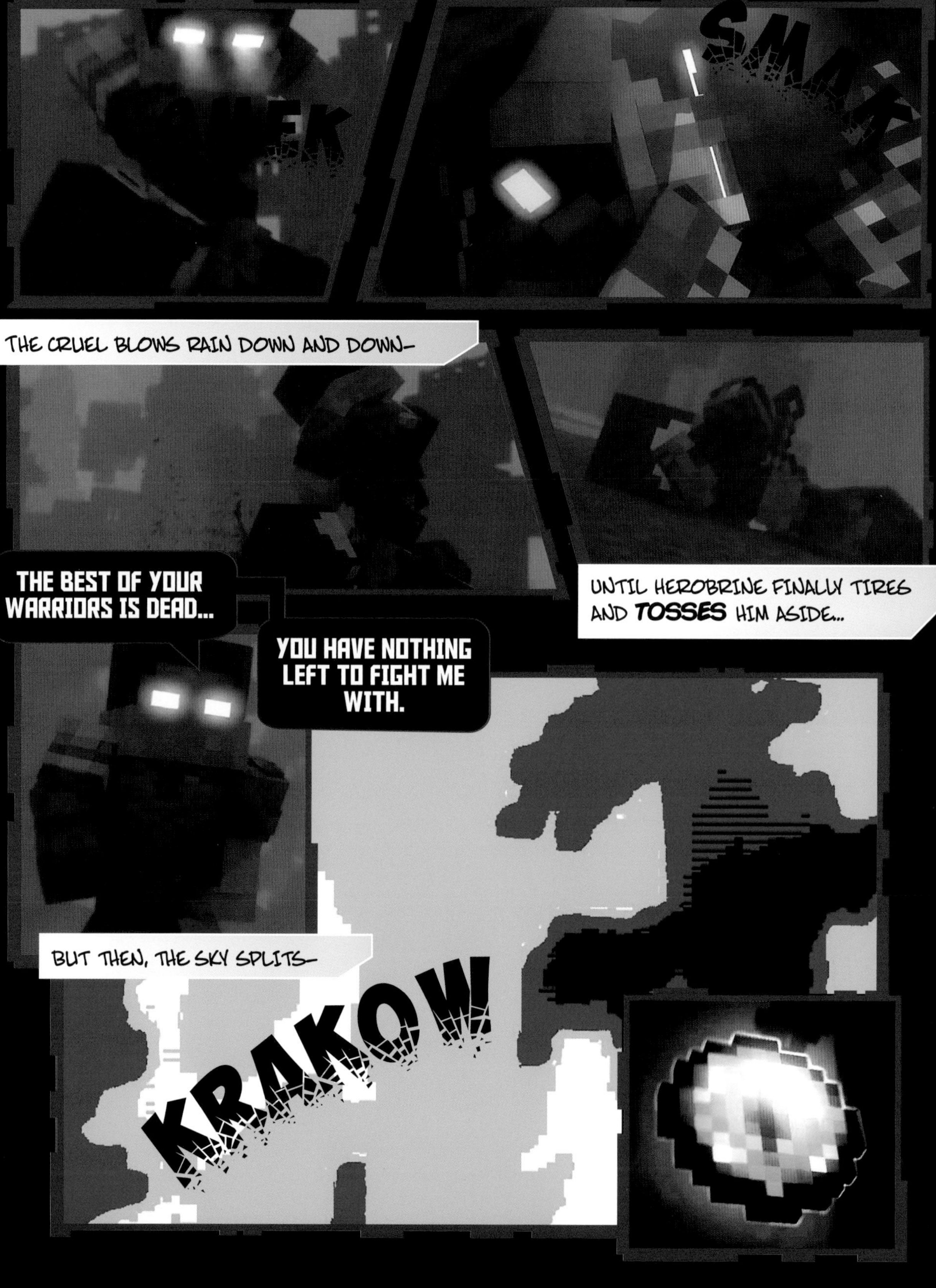
SMAK
THE CRUEL BLOWS RAIN DOWN AND DOWN—
UNTIL HEROBRINE FINALLY TIRES AND **TOSSES** HIM ASIDE...
THE BEST OF YOUR WARRIORS IS DEAD...
YOU HAVE NOTHING LEFT TO FIGHT ME WITH.
BUT THEN, THE SKY SPLITS—
KRAKOW

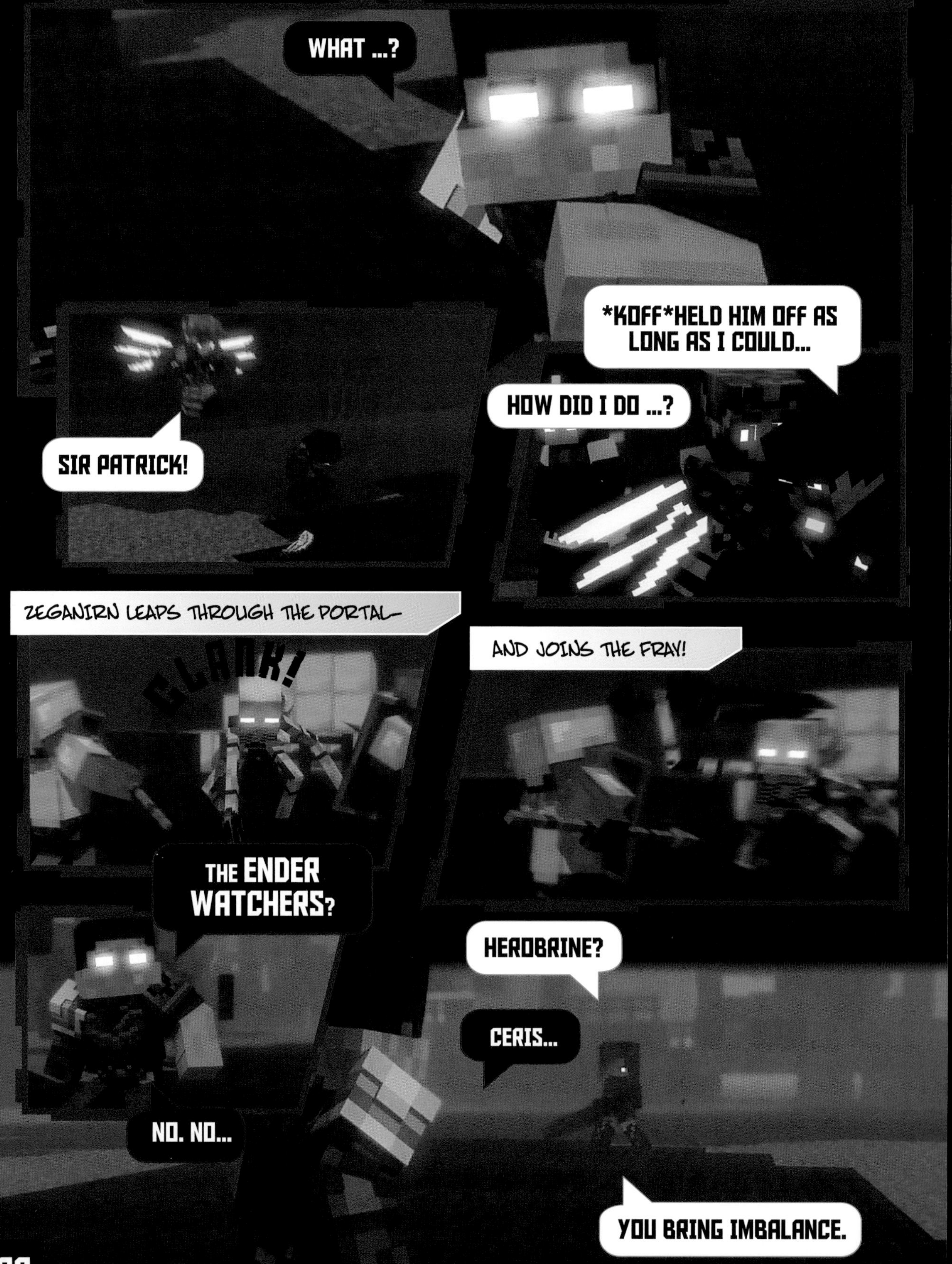
WHAT ...?
SIR PATRICK!
*KOFF*HELD HIM OFF AS LONG AS I COULD...
HOW DID I DO ...?
ZEGANIRN LEAPS THROUGH THE PORTAL–
AND JOINS THE FRAY!
THE ENDER WATCHERS?
HEROBRINE?
CERIS...
NO. NO...
YOU BRING IMBALANCE.

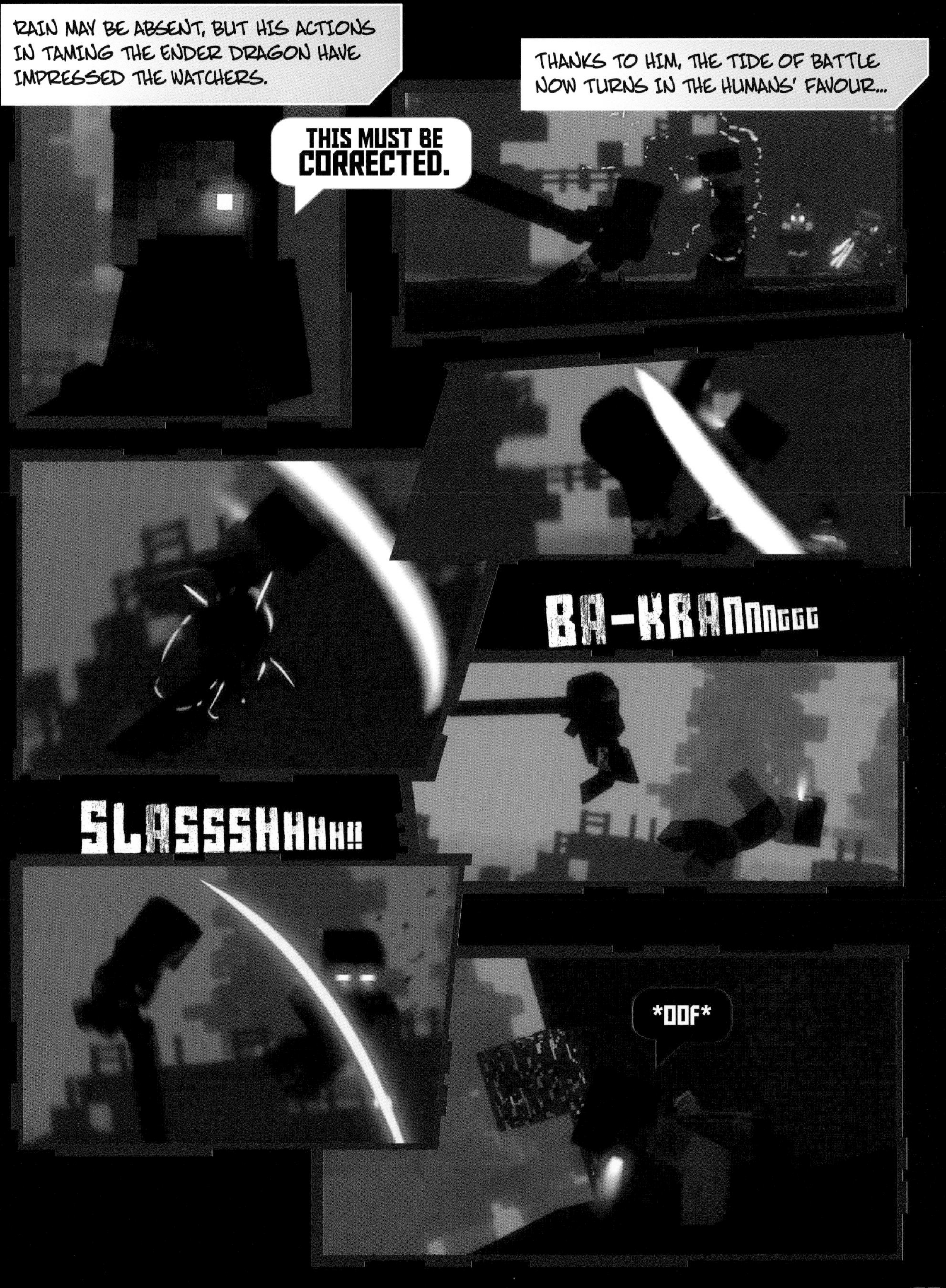

RAIN MAY BE ABSENT, BUT HIS ACTIONS IN TAMING THE ENDER DRAGON HAVE IMPRESSED THE WATCHERS.
THANKS TO HIM, THE TIDE OF BATTLE NOW TURNS IN THE HUMANS' FAVOUR...
THIS MUST BE CORRECTED.
BA-KRANNNGGG
SLASSSHHHH!!
OOF

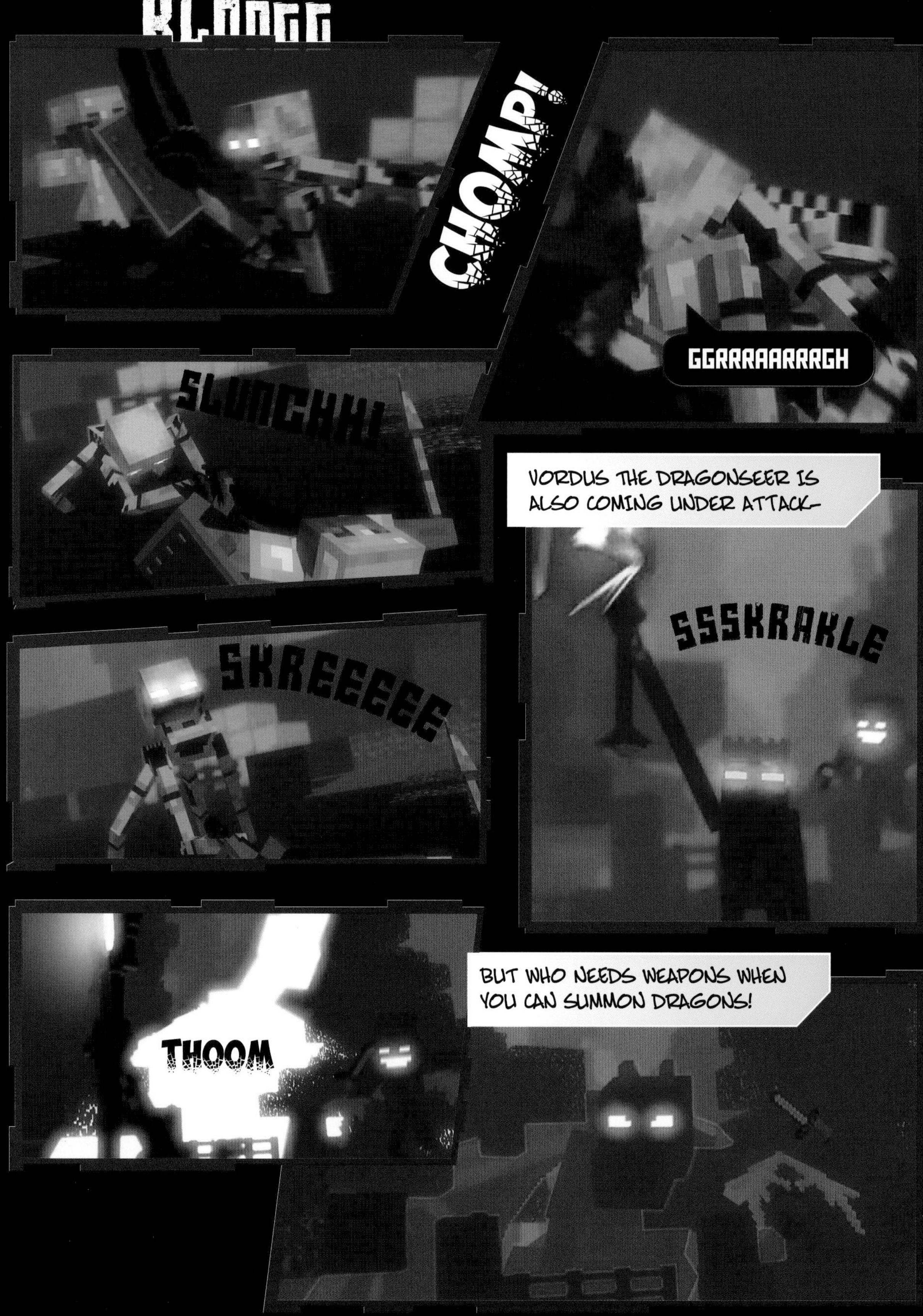
KLANGG
CHOMP!
GGRRRAARRRGH
SLUNCHH!
SKREEEEEE
VORDUS THE DRAGONSEER IS ALSO COMING UNDER ATTACK–
SSSKRAKLE
THOOM
BUT WHO NEEDS WEAPONS WHEN YOU CAN SUMMON DRAGONS!

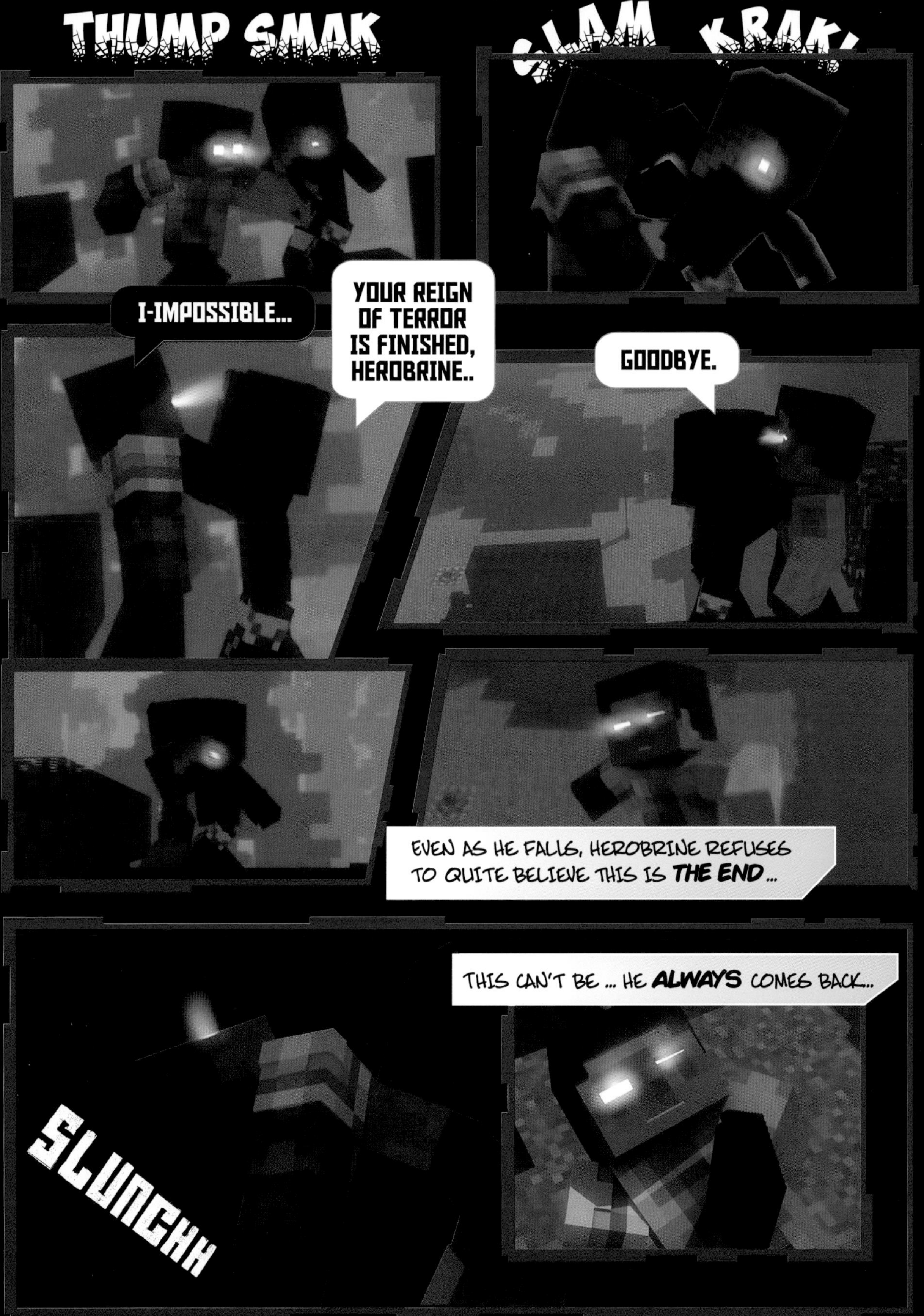
THUMP SMAK
SLAM KRAK!
I-IMPOSSIBLE...
YOUR REIGN OF TERROR IS FINISHED, HEROBRINE..
GOODBYE.
EVEN AS HE FALLS, HEROBRINE REFUSES TO QUITE BELIEVE THIS IS **THE END**...
THIS CAN'T BE ... HE **ALWAYS** COMES BACK...
SLUNCHH

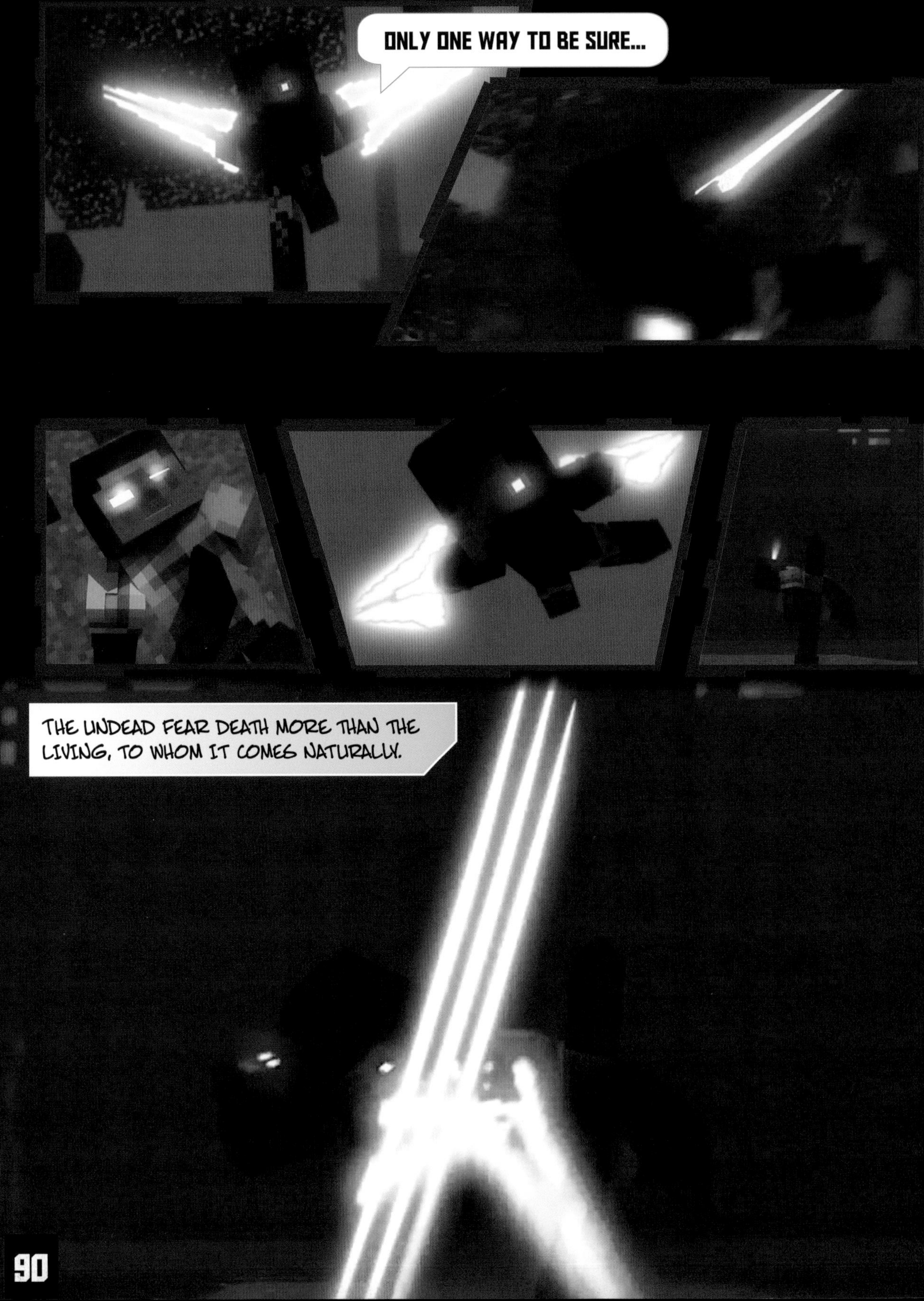
ONLY ONE WAY TO BE SURE...
THE UNDEAD FEAR DEATH MORE THAN THE LIVING, TO WHOM IT COMES NATURALLY.

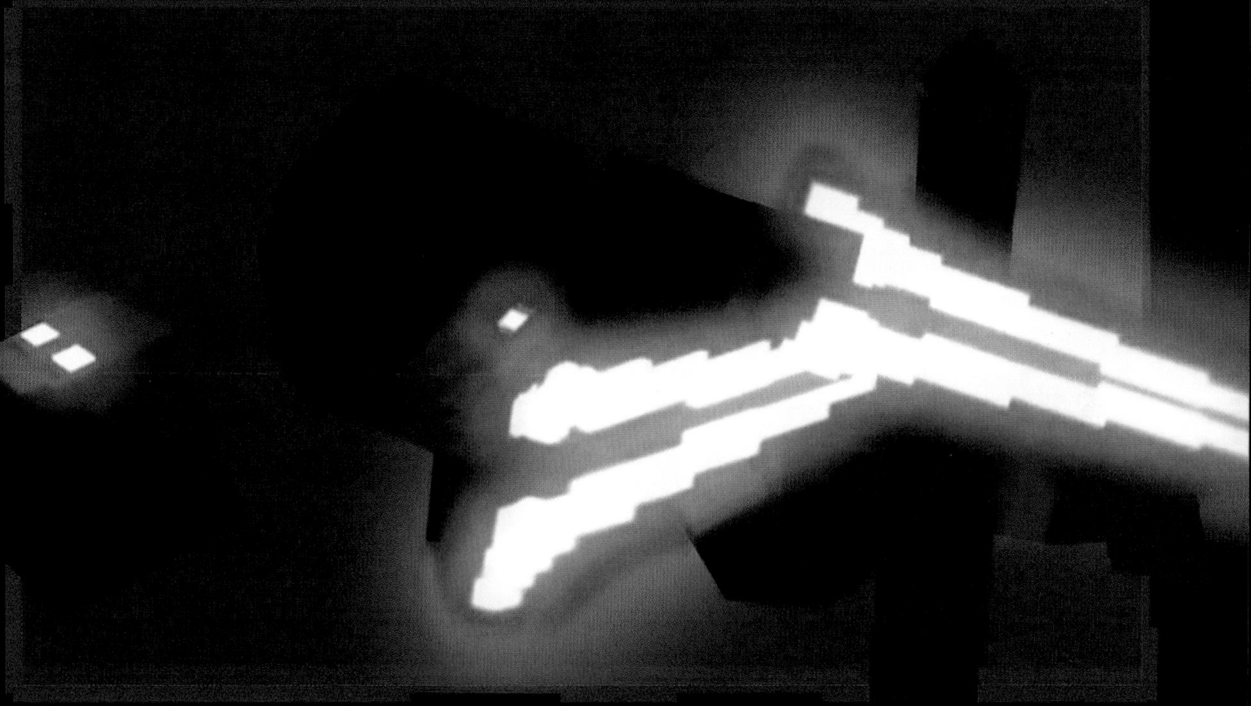

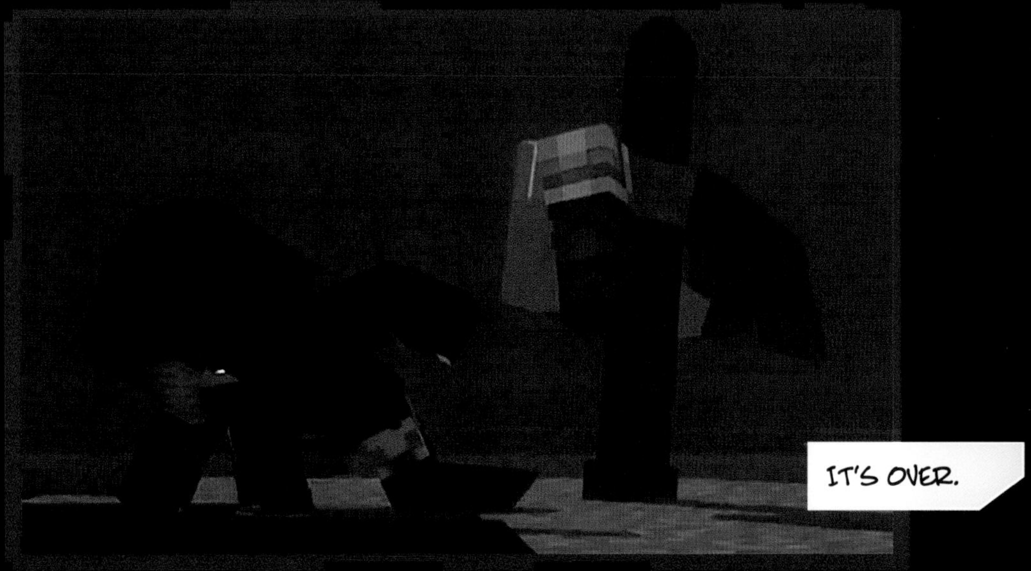
IT'S OVER.

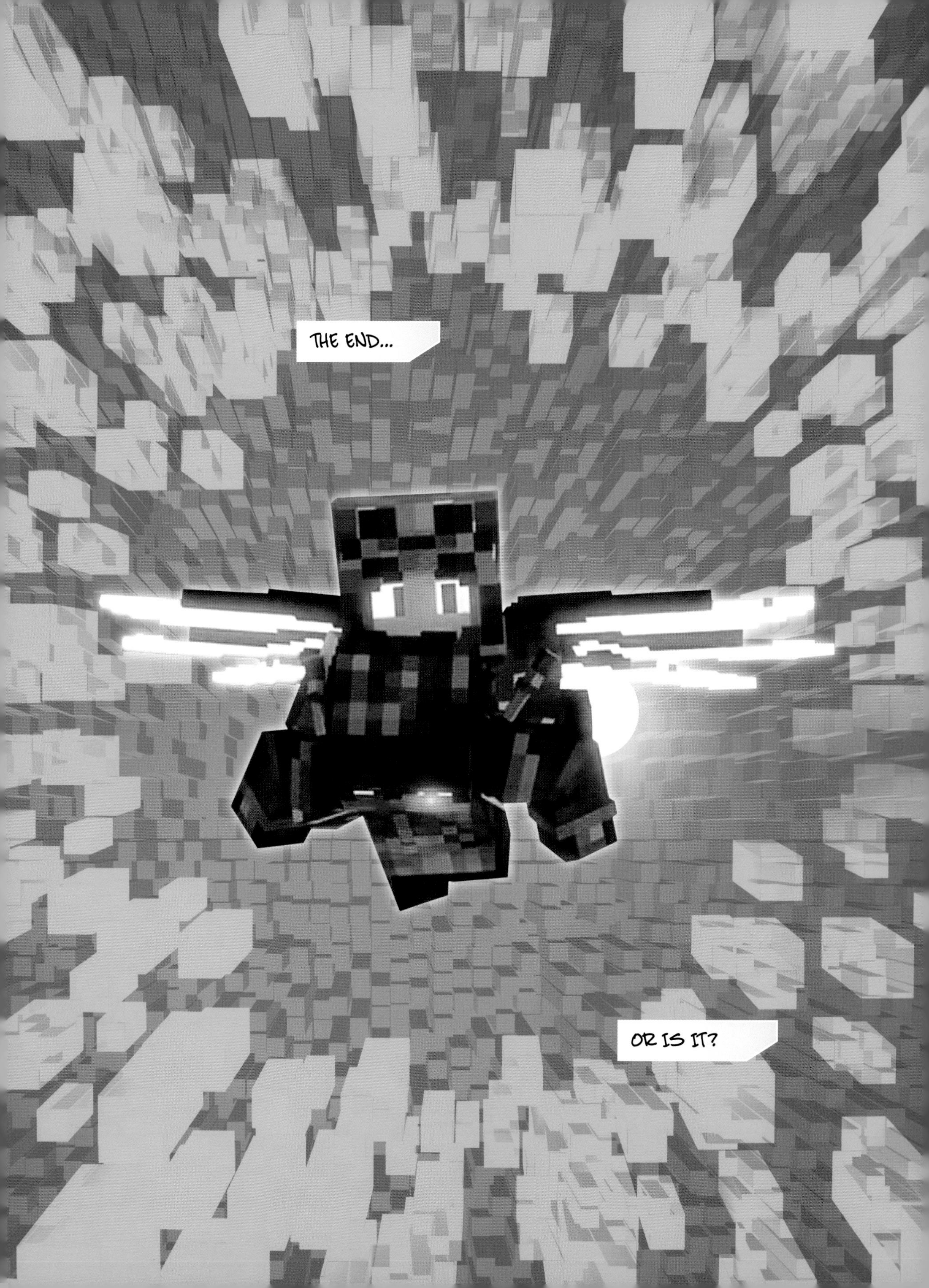
THE END...
OR IS IT?

REIGN OF TERROR

PART 2

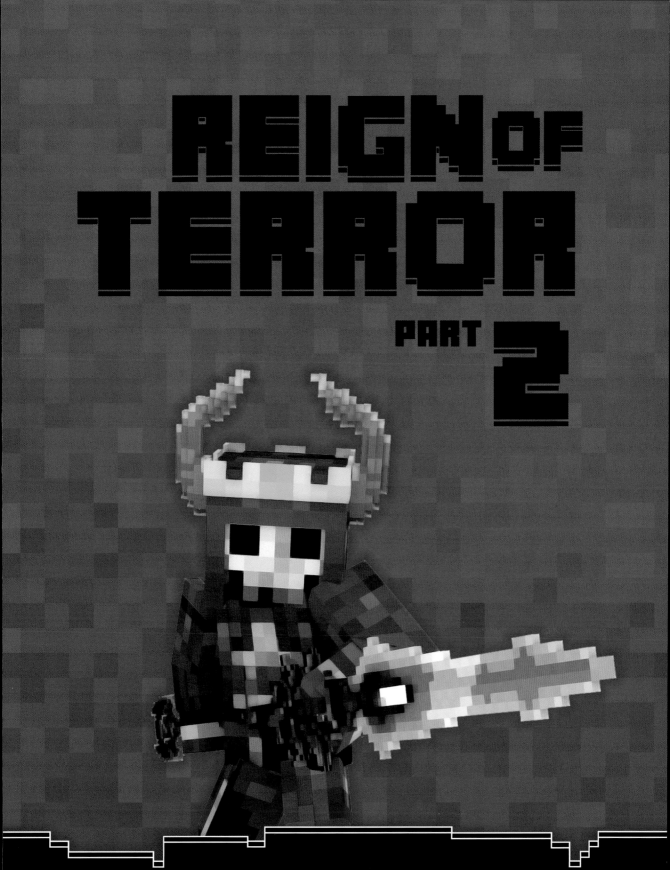

THE STORY SO FAR...

THE OVERWORLD HAS SURVIVED THE ONSLAUGHT OF **HEROBRINE'S** FORCES... BUT NOW, A NEW EVIL RISES TO TAKE ITS PLACE.

GENERAL NAEUS AIMS TO UNITE THE NETHER'S HORRIFIC INHABITANTS, AND THEN ATTACK THE OVERWORLD ONCE MORE. IF HE GAINS **HEROBRINE'S** POWER, HE WILL BE UNSTOPPABLE.

THE OVERWORLD'S GREATEST HERO, **RAIN THE DRAGON TAMER**, HAS BEEN LOST IN THE NETHER. NOW, **LADY AZURA** PLANS A DARING RAID, FOR THE FATE OF ALL HEROES HANGS IN THE BALANCE...

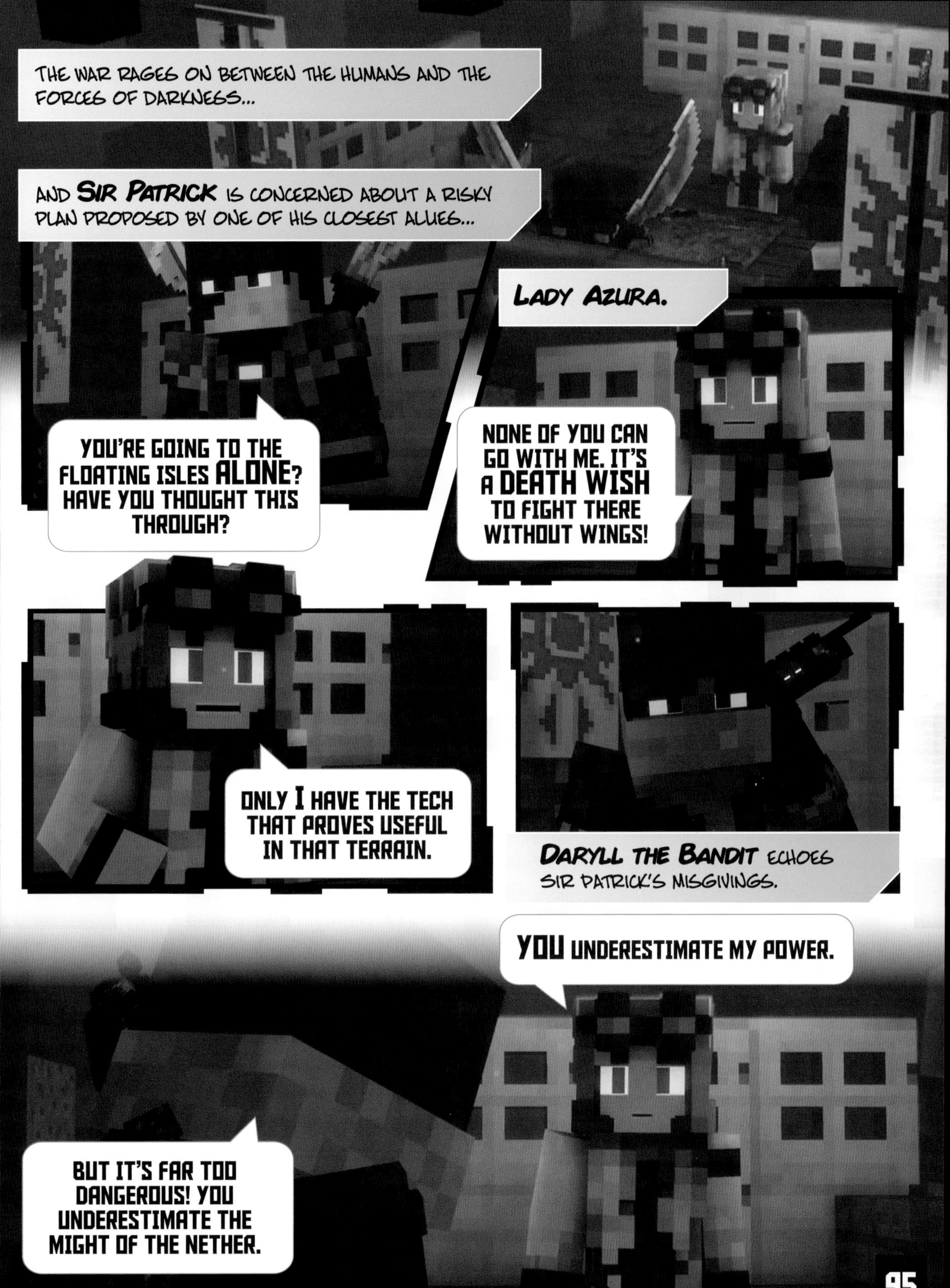
THE WAR RAGES ON BETWEEN THE HUMANS AND THE FORCES OF DARKNESS...
AND SIR PATRICK IS CONCERNED ABOUT A RISKY PLAN PROPOSED BY ONE OF HIS CLOSEST ALLIES...
LADY AZURA.
YOU'RE GOING TO THE FLOATING ISLES ALONE? HAVE YOU THOUGHT THIS THROUGH?
NONE OF YOU CAN GO WITH ME. IT'S A DEATH WISH TO FIGHT THERE WITHOUT WINGS!
ONLY I HAVE THE TECH THAT PROVES USEFUL IN THAT TERRAIN.
DARYLL THE BANDIT ECHOES SIR PATRICK'S MISGIVINGS.
YOU UNDERESTIMATE MY POWER.
BUT IT'S FAR TOO DANGEROUS! YOU UNDERESTIMATE THE MIGHT OF THE NETHER.

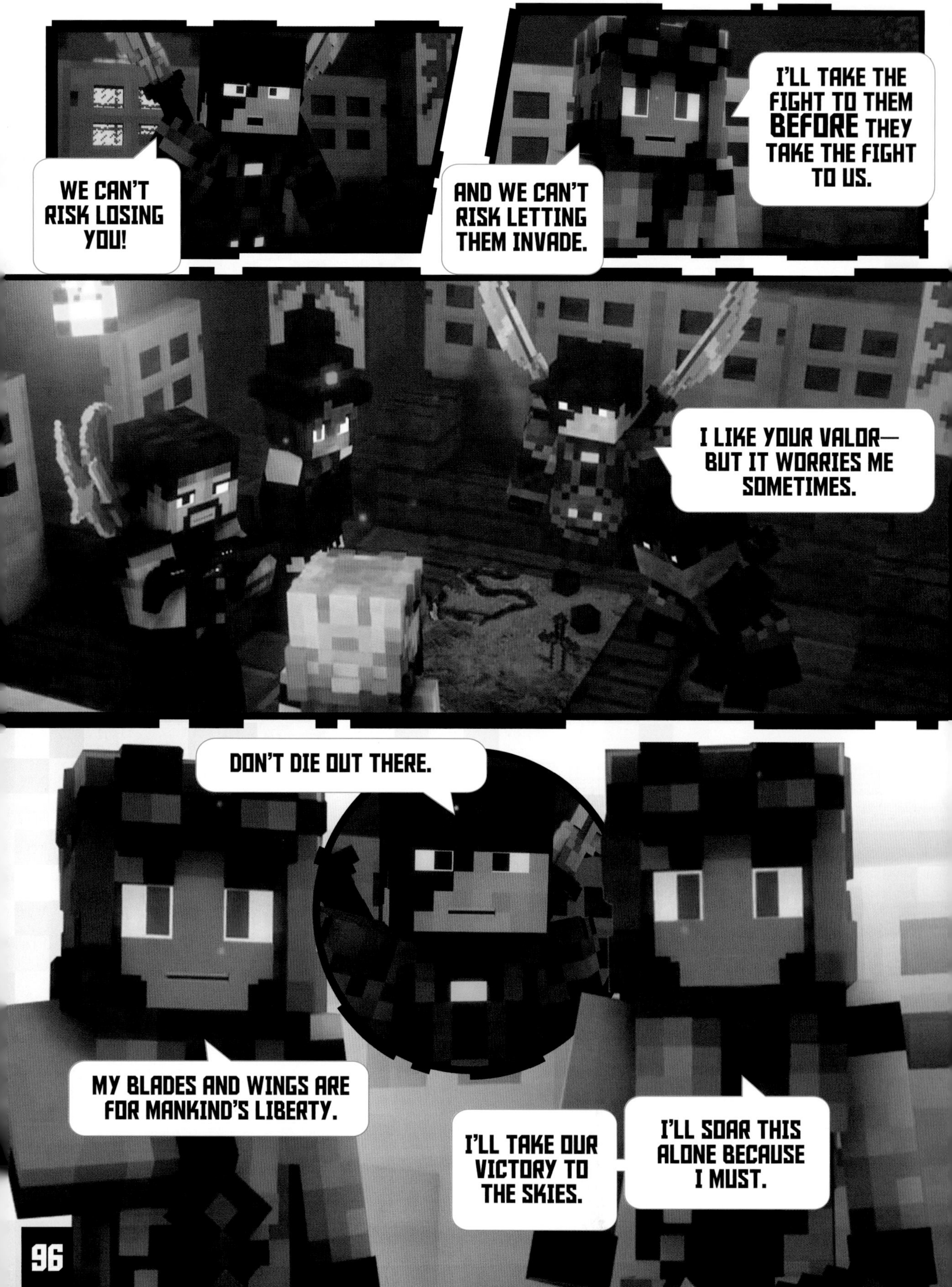
WE CAN'T RISK LOSING YOU!
AND WE CAN'T RISK LETTING THEM INVADE.
I'LL TAKE THE FIGHT TO THEM BEFORE THEY TAKE THE FIGHT TO US.
I LIKE YOUR VALOR— BUT IT WORRIES ME SOMETIMES.
DON'T DIE OUT THERE.
MY BLADES AND WINGS ARE FOR MANKIND'S LIBERTY.
I'LL TAKE OUR VICTORY TO THE SKIES.
I'LL SOAR THIS ALONE BECAUSE I MUST.

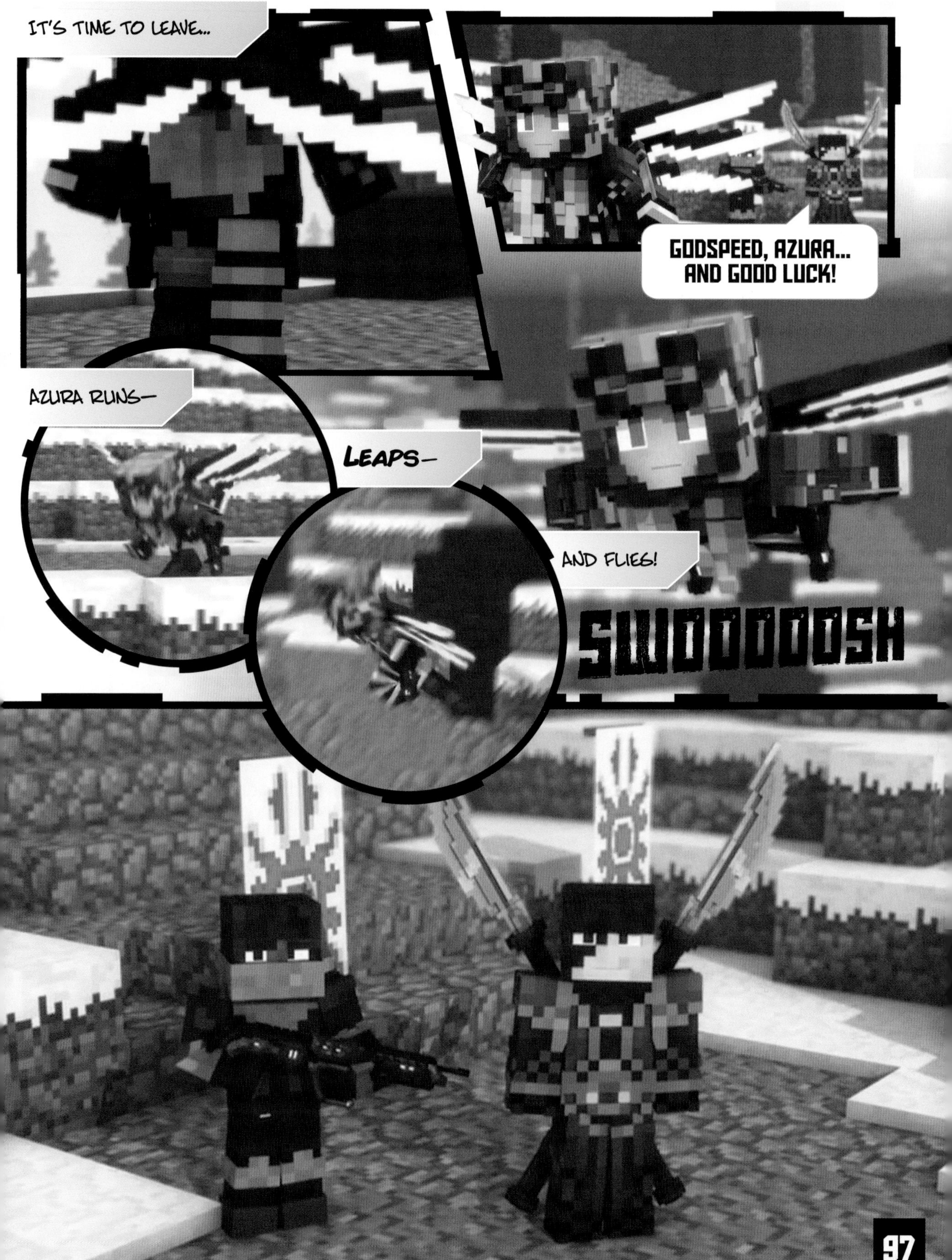
IT'S TIME TO LEAVE...
GODSPEED, AZURA... AND GOOD LUCK!
AZURA RUNS—
LEAPS—
AND FLIES!
SWOOOOOOSH

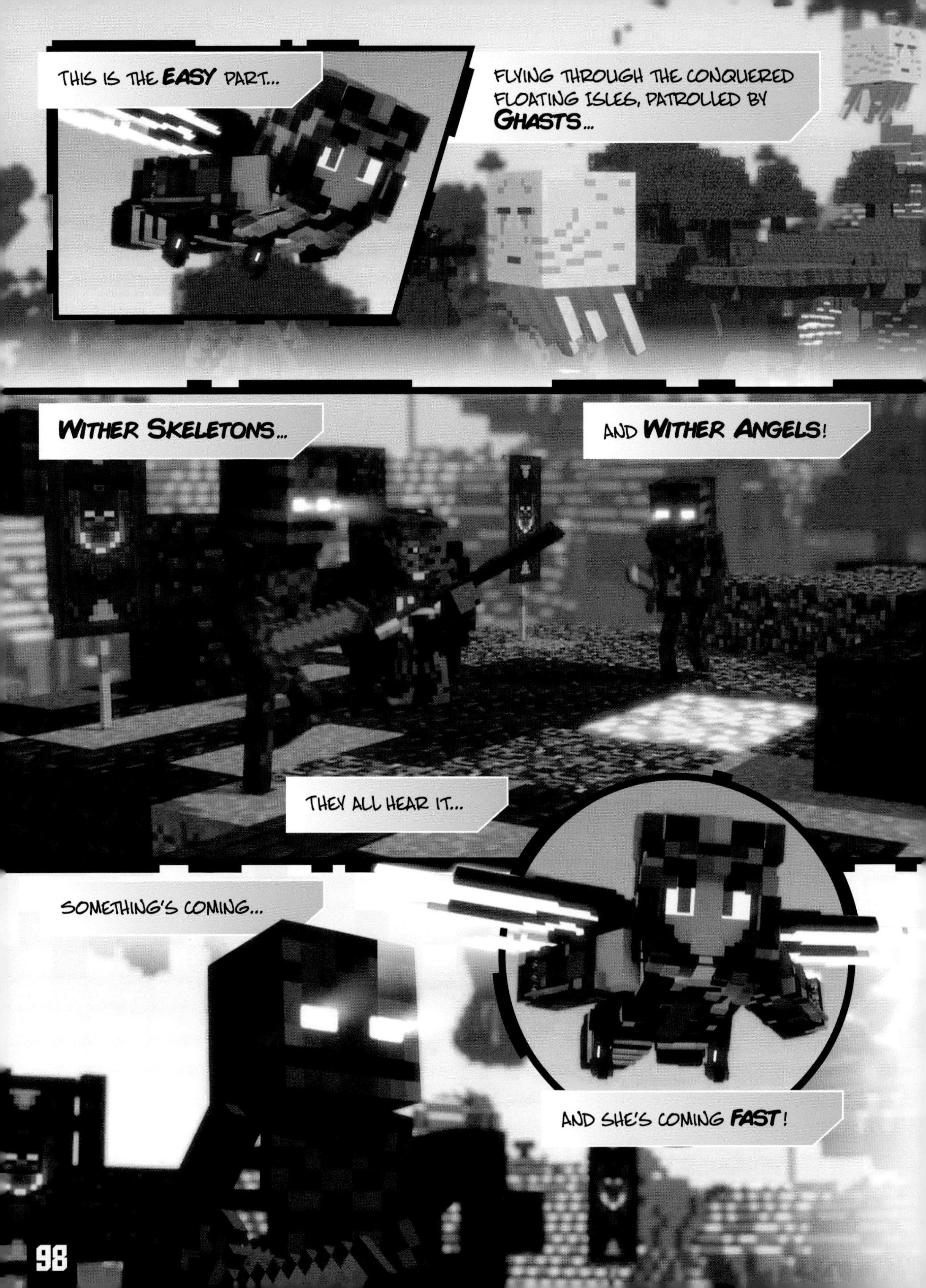
THIS IS THE EASY PART...
FLYING THROUGH THE CONQUERED FLOATING ISLES, PATROLLED BY GHASTS...
WITHER SKELETONS...
AND WITHER ANGELS!
THEY ALL HEAR IT...
SOMETHING'S COMING...
AND SHE'S COMING FAST!

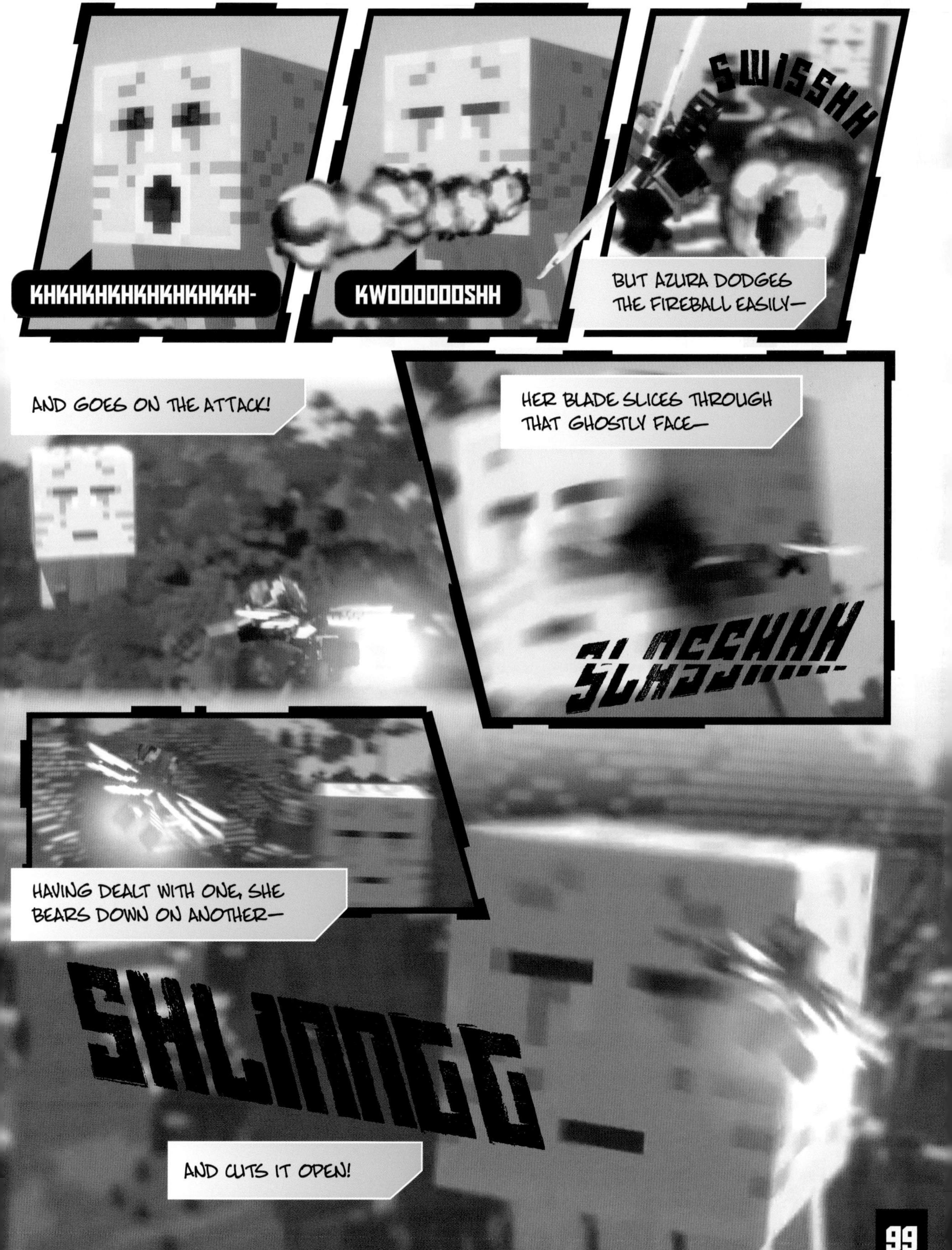

KHKHKHKHKHKHKHKKH-
KWOOOOOOSHH
SWISSHH
BUT AZURA DODGES THE FIREBALL EASILY—
AND GOES ON THE ATTACK!
HER BLADE SLICES THROUGH THAT GHOSTLY FACE—
SLASSHHH
HAVING DEALT WITH ONE, SHE BEARS DOWN ON ANOTHER—
SHLINNGG
AND CUTS IT OPEN!

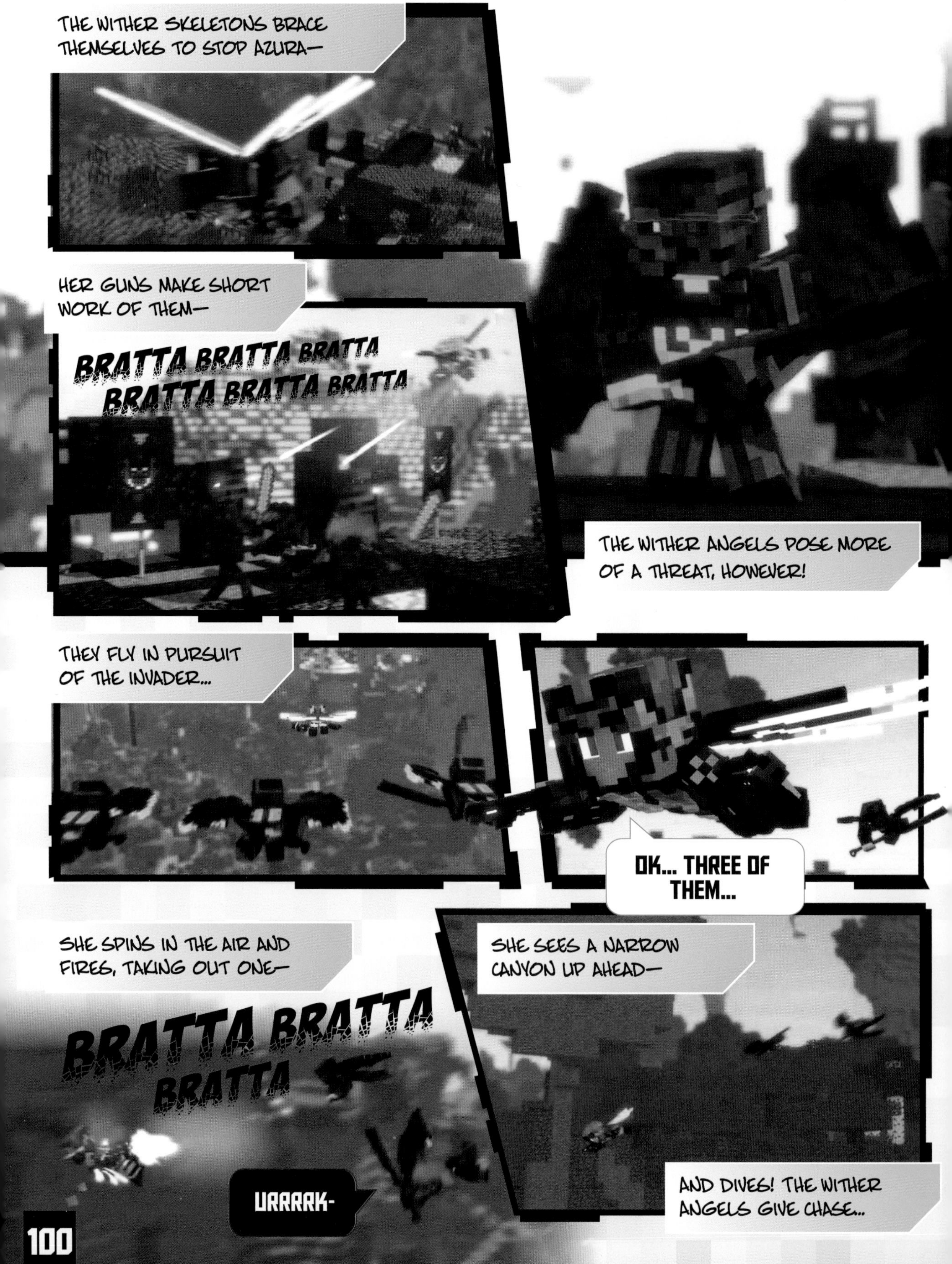

THE WITHER SKELETONS BRACE THEMSELVES TO STOP AZURA—
HER GUNS MAKE SHORT WORK OF THEM—
BRATTA BRATTA BRATTA BRATTA BRATTA BRATTA
THE WITHER ANGELS POSE MORE OF A THREAT, HOWEVER!
THEY FLY IN PURSUIT OF THE INVADER...
OK... THREE OF THEM...
SHE SPINS IN THE AIR AND FIRES, TAKING OUT ONE—
BRATTA BRATTA BRATTA
URRRRK-
SHE SEES A NARROW CANYON UP AHEAD—
AND DIVES! THE WITHER ANGELS GIVE CHASE...

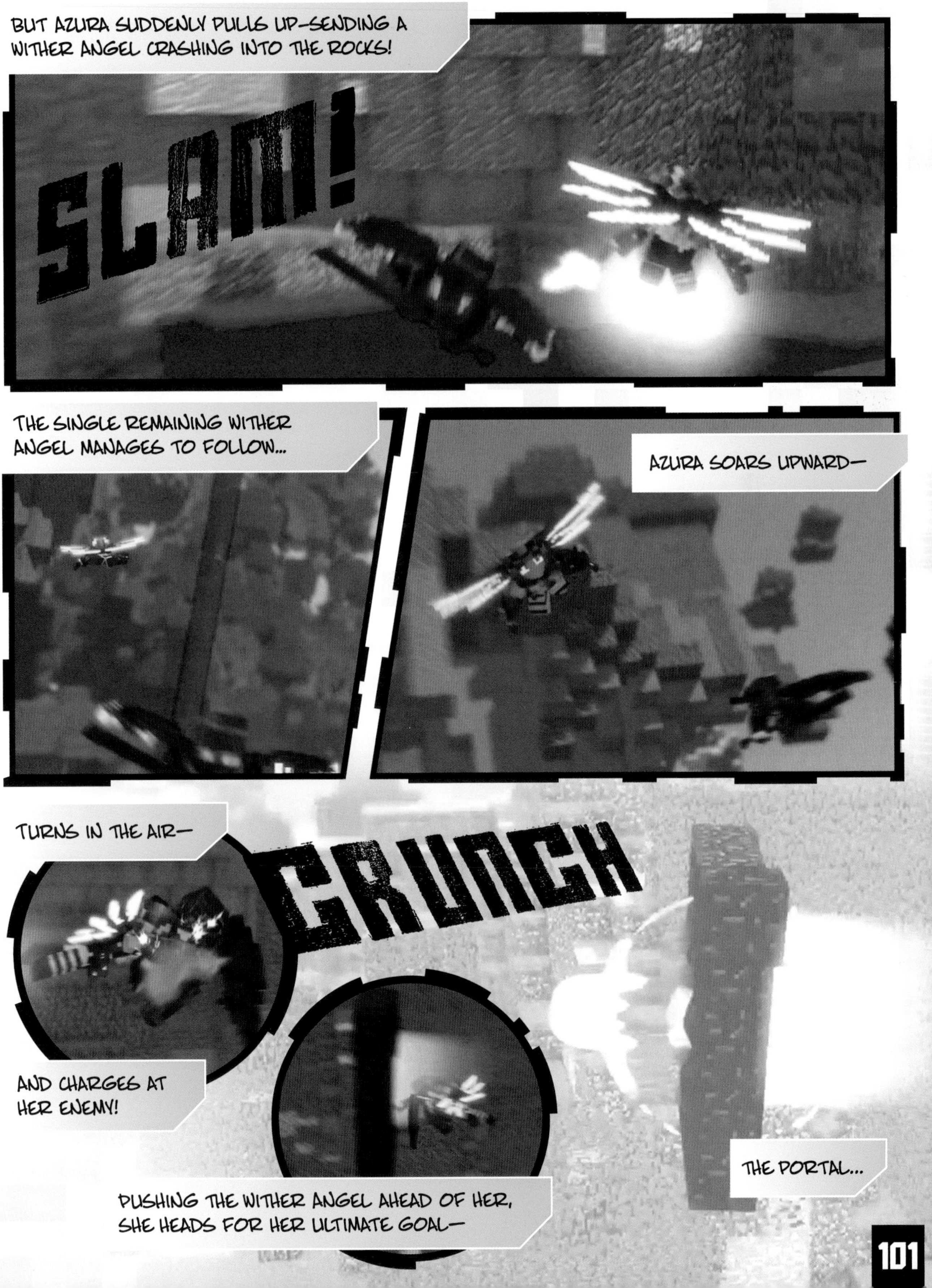
BUT AZURA SUDDENLY PULLS UP—SENDING A WITHER ANGEL CRASHING INTO THE ROCKS!
SLAM!
THE SINGLE REMAINING WITHER ANGEL MANAGES TO FOLLOW...
AZURA SOARS UPWARD—
TURNS IN THE AIR—
CRUNCH
AND CHARGES AT HER ENEMY!
PUSHING THE WITHER ANGEL AHEAD OF HER, SHE HEADS FOR HER ULTIMATE GOAL—
THE PORTAL...

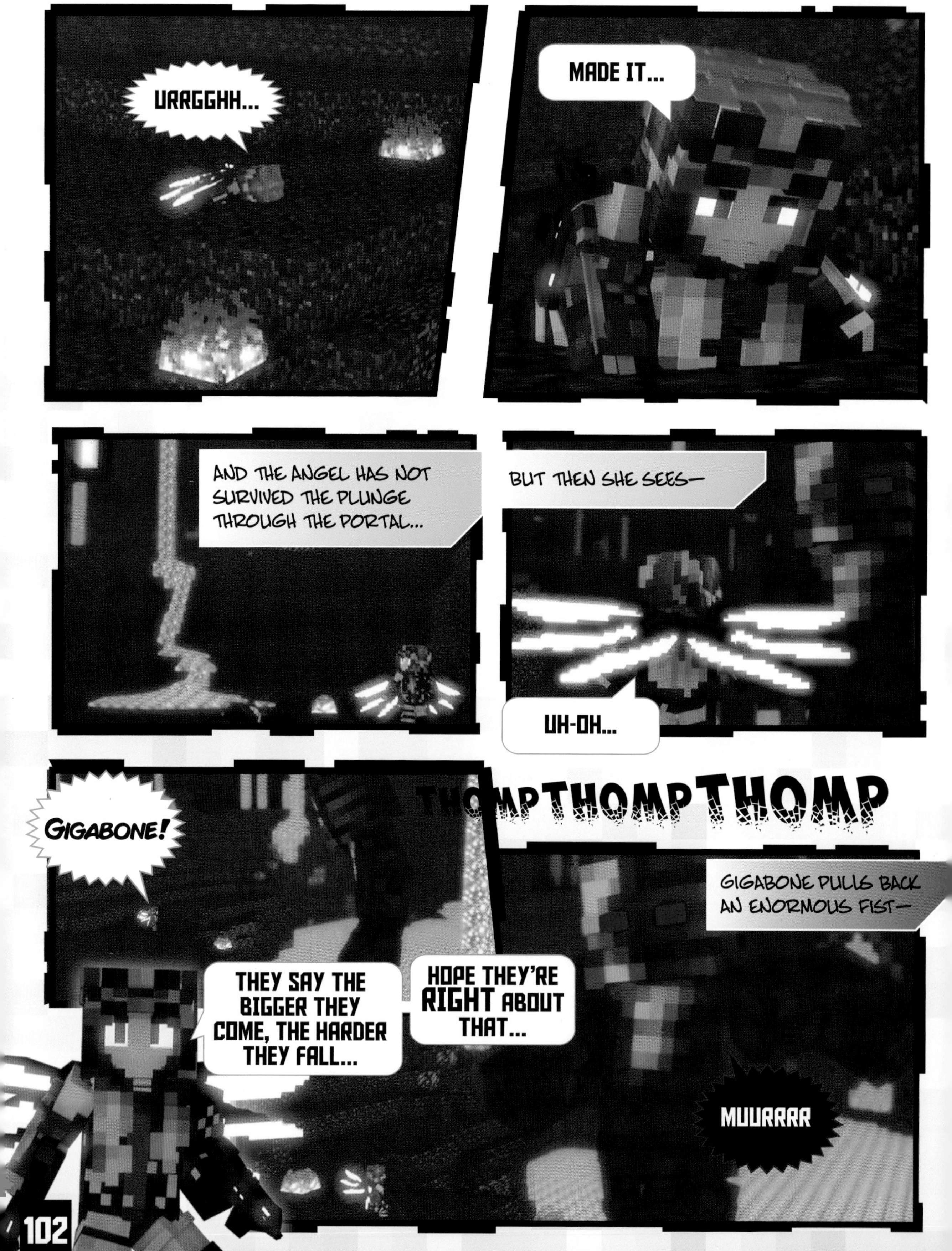
URRGGHH...
MADE IT...
AND THE ANGEL HAS NOT SURVIVED THE PLUNGE THROUGH THE PORTAL...
BUT THEN SHE SEES—
UH-OH...
GIGABONE!
THOMPTHOMPTHOMP
GIGABONE PULLS BACK AN ENORMOUS FIST—
THEY SAY THE BIGGER THEY COME, THE HARDER THEY FALL...
HOPE THEY'RE RIGHT ABOUT THAT...
MUURRRR

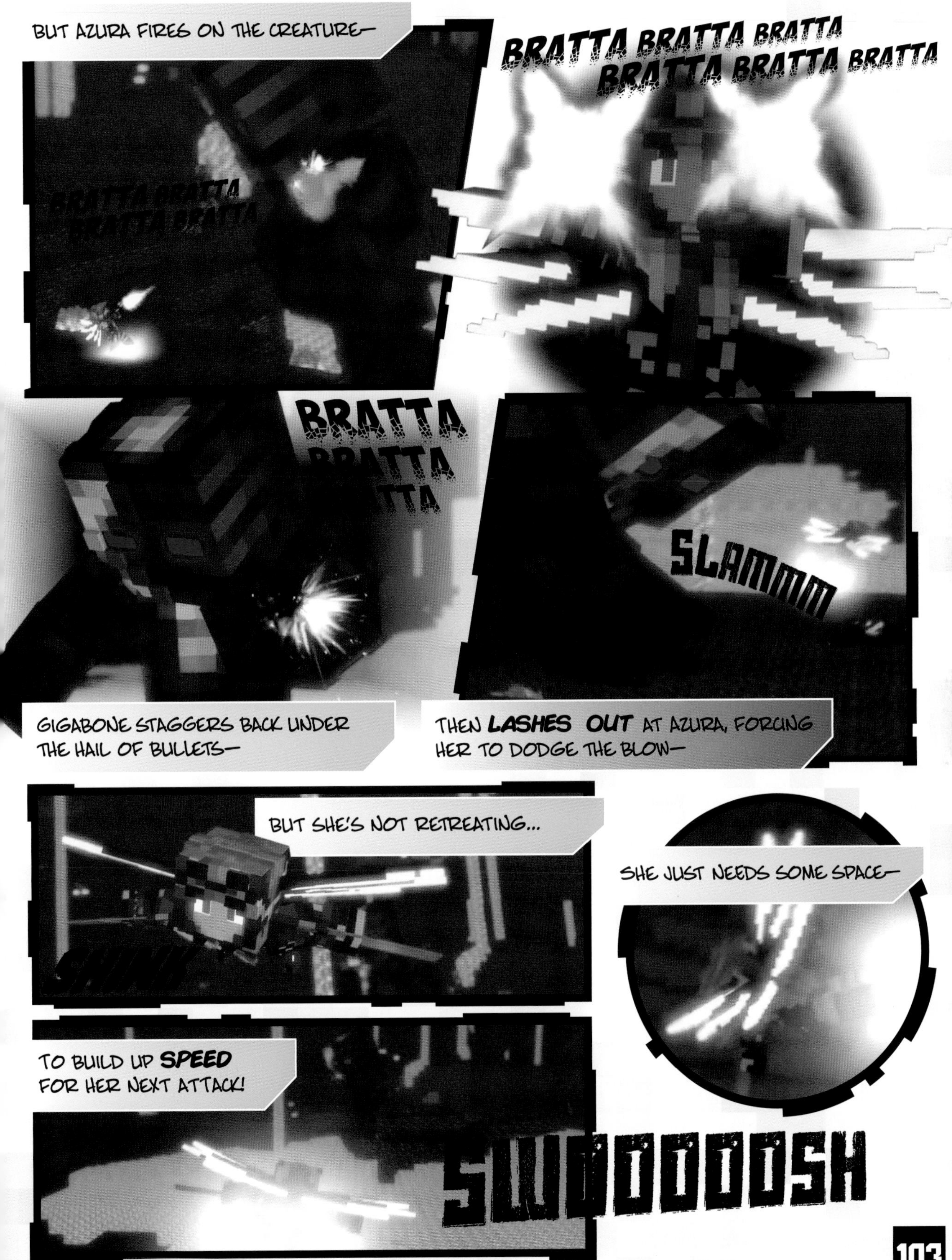

BUT AZURA FIRES ON THE CREATURE—
BRATTA BRATTA
BRATTA BRATTA
BRATTA BRATTA BRATTA
BRATTA BRATTA BRATTA
BRATTA
BRATTA
BRATTA
SLAMMM
GIGABONE STAGGERS BACK UNDER THE HAIL OF BULLETS—
THEN **LASHES OUT** AT AZURA, FORCING HER TO DODGE THE BLOW—
BUT SHE'S NOT RETREATING...
SHE JUST NEEDS SOME SPACE—
TO BUILD UP **SPEED** FOR HER NEXT ATTACK!

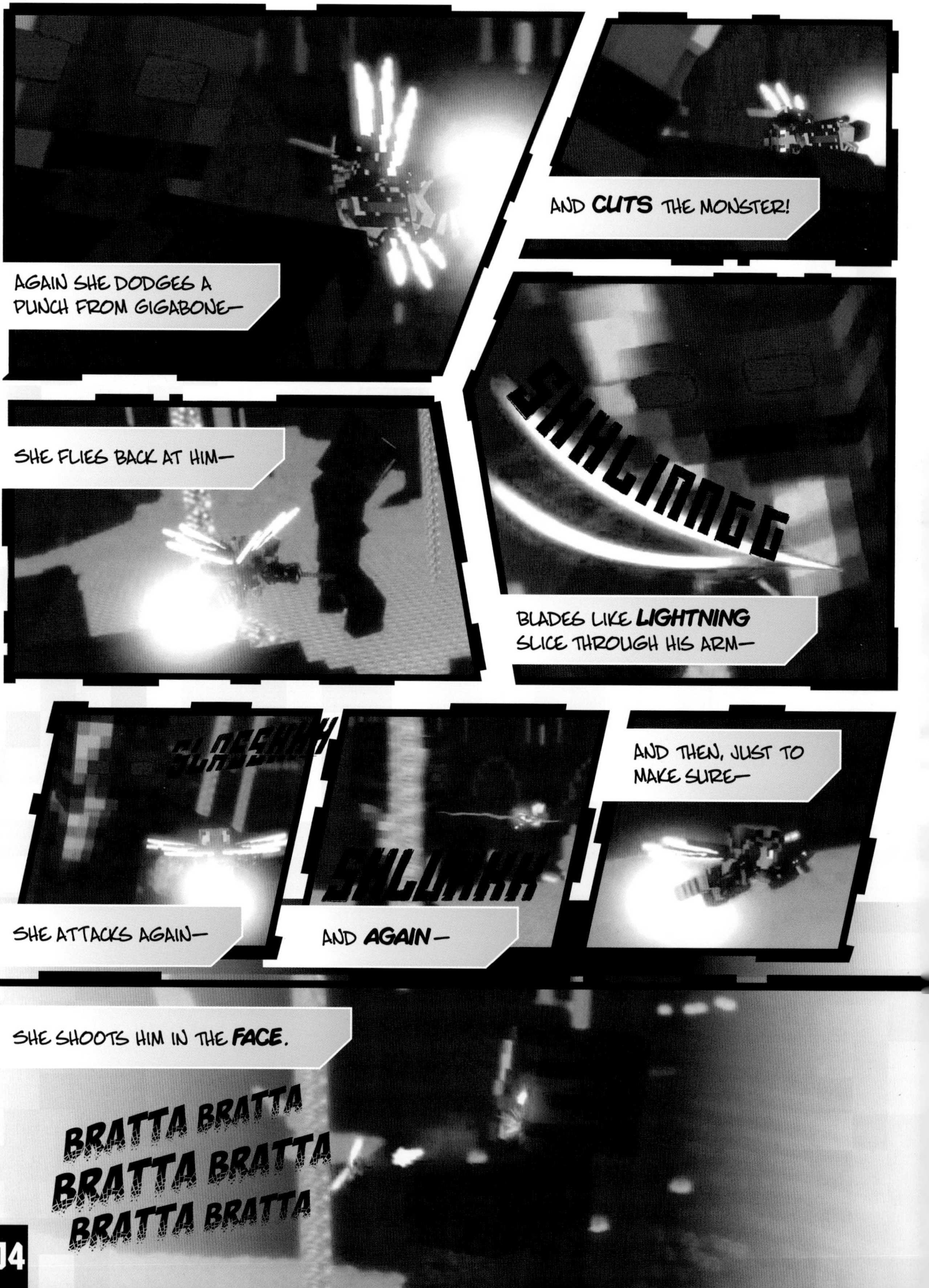
AGAIN SHE DODGES A PUNCH FROM GIGABONE—
AND CUTS THE MONSTER!
SHE FLIES BACK AT HIM—
SHHLINNGG
BLADES LIKE LIGHTNING SLICE THROUGH HIS ARM—
SLASHHH
SHE ATTACKS AGAIN—
AND AGAIN—
AND THEN, JUST TO MAKE SURE—
SHE SHOOTS HIM IN THE FACE.
BRATTA BRATTA
BRATTA BRATTA
BRATTA BRATTA

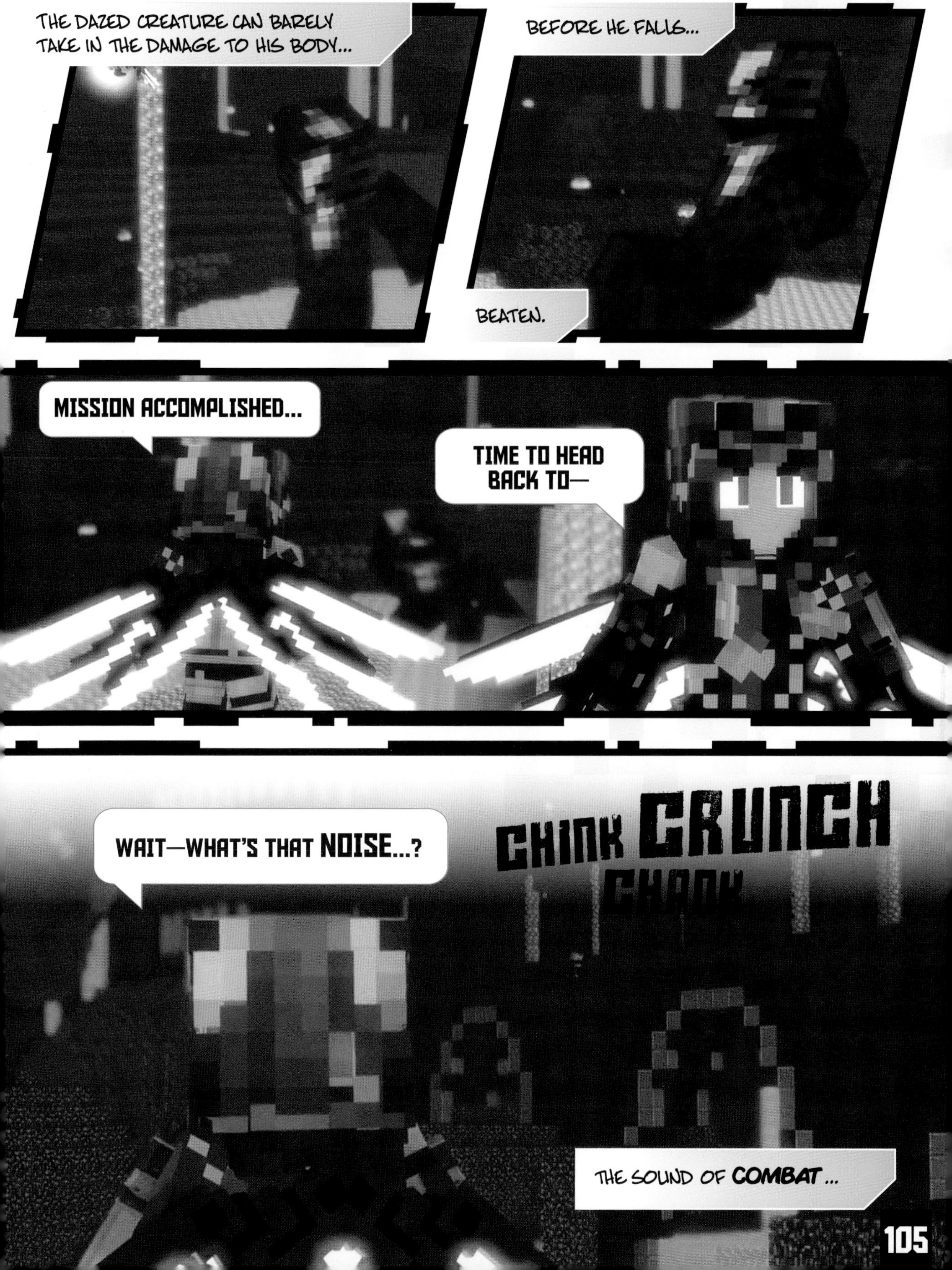
THE DAZED CREATURE CAN BARELY TAKE IN THE DAMAGE TO HIS BODY...
BEFORE HE FALLS...
BEATEN.
MISSION ACCOMPLISHED...
TIME TO HEAD BACK TO—
WAIT—WHAT'S THAT NOISE...?
CHINK CRUNCH CHANK
THE SOUND OF COMBAT...

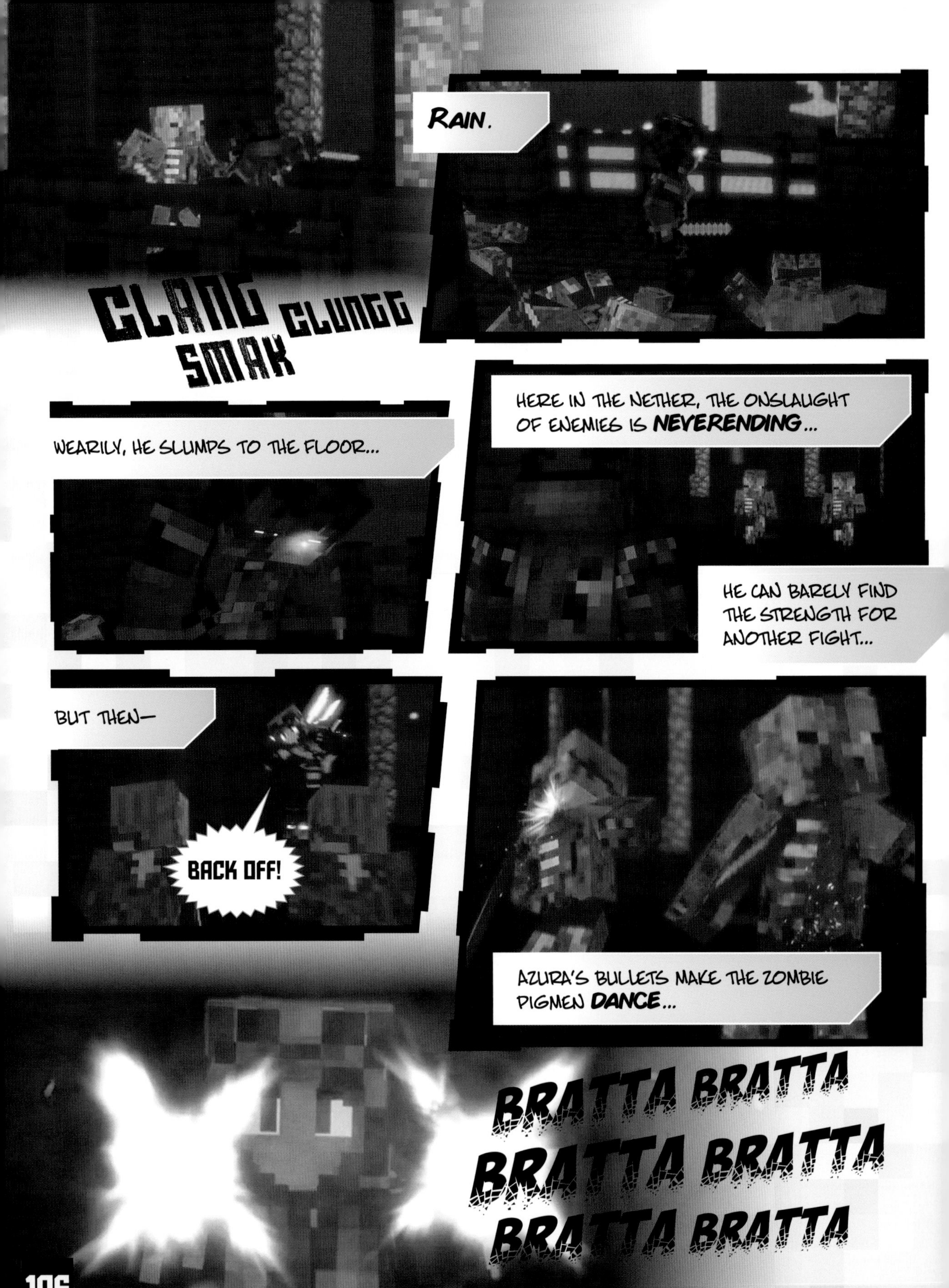

RAIN.
CLANG
CLUNGG
SMAK
HERE IN THE NETHER, THE ONSLAUGHT OF ENEMIES IS **NEVERENDING**...
WEARILY, HE SLUMPS TO THE FLOOR...
HE CAN BARELY FIND THE STRENGTH FOR ANOTHER FIGHT...
BUT THEN—
BACK OFF!
AZURA'S BULLETS MAKE THE ZOMBIE PIGMEN **DANCE**...
BRATTA BRATTA
BRATTA BRATTA
BRATTA BRATTA

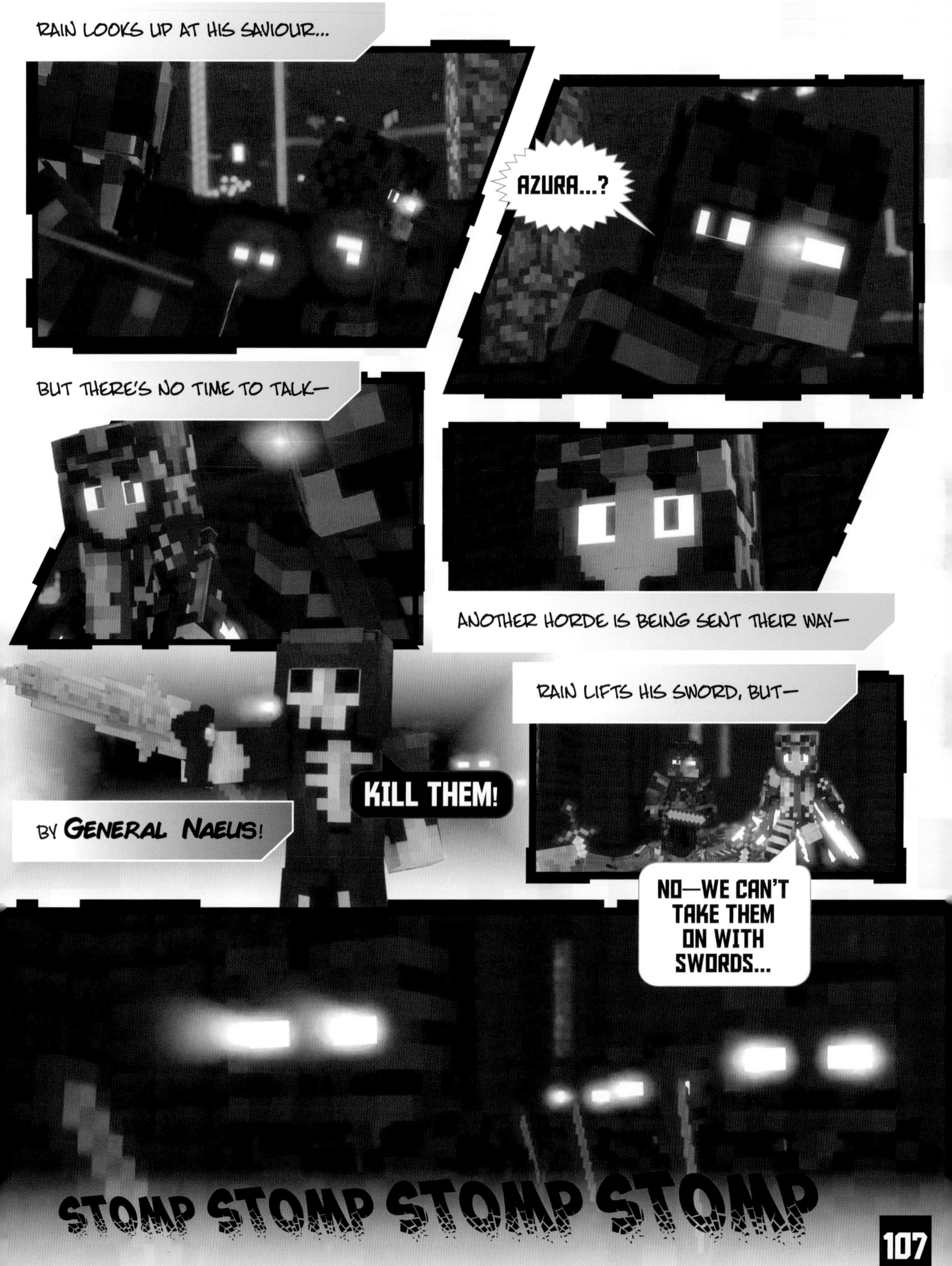
RAIN LOOKS UP AT HIS SAVIOUR...
AZURA...?
BUT THERE'S NO TIME TO TALK—
ANOTHER HORDE IS BEING SENT THEIR WAY—
BY GENERAL NAEUS!
KILL THEM!
RAIN LIFTS HIS SWORD, BUT—
NO—WE CAN'T TAKE THEM ON WITH SWORDS...
STOMP STOMP STOMP STOMP

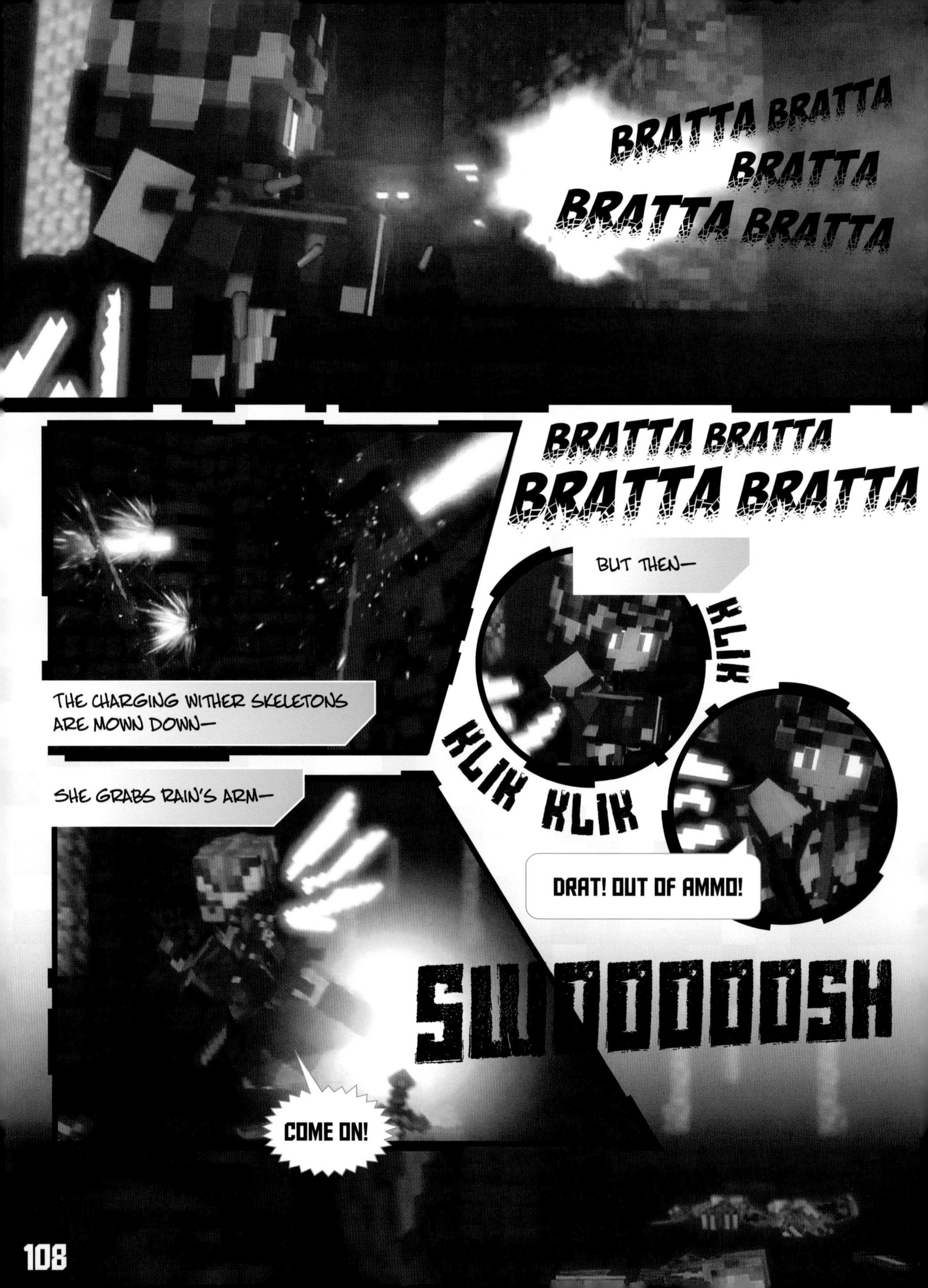
BRATTA BRATTA
BRATTA
BRATTA BRATTA
BRATTA BRATTA
BRATTA BRATTA
THE CHARGING WITHER SKELETONS ARE MOWN DOWN—
BUT THEN—
KLIK
KLIK KLIK
DRAT! OUT OF AMMO!
SHE GRABS RAIN'S ARM—
SWOOOOSH
COME ON!

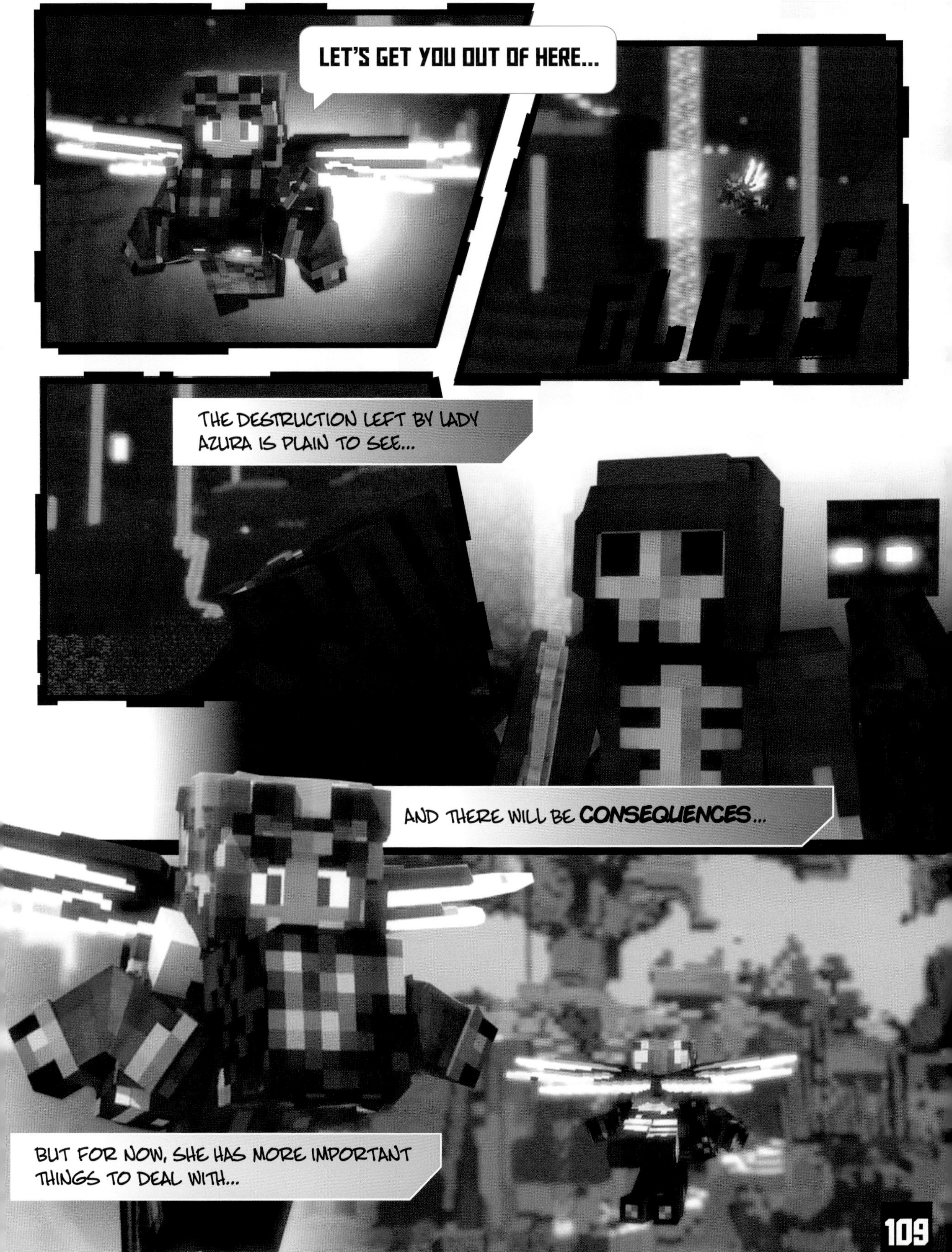

LET'S GET YOU OUT OF HERE...
GLISS
THE DESTRUCTION LEFT BY LADY AZURA IS PLAIN TO SEE...
AND THERE WILL BE **CONSEQUENCES**...
BUT FOR NOW, SHE HAS MORE IMPORTANT THINGS TO DEAL WITH...

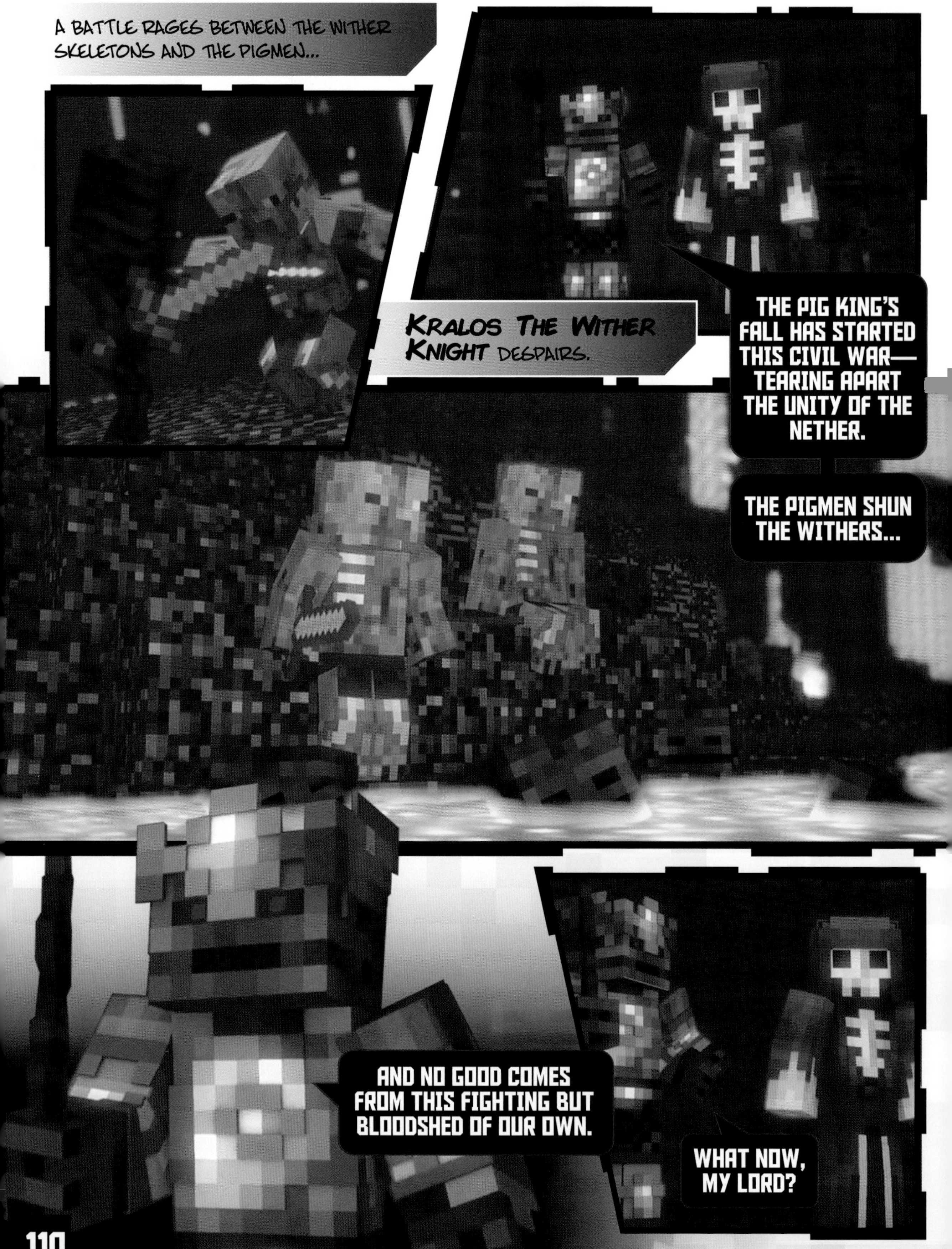
A BATTLE RAGES BETWEEN THE WITHER SKELETONS AND THE PIGMEN...
KRALOS THE WITHER KNIGHT DESPAIRS.
THE PIG KING'S FALL HAS STARTED THIS CIVIL WAR— TEARING APART THE UNITY OF THE NETHER.
THE PIGMEN SHUN THE WITHERS...
AND NO GOOD COMES FROM THIS FIGHTING BUT BLOODSHED OF OUR OWN.
WHAT NOW, MY LORD?

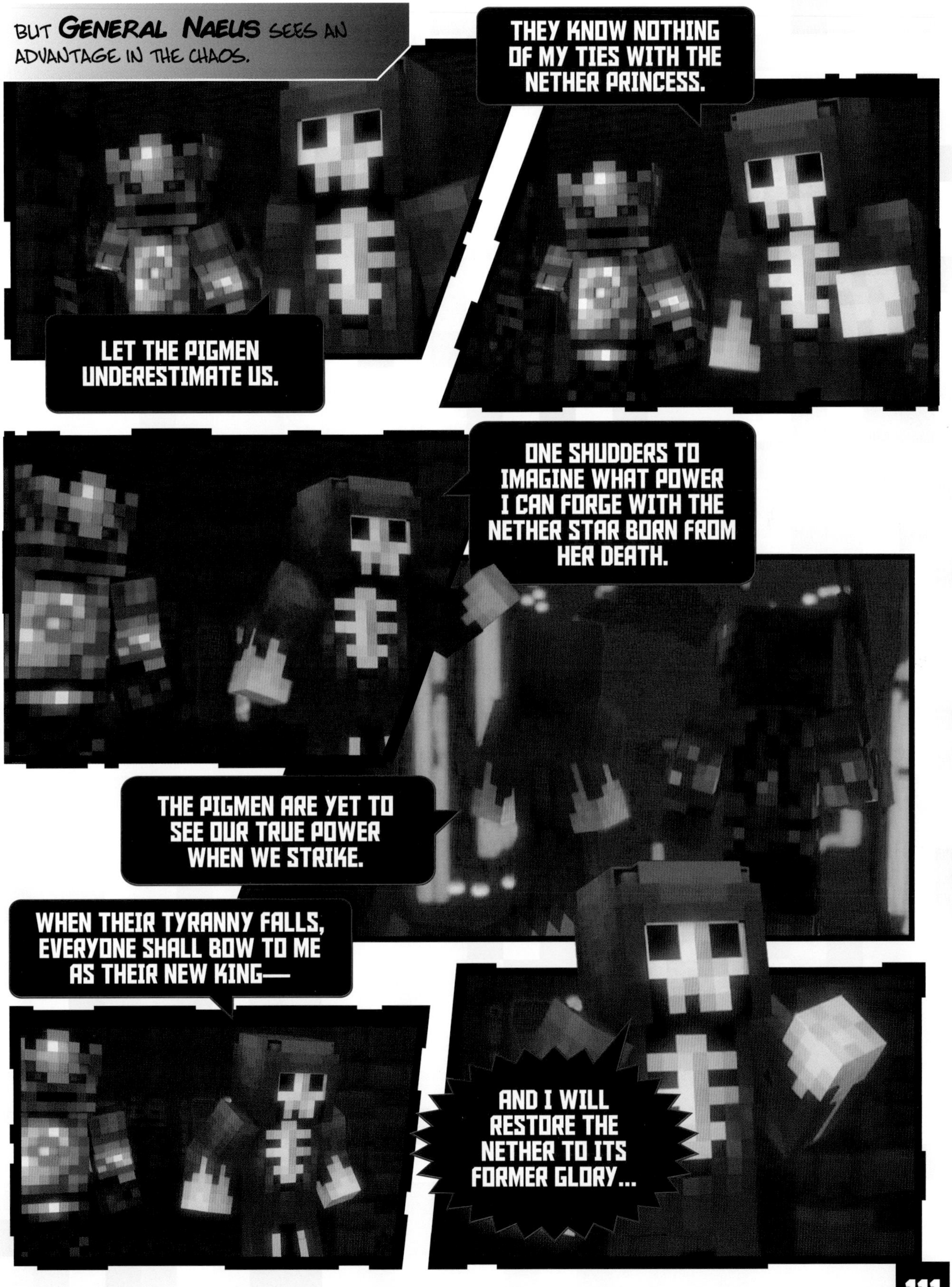
BUT GENERAL NAEUS SEES AN ADVANTAGE IN THE CHAOS.
LET THE PIGMEN UNDERESTIMATE US.
THEY KNOW NOTHING OF MY TIES WITH THE NETHER PRINCESS.
ONE SHUDDERS TO IMAGINE WHAT POWER I CAN FORGE WITH THE NETHER STAR BORN FROM HER DEATH.
THE PIGMEN ARE YET TO SEE OUR TRUE POWER WHEN WE STRIKE.
WHEN THEIR TYRANNY FALLS, EVERYONE SHALL BOW TO ME AS THEIR NEW KING—
AND I WILL RESTORE THE NETHER TO ITS FORMER GLORY...

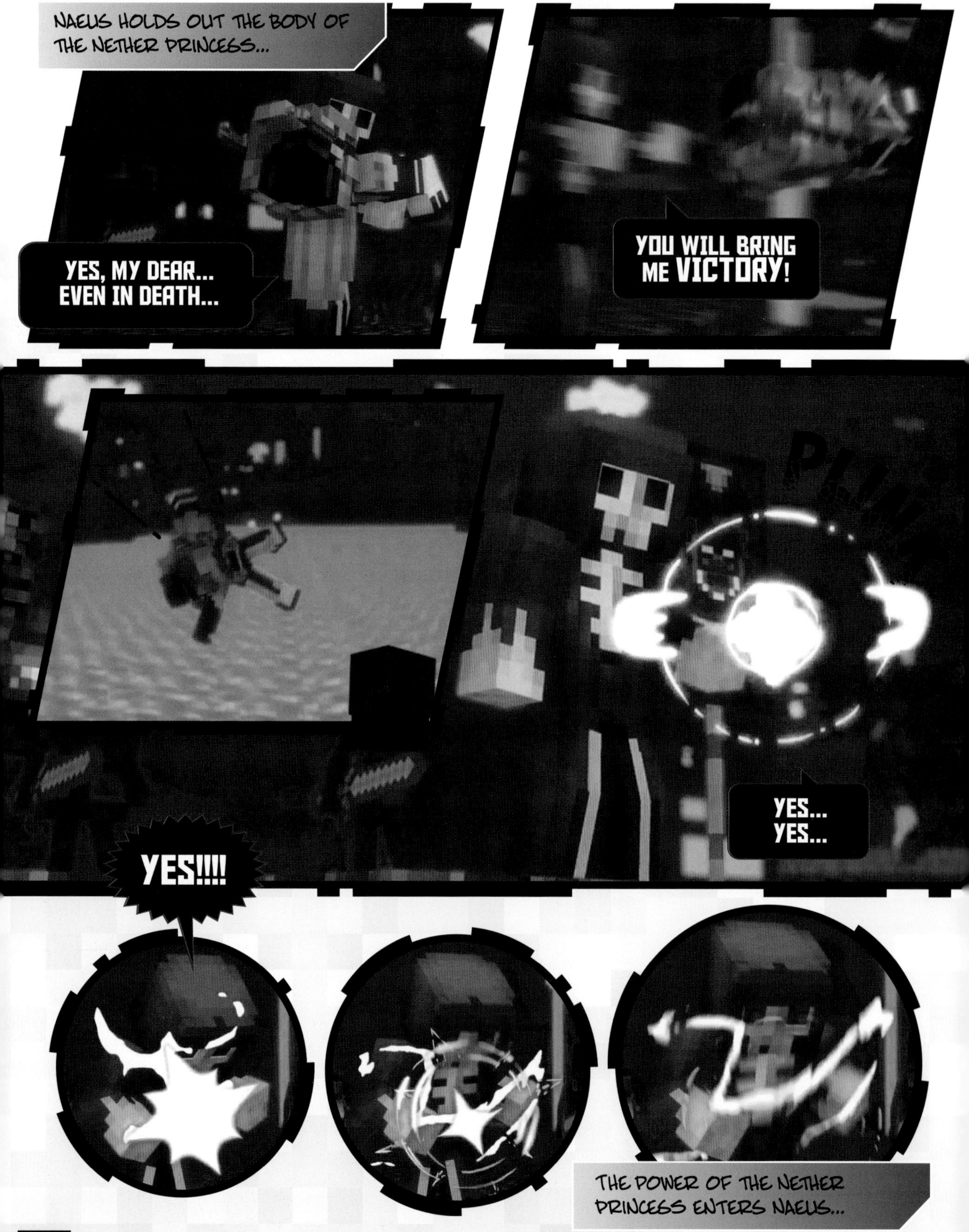
NAEUS HOLDS OUT THE BODY OF THE NETHER PRINCESS...
YES, MY DEAR... EVEN IN DEATH...
YOU WILL BRING ME VICTORY!
YES... YES...
YES!!!!
THE POWER OF THE NETHER PRINCESS ENTERS NAEUS...

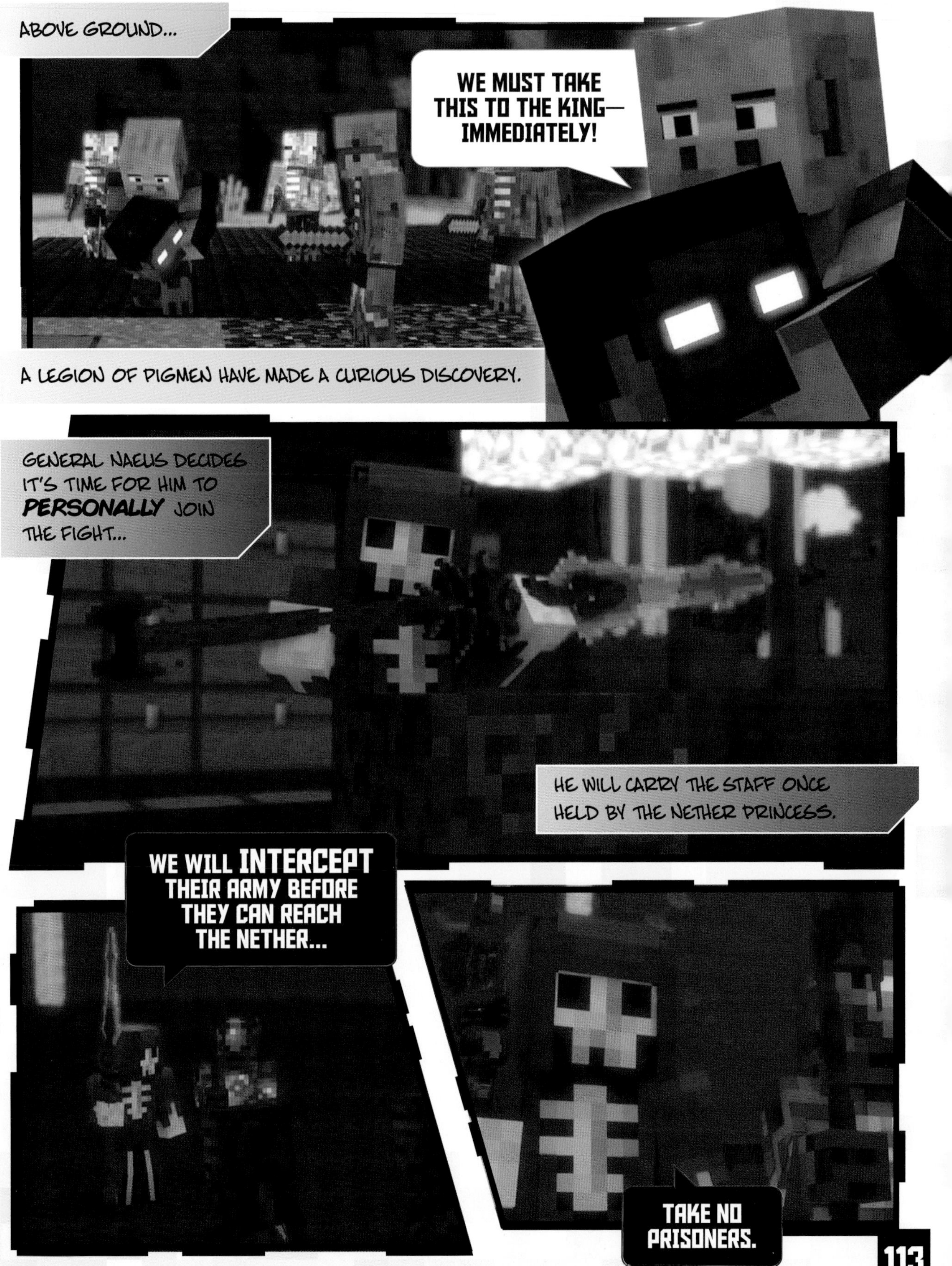
ABOVE GROUND...
WE MUST TAKE THIS TO THE KING—IMMEDIATELY!
A LEGION OF PIGMEN HAVE MADE A CURIOUS DISCOVERY.
GENERAL NAEUS DECIDES IT'S TIME FOR HIM TO **PERSONALLY** JOIN THE FIGHT...
HE WILL CARRY THE STAFF ONCE HELD BY THE NETHER PRINCESS.
WE WILL INTERCEPT THEIR ARMY BEFORE THEY CAN REACH THE NETHER...
TAKE NO PRISONERS.

STOMP STOMP STOMP

WAIT!

WHY IS A **PORTAL** HERE...?

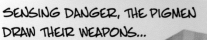

SENSING DANGER, THE PIGMEN DRAW THEIR WEAPONS...

THE WITHER SKELETONS RUN FROM HIDING—

AMBUSH!

BUT EVEN THEY'RE NOT EXPECTING TO BE AMBUSHED BY GENERAL NAEUS HIMSELF...

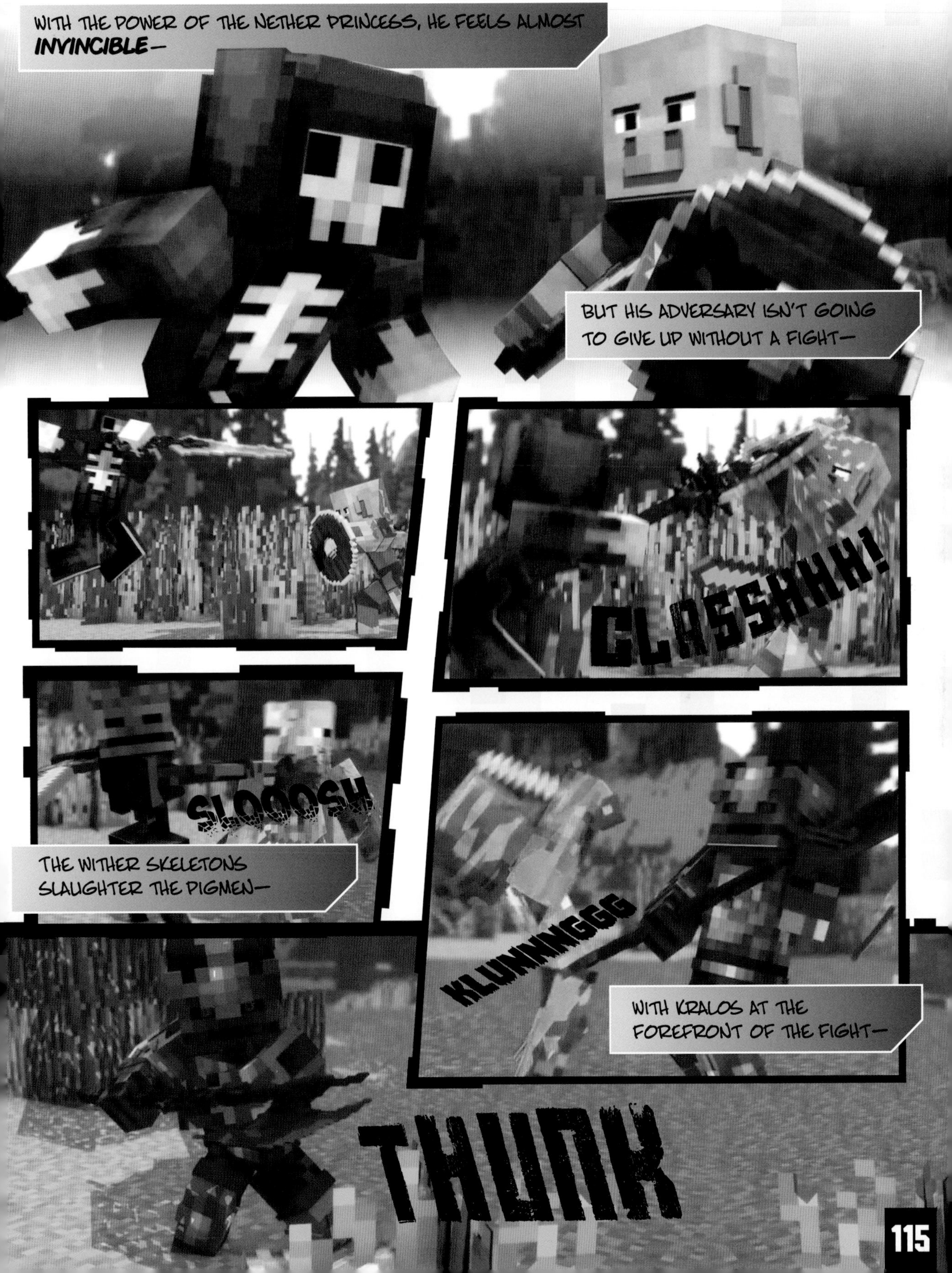
WITH THE POWER OF THE NETHER PRINCESS, HE FEELS ALMOST **INVINCIBLE**–
BUT HIS ADVERSARY ISN'T GOING TO GIVE UP WITHOUT A FIGHT–
CLASSHHH!
SLOOOSH
THE WITHER SKELETONS SLAUGHTER THE PIGMEN–
KLUNNNGGG
WITH KRALOS AT THE FOREFRONT OF THE FIGHT–
THUNK

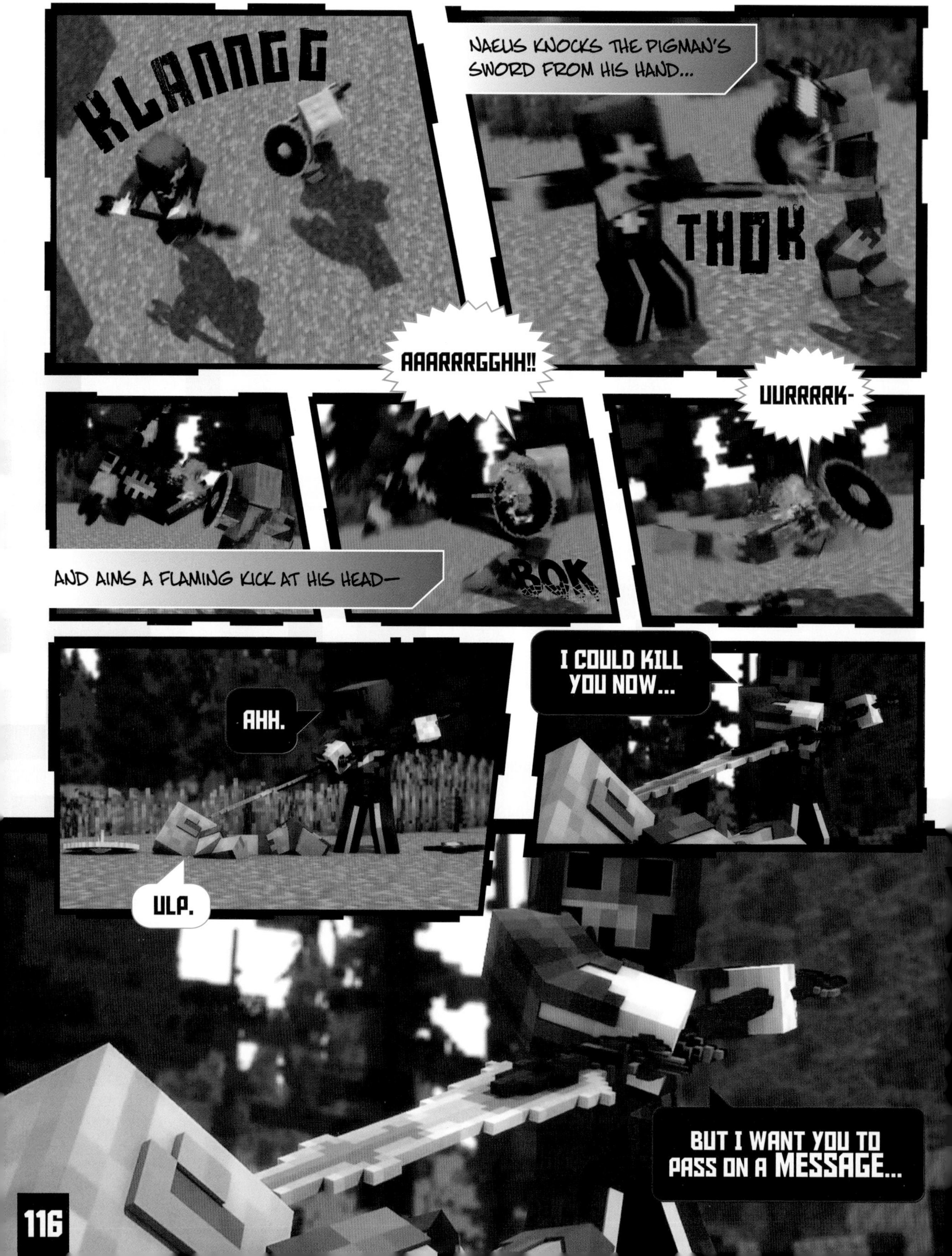

KLANNGG
NAEUS KNOCKS THE PIGMAN'S SWORD FROM HIS HAND...
THOK
AAARRRGGHH!!
AND AIMS A FLAMING KICK AT HIS HEAD—
BOK
UURRRRK-
AHH.
ULP.
I COULD KILL YOU NOW...
BUT I WANT YOU TO PASS ON A MESSAGE...

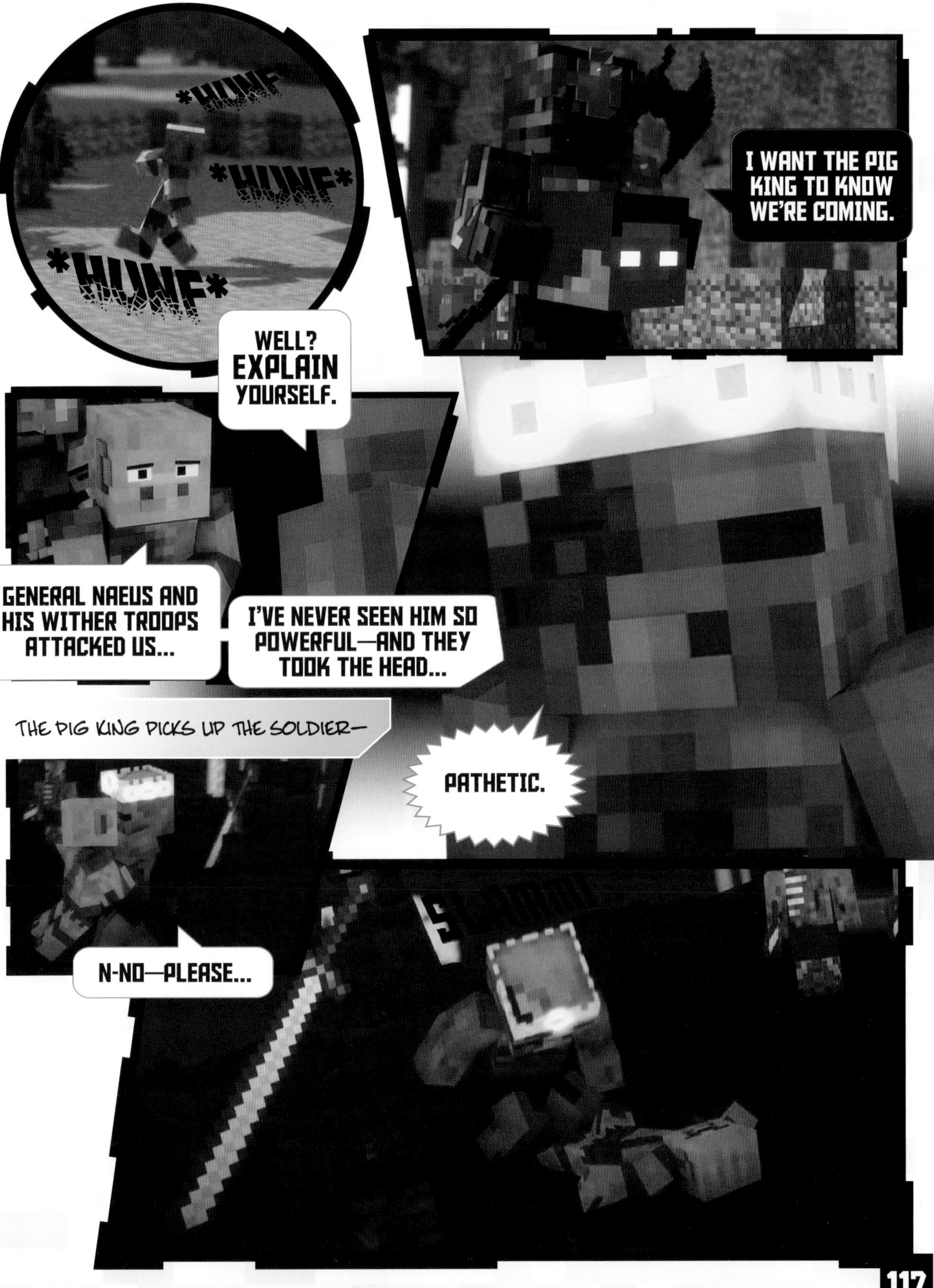
HUNF
HUNF
HUNF
I WANT THE PIG KING TO KNOW WE'RE COMING.
WELL? EXPLAIN YOURSELF.
GENERAL NAEUS AND HIS WITHER TROOPS ATTACKED US...
I'VE NEVER SEEN HIM SO POWERFUL—AND THEY TOOK THE HEAD...
PATHETIC.
THE PIG KING PICKS UP THE SOLDIER—
N-NO—PLEASE...

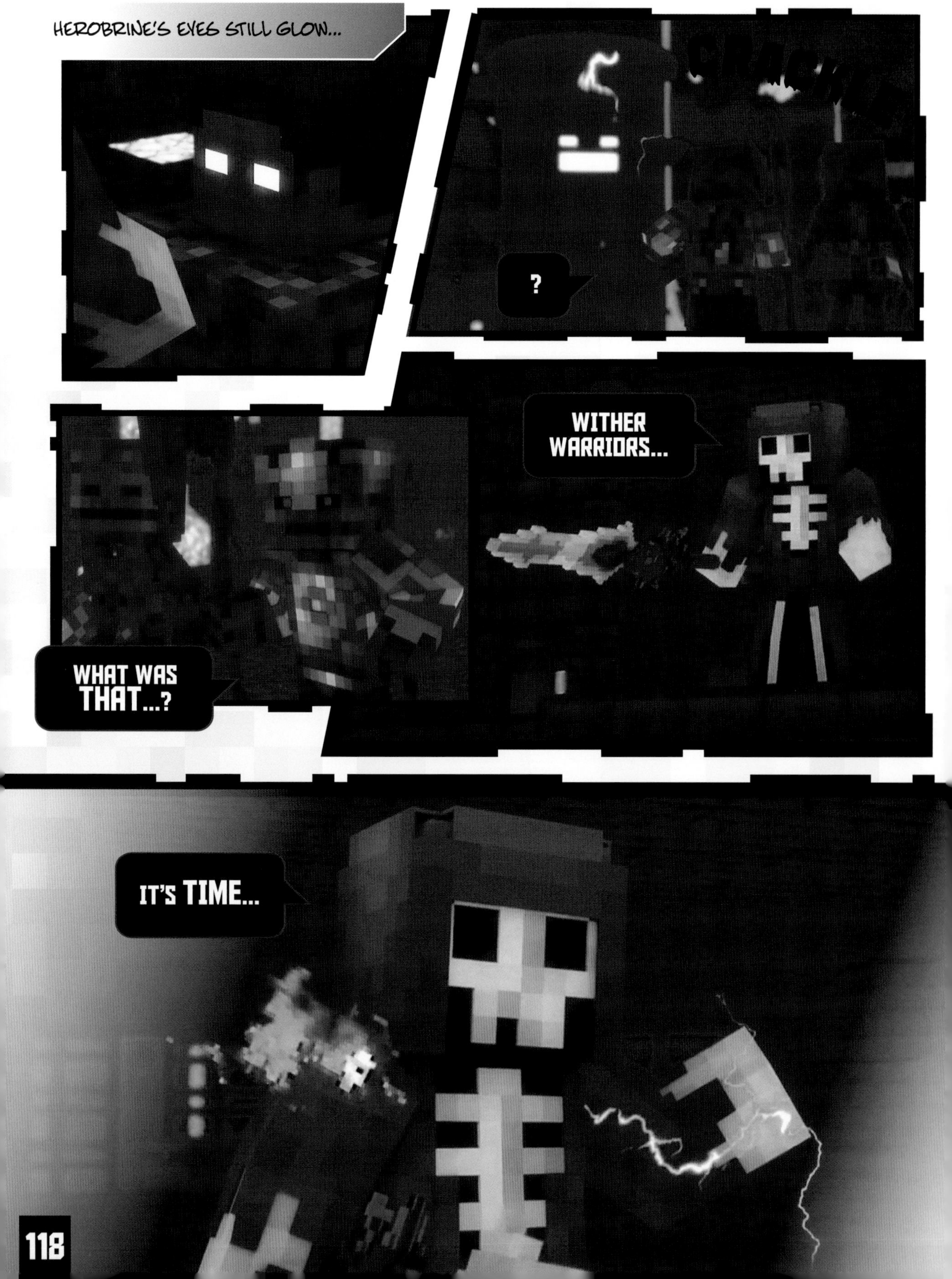
HEROBRINE'S EYES STILL GLOW...
?
WHAT WAS THAT...?
WITHER WARRIORS...
IT'S TIME...

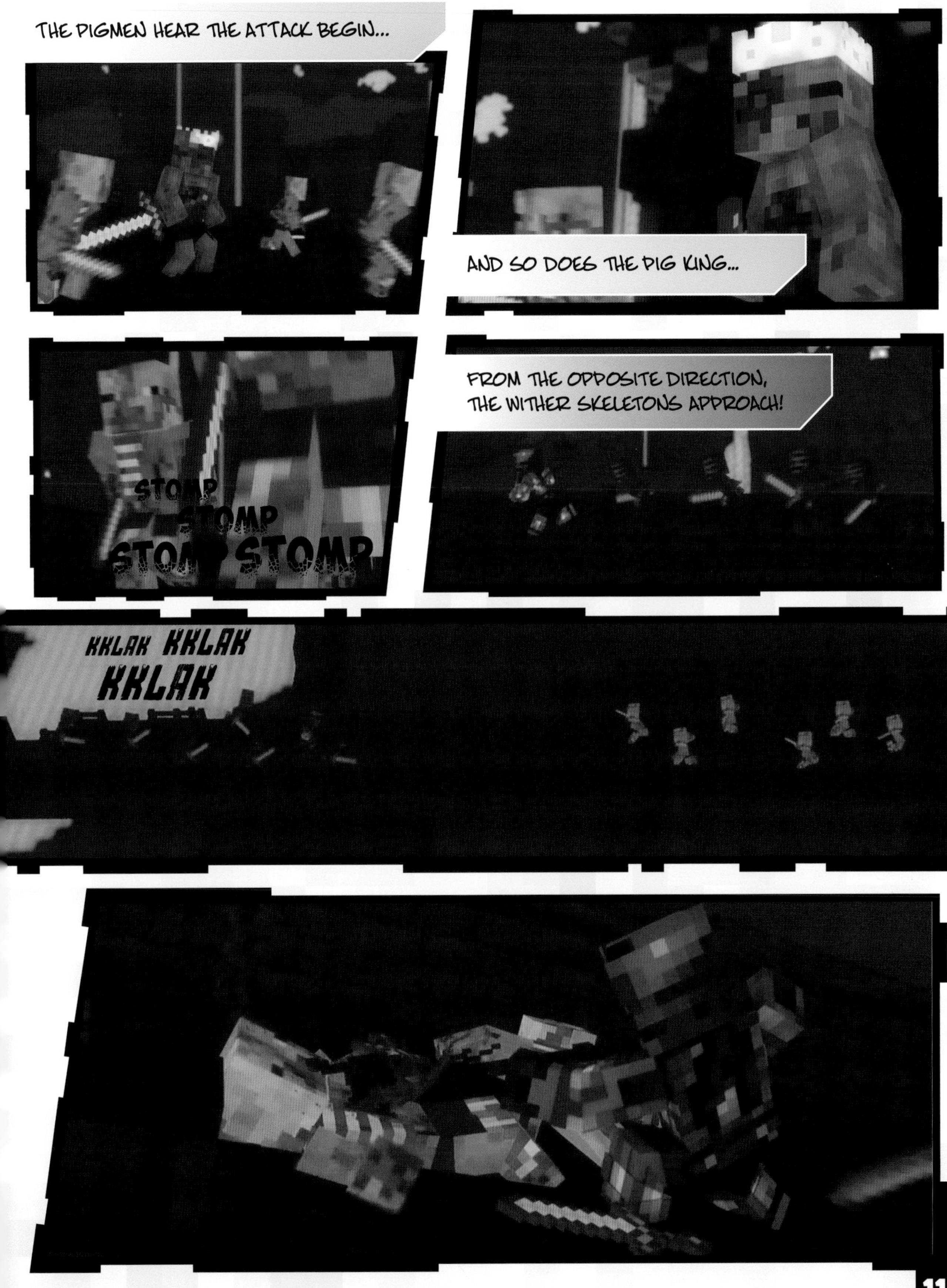
THE PIGMEN HEAR THE ATTACK BEGIN...
AND SO DOES THE PIG KING...
STOMP STOMP STOMP STOMP
FROM THE OPPOSITE DIRECTION, THE WITHER SKELETONS APPROACH!
KKLAK KKLAK KKLAK

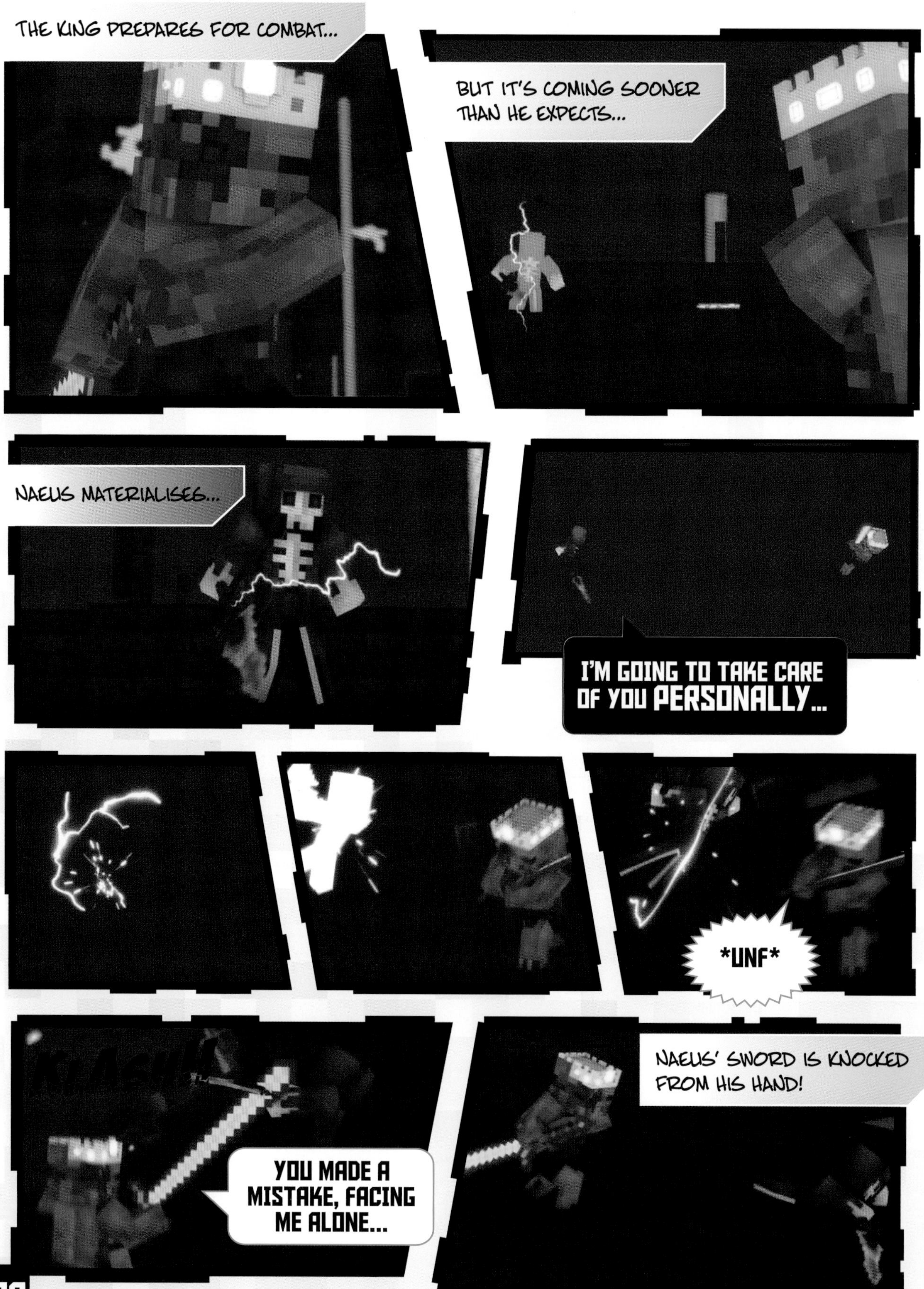
THE KING PREPARES FOR COMBAT...
BUT IT'S COMING SOONER THAN HE EXPECTS...
NAEUS MATERIALISES...
I'M GOING TO TAKE CARE OF YOU PERSONALLY...
UNF
YOU MADE A MISTAKE, FACING ME ALONE...
NAEUS' SWORD IS KNOCKED FROM HIS HAND!

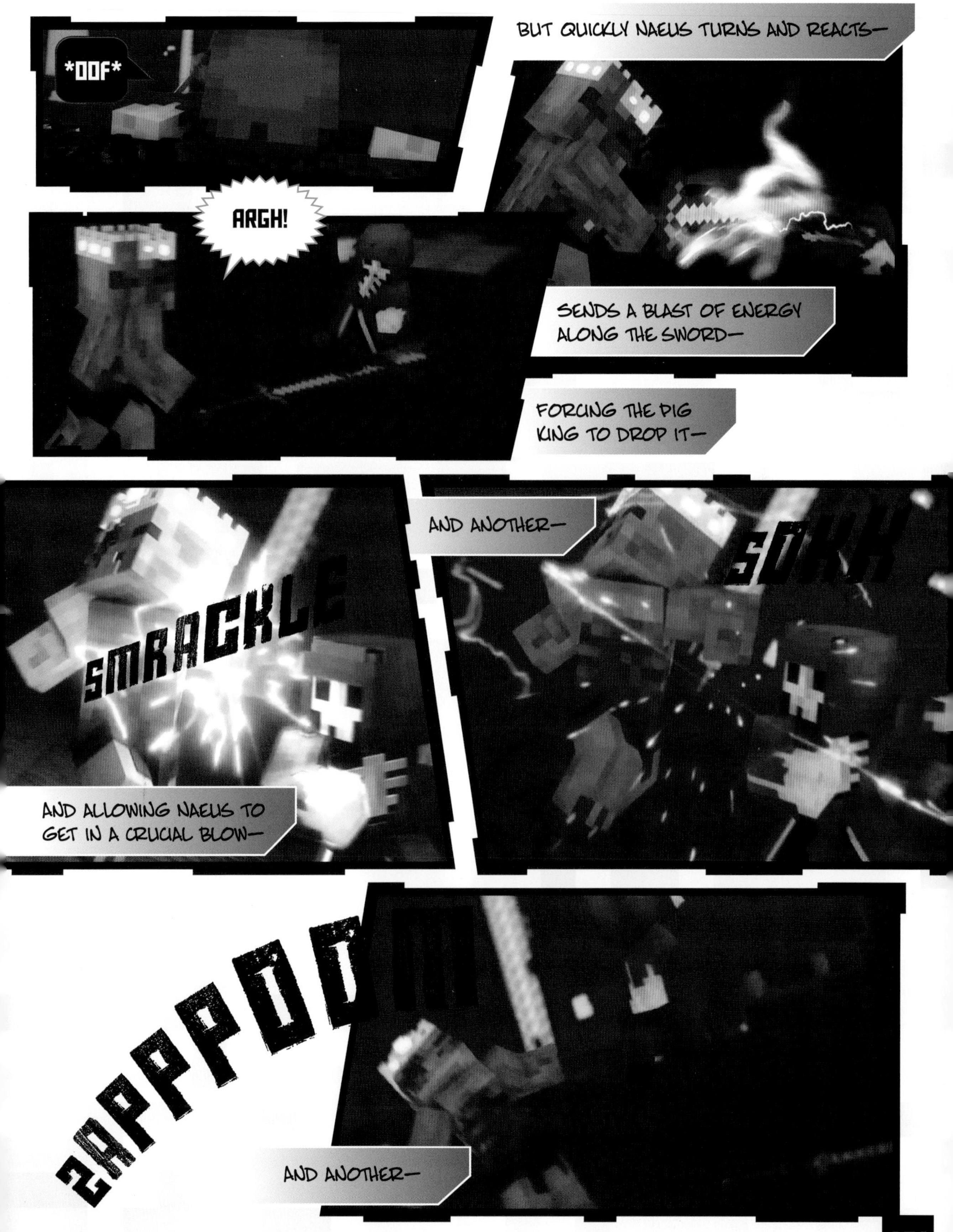
OOF
BUT QUICKLY NAEUS TURNS AND REACTS—
ARGH!
SENDS A BLAST OF ENERGY ALONG THE SWORD—
FORCING THE PIG KING TO DROP IT—
SMRACKLE
AND ALLOWING NAEUS TO GET IN A CRUCIAL BLOW—
AND ANOTHER—
SOKK
ZAPPOOM
AND ANOTHER—

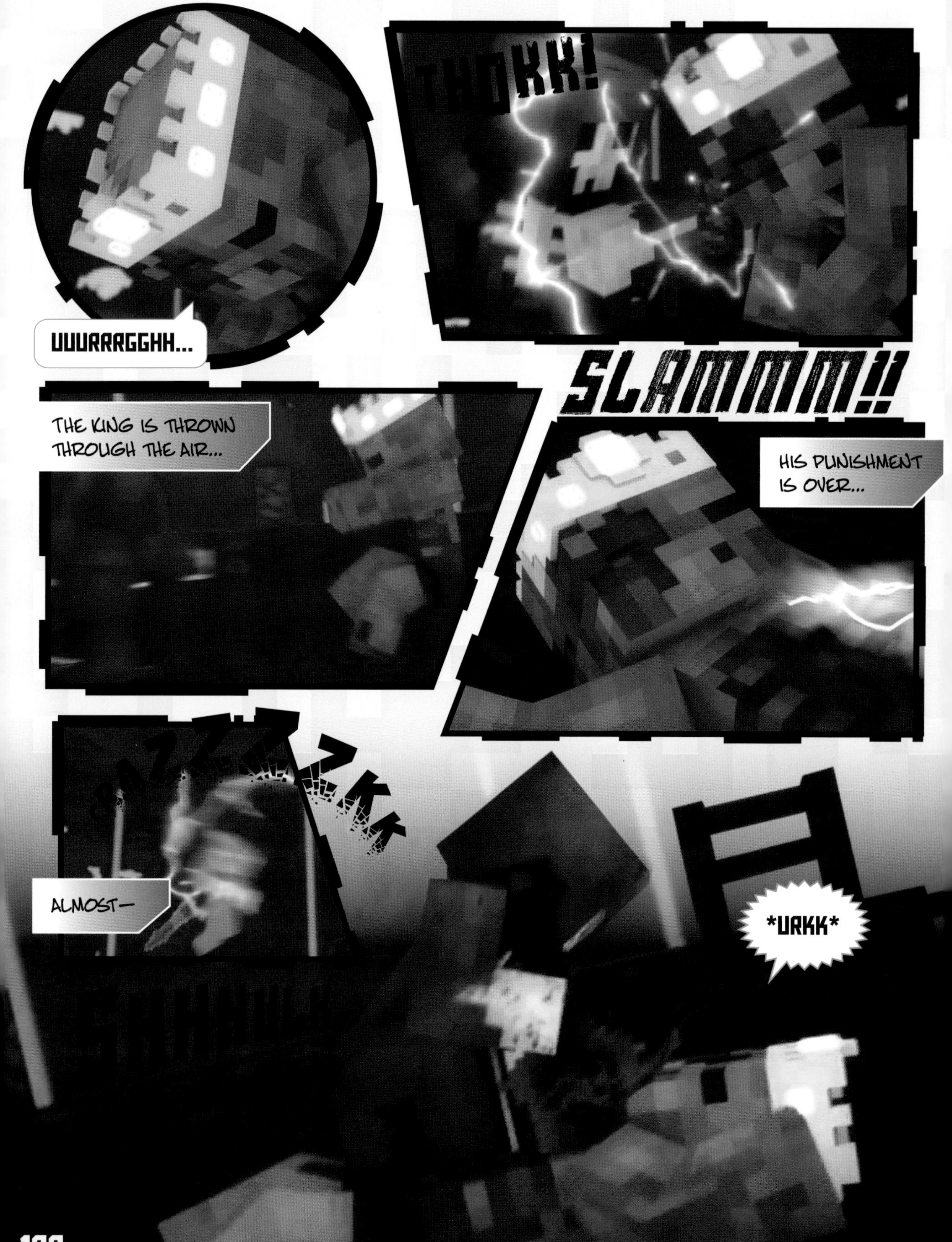
UUURRRGGHH...
THOKK!
SLAMMM!!
THE KING IS THROWN THROUGH THE AIR...
HIS PUNISHMENT IS OVER...
ALMOST—
URKK

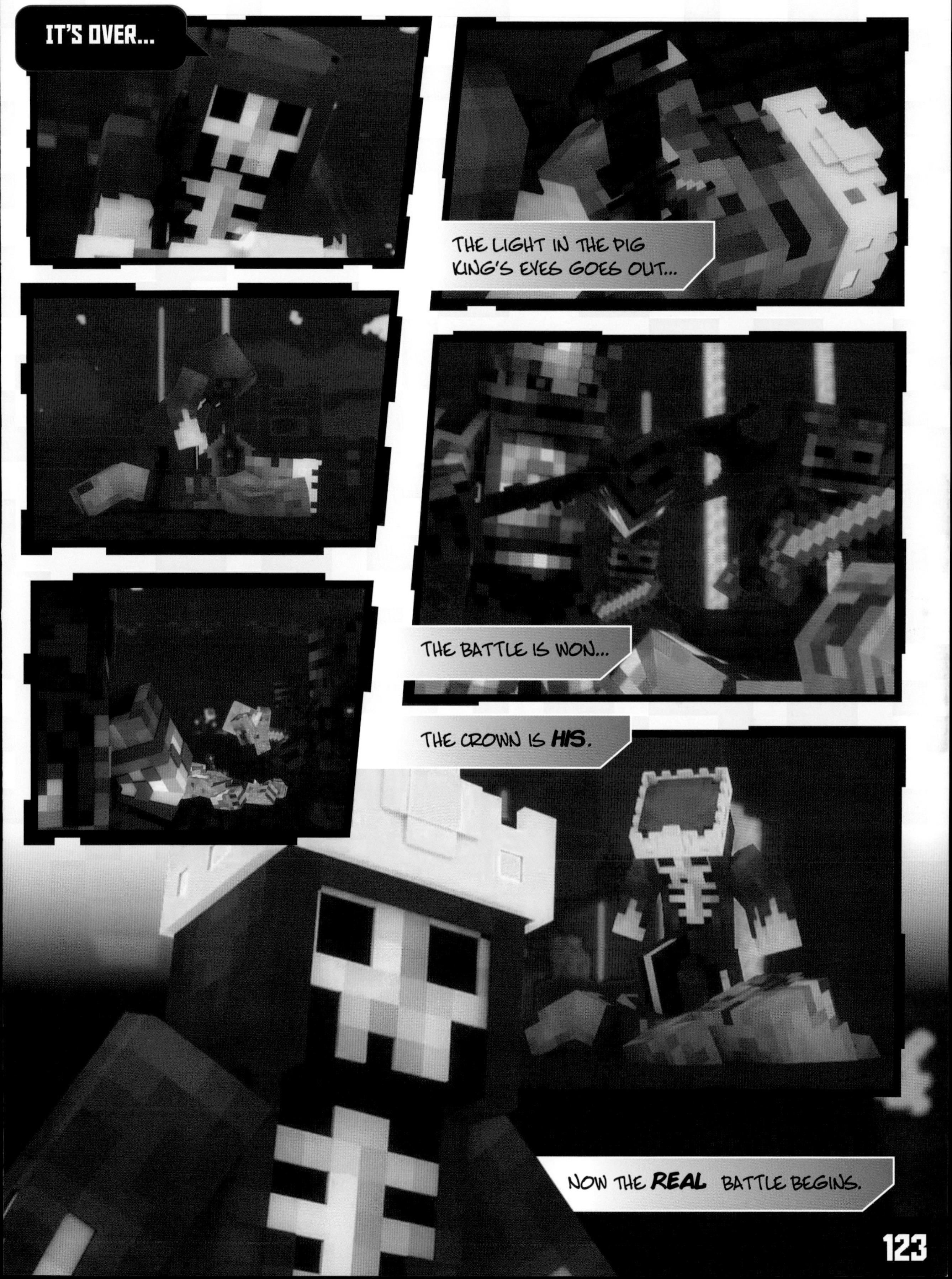

IT'S OVER...
THE LIGHT IN THE PIG KING'S EYES GOES OUT...
THE BATTLE IS WON...
THE CROWN IS **HIS**.
NOW THE **REAL** BATTLE BEGINS.

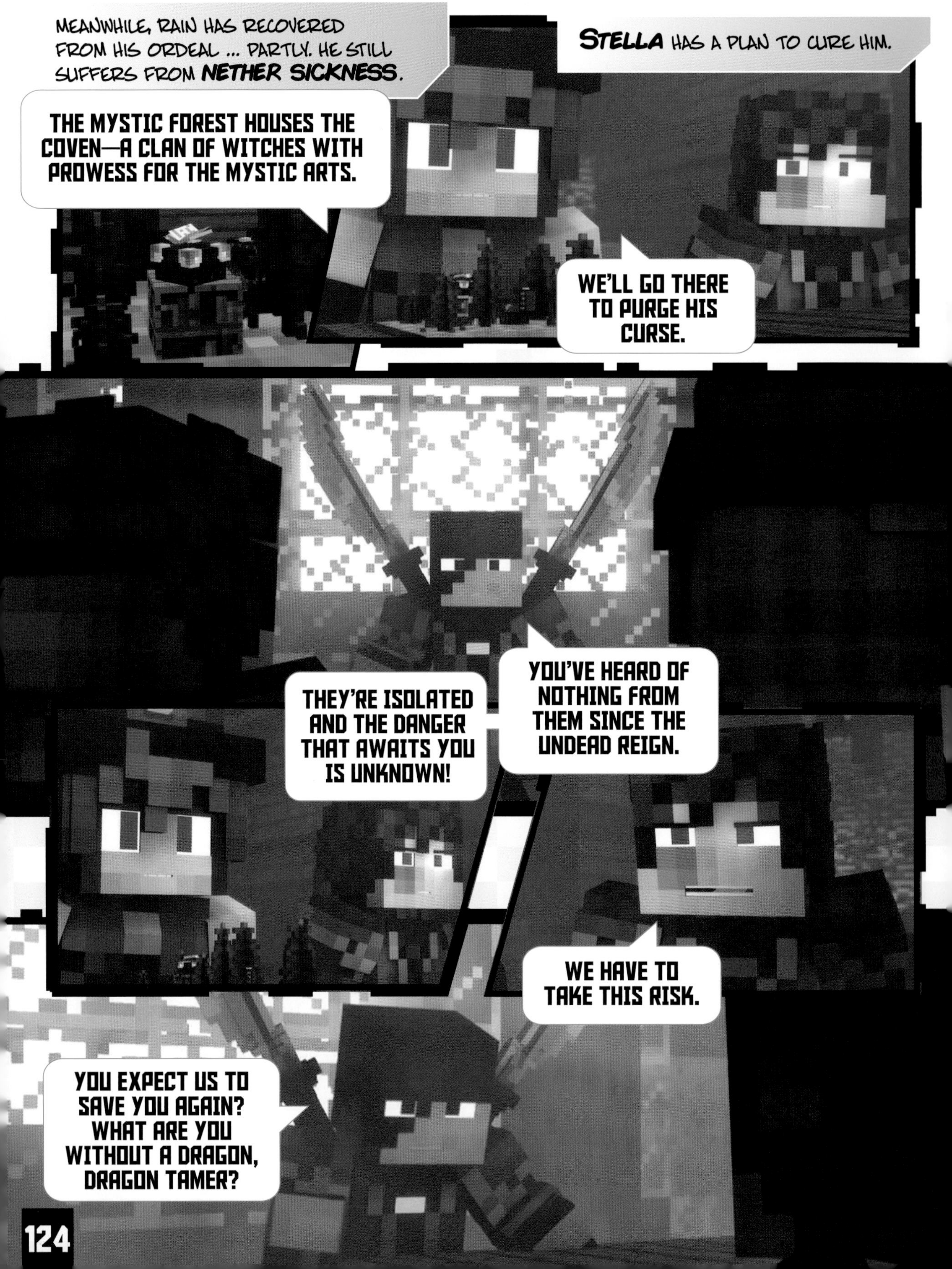

MEANWHILE, RAIN HAS RECOVERED FROM HIS ORDEAL ... PARTLY. HE STILL SUFFERS FROM **NETHER SICKNESS**.
STELLA HAS A PLAN TO CURE HIM.
THE MYSTIC FOREST HOUSES THE COVEN—A CLAN OF WITCHES WITH PROWESS FOR THE MYSTIC ARTS.
WE'LL GO THERE TO PURGE HIS CURSE.
YOU'VE HEARD OF NOTHING FROM THEM SINCE THE UNDEAD REIGN.
THEY'RE ISOLATED AND THE DANGER THAT AWAITS YOU IS UNKNOWN!
WE HAVE TO TAKE THIS RISK.
YOU EXPECT US TO SAVE YOU AGAIN? WHAT ARE YOU WITHOUT A DRAGON, DRAGON TAMER?

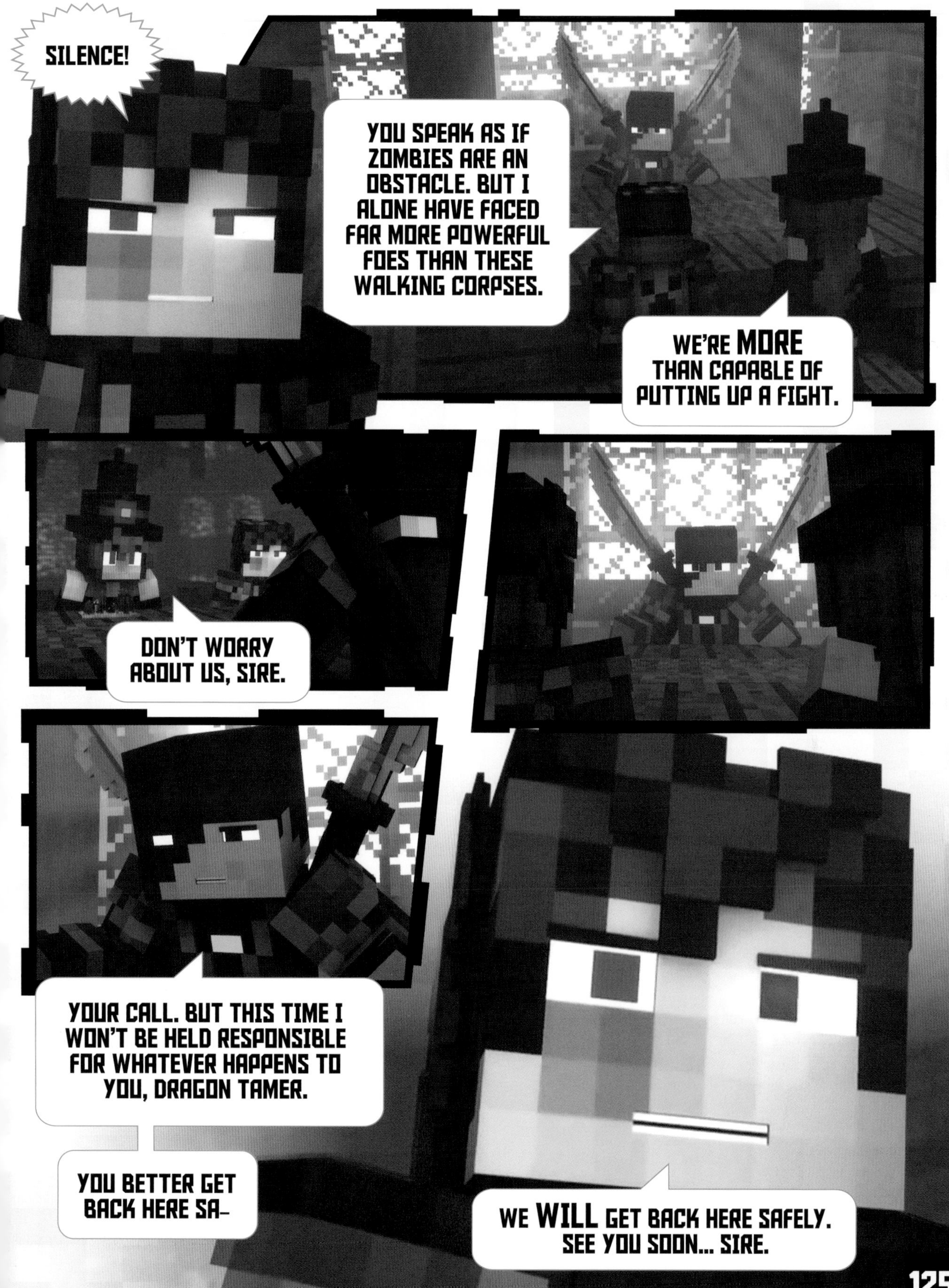
SILENCE!
YOU SPEAK AS IF ZOMBIES ARE AN OBSTACLE. BUT I ALONE HAVE FACED FAR MORE POWERFUL FOES THAN THESE WALKING CORPSES.
WE'RE MORE THAN CAPABLE OF PUTTING UP A FIGHT.
DON'T WORRY ABOUT US, SIRE.
YOUR CALL. BUT THIS TIME I WON'T BE HELD RESPONSIBLE FOR WHATEVER HAPPENS TO YOU, DRAGON TAMER.
YOU BETTER GET BACK HERE SA–
WE WILL GET BACK HERE SAFELY. SEE YOU SOON... SIRE.

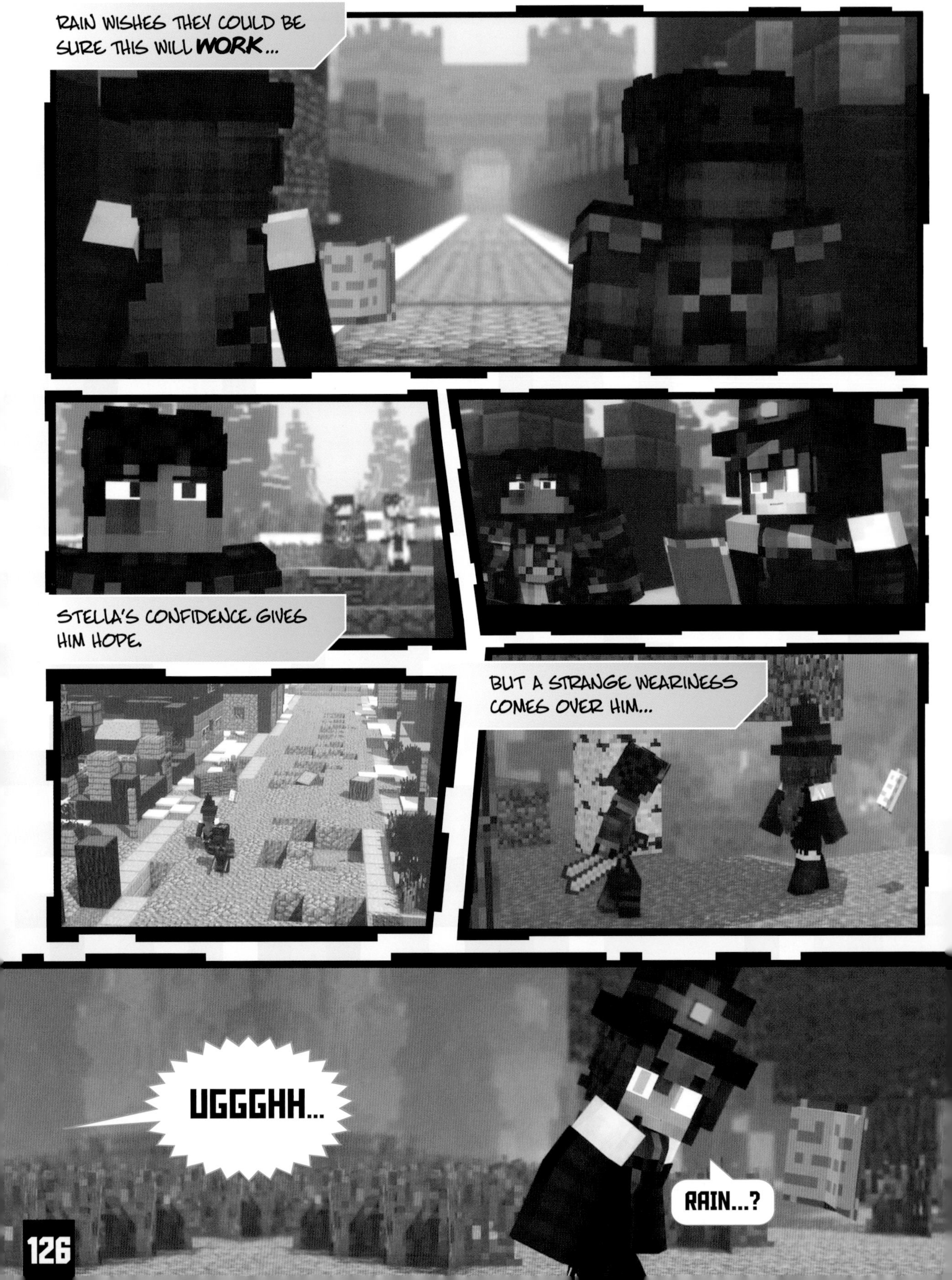
RAIN WISHES THEY COULD BE SURE THIS WILL **WORK**...
STELLA'S CONFIDENCE GIVES HIM HOPE.
BUT A STRANGE WEARINESS COMES OVER HIM...
UGGGHH...
RAIN...?

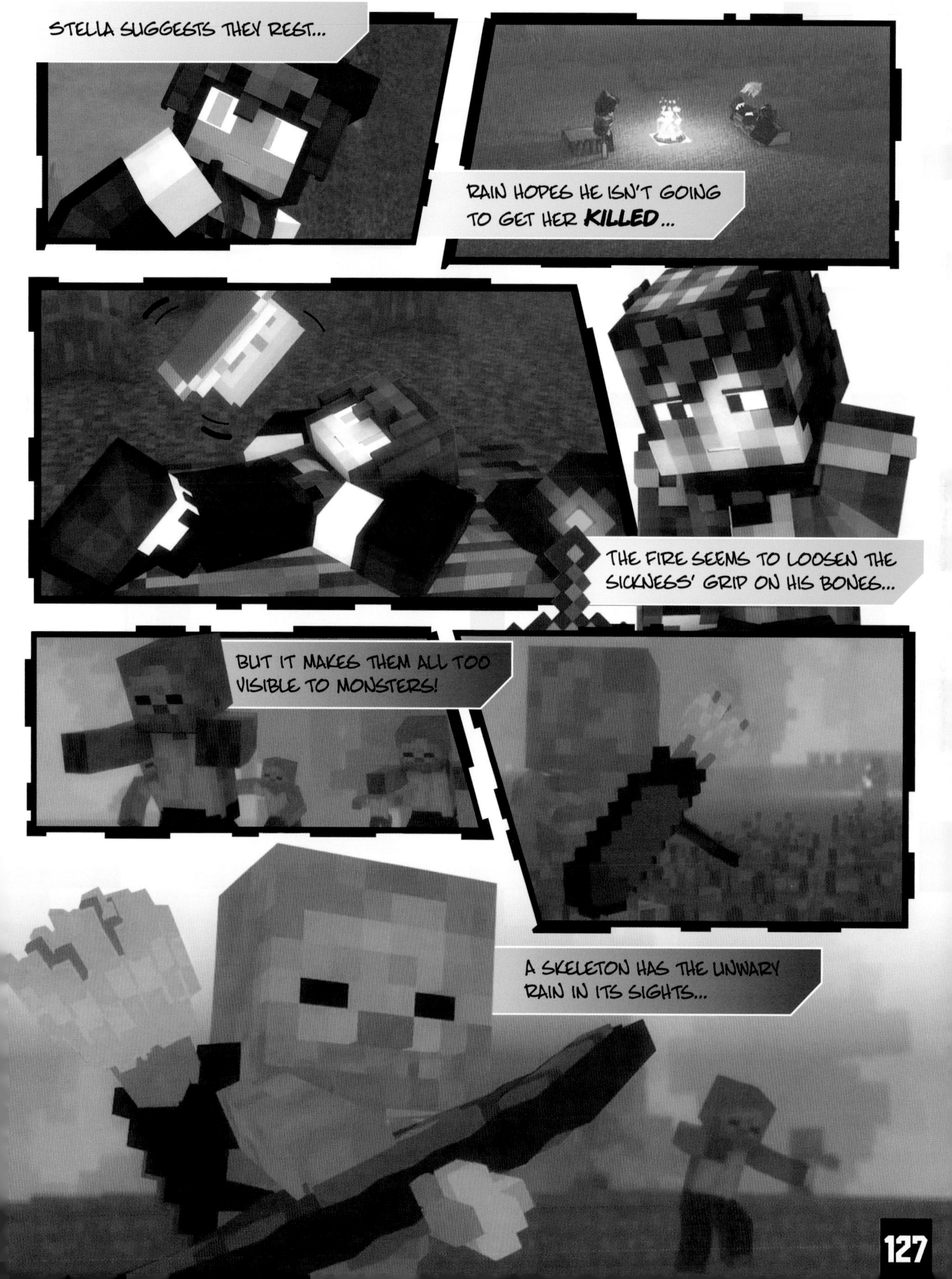
STELLA SUGGESTS THEY REST...
RAIN HOPES HE ISN'T GOING TO GET HER KILLED...
THE FIRE SEEMS TO LOOSEN THE SICKNESS' GRIP ON HIS BONES...
BUT IT MAKES THEM ALL TOO VISIBLE TO MONSTERS!
A SKELETON HAS THE UNWARY RAIN IN ITS SIGHTS...

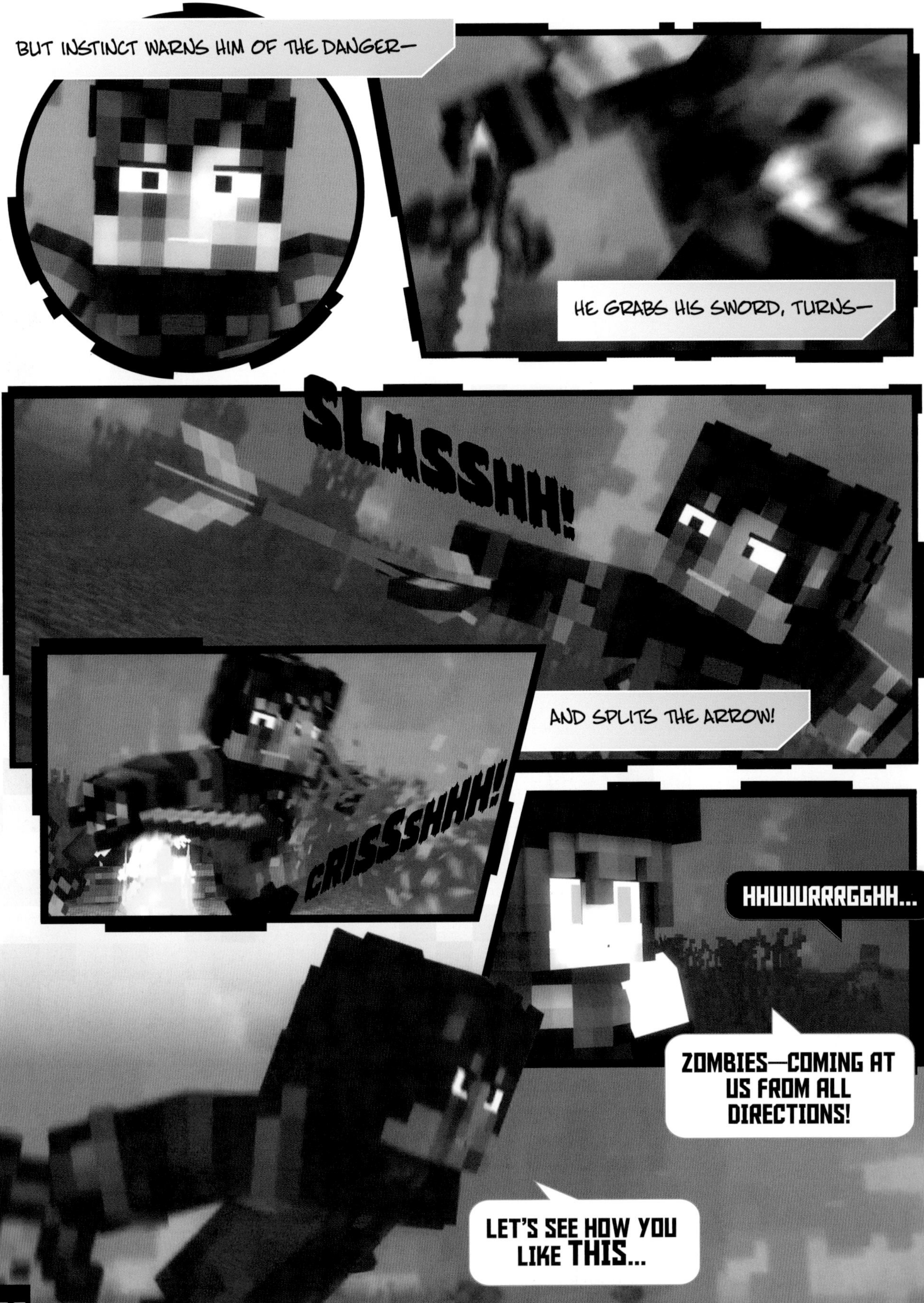
BUT INSTINCT WARNS HIM OF THE DANGER—
HE GRABS HIS SWORD, TURNS—
SLASSHH!
AND SPLITS THE ARROW!
CRISSSHHH!
HHUUURRRGGHH...
ZOMBIES—COMING AT US FROM ALL DIRECTIONS!
LET'S SEE HOW YOU LIKE THIS...

RAIN FEELS A RUSH OF ADRENALINE—

SLASSHH!

SLASSHH

HE FORGETS HIS EARLIER TIREDNESS—

SPECTACULAR SWORDSMANSHIP DISPATCHES ONE WAVE OF ZOMBIES—

SWISHAWISHAWISH

HE FLINGS HIS SWORD—

CRUNCH

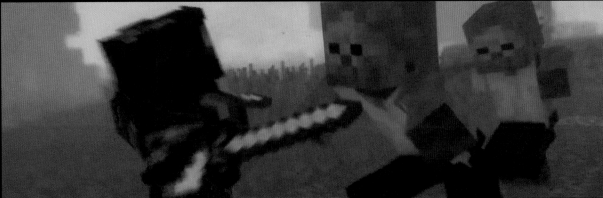

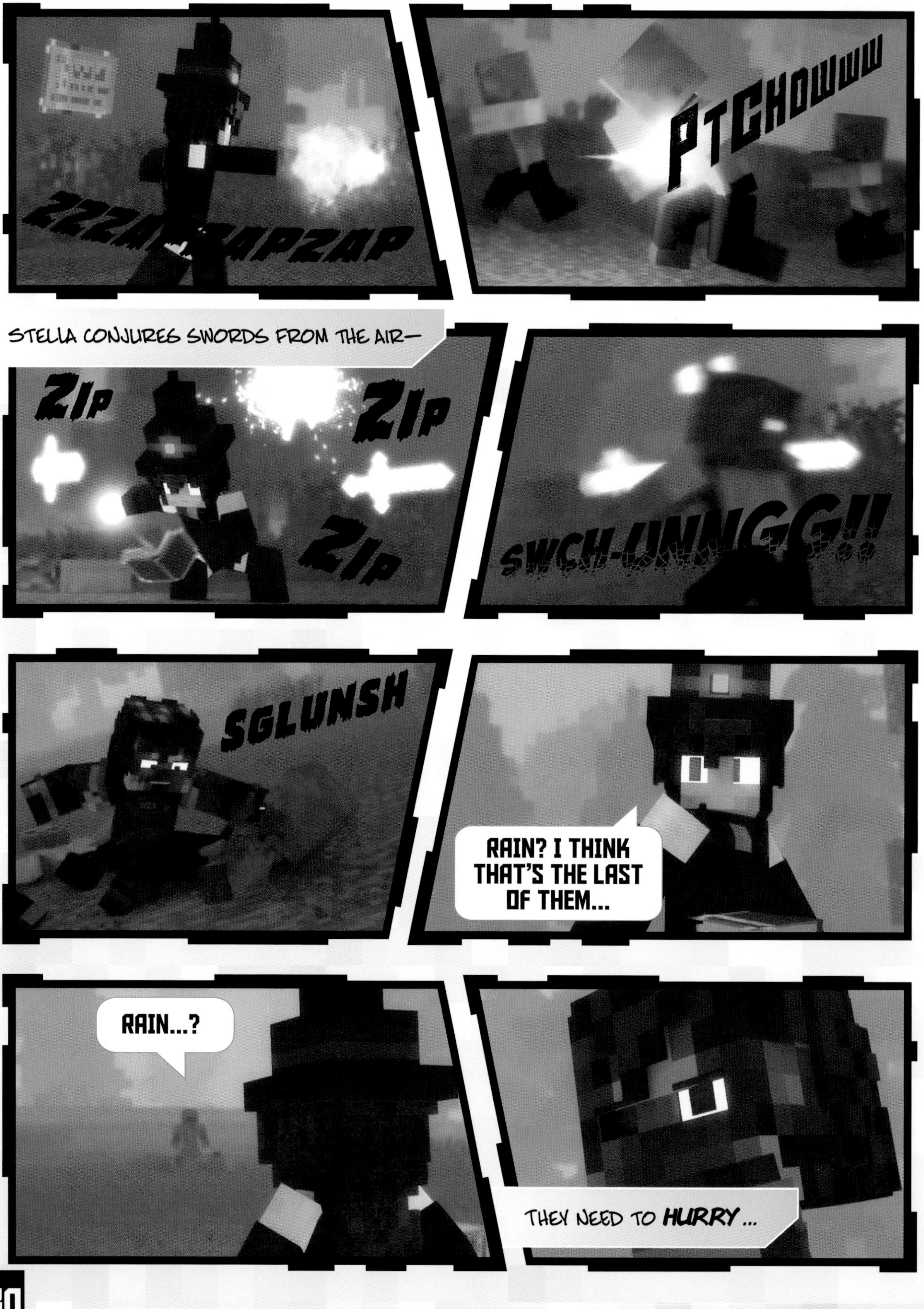
PTCHOWWW
STELLA CONJURES SWORDS FROM THE AIR—
ZIP
ZIP
ZIP
SWCH-UNNGG!!
SGLUNSH
RAIN? I THINK THAT'S THE LAST OF THEM...
RAIN...?
THEY NEED TO **HURRY**...

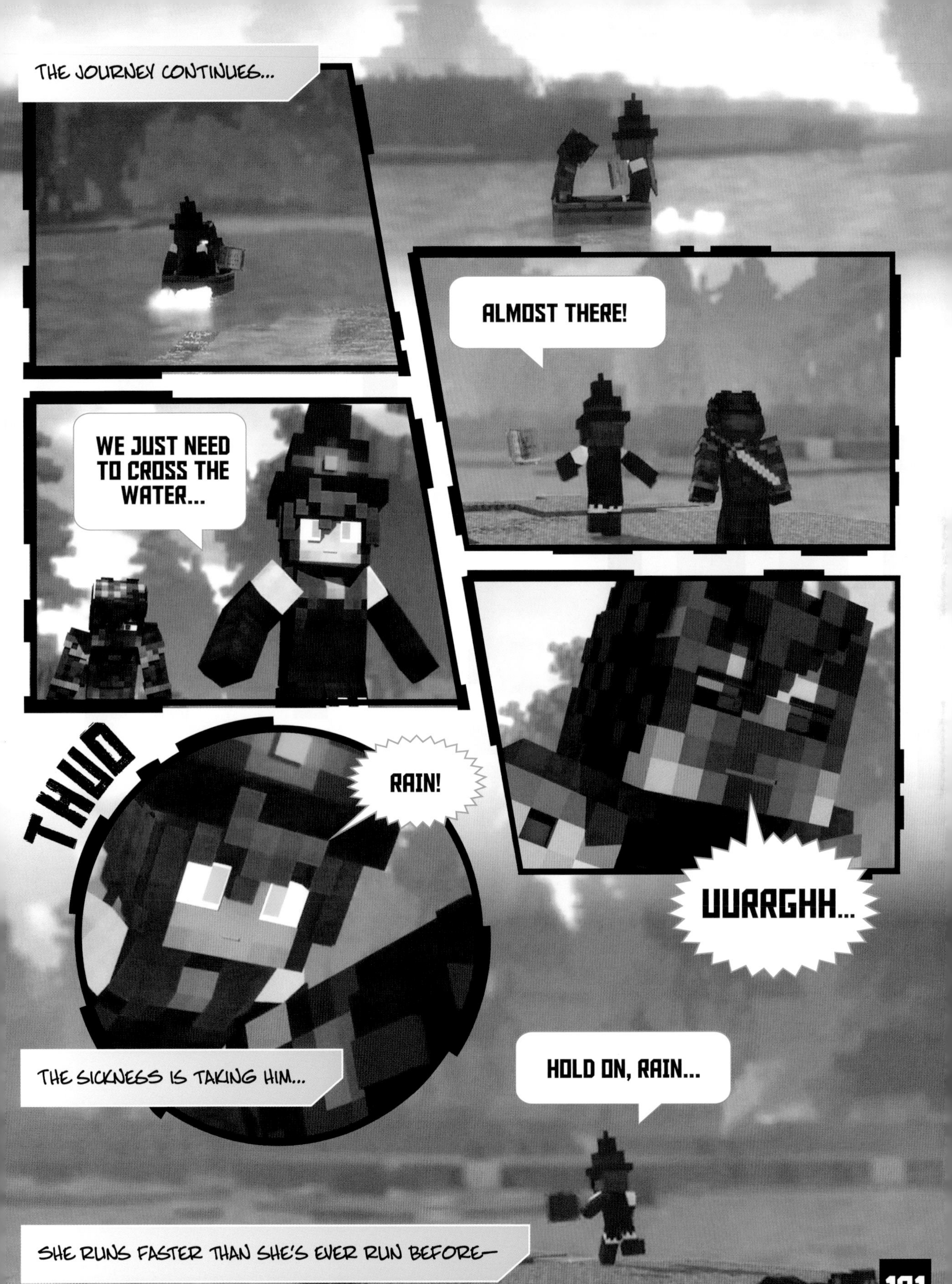
THE JOURNEY CONTINUES...
ALMOST THERE!
WE JUST NEED TO CROSS THE WATER...
THUD
RAIN!
UURRGHH...
THE SICKNESS IS TAKING HIM...
HOLD ON, RAIN...
SHE RUNS FASTER THAN SHE'S EVER RUN BEFORE—

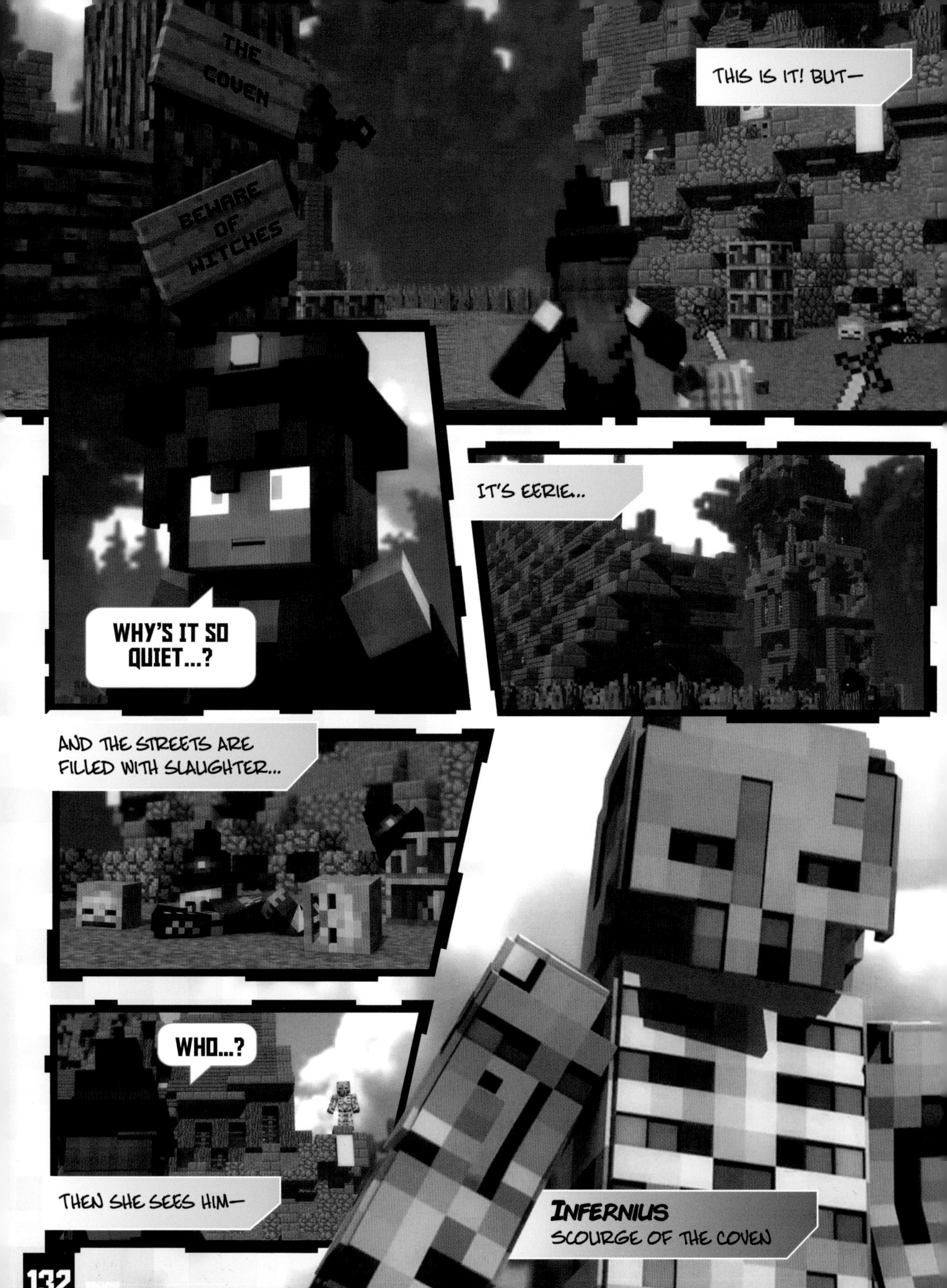
THE COVEN
BEWARE OF WITCHES
THIS IS IT! BUT—
IT'S EERIE...
WHY'S IT SO QUIET...?
AND THE STREETS ARE FILLED WITH SLAUGHTER...
WHO...?
THEN SHE SEES HIM—
INFERNIUS
SCOURGE OF THE COVEN

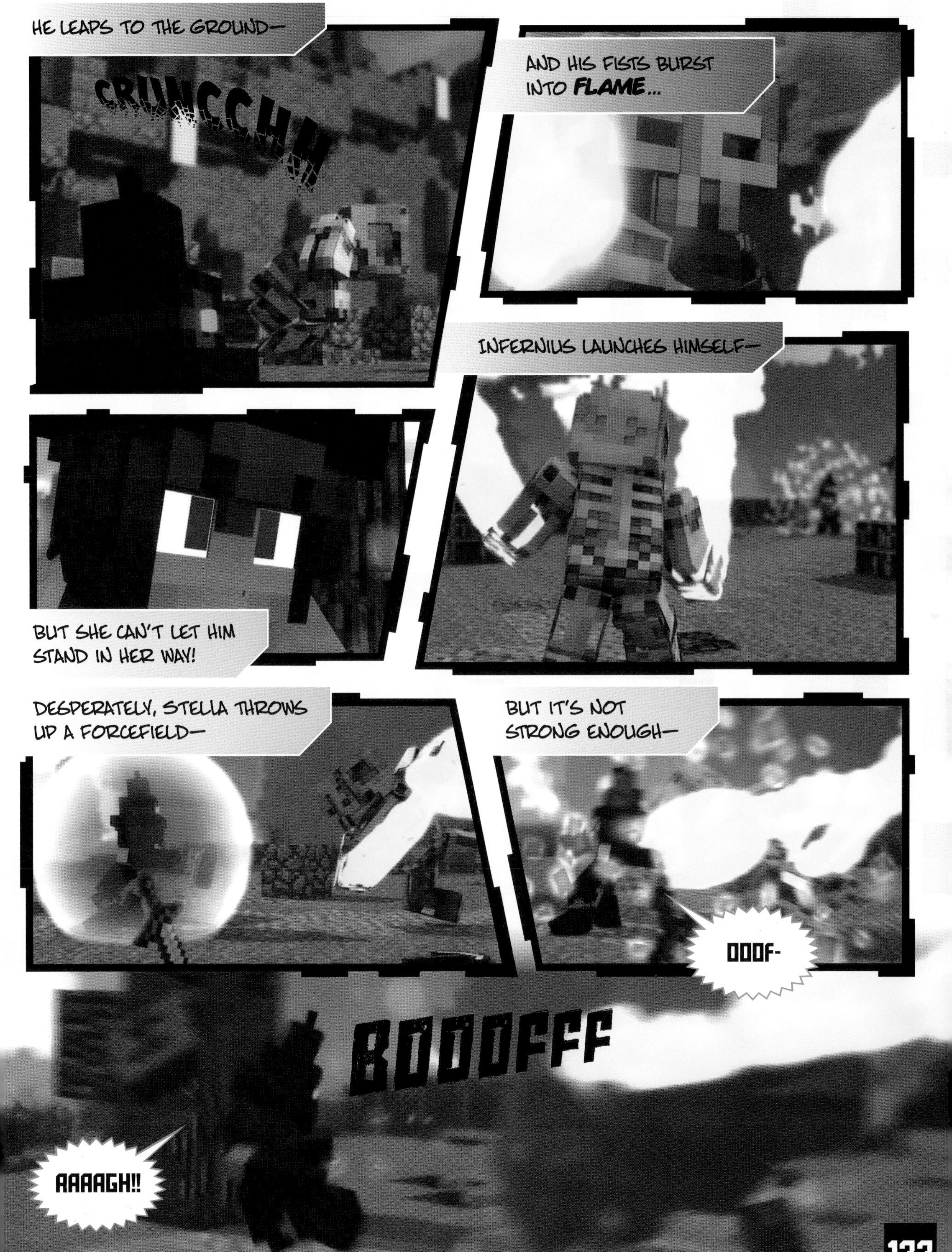
HE LEAPS TO THE GROUND—
CRUNCCHH!!
AND HIS FISTS BURST INTO **FLAME**...
INFERNIUS LAUNCHES HIMSELF—
BUT SHE CAN'T LET HIM STAND IN HER WAY!
DESPERATELY, STELLA THROWS UP A FORCEFIELD—
BUT IT'S NOT STRONG ENOUGH—
OOOF-
BOOOFFF
AAAAGH!!

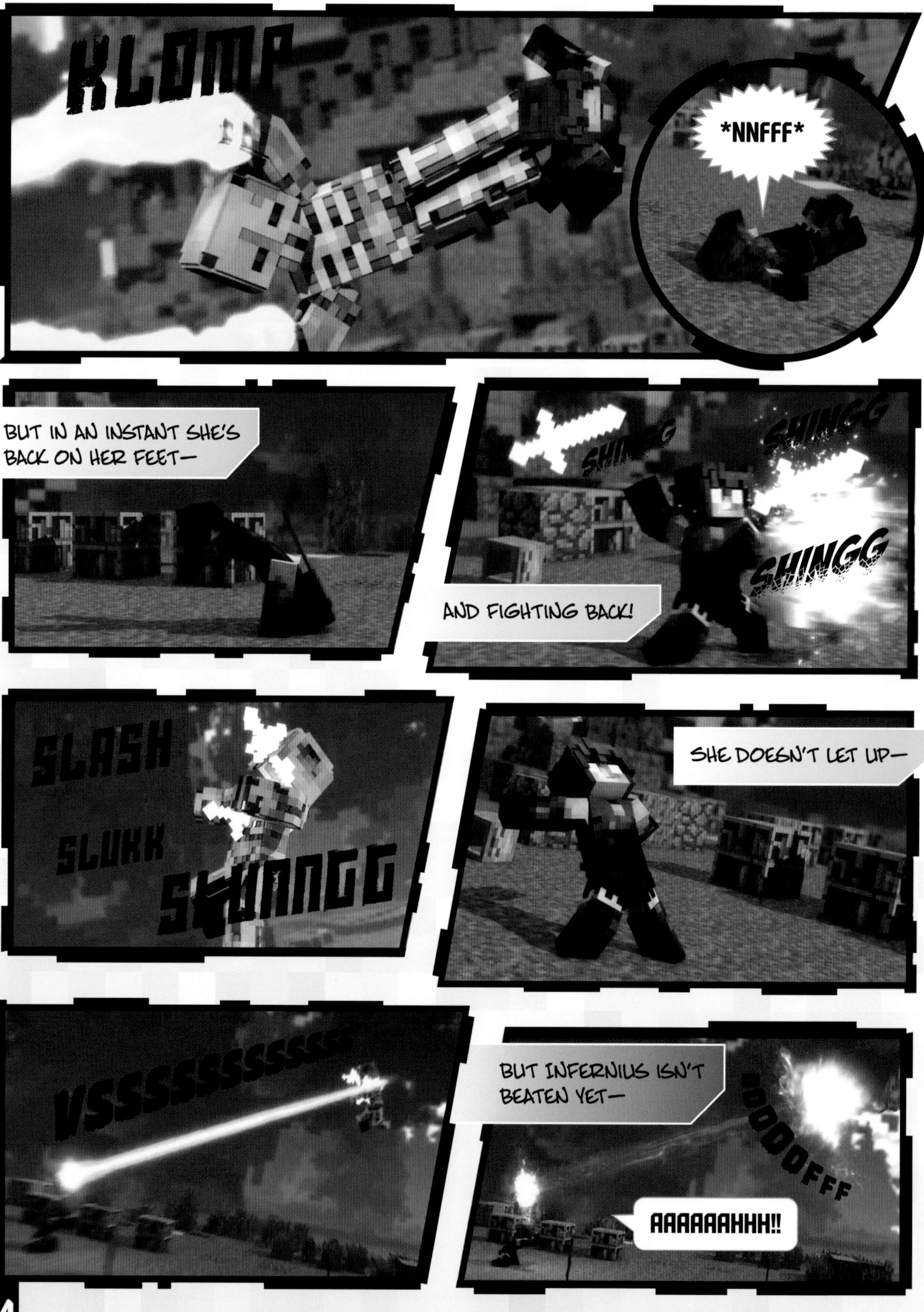
KLOMP
NNFFF
BUT IN AN INSTANT SHE'S BACK ON HER FEET—
SHINGG
SHINGG
SHINGG
AND FIGHTING BACK!
SLASH
SLUKK
SHE DOESN'T LET UP—
BUT INFERNIUS ISN'T BEATEN YET—
AAAAAAHHH!!

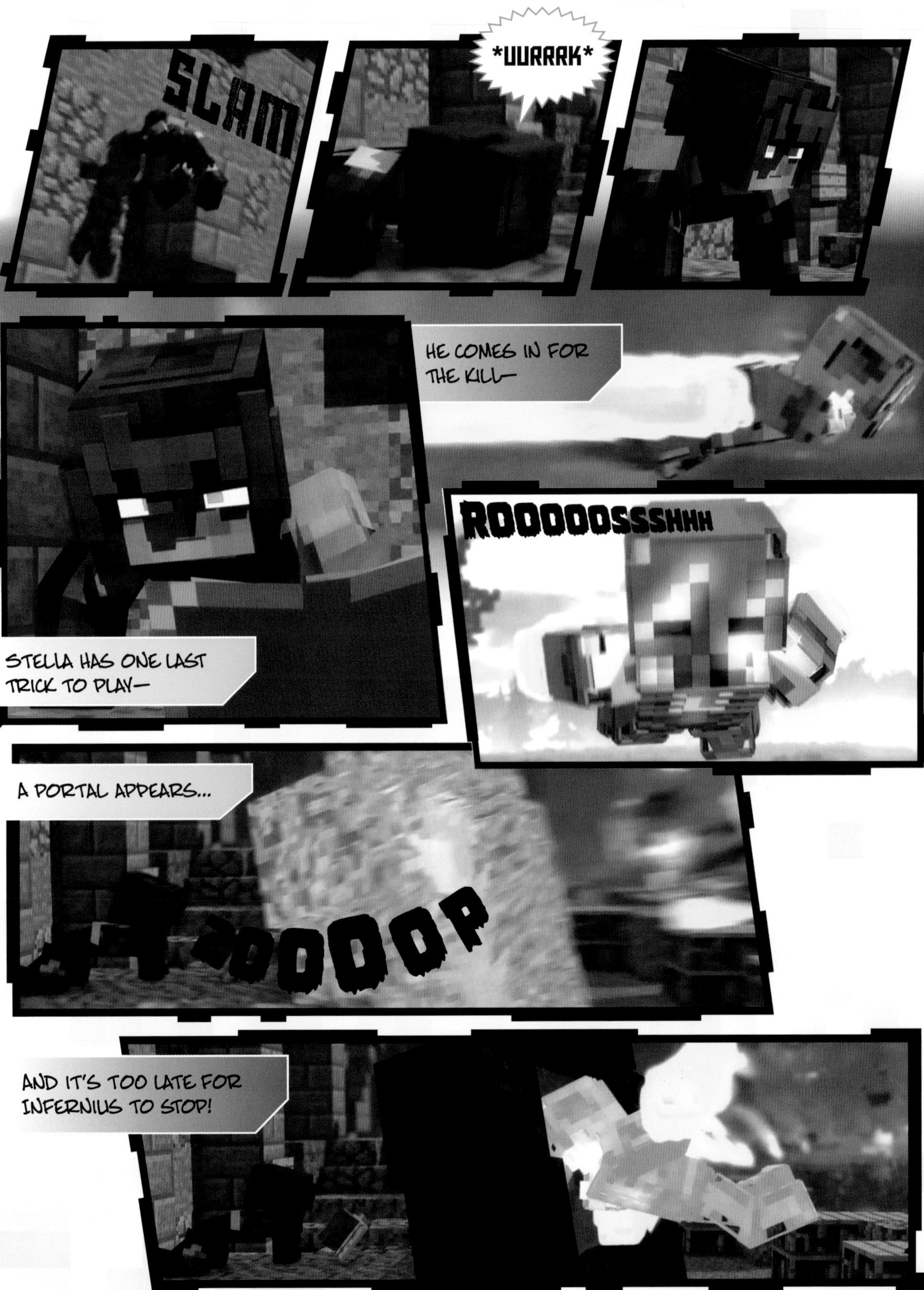
SLAM
UURRRK
HE COMES IN FOR THE KILL—
STELLA HAS ONE LAST TRICK TO PLAY—
ROOOOOOSSSHHH
A PORTAL APPEARS...
OOOOP
AND IT'S TOO LATE FOR INFERNIUS TO STOP!

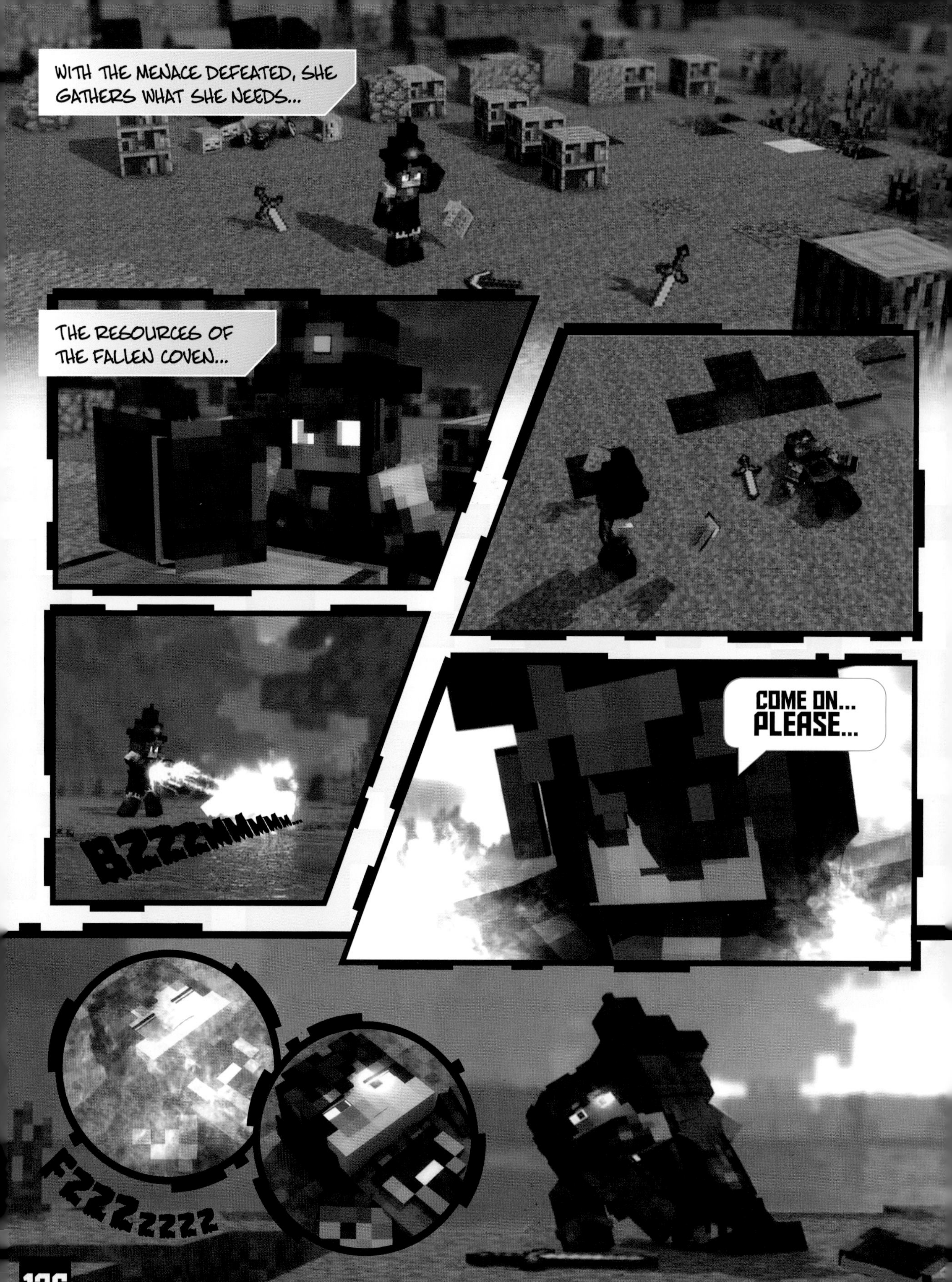

WITH THE MENACE DEFEATED, SHE GATHERS WHAT SHE NEEDS...
THE RESOURCES OF THE FALLEN COVEN...
BZZZMMMMM...
COME ON... PLEASE...
FZZZzzzz

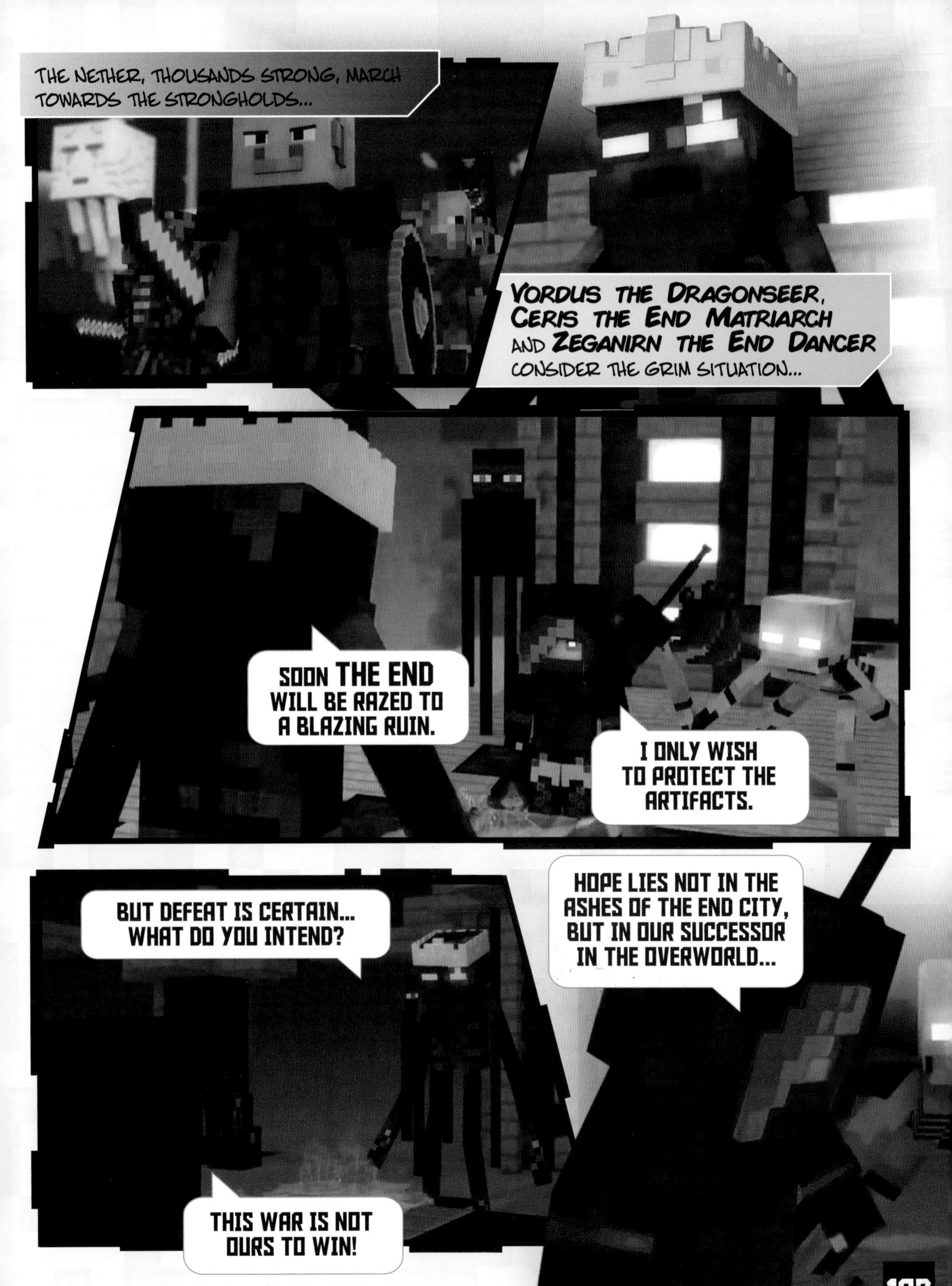
THE NETHER, THOUSANDS STRONG, MARCH TOWARDS THE STRONGHOLDS...
VORDUS THE DRAGONSEER, CERIS THE END MATRIARCH AND ZEGANIRN THE END DANCER CONSIDER THE GRIM SITUATION...
SOON THE END WILL BE RAZED TO A BLAZING RUIN.
I ONLY WISH TO PROTECT THE ARTIFACTS.
BUT DEFEAT IS CERTAIN... WHAT DO YOU INTEND?
HOPE LIES NOT IN THE ASHES OF THE END CITY, BUT IN OUR SUCCESSOR IN THE OVERWORLD...
THIS WAR IS NOT OURS TO WIN!

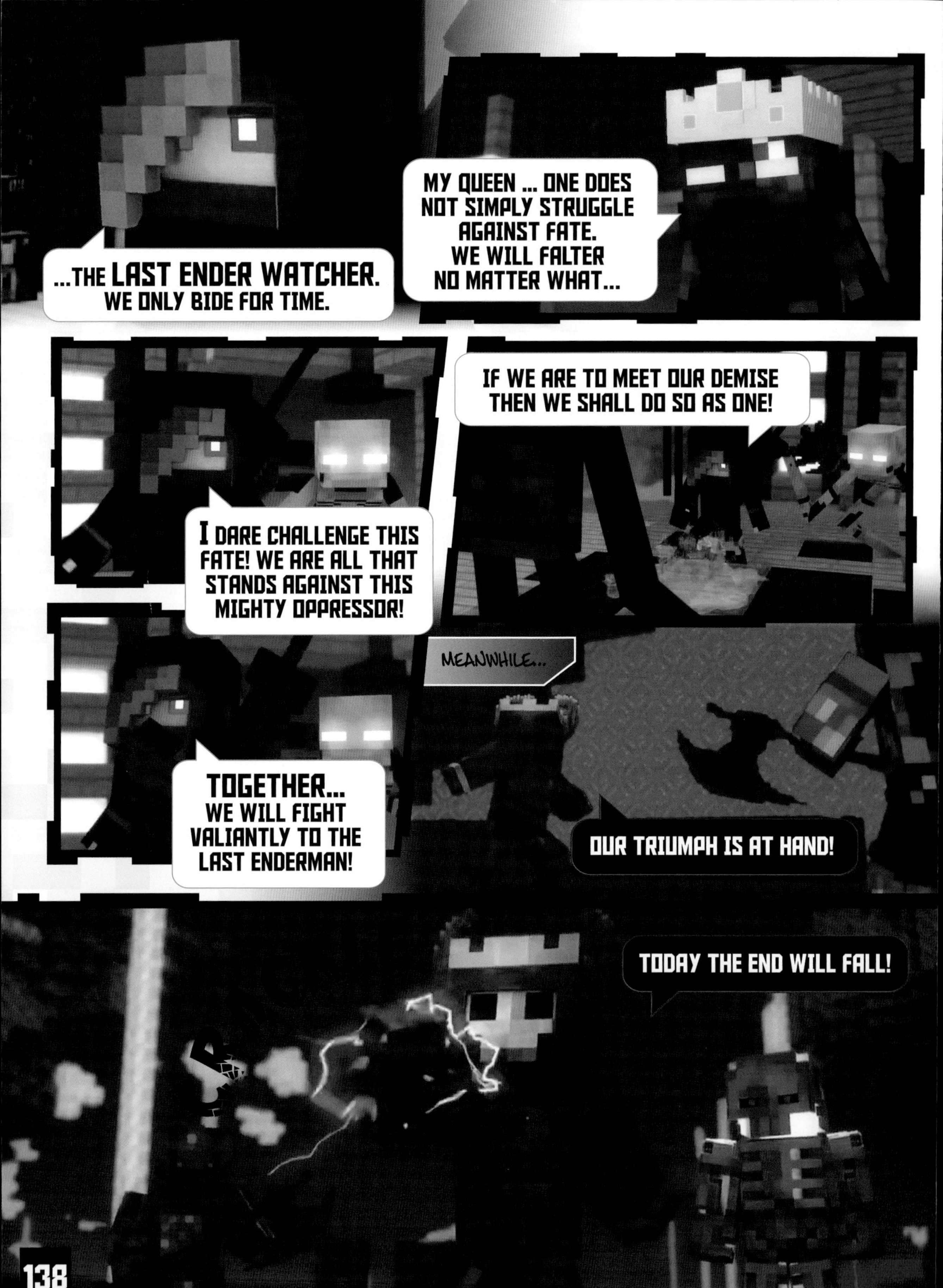

...THE LAST ENDER WATCHER. WE ONLY BIDE FOR TIME.
MY QUEEN ... ONE DOES NOT SIMPLY STRUGGLE AGAINST FATE. WE WILL FALTER NO MATTER WHAT...
I DARE CHALLENGE THIS FATE! WE ARE ALL THAT STANDS AGAINST THIS MIGHTY OPPRESSOR!
IF WE ARE TO MEET OUR DEMISE THEN WE SHALL DO SO AS ONE!
TOGETHER... WE WILL FIGHT VALIANTLY TO THE LAST ENDERMAN!
MEANWHILE...
OUR TRIUMPH IS AT HAND!
TODAY THE END WILL FALL!

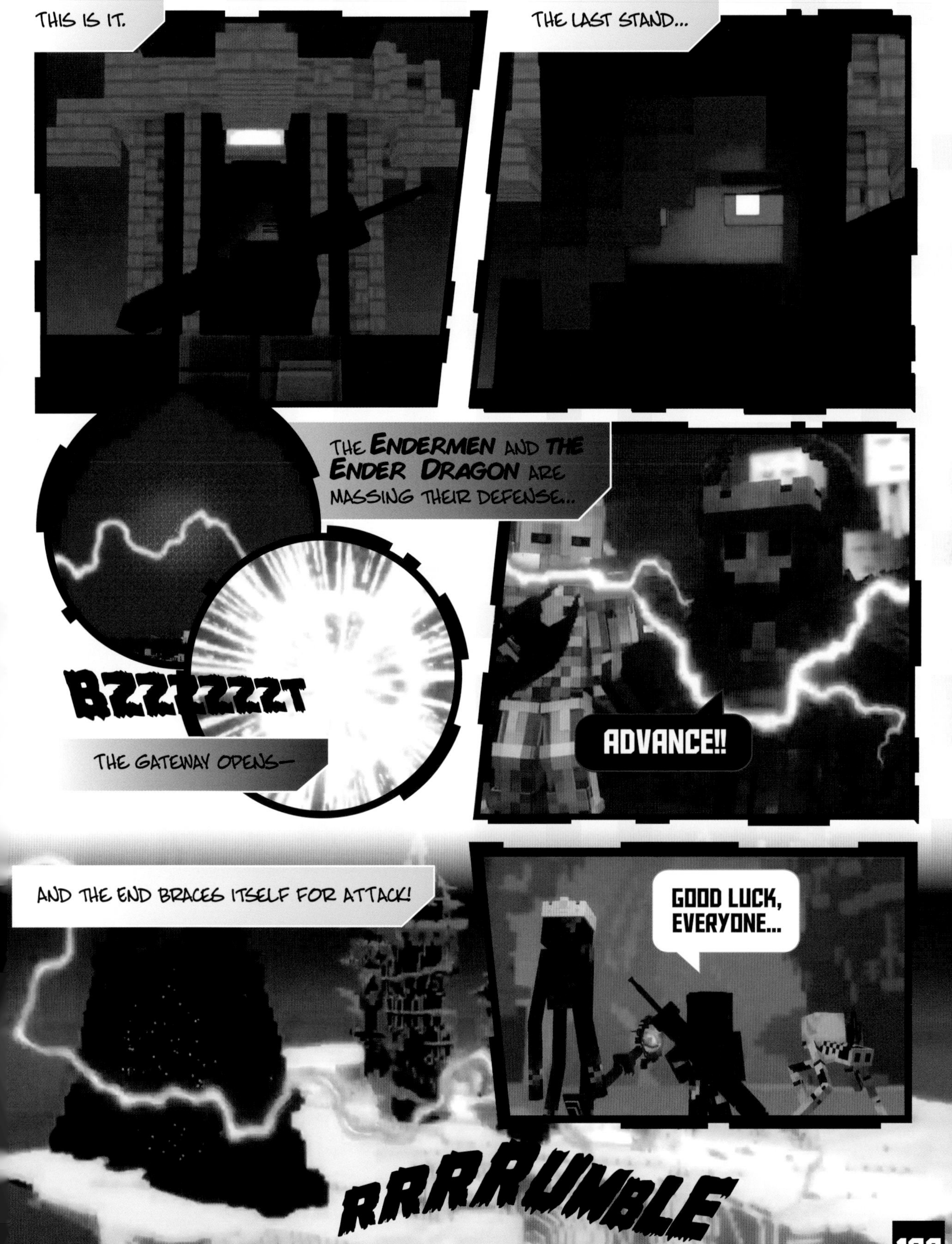
THIS IS IT.
THE LAST STAND...
THE ENDERMEN AND THE ENDER DRAGON ARE MASSING THEIR DEFENSE...
BZZZZZZZT
THE GATEWAY OPENS—
ADVANCE!!
AND THE END BRACES ITSELF FOR ATTACK!
GOOD LUCK, EVERYONE...
RRRRUMBLE

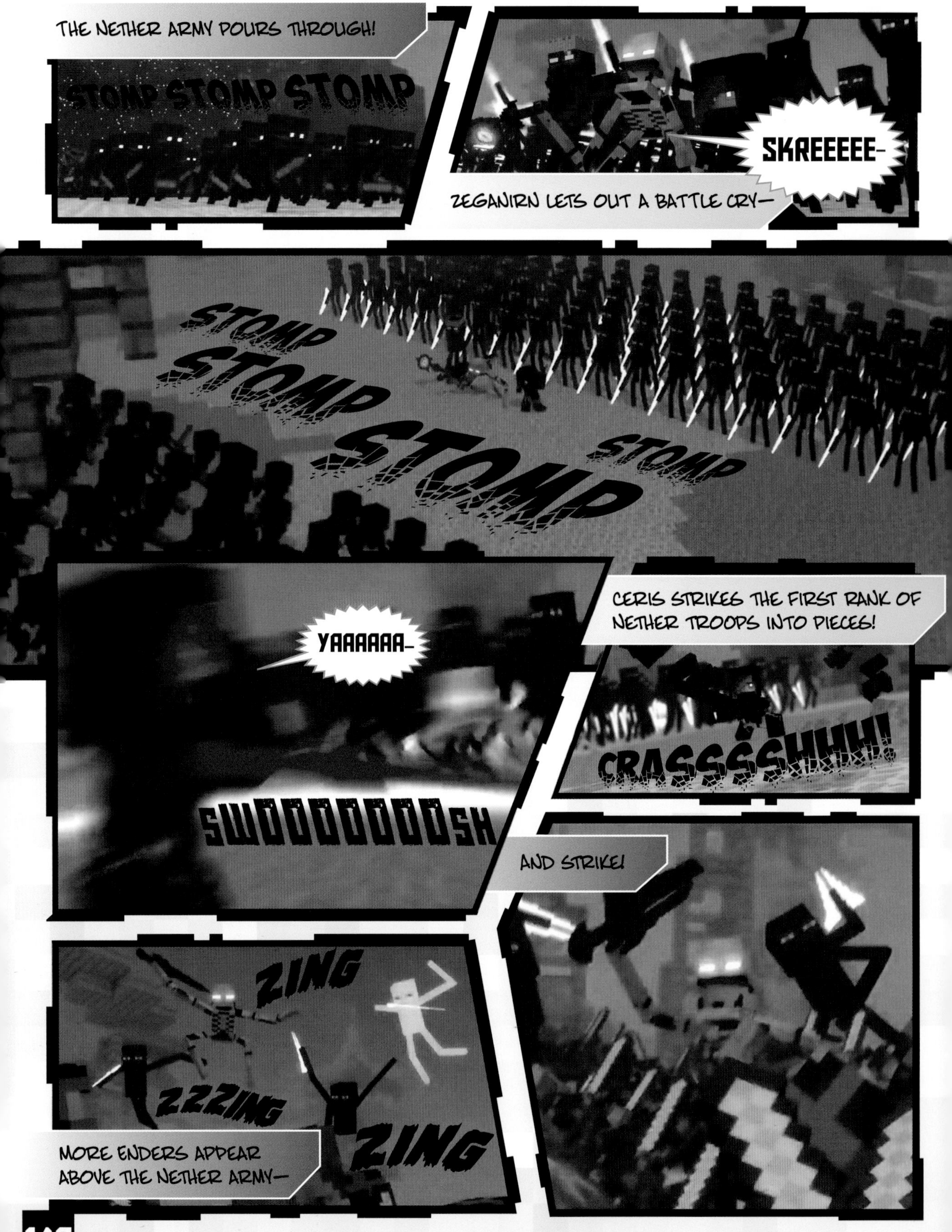
THE NETHER ARMY POURS THROUGH!
STOMP STOMP STOMP
SKREEEEE-
ZEGANIRN LETS OUT A BATTLE CRY—
STOMP
STOMP
STOMP
STOMP
CERIS STRIKES THE FIRST RANK OF NETHER TROOPS INTO PIECES!
YAAAAAA-
CRASSSSHHH!
SWOOOOOOOOSH
AND STRIKE!
ZING
ZZZING
ZING
MORE ENDERS APPEAR ABOVE THE NETHER ARMY—

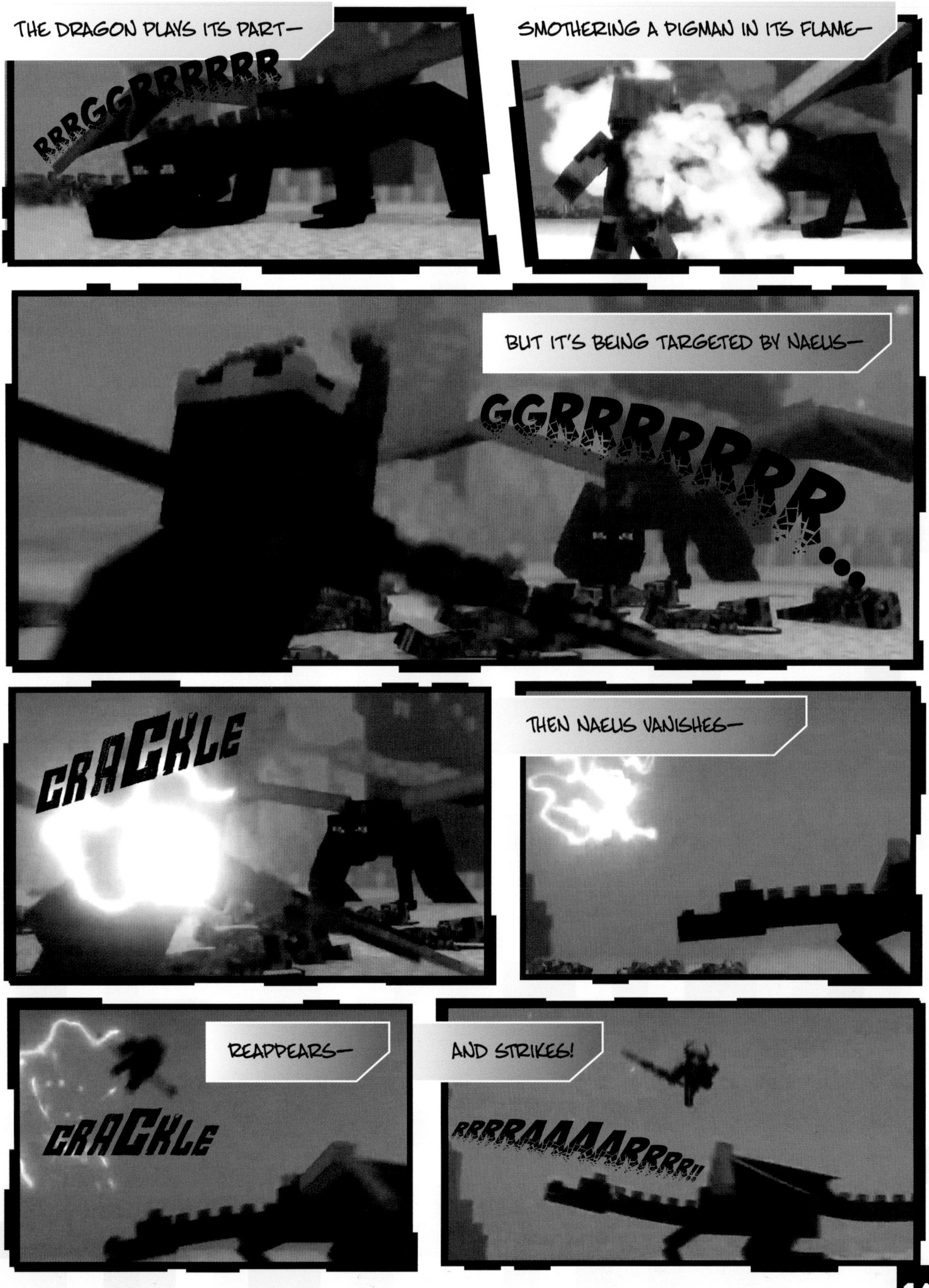
THE DRAGON PLAYS ITS PART—
RRRGGRRRRRRR
SMOTHERING A PIGMAN IN ITS FLAME—
BUT IT'S BEING TARGETED BY NAEUS—
GGRRRRRRRRR...
CRACKLE
THEN NAEUS VANISHES—
REAPPEARS—
CRACKLE
AND STRIKES!
RRRRAAAAARRRR!!

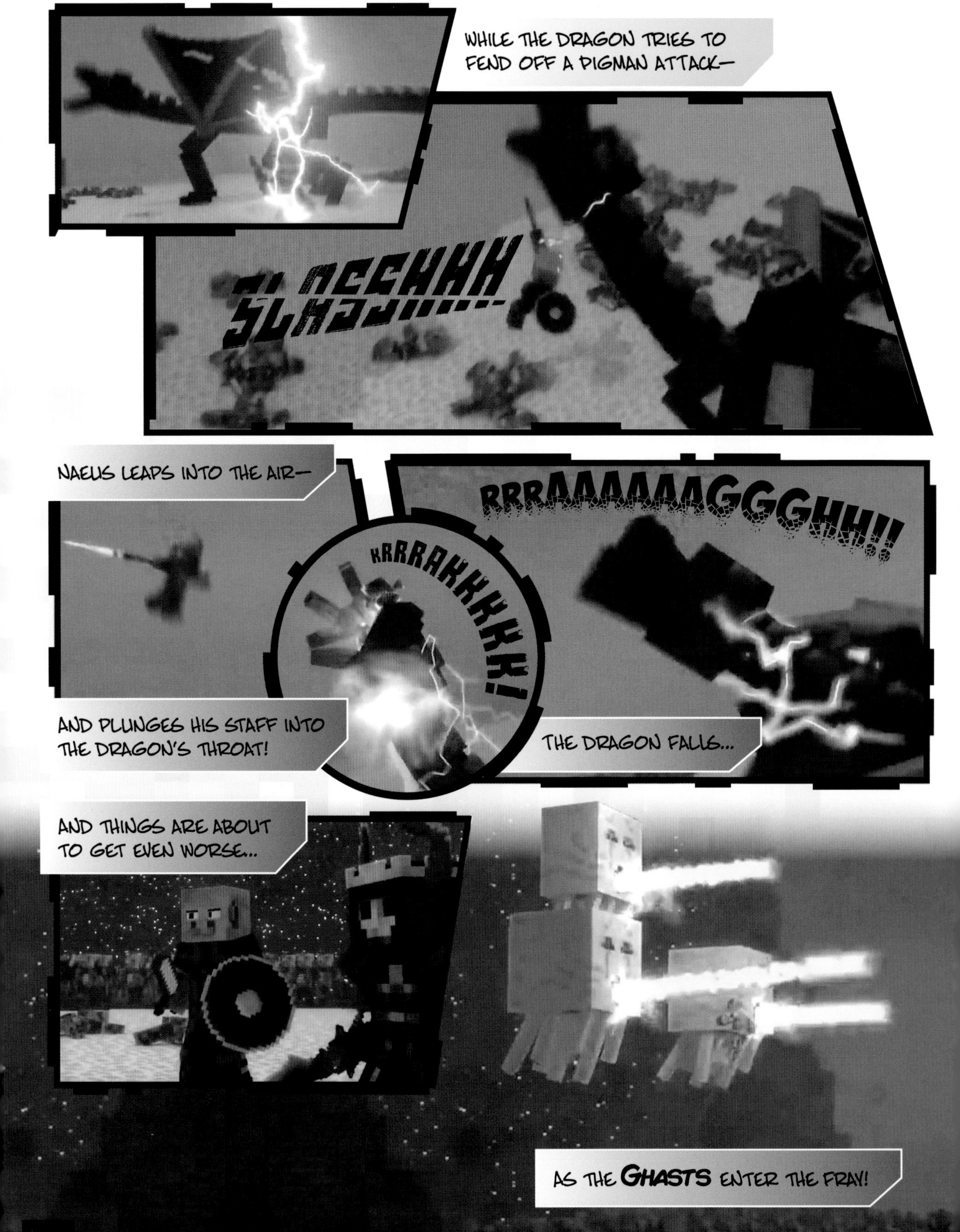

WHILE THE DRAGON TRIES TO FEND OFF A PIGMAN ATTACK—
NAEUS LEAPS INTO THE AIR—
KRRRRAKKKKKK!
RRRAAAAAAAGGGHH!!
AND PLUNGES HIS STAFF INTO THE DRAGON'S THROAT!
THE DRAGON FALLS...
AND THINGS ARE ABOUT TO GET EVEN WORSE...
AS THE GHASTS ENTER THE FRAY!

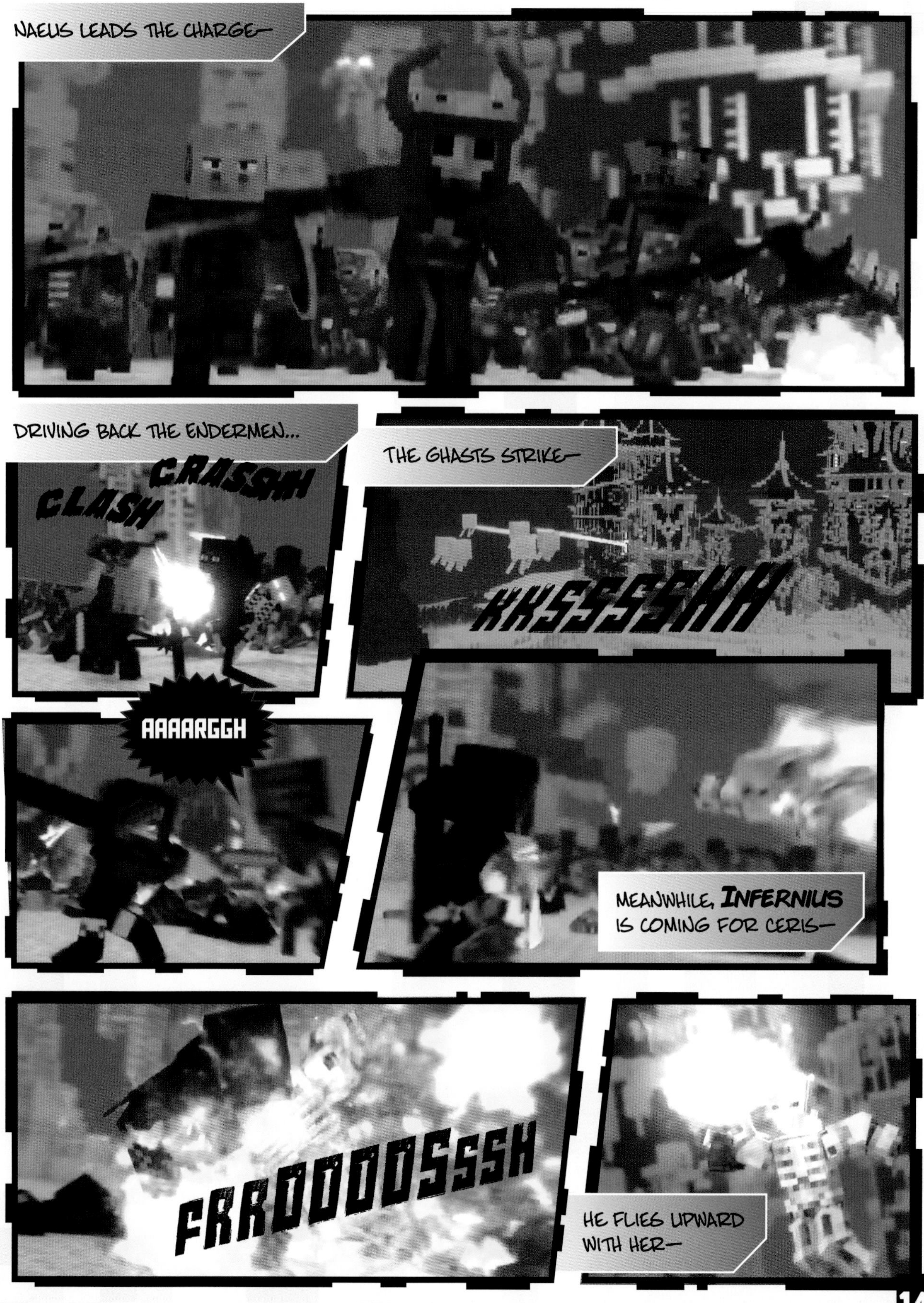

NAEUS LEADS THE CHARGE—
DRIVING BACK THE ENDERMEN...
CLASH
CRASSHH
THE GHASTS STRIKE—
KKSSSSSHH
AAAARGGH
MEANWHILE, INFERNIUS IS COMING FOR CERIS—
FRROOOOSSSH
HE FLIES UPWARD WITH HER—

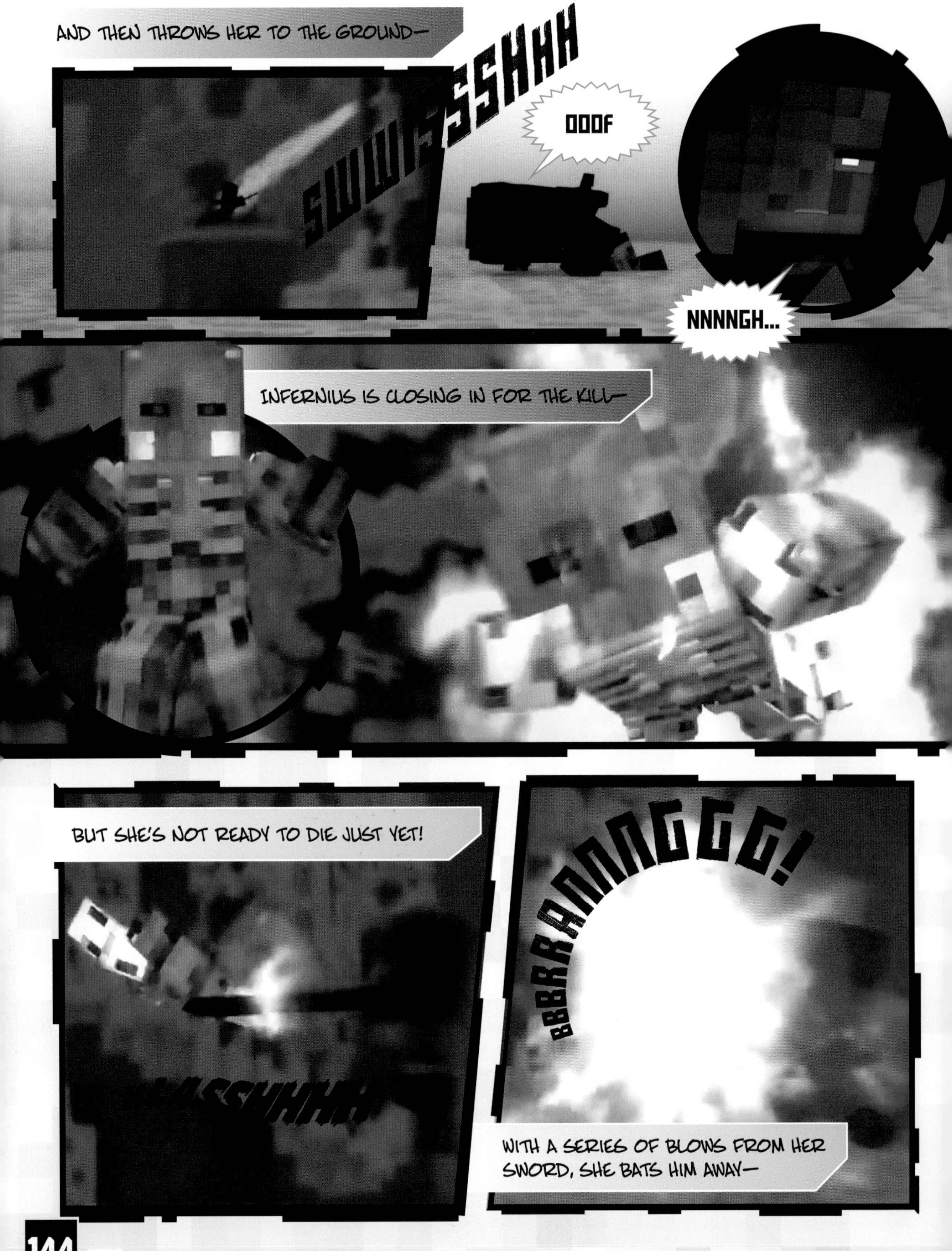
AND THEN THROWS HER TO THE GROUND—
SWWISSSHHH
OOOF
NNNNGH...
INFERNIUS IS CLOSING IN FOR THE KILL—
BUT SHE'S NOT READY TO DIE JUST YET!
BBBBRANNGGG!
WITH A SERIES OF BLOWS FROM HER SWORD, SHE BATS HIM AWAY—

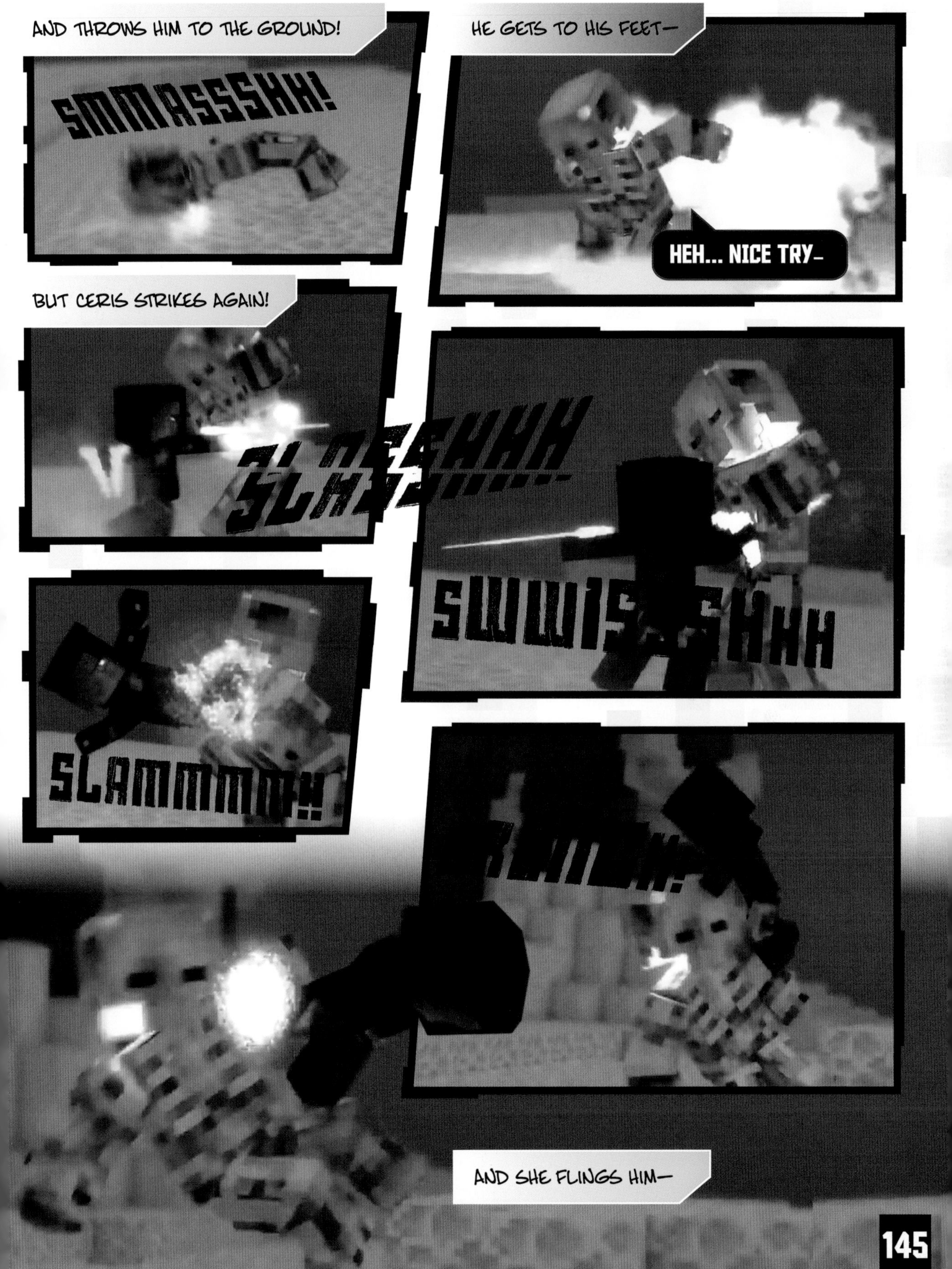
AND THROWS HIM TO THE GROUND!
SMMASSSHH!
HE GETS TO HIS FEET—
HEH... NICE TRY—
BUT CERIS STRIKES AGAIN!
SLAMMMMM!!
AND SHE FLINGS HIM—

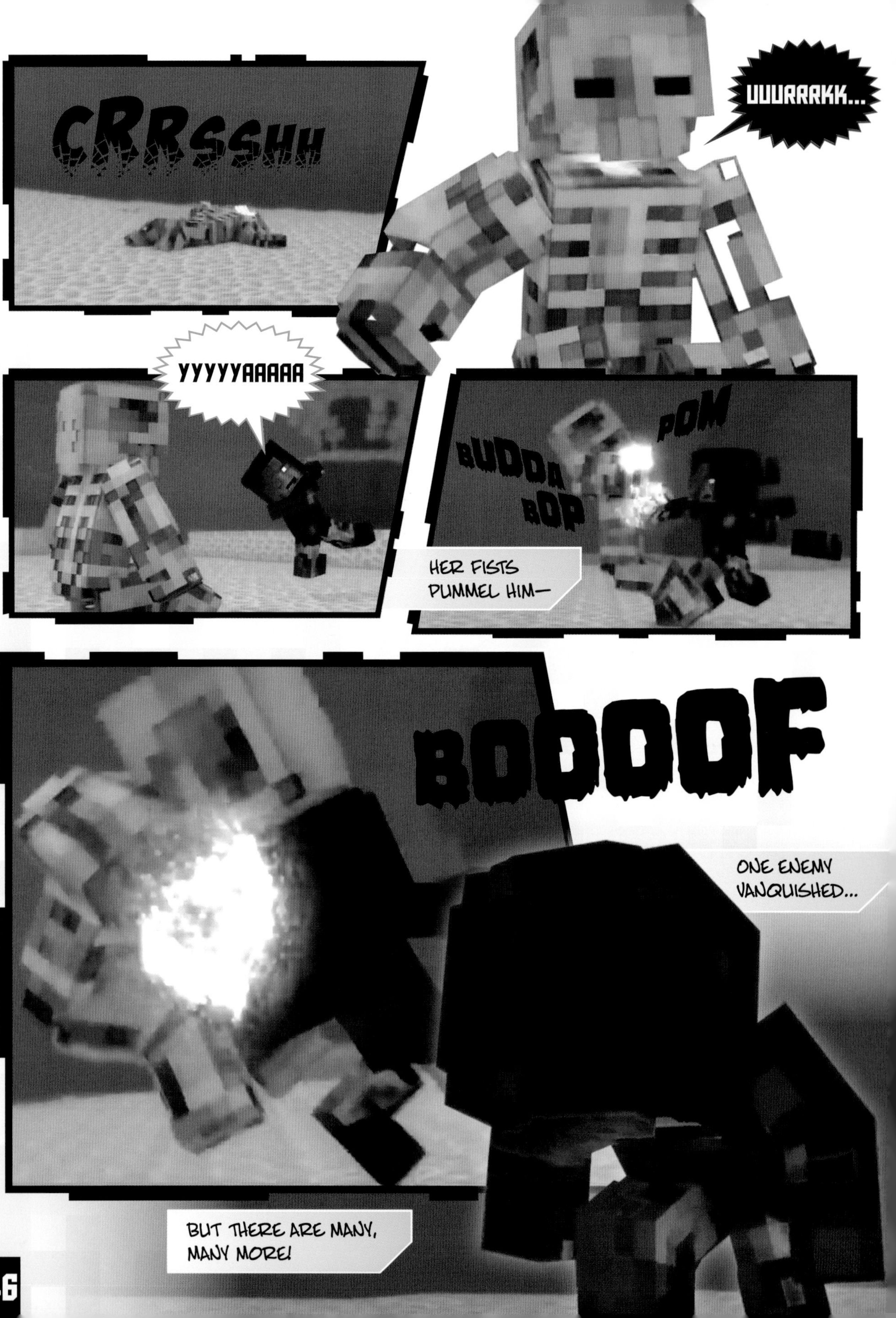
CRRSSHH
UUURRRKK...
YYYYYAAAAA
BUDDA
BOP
POM
HER FISTS PUMMEL HIM—
BOOOOF
ONE ENEMY VANQUISHED...
BUT THERE ARE MANY, MANY MORE!

VORDUS LIES DEAD ON THE BATTLEFIELD... AN ENDER PEARL IS RELEASED—
SHHHRRRRRSSSSHHH...
AND WHILE CERIS MAINTAINS HER PLEDGE TO PROTECT THE ARTIFACTS, ANOTHER FOE LOOMS—
NAEUS...
I WANT THE ARTIFACTS. I WILL TAKE THEM.

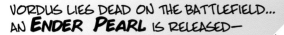

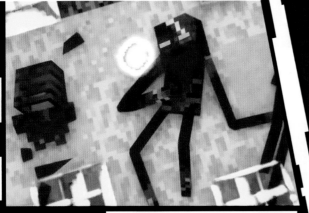

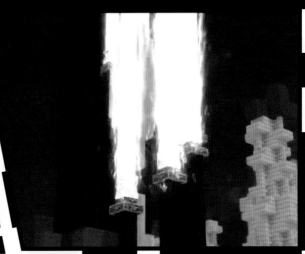

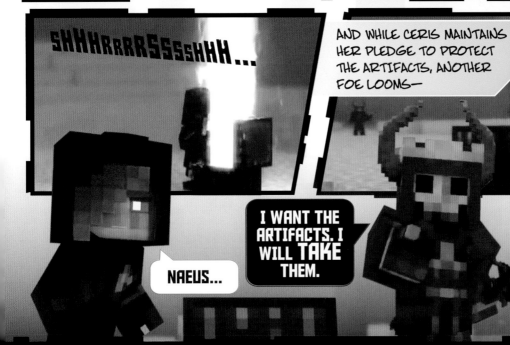

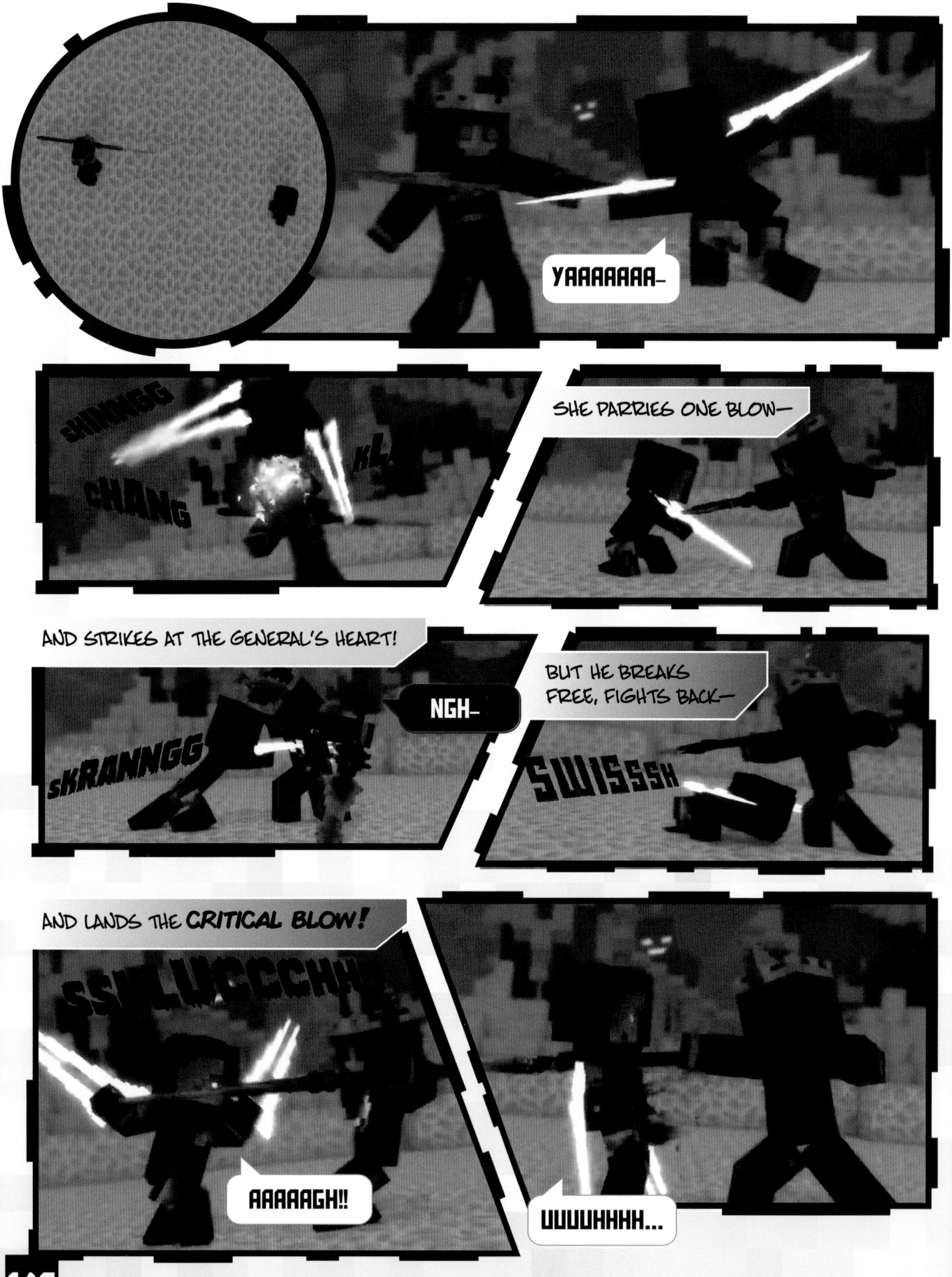

YAAAAAAA–
SHINNGG
CHANG
SHE PARRIES ONE BLOW–
AND STRIKES AT THE GENERAL'S HEART!
NGH–
sKRANNGG
BUT HE BREAKS FREE, FIGHTS BACK–
SWISSSH
AND LANDS THE CRITICAL BLOW!
AAAAAGH!!
UUUUHHHH...

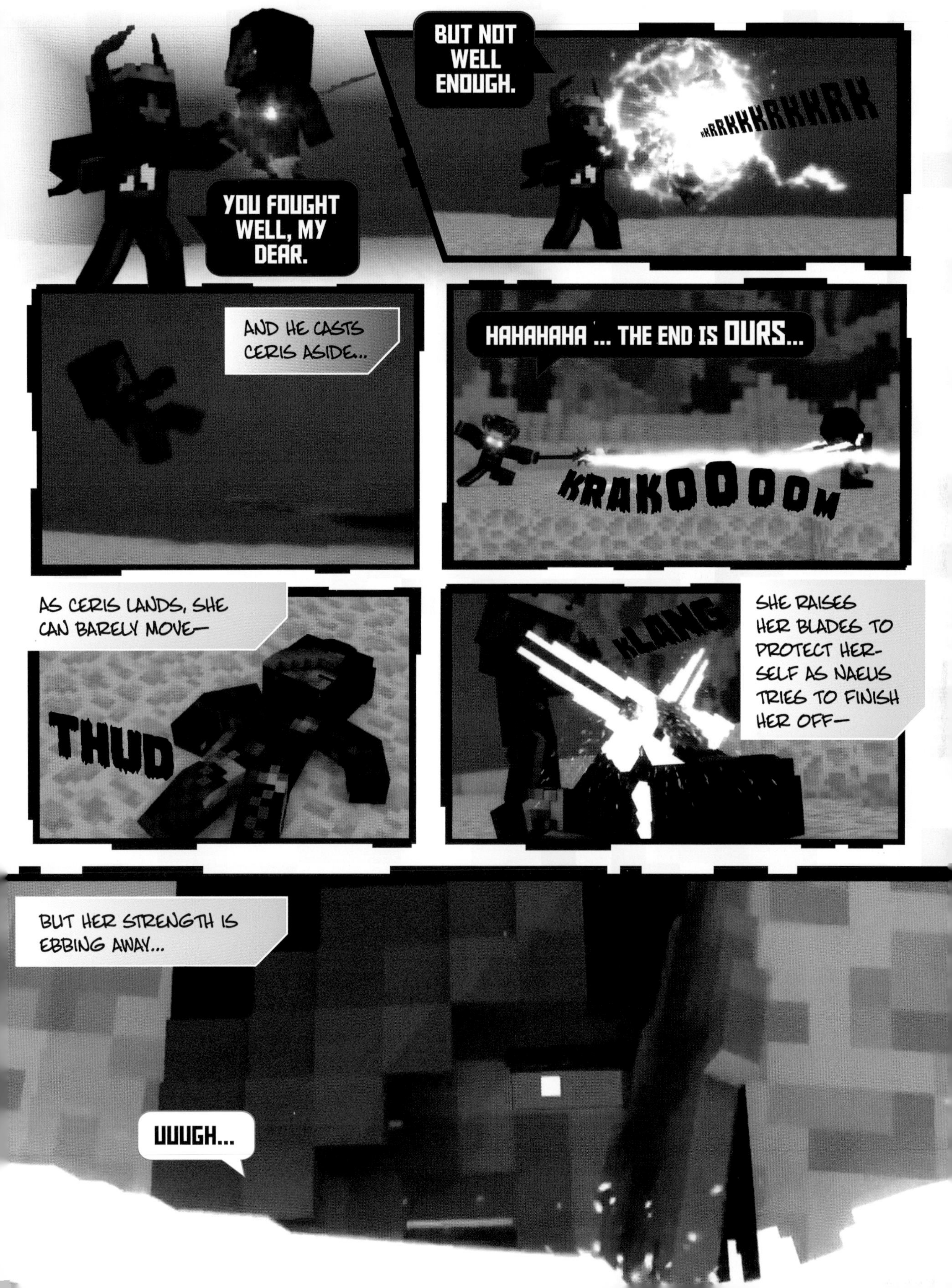
YOU FOUGHT WELL, MY DEAR.
BUT NOT WELL ENOUGH.
KRRKKKRKKKRK
AND HE CASTS CERIS ASIDE...
HAHAHAHA ... THE END IS OURS...
KRAKOOOOOM
AS CERIS LANDS, SHE CAN BARELY MOVE—
THUD
SHE RAISES HER BLADES TO PROTECT HER-SELF AS NAEUS TRIES TO FINISH HER OFF—
KLANG
BUT HER STRENGTH IS EBBING AWAY...
UUUGH...

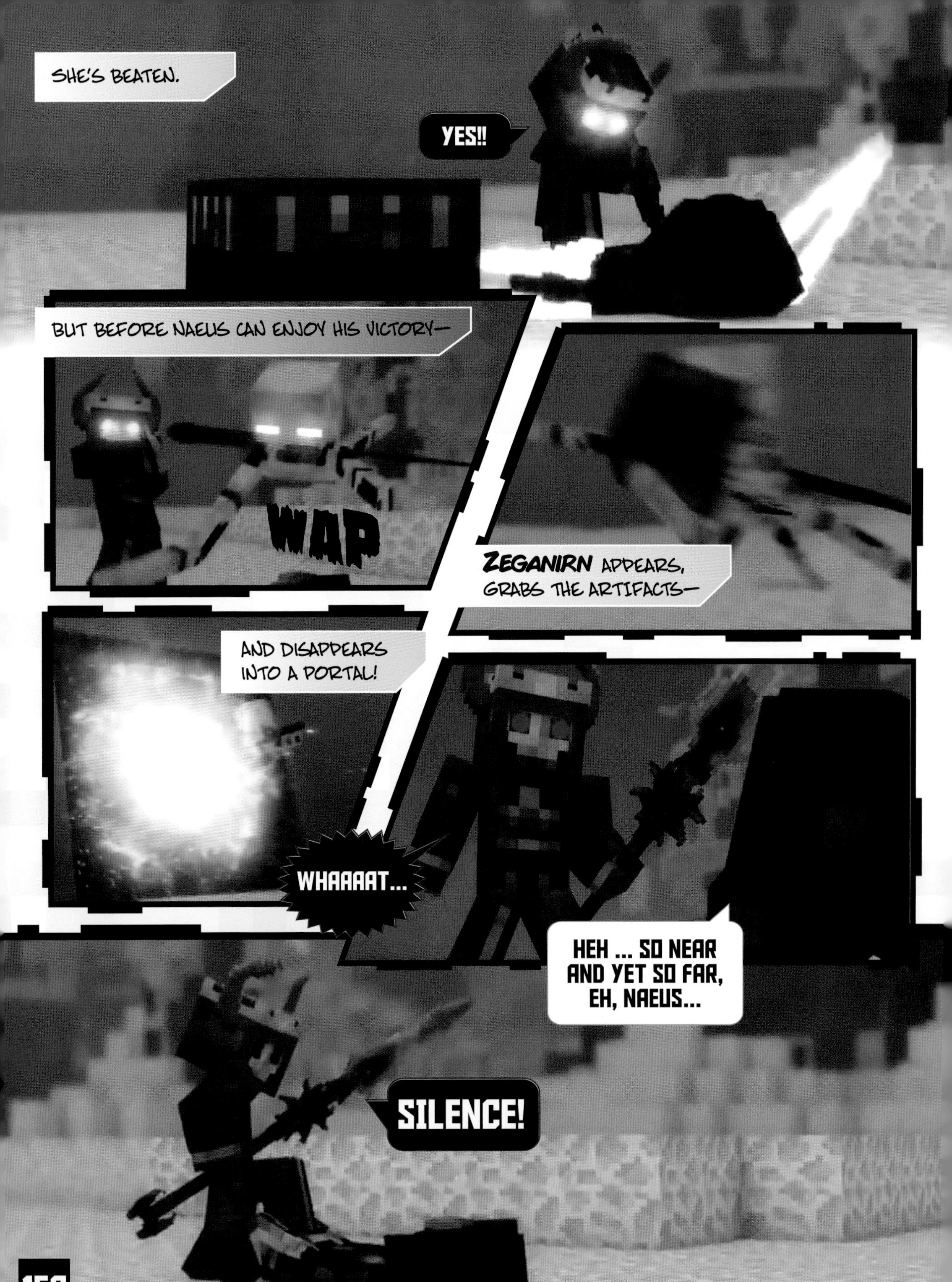
SHE'S BEATEN.
YES!!
BUT BEFORE NAEUS CAN ENJOY HIS VICTORY—
WAP
ZEGANIRN APPEARS, GRABS THE ARTIFACTS—
AND DISAPPEARS INTO A PORTAL!
WHAAAAT...
HEH ... SO NEAR AND YET SO FAR, EH, NAEUS...
SILENCE!

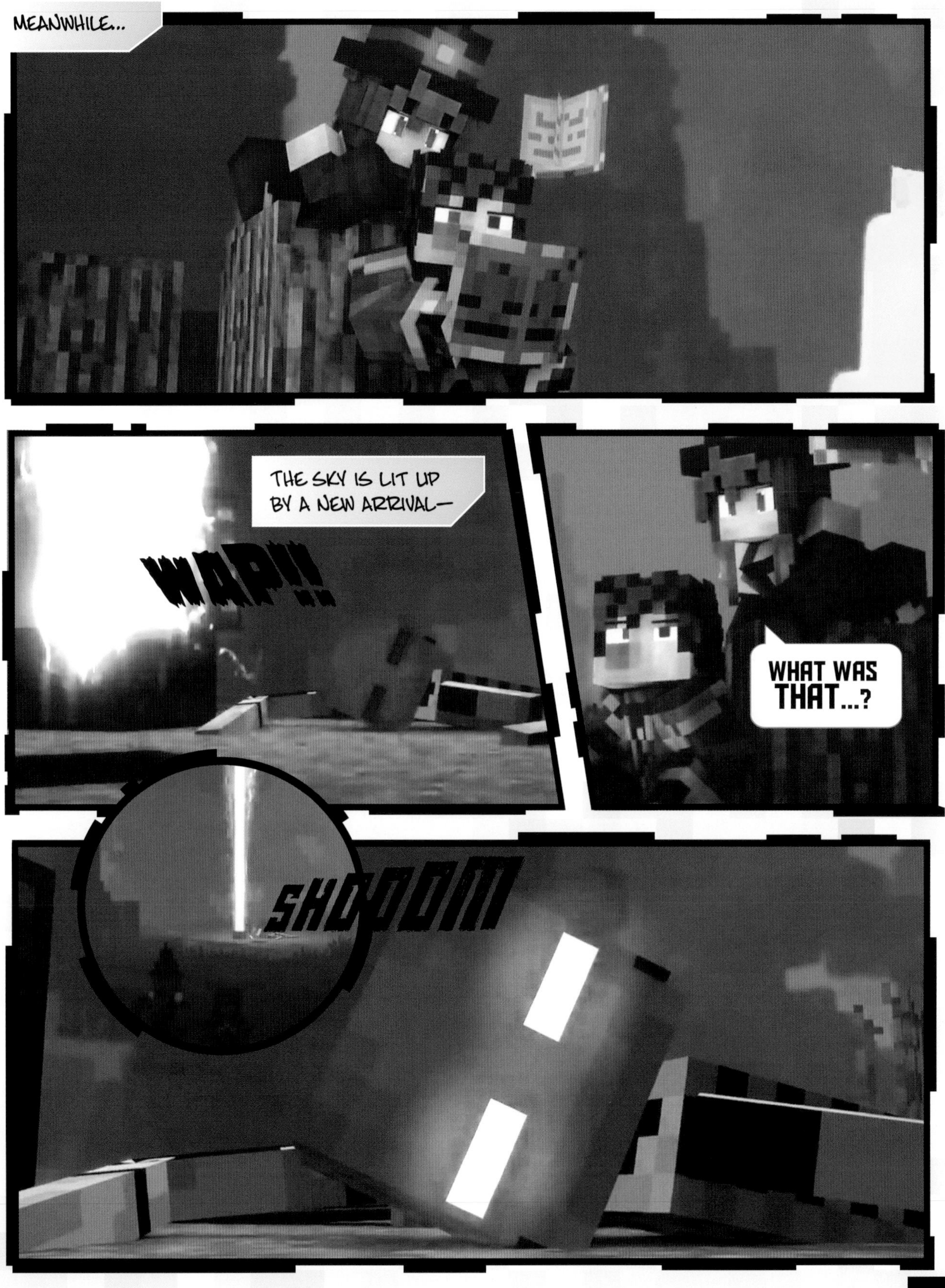
MEANWHILE...
THE SKY IS LIT UP BY A NEW ARRIVAL—
WARP!!
WHAT WAS THAT...?
SHOOOM

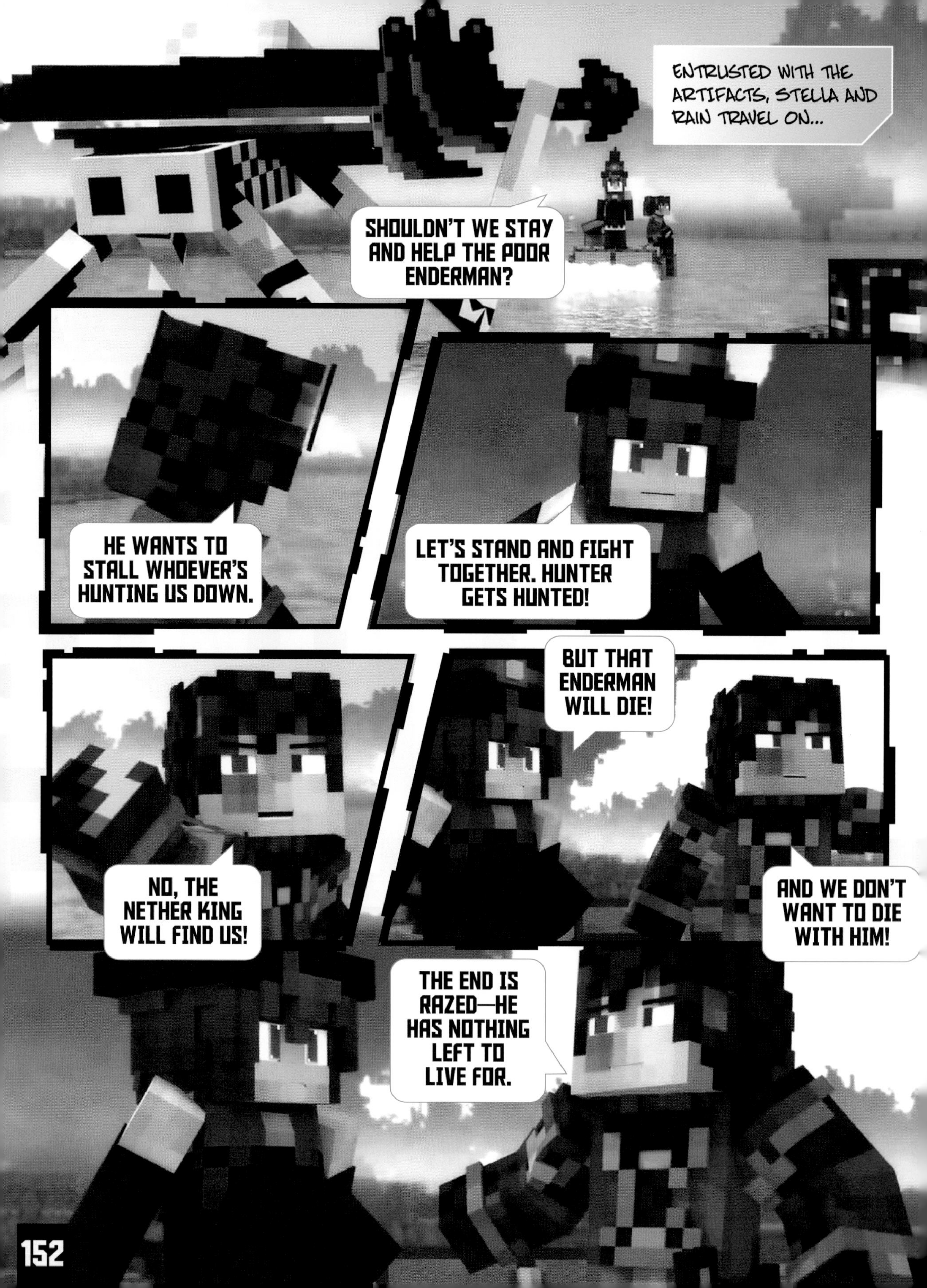
ENTRUSTED WITH THE ARTIFACTS, STELLA AND RAIN TRAVEL ON...
SHOULDN'T WE STAY AND HELP THE POOR ENDERMAN?
HE WANTS TO STALL WHOEVER'S HUNTING US DOWN.
LET'S STAND AND FIGHT TOGETHER. HUNTER GETS HUNTED!
NO, THE NETHER KING WILL FIND US!
BUT THAT ENDERMAN WILL DIE!
AND WE DON'T WANT TO DIE WITH HIM!
THE END IS RAZED—HE HAS NOTHING LEFT TO LIVE FOR.

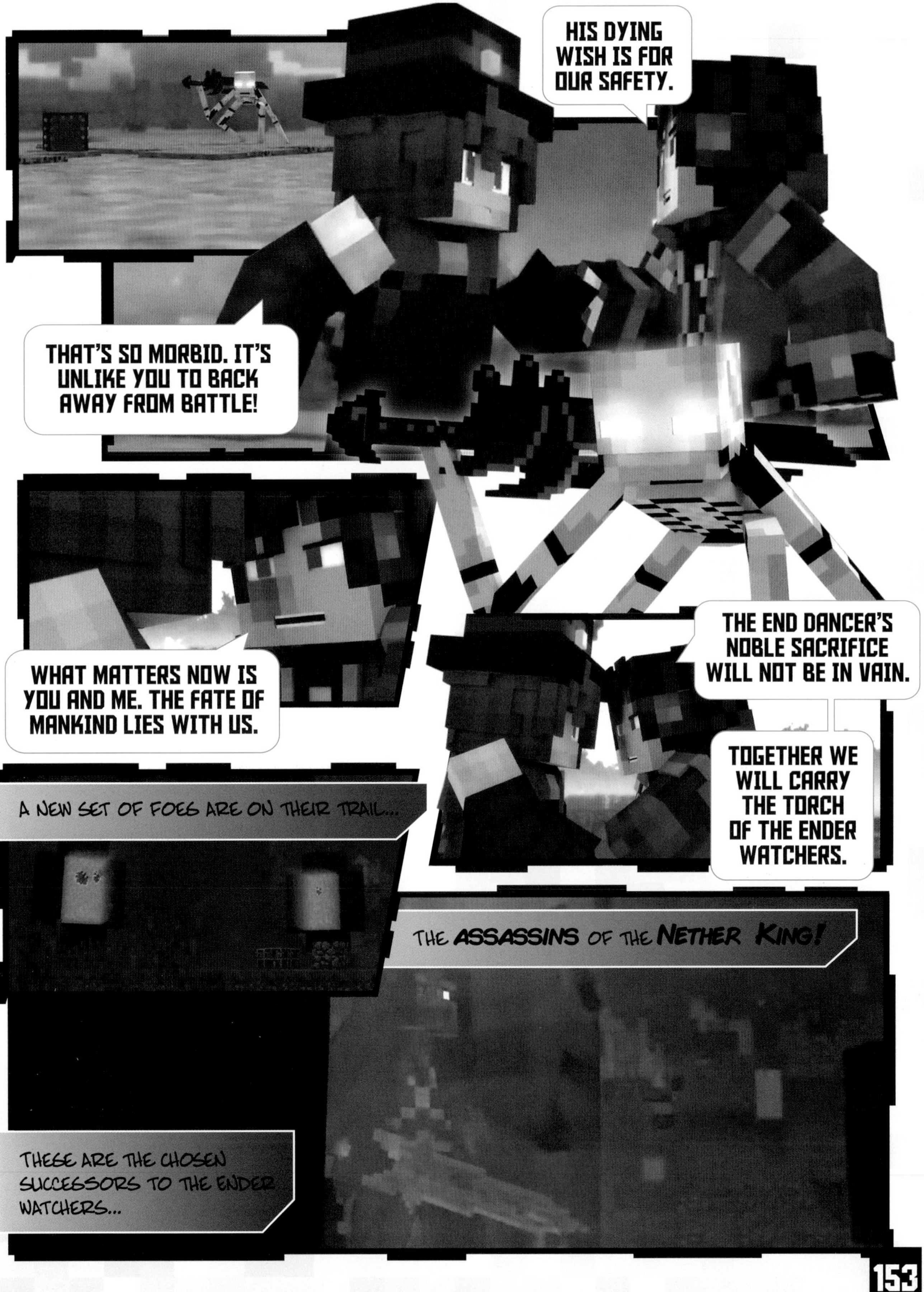
HIS DYING WISH IS FOR OUR SAFETY.
THAT'S SO MORBID. IT'S UNLIKE YOU TO BACK AWAY FROM BATTLE!
WHAT MATTERS NOW IS YOU AND ME. THE FATE OF MANKIND LIES WITH US.
THE END DANCER'S NOBLE SACRIFICE WILL NOT BE IN VAIN.
TOGETHER WE WILL CARRY THE TORCH OF THE ENDER WATCHERS.
A NEW SET OF FOES ARE ON THEIR TRAIL...
THE ASSASSINS OF THE NETHER KING!
THESE ARE THE CHOSEN SUCCESSORS TO THE ENDER WATCHERS...

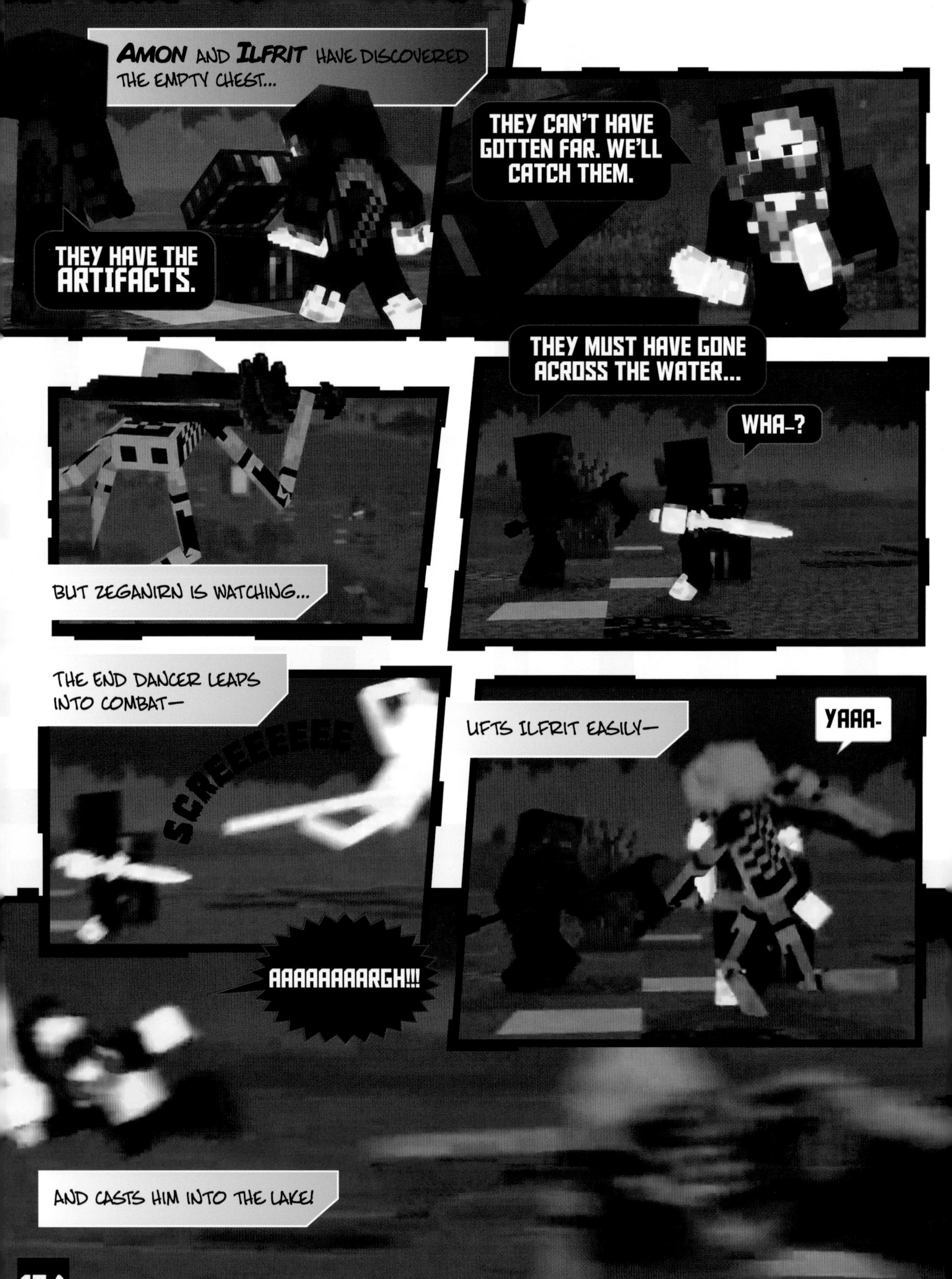

AMON AND ILFRIT HAVE DISCOVERED THE EMPTY CHEST...
THEY HAVE THE ARTIFACTS.
THEY CAN'T HAVE GOTTEN FAR. WE'LL CATCH THEM.
BUT ZEGANIRN IS WATCHING...
THEY MUST HAVE GONE ACROSS THE WATER...
WHA-?
THE END DANCER LEAPS INTO COMBAT—
SCREEEEEEE
LIFTS ILFRIT EASILY—
YAAA-
AAAAAAAARGH!!!
AND CASTS HIM INTO THE LAKE!

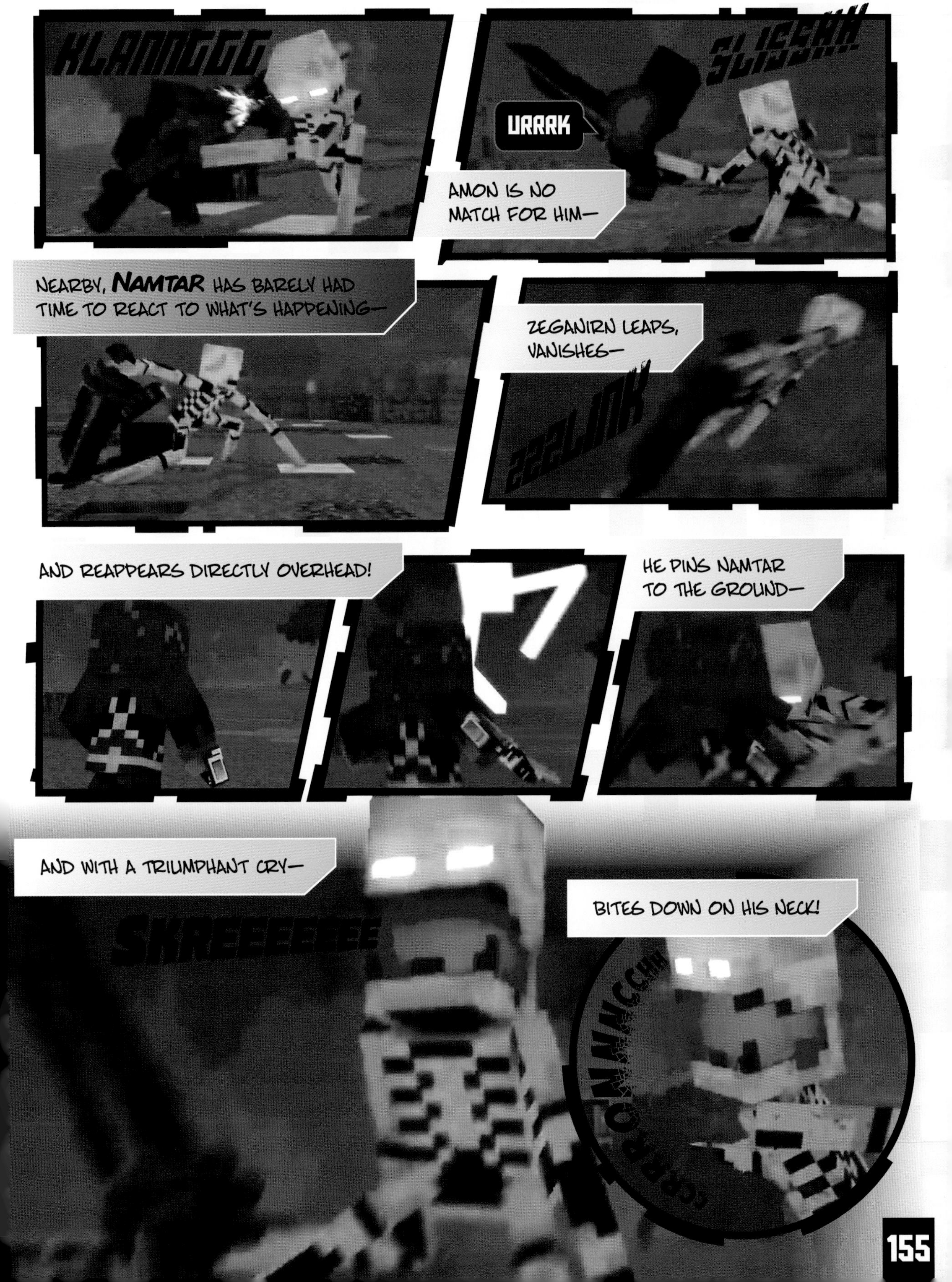
KLANNGGG
SLISCHH!!
URRRK
AMON IS NO MATCH FOR HIM—
NEARBY, **NAMTAR** HAS BARELY HAD TIME TO REACT TO WHAT'S HAPPENING—
ZEGANIRN LEAPS, VANISHES—
ZZZLINK
AND REAPPEARS DIRECTLY OVERHEAD!
HE PINS NAMTAR TO THE GROUND—
AND WITH A TRIUMPHANT CRY—
SKREEEEEEEE
BITES DOWN ON HIS NECK!

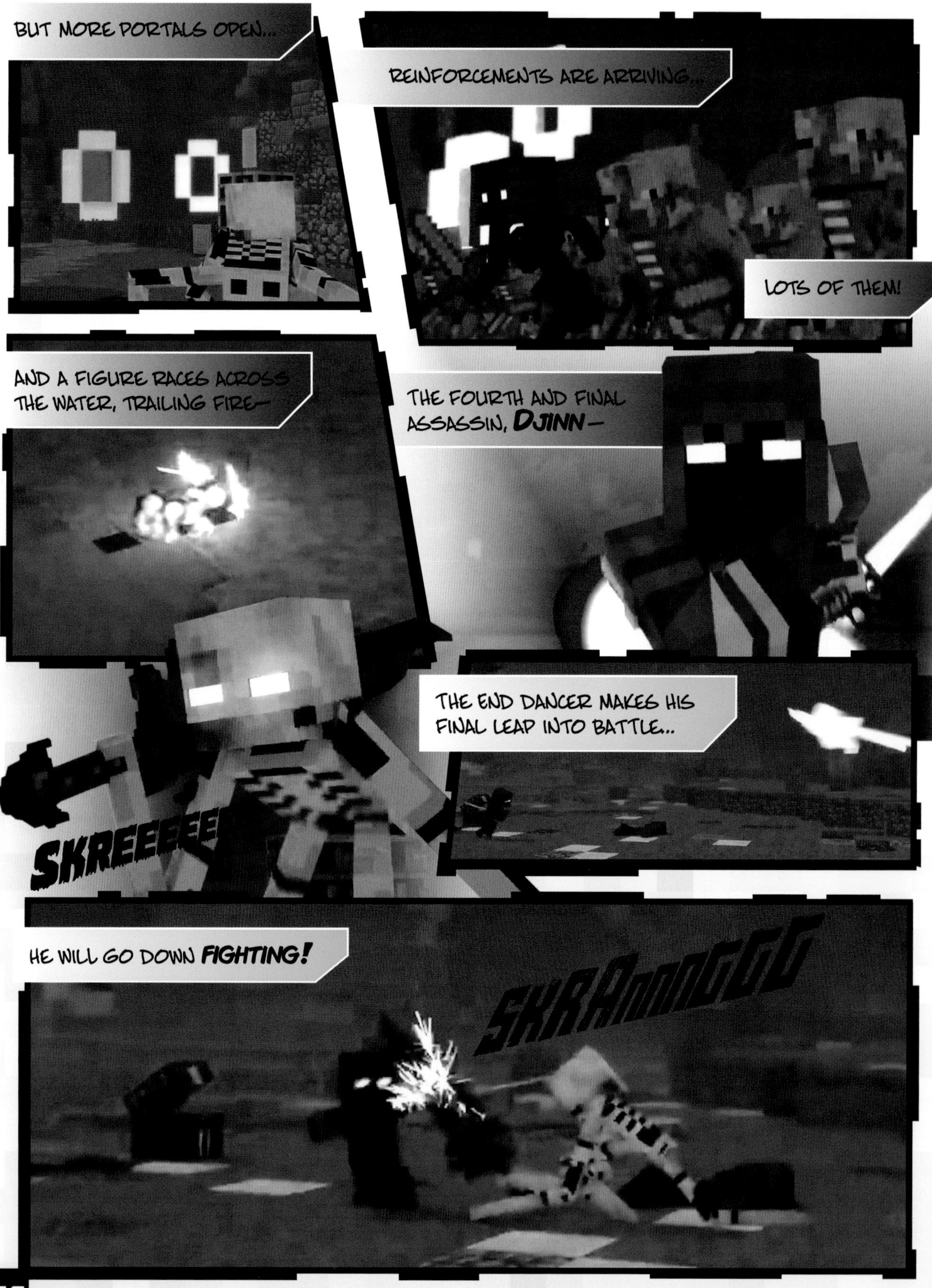
BUT MORE PORTALS OPEN...
REINFORCEMENTS ARE ARRIVING...
LOTS OF THEM!
AND A FIGURE RACES ACROSS THE WATER, TRAILING FIRE—
THE FOURTH AND FINAL ASSASSIN, **DJINN**—
SKREEEEEE
THE END DANCER MAKES HIS FINAL LEAP INTO BATTLE...
HE WILL GO DOWN **FIGHTING!**
SKRAnnnGGG

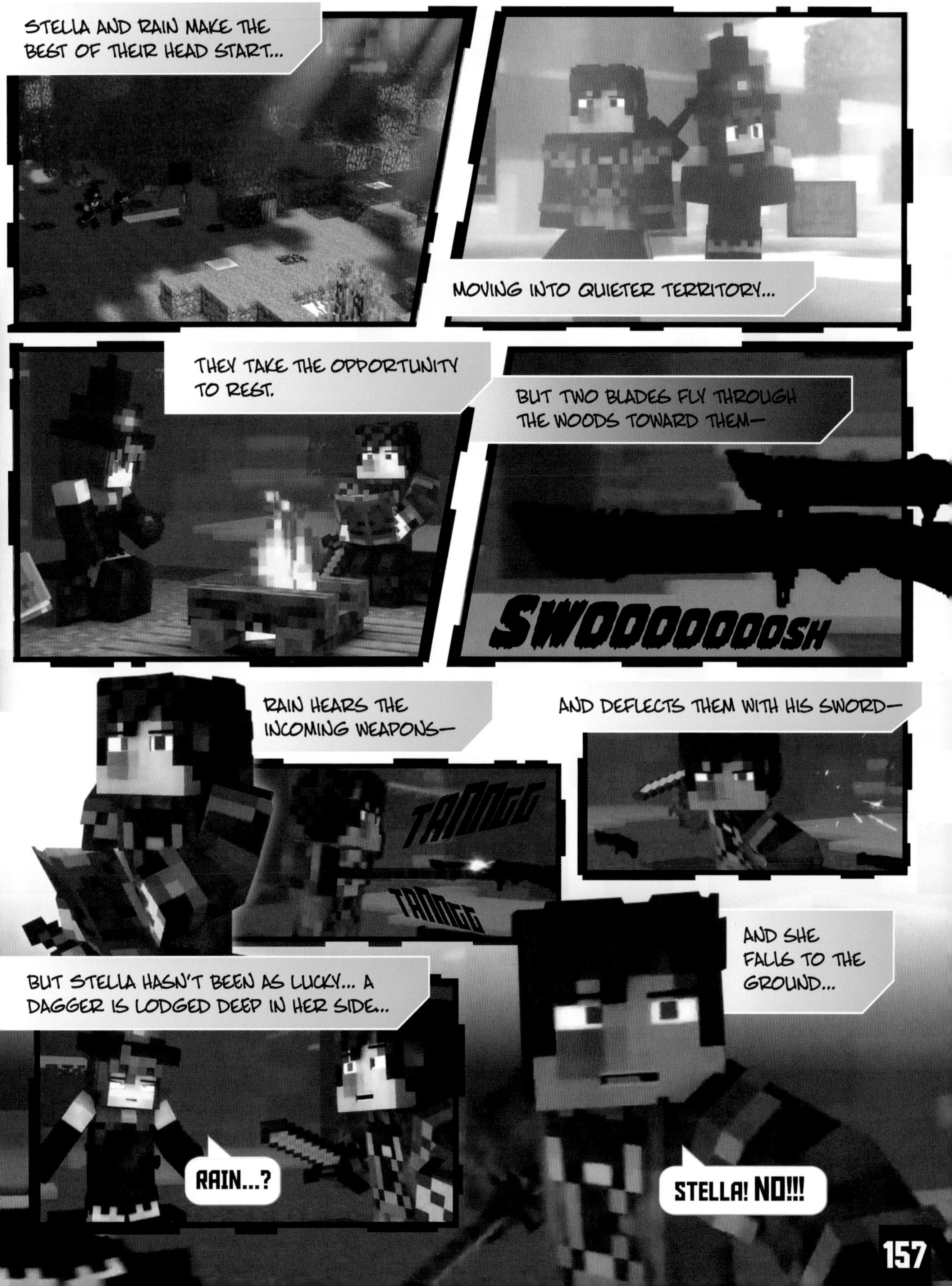

STELLA AND RAIN MAKE THE BEST OF THEIR HEAD START...
MOVING INTO QUIETER TERRITORY...
THEY TAKE THE OPPORTUNITY TO REST.
BUT TWO BLADES FLY THROUGH THE WOODS TOWARD THEM—
SWOOOOOOOSH
RAIN HEARS THE INCOMING WEAPONS—
TANNGG
TANNGG
AND DEFLECTS THEM WITH HIS SWORD—
BUT STELLA HASN'T BEEN AS LUCKY... A DAGGER IS LODGED DEEP IN HER SIDE...
RAIN...?
AND SHE FALLS TO THE GROUND...
STELLA! NO!!!

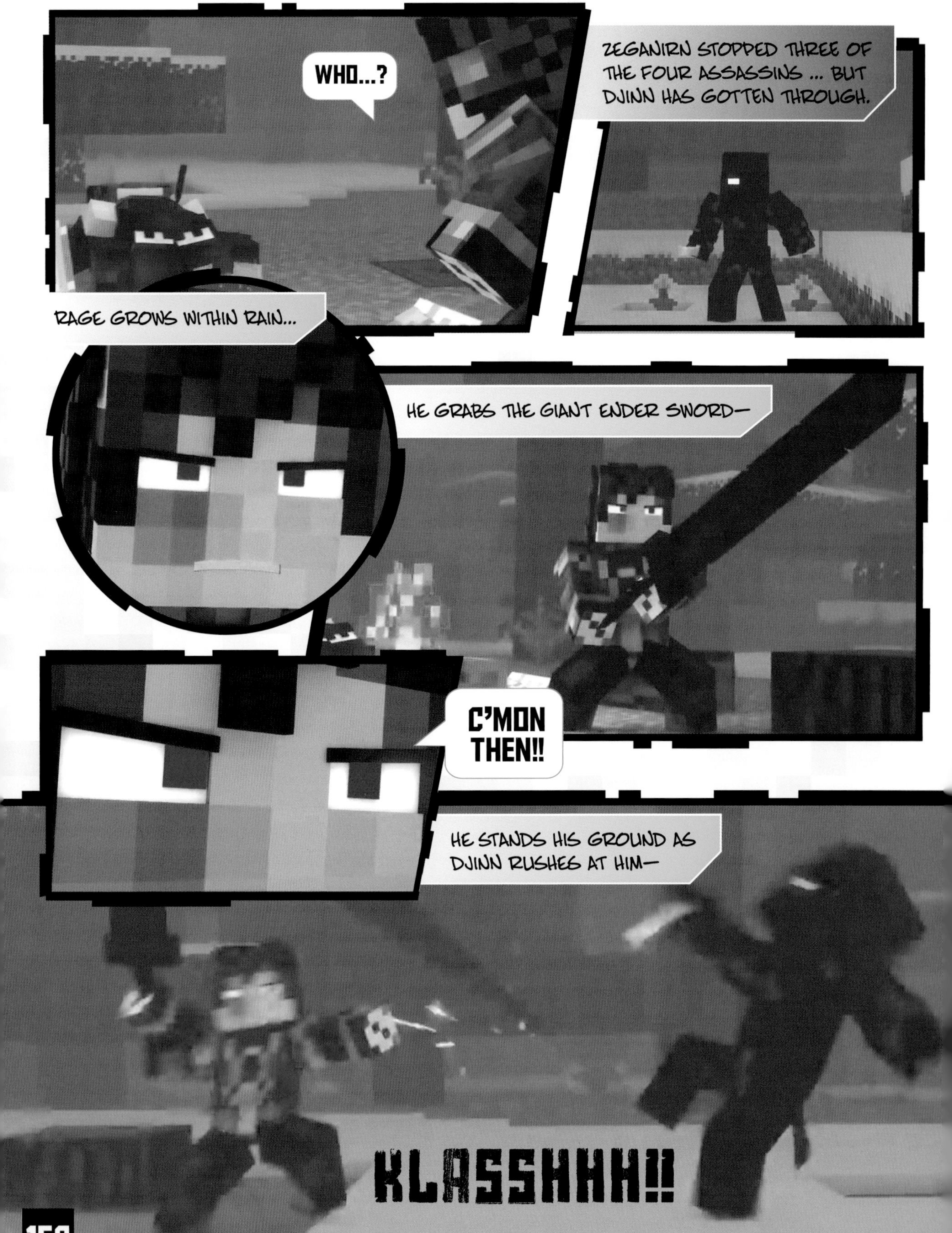
WHO...?
ZEGANIRN STOPPED THREE OF THE FOUR ASSASSINS ... BUT DJINN HAS GOTTEN THROUGH.
RAGE GROWS WITHIN RAIN...
HE GRABS THE GIANT ENDER SWORD—
C'MON THEN!!
HE STANDS HIS GROUND AS DJINN RUSHES AT HIM—
KLASSHHH!!

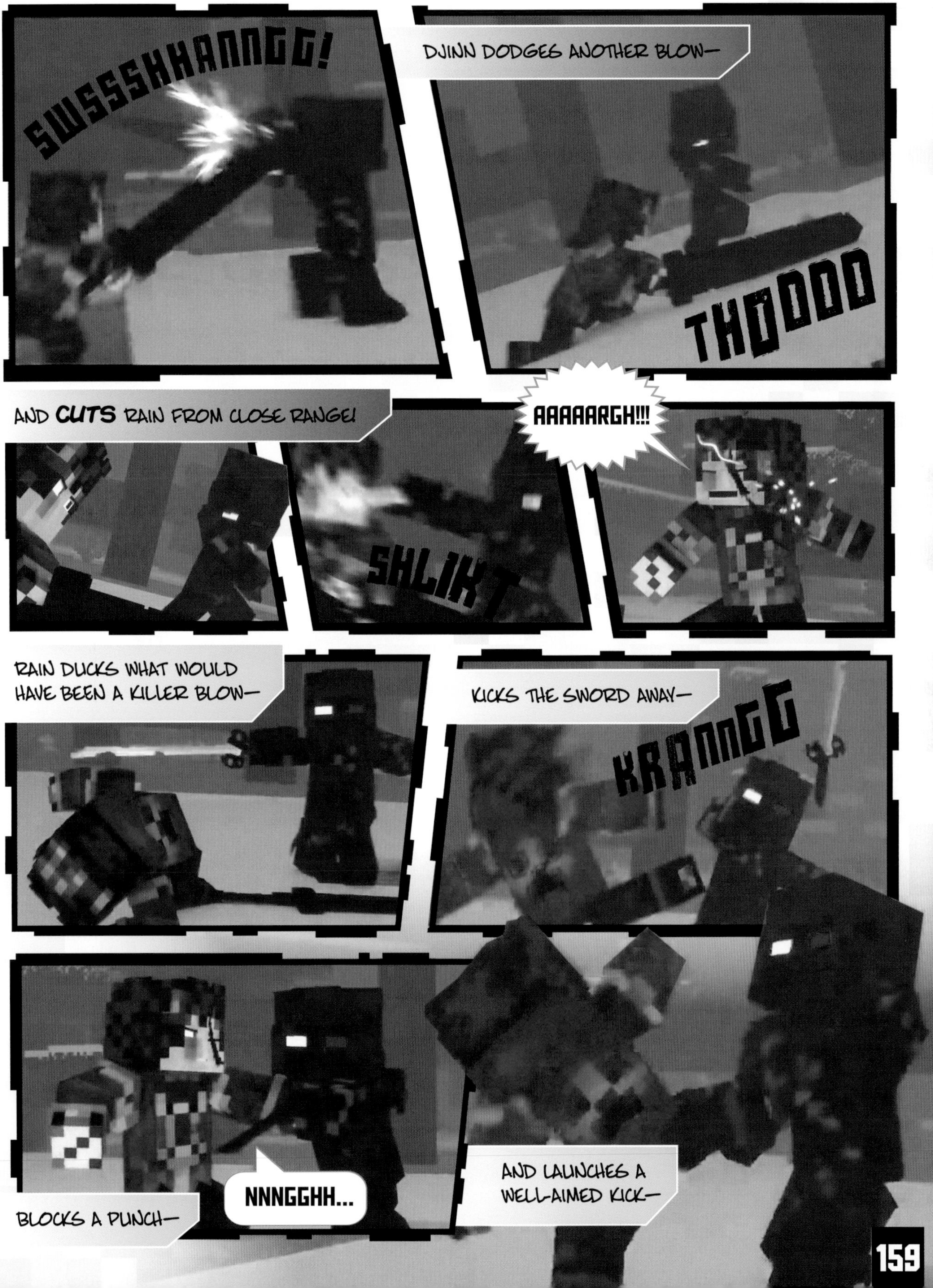
SWSSSHHANNGG!
DJINN DODGES ANOTHER BLOW—
THDDDD
AND CUTS RAIN FROM CLOSE RANGE!
SHLIKT
AAAAARGH!!!
RAIN DUCKS WHAT WOULD HAVE BEEN A KILLER BLOW—
KICKS THE SWORD AWAY—
KRANNGG
BLOCKS A PUNCH—
NNNGGHH...
AND LAUNCHES A WELL-AIMED KICK—

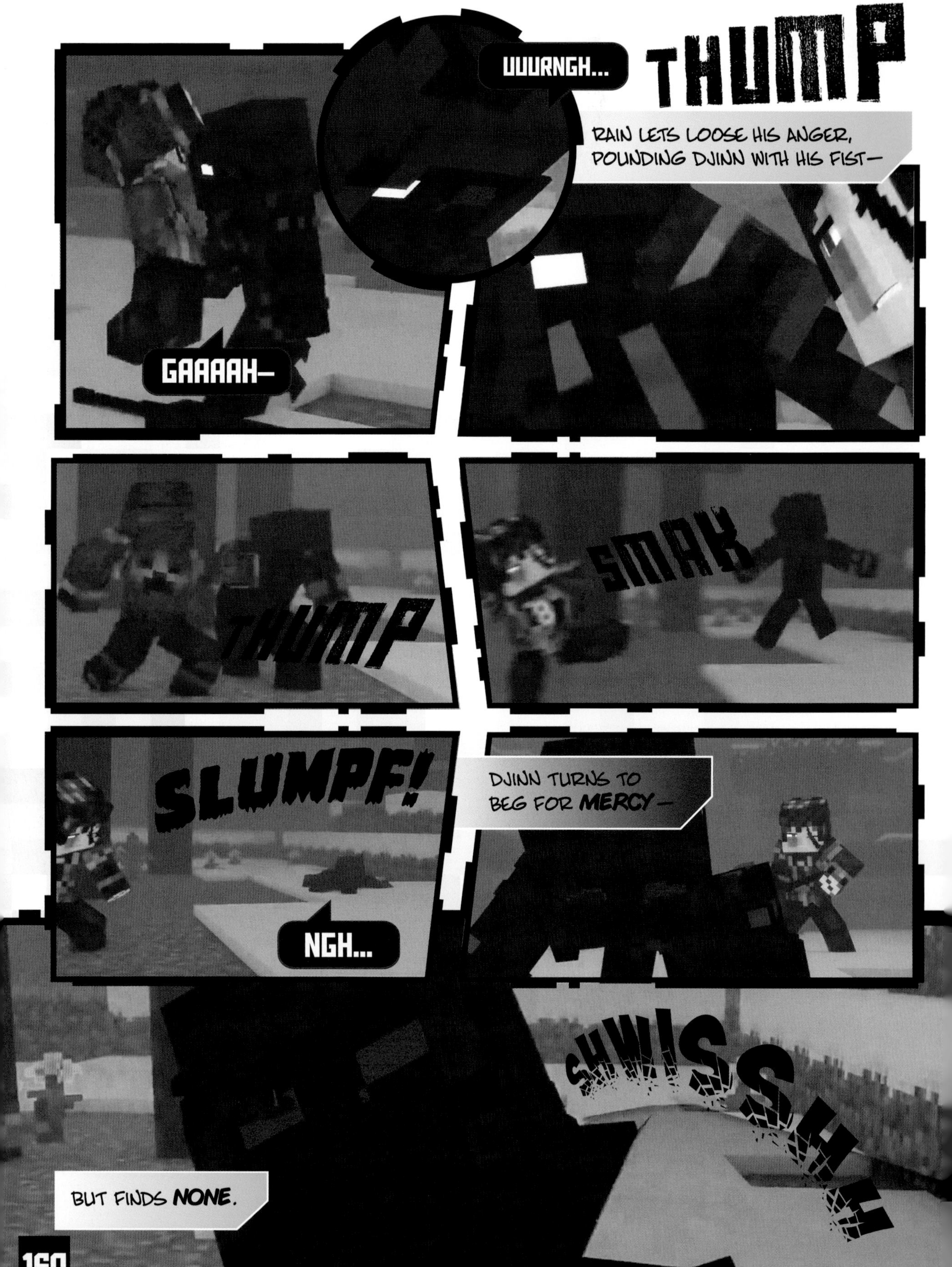

UUURNGH...
THUMP
RAIN LETS LOOSE HIS ANGER, POUNDING DJINN WITH HIS FIST—
GAAAAH—
THUMP
SMAK
SLUMPF!
NGH...
DJINN TURNS TO BEG FOR **MERCY**—
SHWISSSHM
BUT FINDS **NONE**.

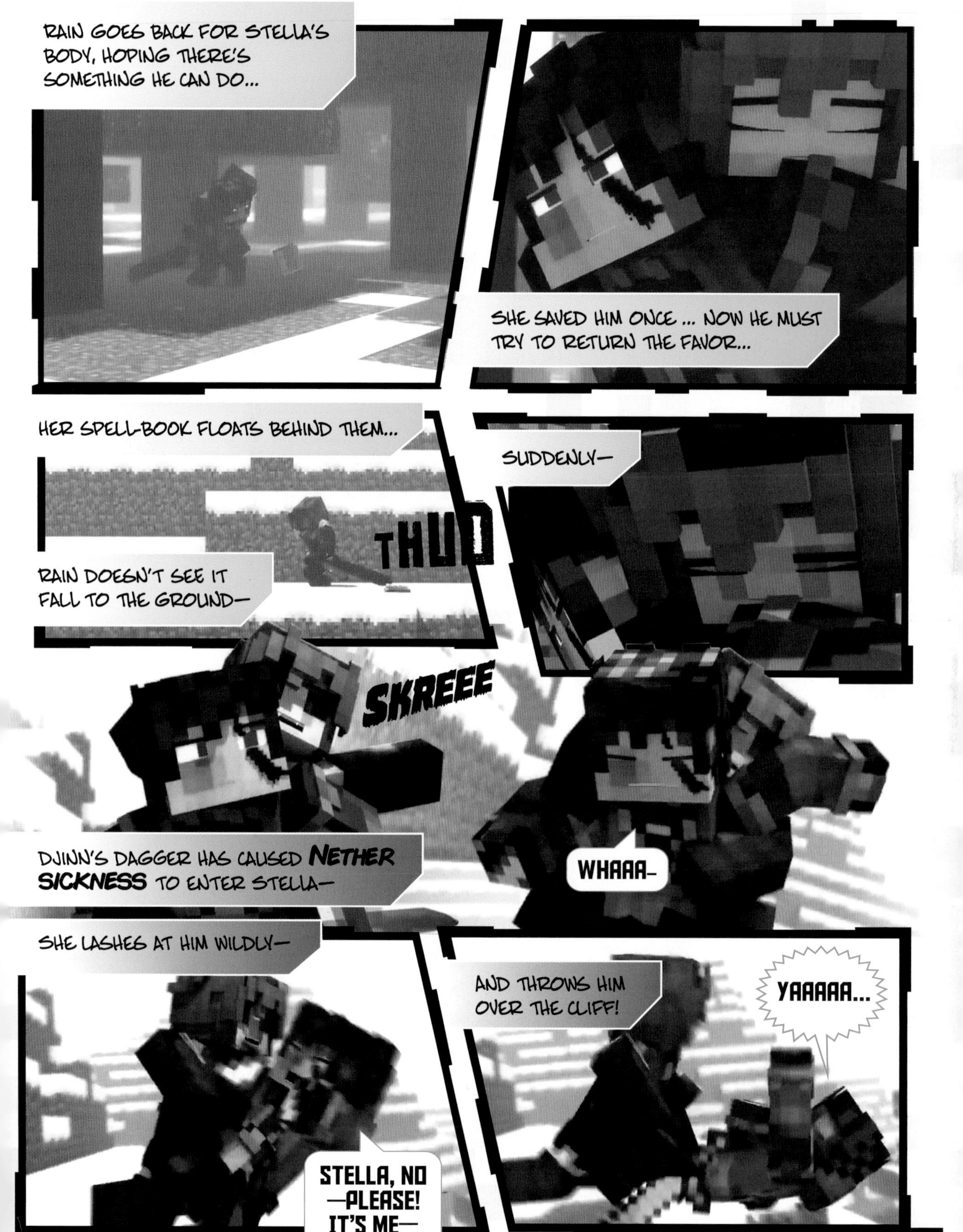

RAIN GOES BACK FOR STELLA'S BODY, HOPING THERE'S SOMETHING HE CAN DO...
SHE SAVED HIM ONCE ... NOW HE MUST TRY TO RETURN THE FAVOR...
HER SPELL-BOOK FLOATS BEHIND THEM...
THUD
RAIN DOESN'T SEE IT FALL TO THE GROUND—
SUDDENLY—
SKREEE
DJINN'S DAGGER HAS CAUSED NETHER SICKNESS TO ENTER STELLA—
WHAAA-
SHE LASHES AT HIM WILDLY—
STELLA, NO —PLEASE! IT'S ME—
AND THROWS HIM OVER THE CLIFF!
YAAAAA...

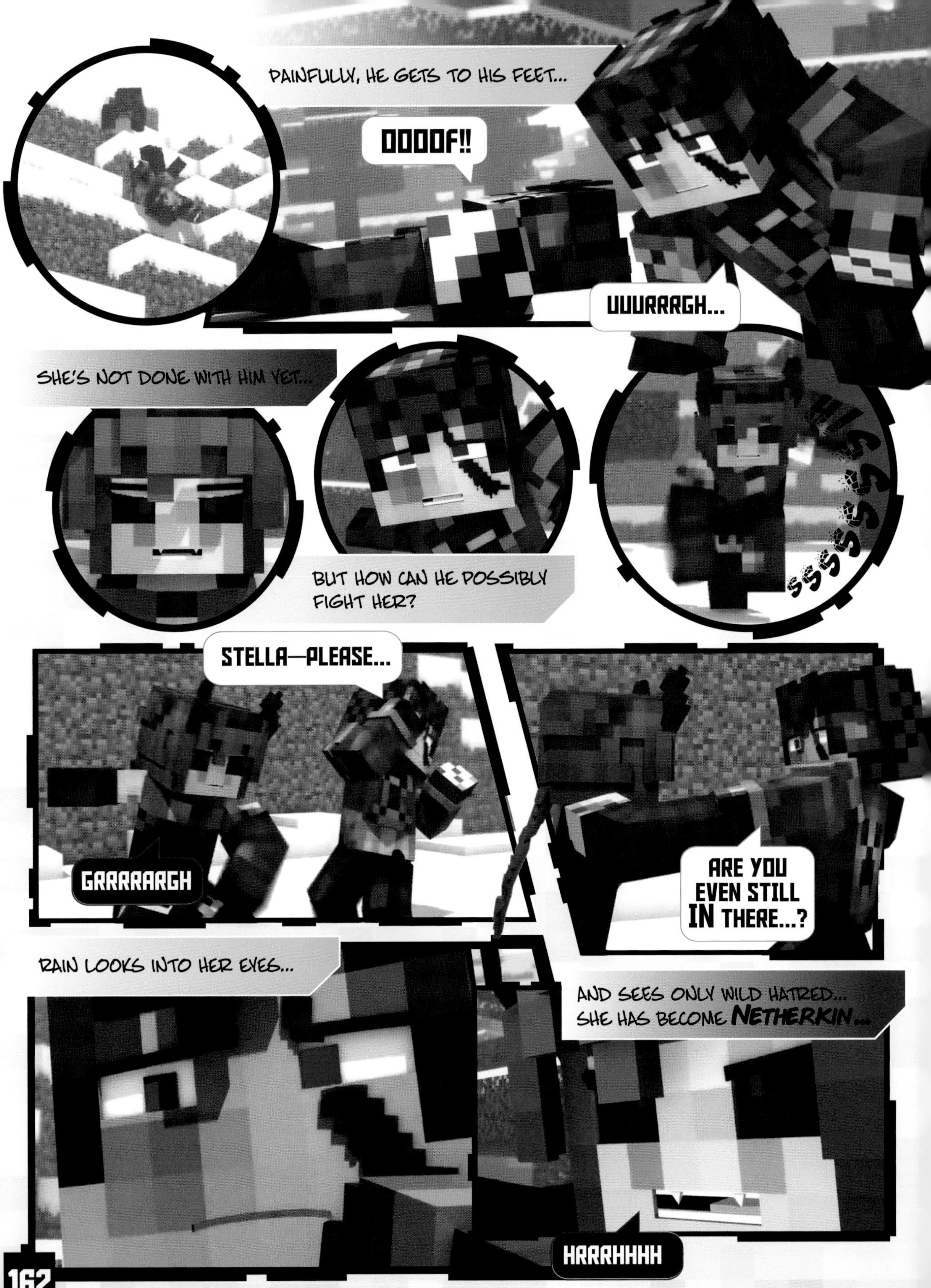
PAINFULLY, HE GETS TO HIS FEET...
OOOOF!!
UUURRRGH...
SHE'S NOT DONE WITH HIM YET...
BUT HOW CAN HE POSSIBLY FIGHT HER?
HISSSSSS
STELLA—PLEASE...
GRRRRARGH
ARE YOU EVEN STILL IN THERE...?
RAIN LOOKS INTO HER EYES...
AND SEES ONLY WILD HATRED... SHE HAS BECOME NETHERKIN...
HRRRHHHH

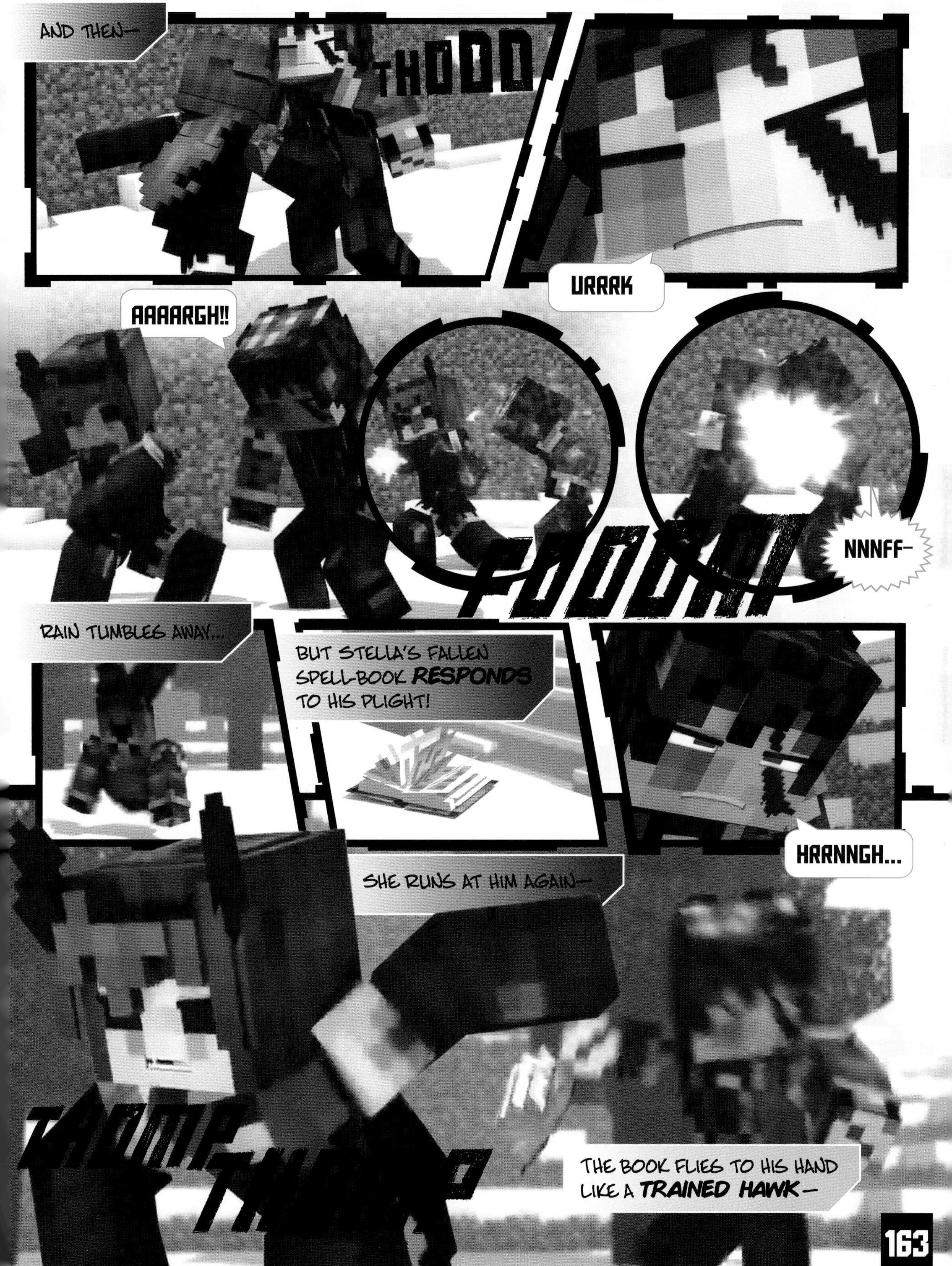
AND THEN—
THODD
URRRK
AAAARGH!!
NNNFF-
RAIN TUMBLES AWAY...
BUT STELLA'S FALLEN SPELL-BOOK RESPONDS TO HIS PLIGHT!
HRRNNGH...
SHE RUNS AT HIM AGAIN—
THE BOOK FLIES TO HIS HAND LIKE A TRAINED HAWK—

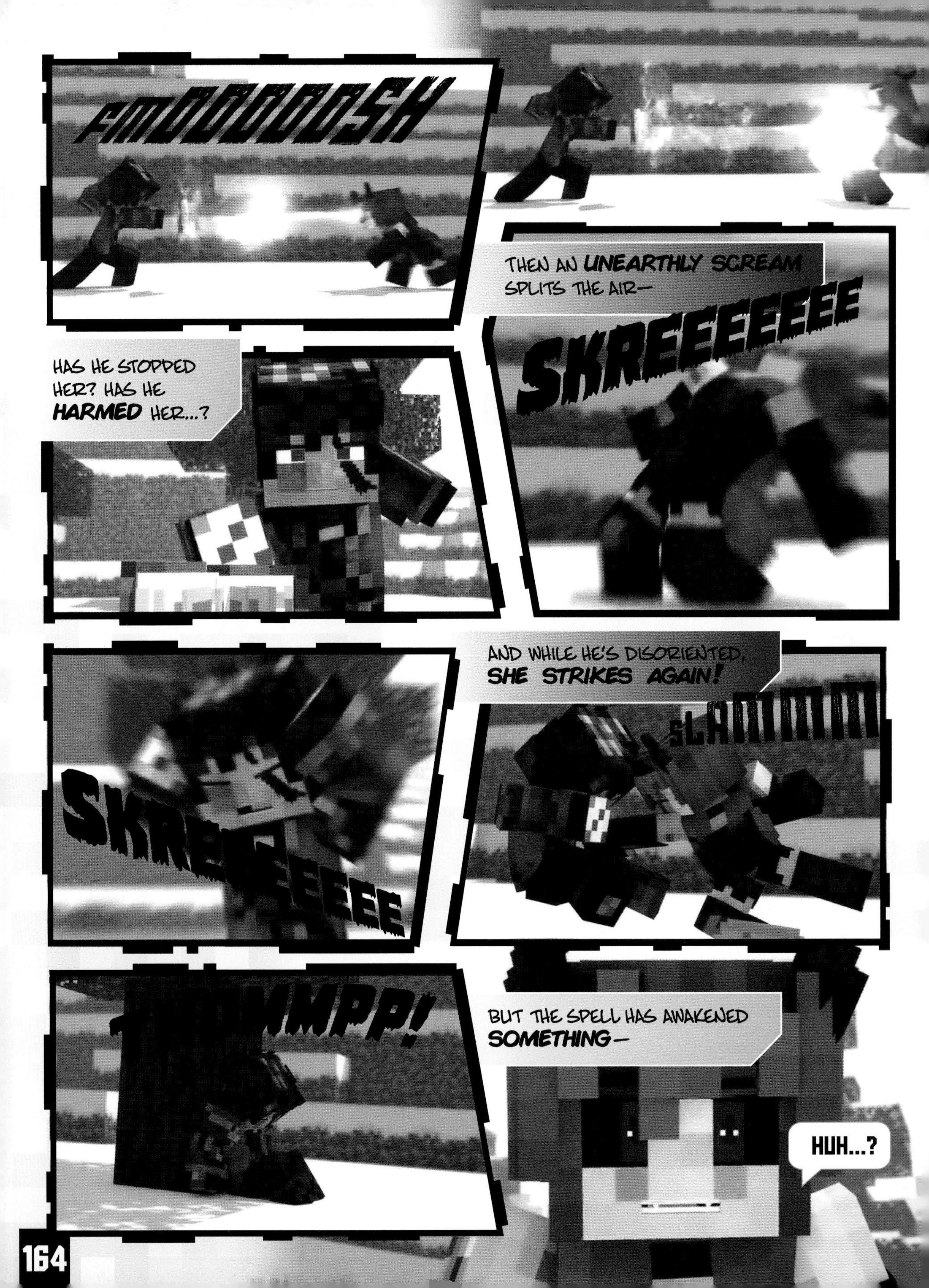
FWOOOOSH
THEN AN **UNEARTHLY** SCREAM SPLITS THE AIR—
SKREEEEEEEE
HAS HE STOPPED HER? HAS HE **HARMED** HER...?
AND WHILE HE'S DISORIENTED, **SHE STRIKES AGAIN!**
SKRE EEEE
SLAMMMM
MMPP!
BUT THE SPELL HAS AWAKENED **SOMETHING**—
HUH...?

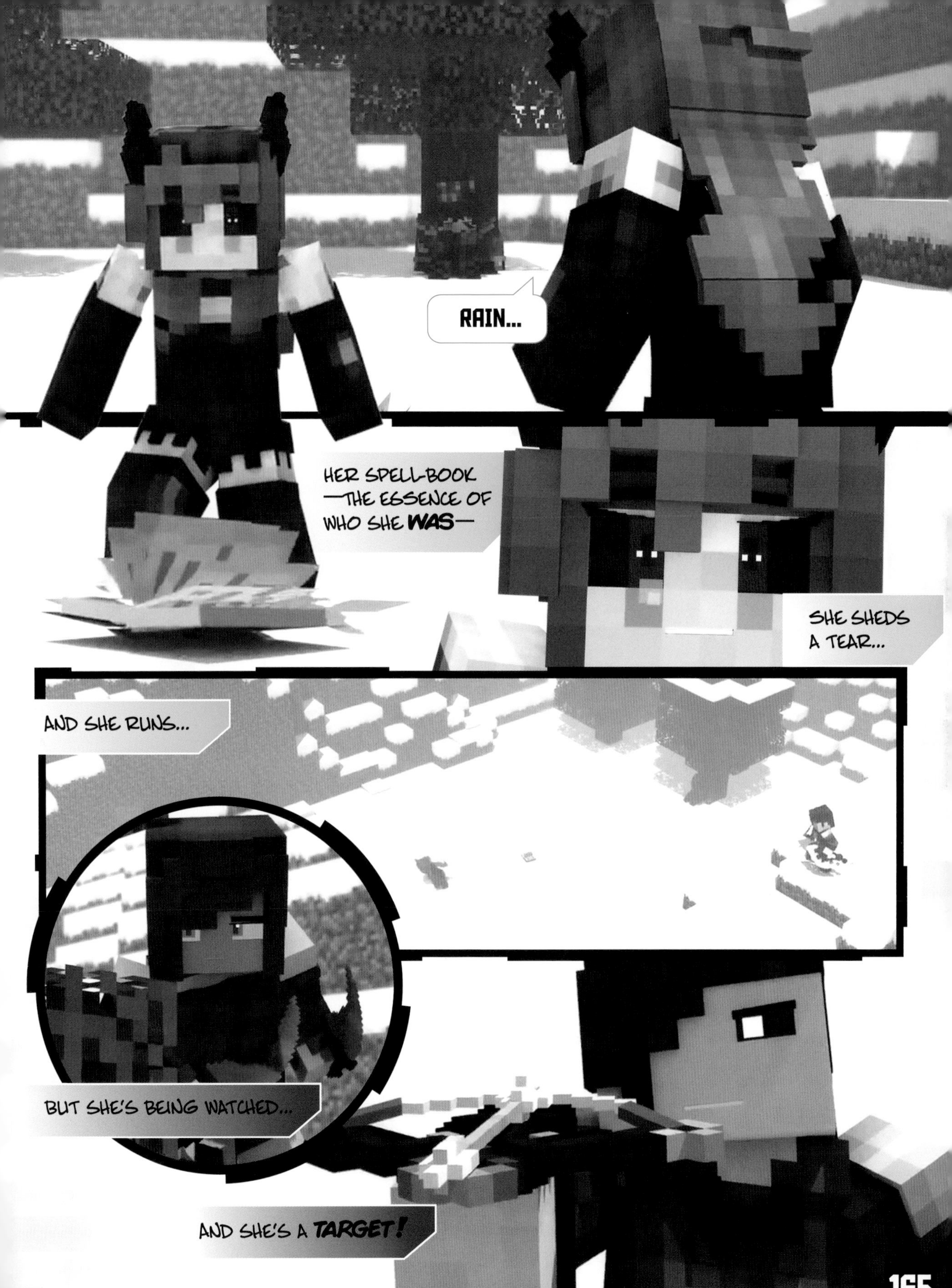
RAIN...
HER SPELL-BOOK —THE ESSENCE OF WHO SHE WAS—
SHE SHEDS A TEAR...
AND SHE RUNS...
BUT SHE'S BEING WATCHED...
AND SHE'S A TARGET!

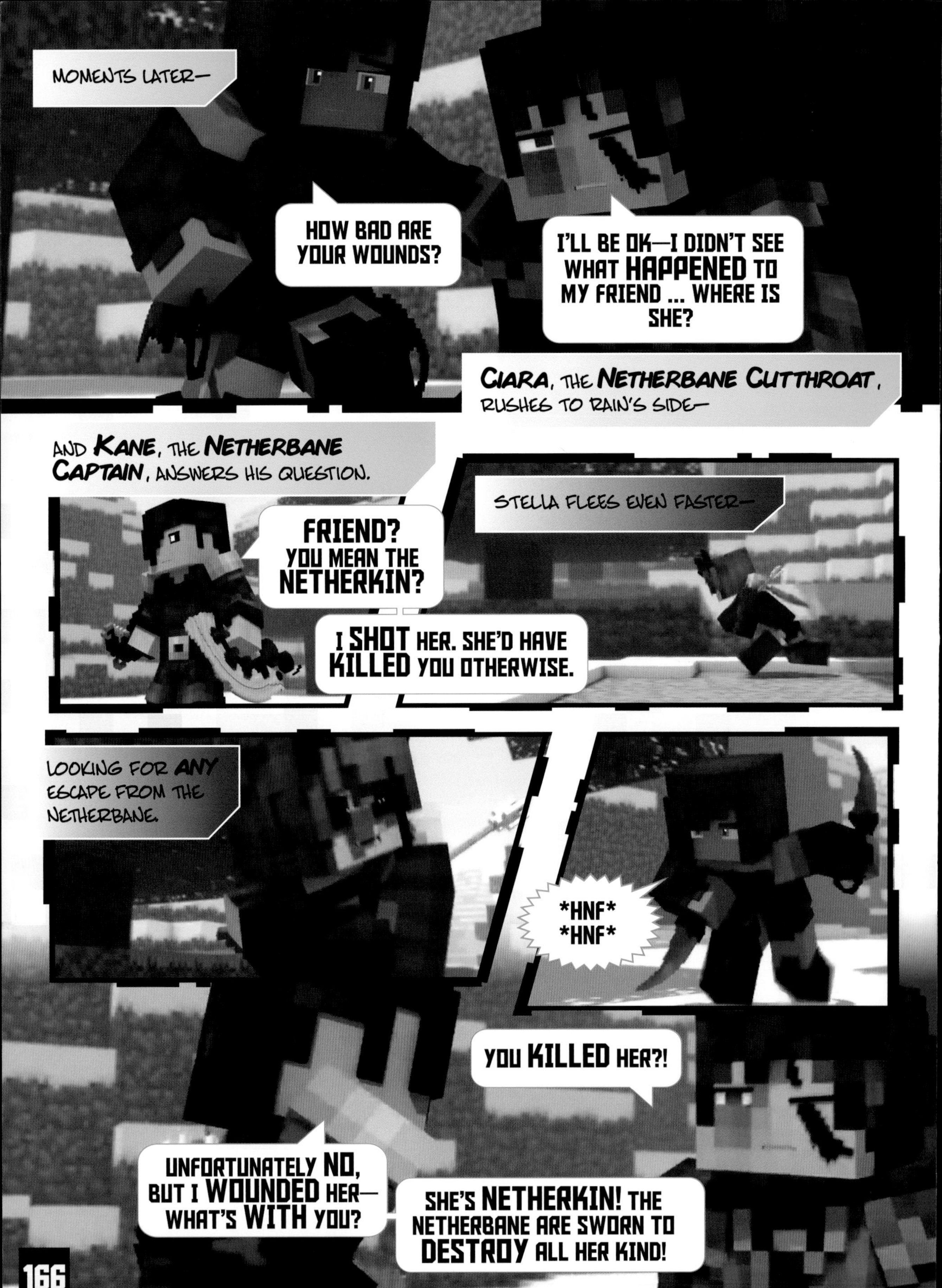
MOMENTS LATER—
HOW BAD ARE YOUR WOUNDS?
I'LL BE OK—I DIDN'T SEE WHAT HAPPENED TO MY FRIEND ... WHERE IS SHE?
CIARA, THE NETHERBANE CUTTHROAT, RUSHES TO RAIN'S SIDE—
AND KANE, THE NETHERBANE CAPTAIN, ANSWERS HIS QUESTION.
FRIEND? YOU MEAN THE NETHERKIN?
I SHOT HER. SHE'D HAVE KILLED YOU OTHERWISE.
STELLA FLEES EVEN FASTER—
LOOKING FOR ANY ESCAPE FROM THE NETHERBANE.
HNF *HNF*
YOU KILLED HER?!
UNFORTUNATELY NO, BUT I WOUNDED HER—WHAT'S WITH YOU?
SHE'S NETHERKIN! THE NETHERBANE ARE SWORN TO DESTROY ALL HER KIND!

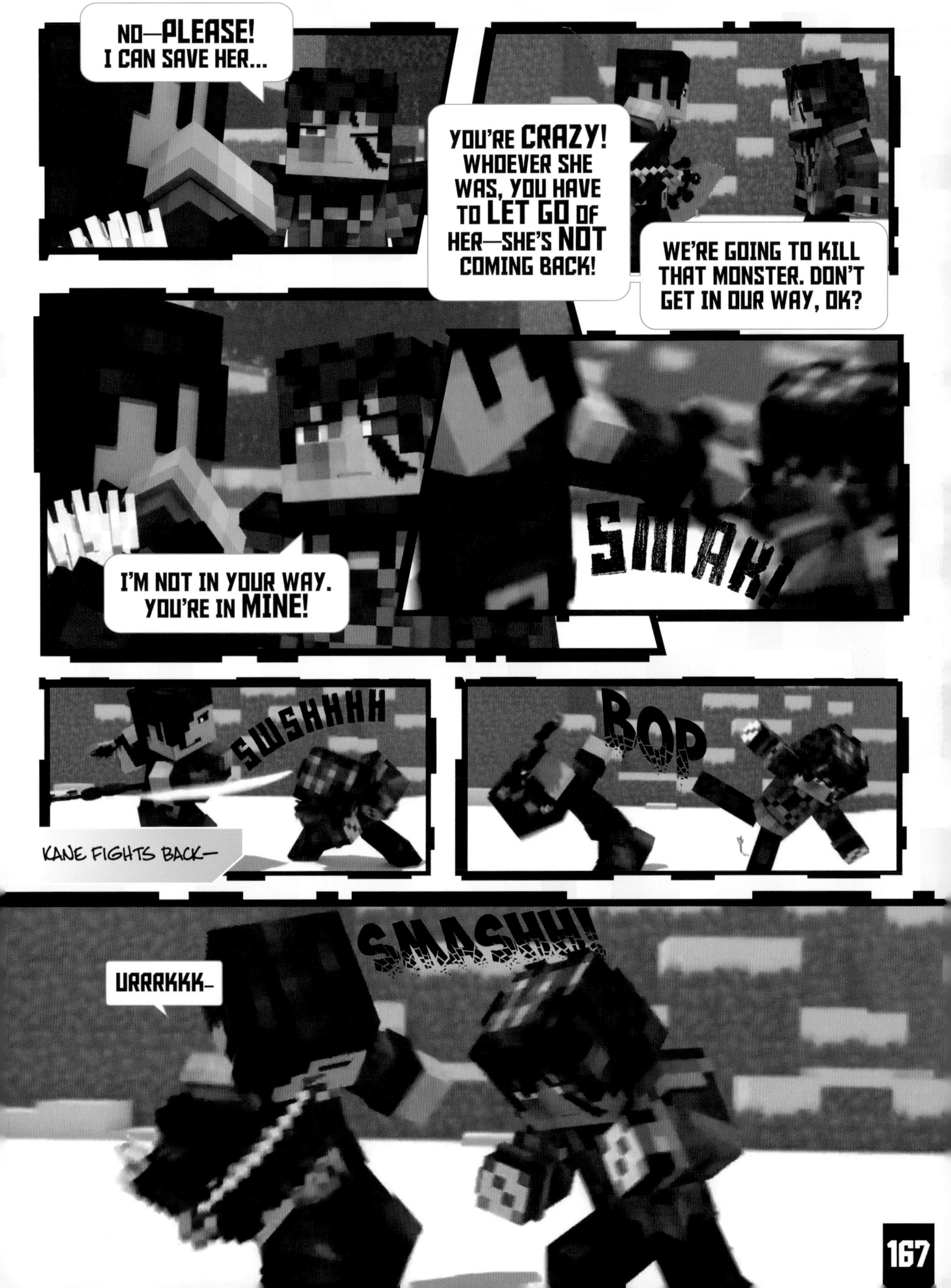
NO—PLEASE! I CAN SAVE HER...
YOU'RE CRAZY! WHOEVER SHE WAS, YOU HAVE TO LET GO OF HER—SHE'S NOT COMING BACK!
WE'RE GOING TO KILL THAT MONSTER. DON'T GET IN OUR WAY, OK?
I'M NOT IN YOUR WAY. YOU'RE IN MINE!
SMAK!
KANE FIGHTS BACK—
SWSHHHH
BOP
SMASHH!
URRRKKK-

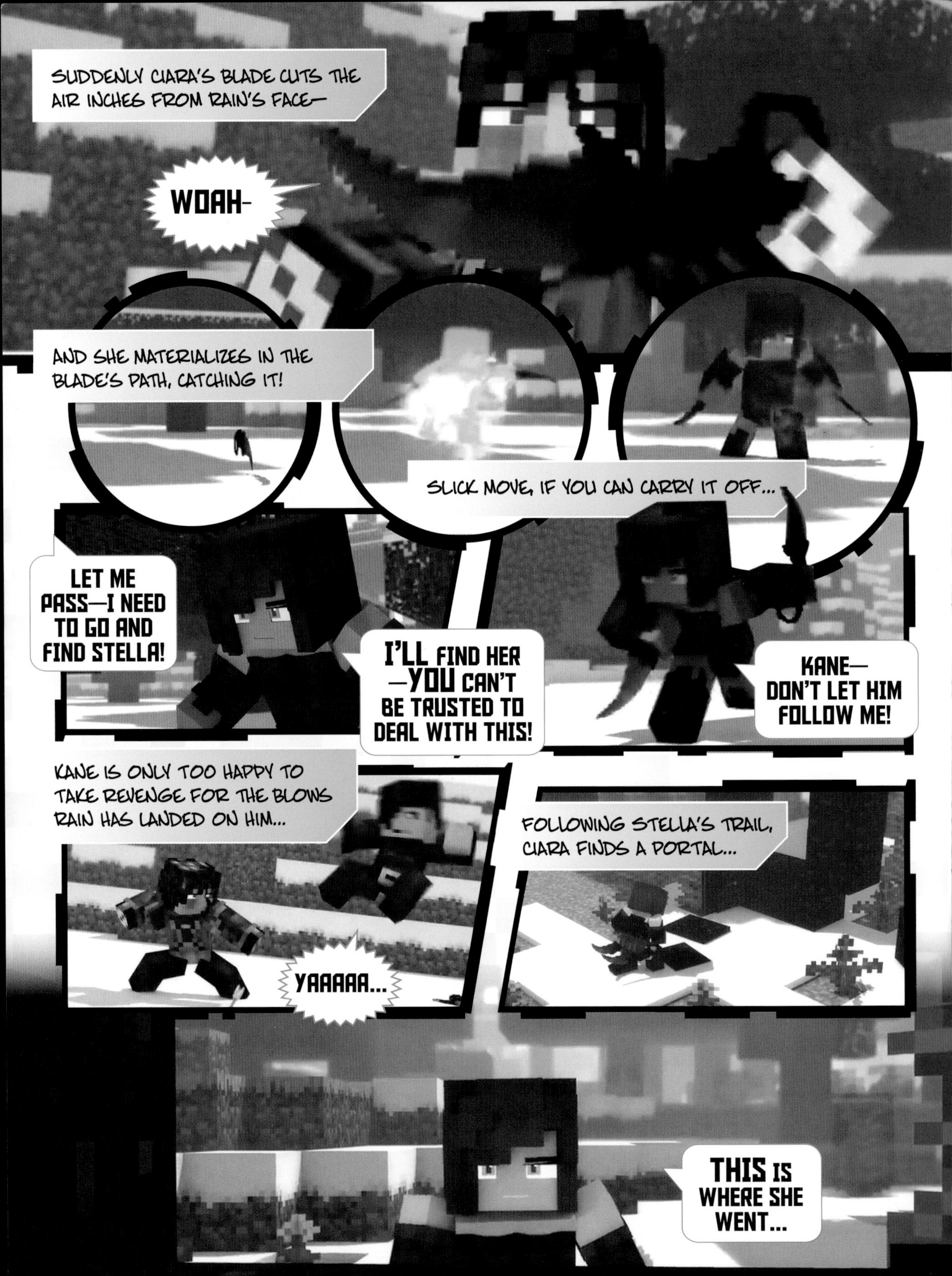
SUDDENLY CIARA'S BLADE CUTS THE AIR INCHES FROM RAIN'S FACE—
WOAH-
AND SHE MATERIALIZES IN THE BLADE'S PATH, CATCHING IT!
SLICK MOVE, IF YOU CAN CARRY IT OFF...
LET ME PASS—I NEED TO GO AND FIND STELLA!
I'LL FIND HER —YOU CAN'T BE TRUSTED TO DEAL WITH THIS!
KANE— DON'T LET HIM FOLLOW ME!
KANE IS ONLY TOO HAPPY TO TAKE REVENGE FOR THE BLOWS RAIN HAS LANDED ON HIM...
YAAAAA...
FOLLOWING STELLA'S TRAIL, CIARA FINDS A PORTAL...
THIS IS WHERE SHE WENT...

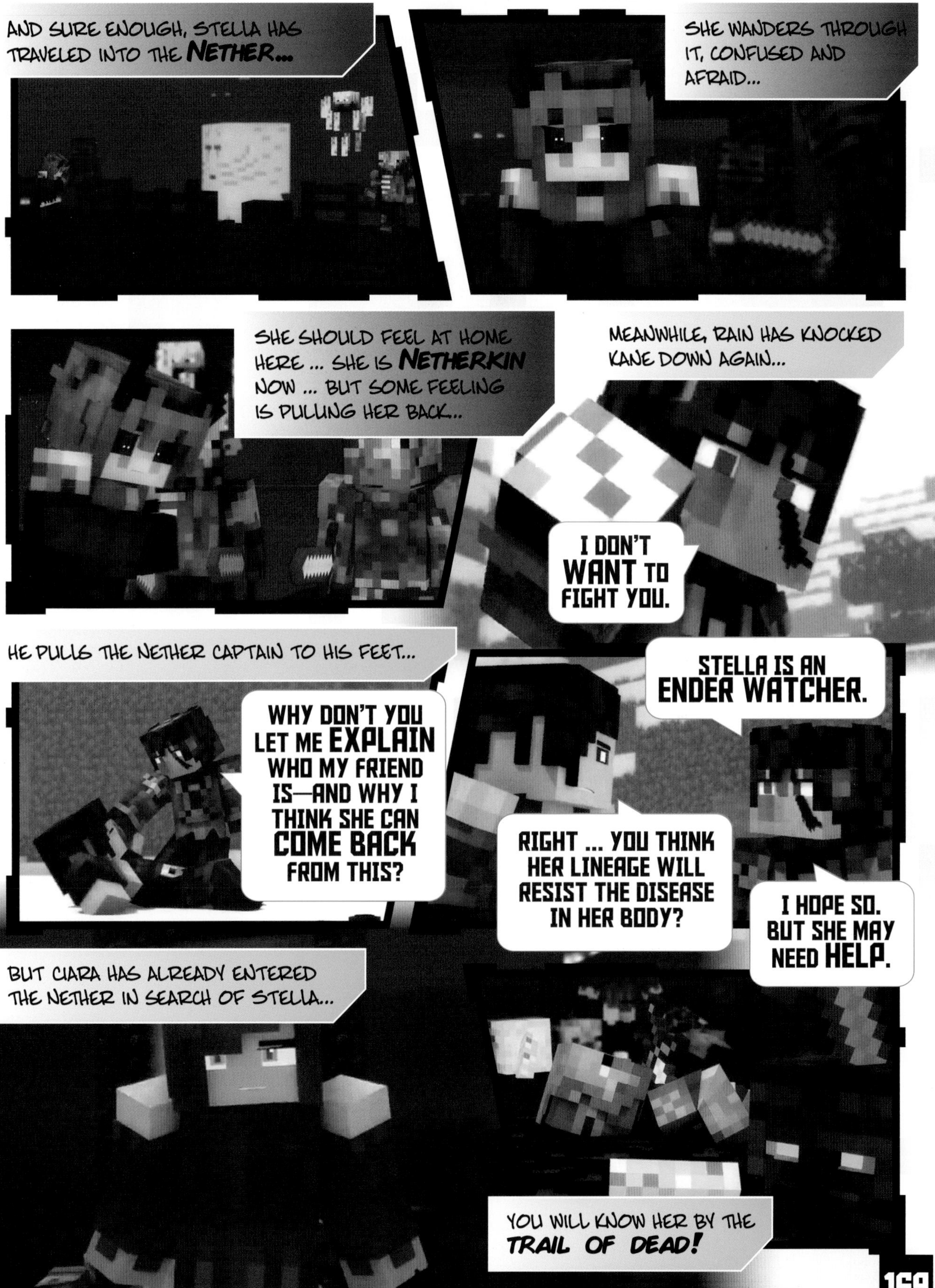
AND SURE ENOUGH, STELLA HAS TRAVELED INTO THE NETHER...
SHE WANDERS THROUGH IT, CONFUSED AND AFRAID...
SHE SHOULD FEEL AT HOME HERE ... SHE IS NETHERKIN NOW ... BUT SOME FEELING IS PULLING HER BACK...
MEANWHILE, RAIN HAS KNOCKED KANE DOWN AGAIN...
I DON'T WANT TO FIGHT YOU.
HE PULLS THE NETHER CAPTAIN TO HIS FEET...
WHY DON'T YOU LET ME EXPLAIN WHO MY FRIEND IS—AND WHY I THINK SHE CAN COME BACK FROM THIS?
STELLA IS AN ENDER WATCHER.
RIGHT ... YOU THINK HER LINEAGE WILL RESIST THE DISEASE IN HER BODY?
I HOPE SO. BUT SHE MAY NEED HELP.
BUT CIARA HAS ALREADY ENTERED THE NETHER IN SEARCH OF STELLA...
YOU WILL KNOW HER BY THE TRAIL OF DEAD!

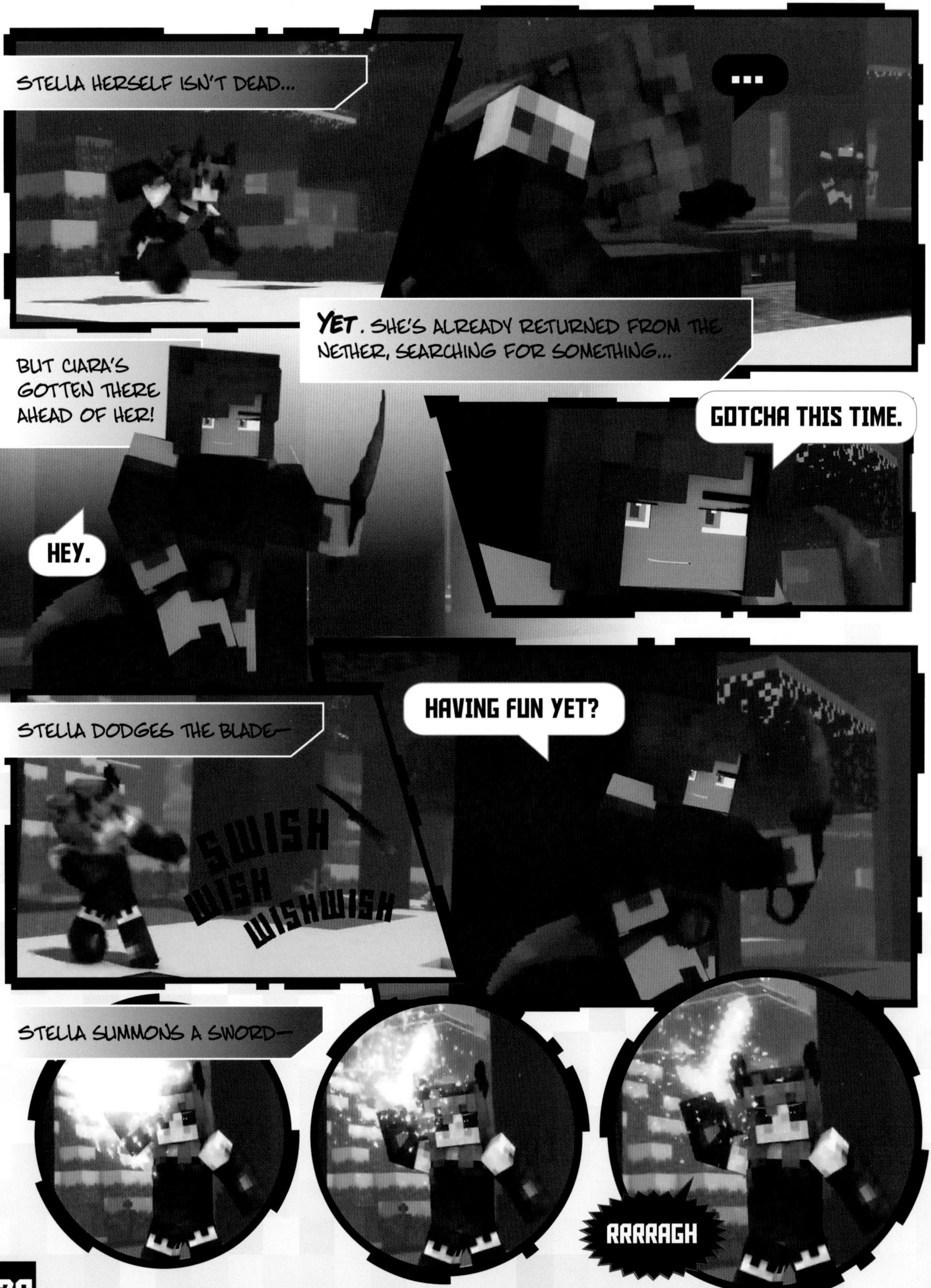
STELLA HERSELF ISN'T DEAD...
...
YET. SHE'S ALREADY RETURNED FROM THE NETHER, SEARCHING FOR SOMETHING...
BUT CIARA'S GOTTEN THERE AHEAD OF HER!
HEY.
GOTCHA THIS TIME.
STELLA DODGES THE BLADE—
SWISH
WISH
WISHWISH
HAVING FUN YET?
STELLA SUMMONS A SWORD—
RRRRAGH

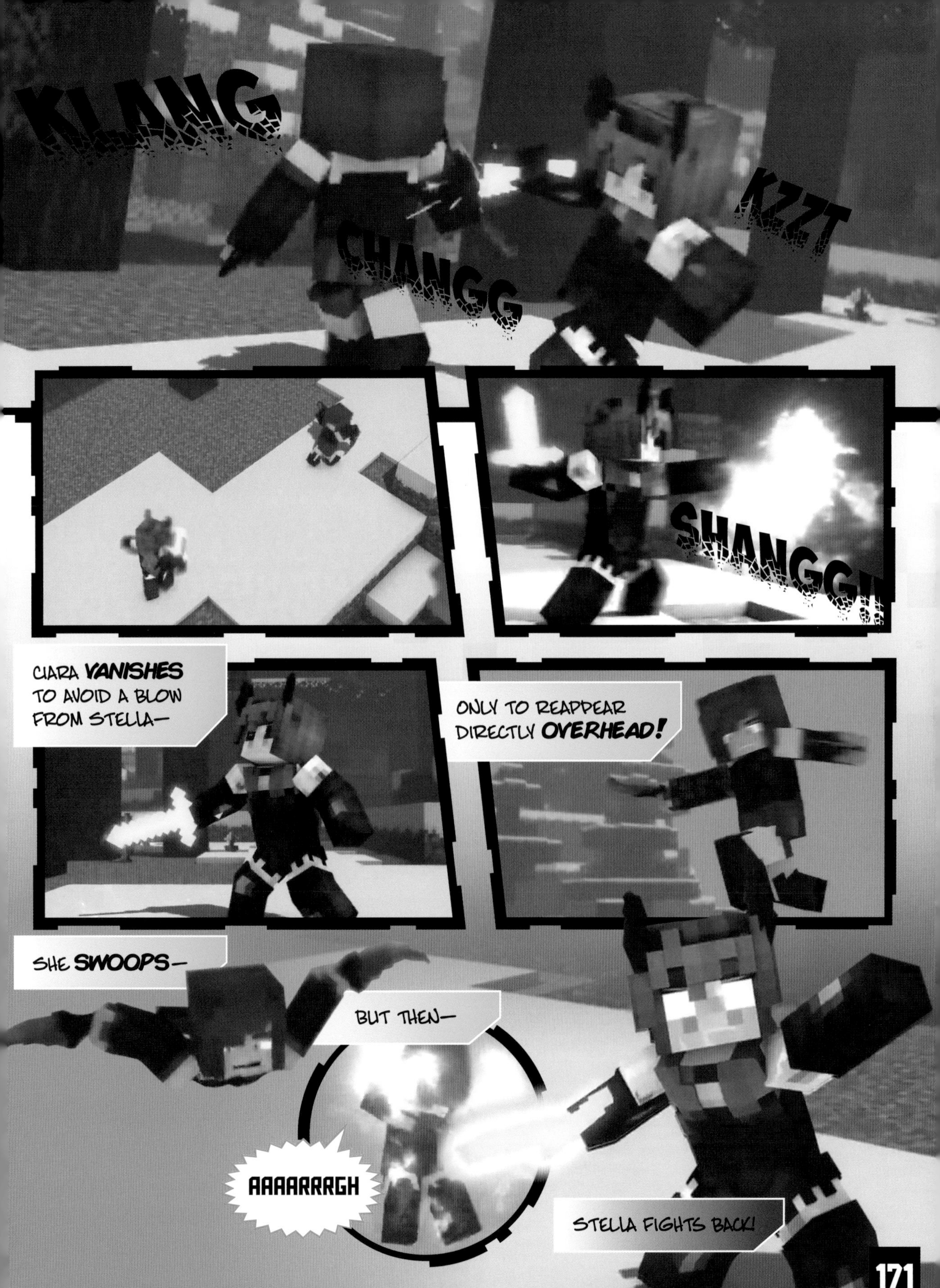
KLANG
CHANGG
KZZT
SHANGG!!
CIARA VANISHES TO AVOID A BLOW FROM STELLA—
ONLY TO REAPPEAR DIRECTLY OVERHEAD!
SHE SWOOPS—
BUT THEN—
AAAAARRRGH
STELLA FIGHTS BACK!

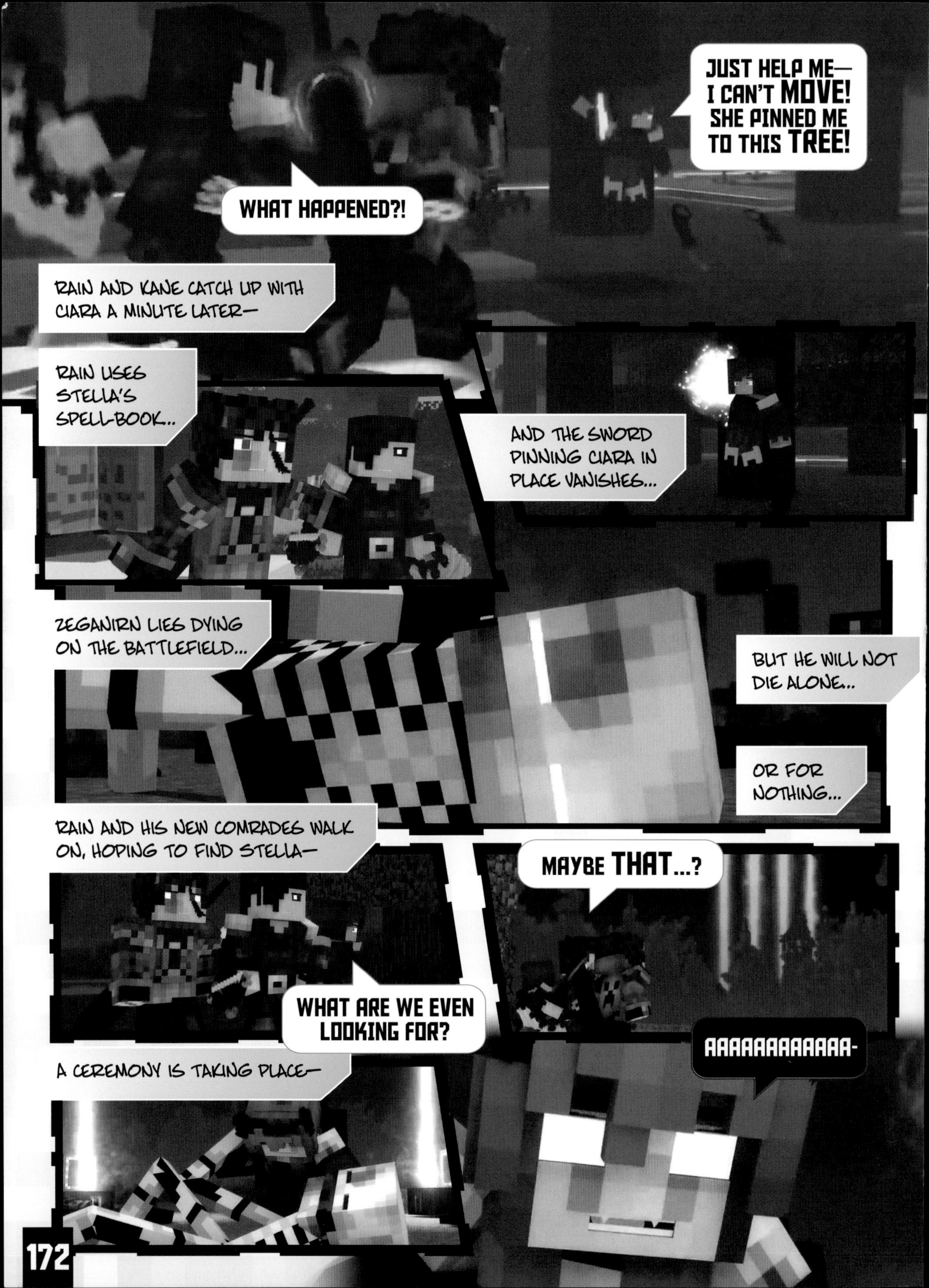

JUST HELP ME— I CAN'T MOVE! SHE PINNED ME TO THIS TREE!
WHAT HAPPENED?!
RAIN AND KANE CATCH UP WITH CIARA A MINUTE LATER—
RAIN USES STELLA'S SPELL-BOOK...
AND THE SWORD PINNING CIARA IN PLACE VANISHES...
ZEGANIRN LIES DYING ON THE BATTLEFIELD...
BUT HE WILL NOT DIE ALONE...
OR FOR NOTHING...
RAIN AND HIS NEW COMRADES WALK ON, HOPING TO FIND STELLA—
WHAT ARE WE EVEN LOOKING FOR?
MAYBE THAT...?
A CEREMONY IS TAKING PLACE—
AAAAAAAAAAAA-

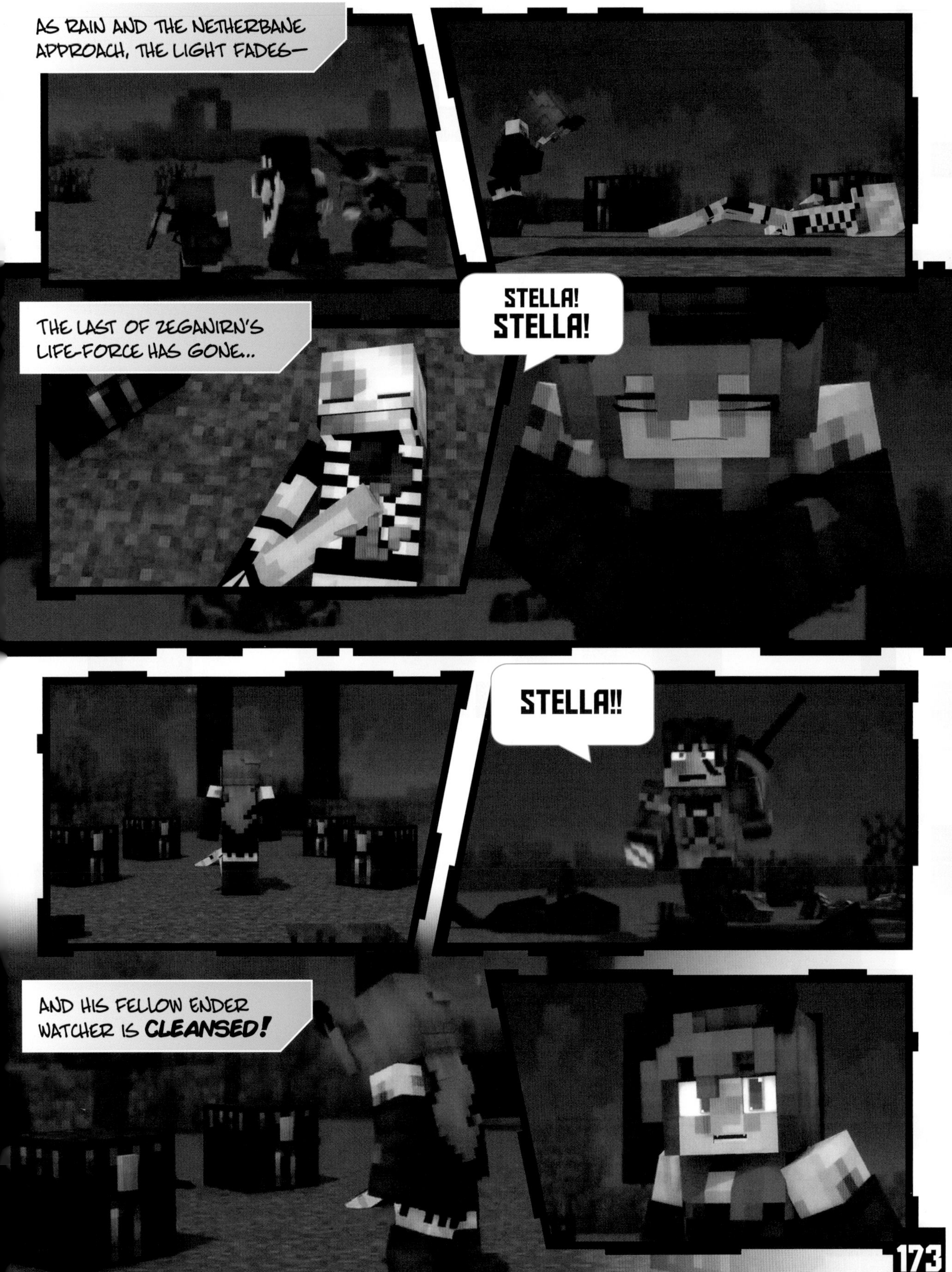
AS RAIN AND THE NETHERBANE APPROACH, THE LIGHT FADES—
THE LAST OF ZEGANIRN'S LIFE-FORCE HAS GONE...
STELLA! STELLA!
STELLA!!
AND HIS FELLOW ENDER WATCHER IS CLEANSED!

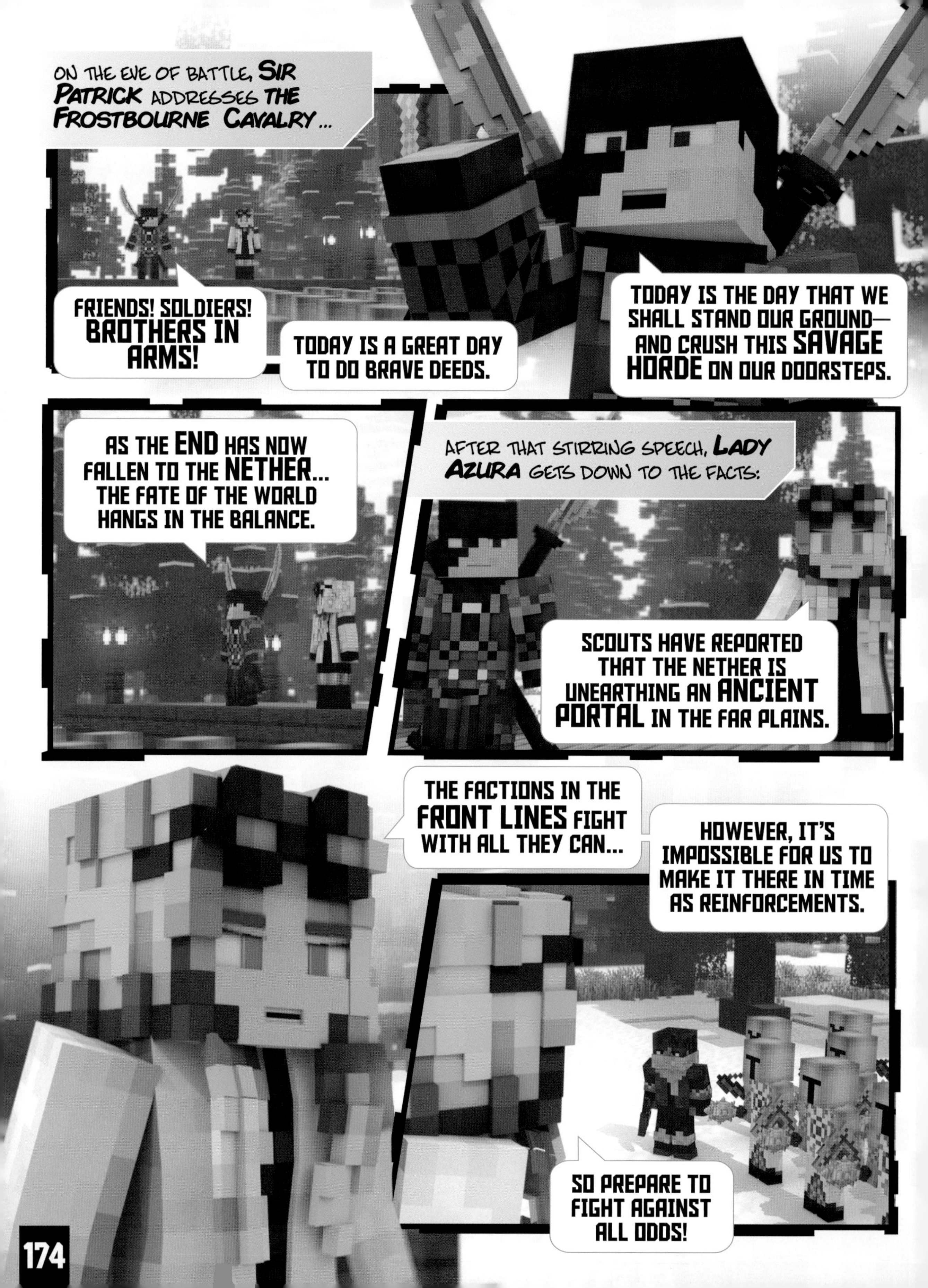
ON THE EVE OF BATTLE, SIR PATRICK ADDRESSES THE FROSTBOURNE CAVALRY...
FRIENDS! SOLDIERS! BROTHERS IN ARMS!
TODAY IS A GREAT DAY TO DO BRAVE DEEDS.
TODAY IS THE DAY THAT WE SHALL STAND OUR GROUND— AND CRUSH THIS SAVAGE HORDE ON OUR DOORSTEPS.
AS THE END HAS NOW FALLEN TO THE NETHER... THE FATE OF THE WORLD HANGS IN THE BALANCE.
AFTER THAT STIRRING SPEECH, LADY AZURA GETS DOWN TO THE FACTS:
SCOUTS HAVE REPORTED THAT THE NETHER IS UNEARTHING AN ANCIENT PORTAL IN THE FAR PLAINS.
THE FACTIONS IN THE FRONT LINES FIGHT WITH ALL THEY CAN...
HOWEVER, IT'S IMPOSSIBLE FOR US TO MAKE IT THERE IN TIME AS REINFORCEMENTS.
SO PREPARE TO FIGHT AGAINST ALL ODDS!

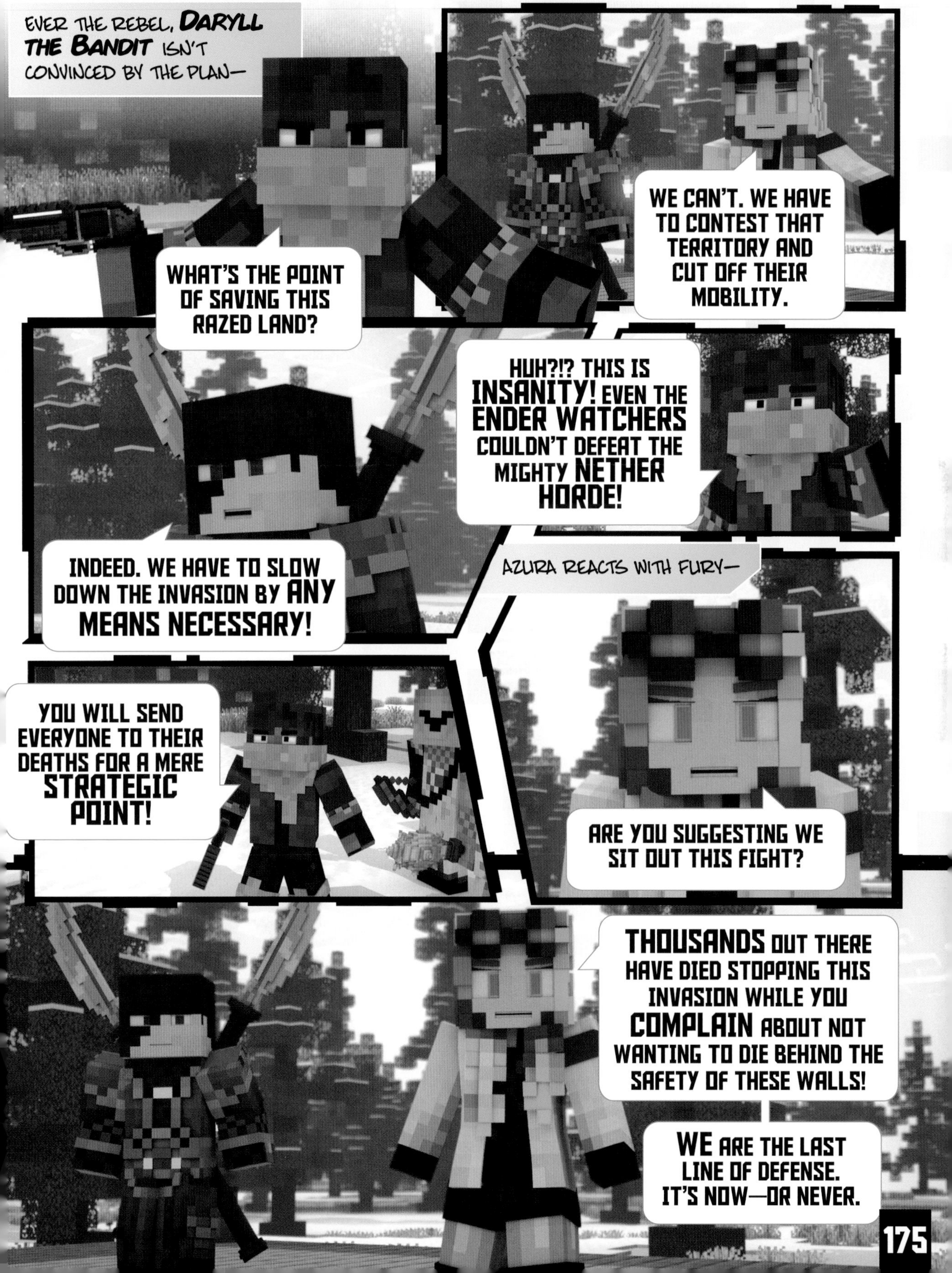
EVER THE REBEL, DARYLL THE BANDIT ISN'T CONVINCED BY THE PLAN—
WHAT'S THE POINT OF SAVING THIS RAZED LAND?
WE CAN'T. WE HAVE TO CONTEST THAT TERRITORY AND CUT OFF THEIR MOBILITY.
HUH?!? THIS IS INSANITY! EVEN THE ENDER WATCHERS COULDN'T DEFEAT THE MIGHTY NETHER HORDE!
INDEED. WE HAVE TO SLOW DOWN THE INVASION BY ANY MEANS NECESSARY!
AZURA REACTS WITH FURY—
YOU WILL SEND EVERYONE TO THEIR DEATHS FOR A MERE STRATEGIC POINT!
ARE YOU SUGGESTING WE SIT OUT THIS FIGHT?
THOUSANDS OUT THERE HAVE DIED STOPPING THIS INVASION WHILE YOU COMPLAIN ABOUT NOT WANTING TO DIE BEHIND THE SAFETY OF THESE WALLS!
WE ARE THE LAST LINE OF DEFENSE. IT'S NOW—OR NEVER.

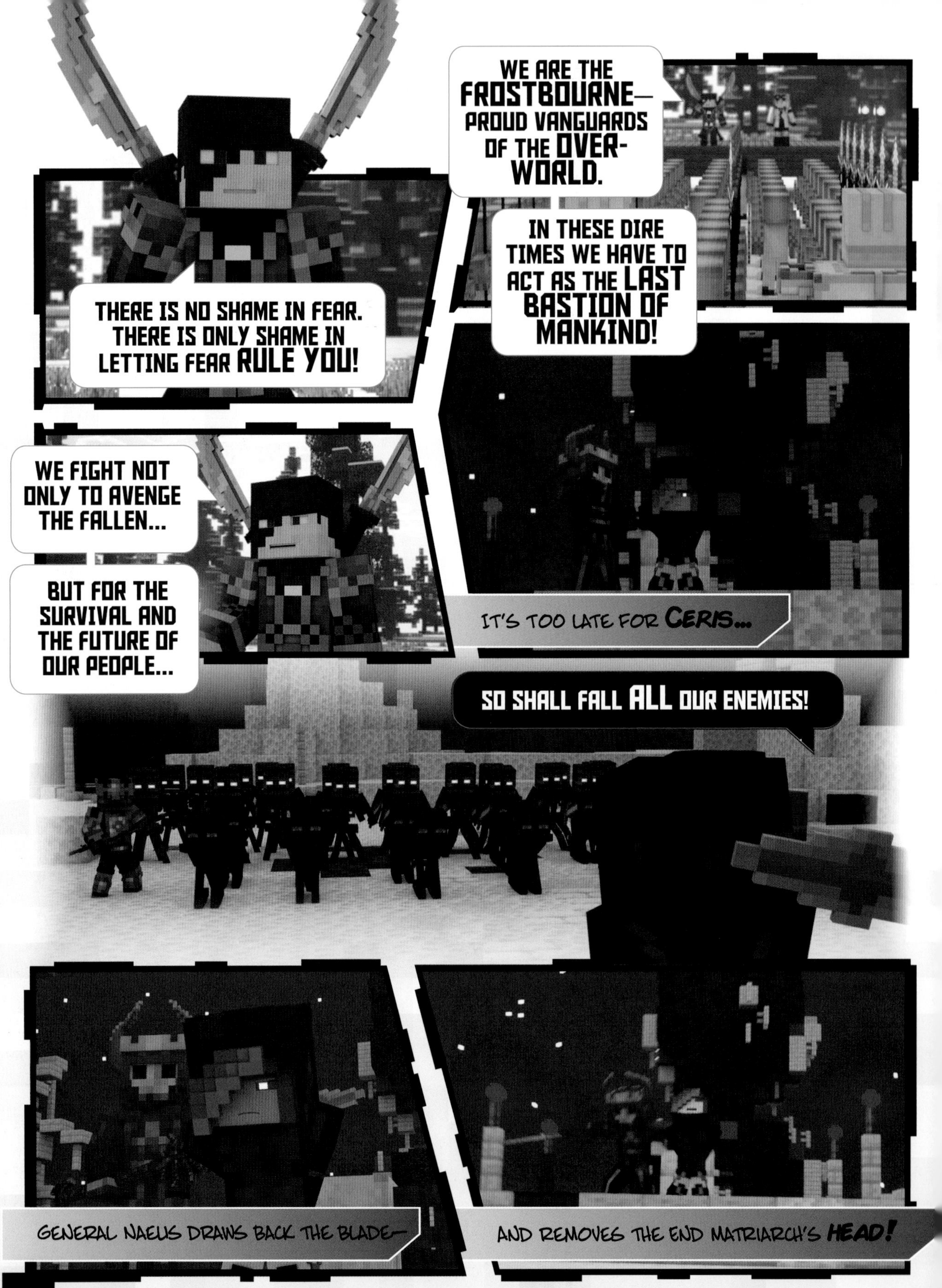

THERE IS NO SHAME IN FEAR. THERE IS ONLY SHAME IN LETTING FEAR RULE YOU!
WE ARE THE FROSTBOURNE—PROUD VANGUARDS OF THE OVER-WORLD.
IN THESE DIRE TIMES WE HAVE TO ACT AS THE LAST BASTION OF MANKIND!
WE FIGHT NOT ONLY TO AVENGE THE FALLEN...
BUT FOR THE SURVIVAL AND THE FUTURE OF OUR PEOPLE...
IT'S TOO LATE FOR CERIS...
SO SHALL FALL ALL OUR ENEMIES!
GENERAL NAEUS DRAWS BACK THE BLADE—
AND REMOVES THE END MATRIARCH'S HEAD!

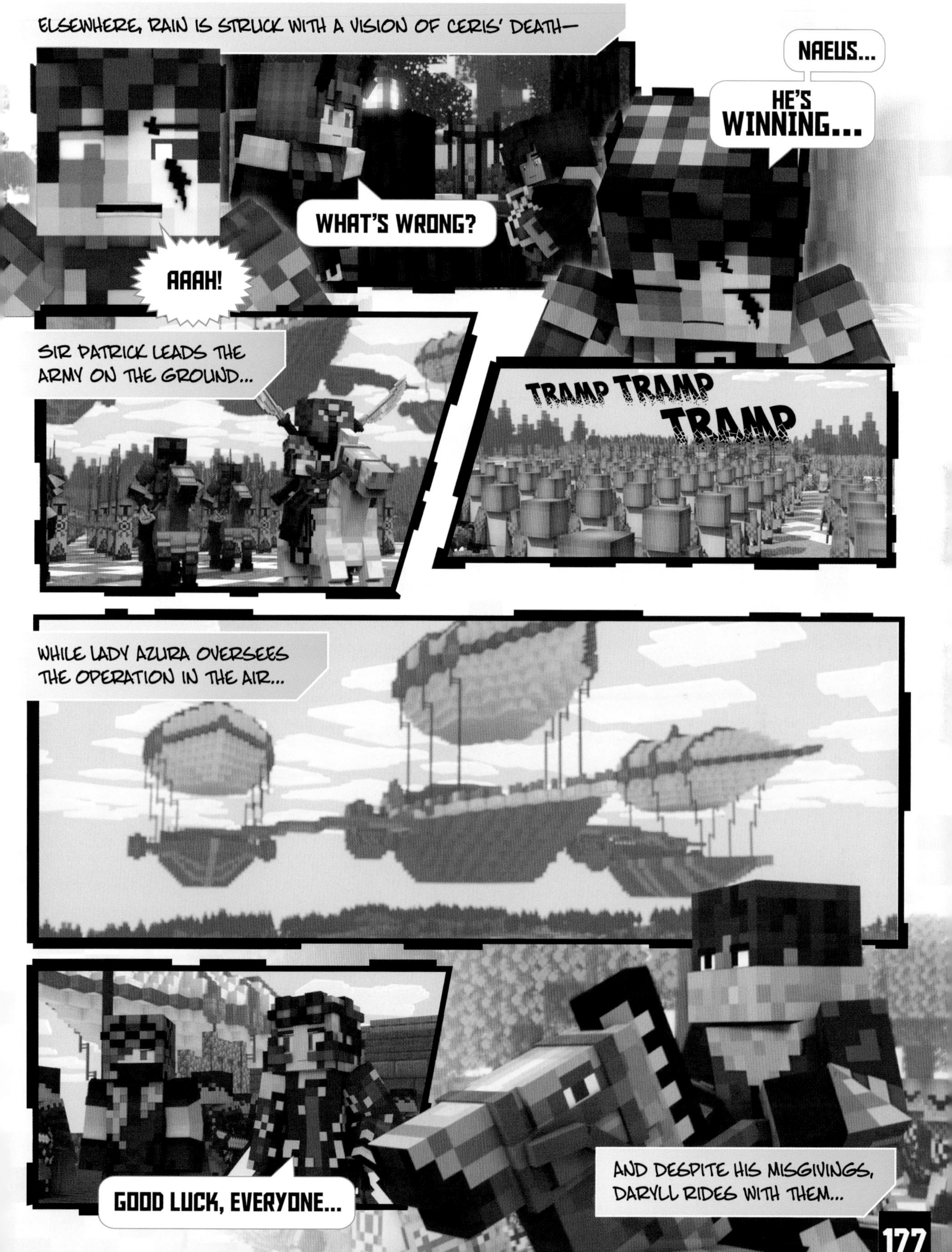
ELSEWHERE, RAIN IS STRUCK WITH A VISION OF CERIS' DEATH—
AAAH!
WHAT'S WRONG?
NAEUS...
HE'S WINNING...
SIR PATRICK LEADS THE ARMY ON THE GROUND...
TRAMP TRAMP TRAMP
WHILE LADY AZURA OVERSEES THE OPERATION IN THE AIR...
GOOD LUCK, EVERYONE...
AND DESPITE HIS MISGIVINGS, DARYLL RIDES WITH THEM...

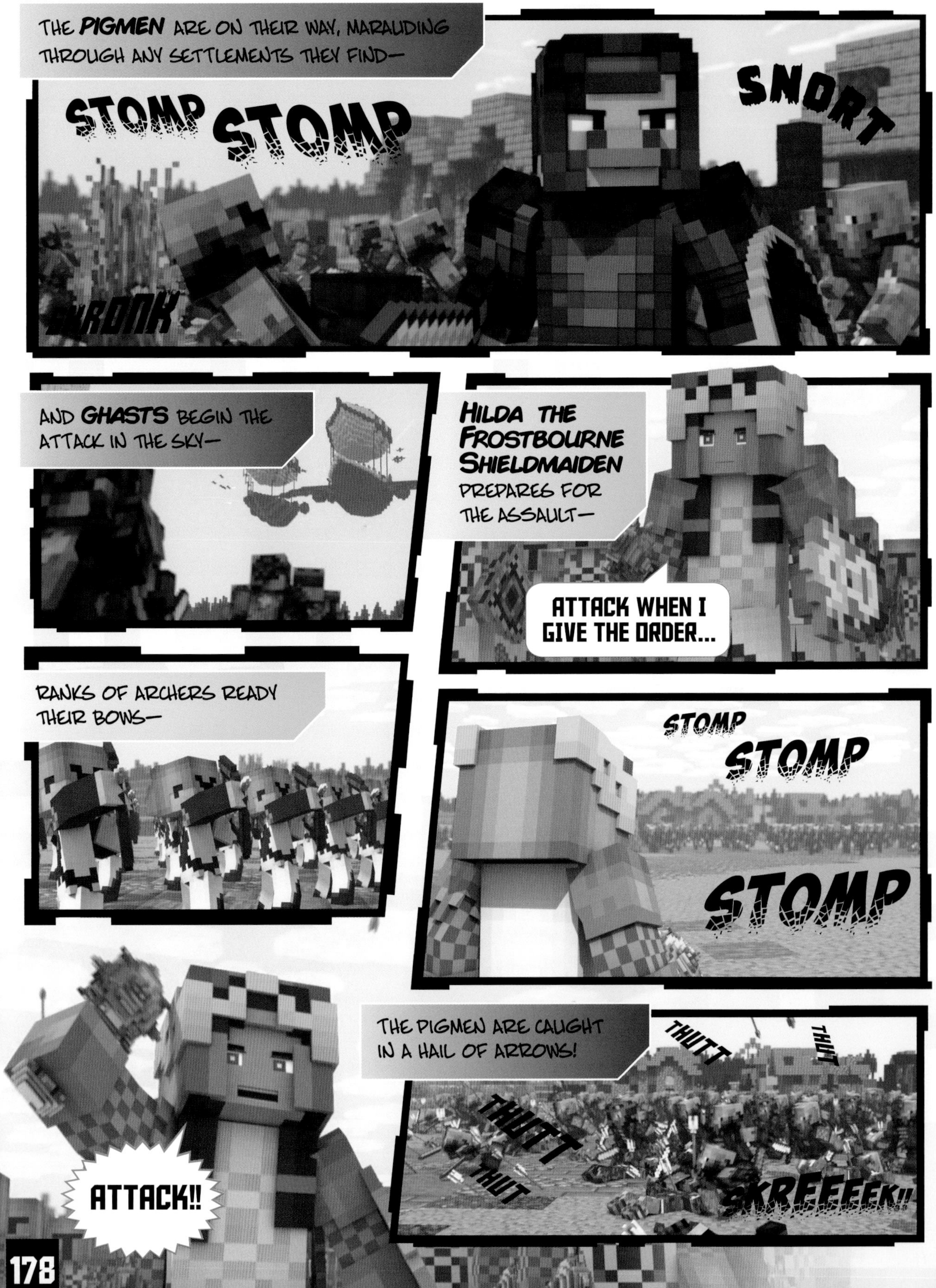

THE PIGMEN ARE ON THEIR WAY, MARAUDING THROUGH ANY SETTLEMENTS THEY FIND—
STOMP STOMP
SNORT
AND GHASTS BEGIN THE ATTACK IN THE SKY—
HILDA THE FROSTBOURNE SHIELDMAIDEN PREPARES FOR THE ASSAULT—
ATTACK WHEN I GIVE THE ORDER...
RANKS OF ARCHERS READY THEIR BOWS—
STOMP
STOMP
STOMP
ATTACK!!
THE PIGMEN ARE CAUGHT IN A HAIL OF ARROWS!
THUTT
THUT
THUTT
THUT
SKREEEEK!!

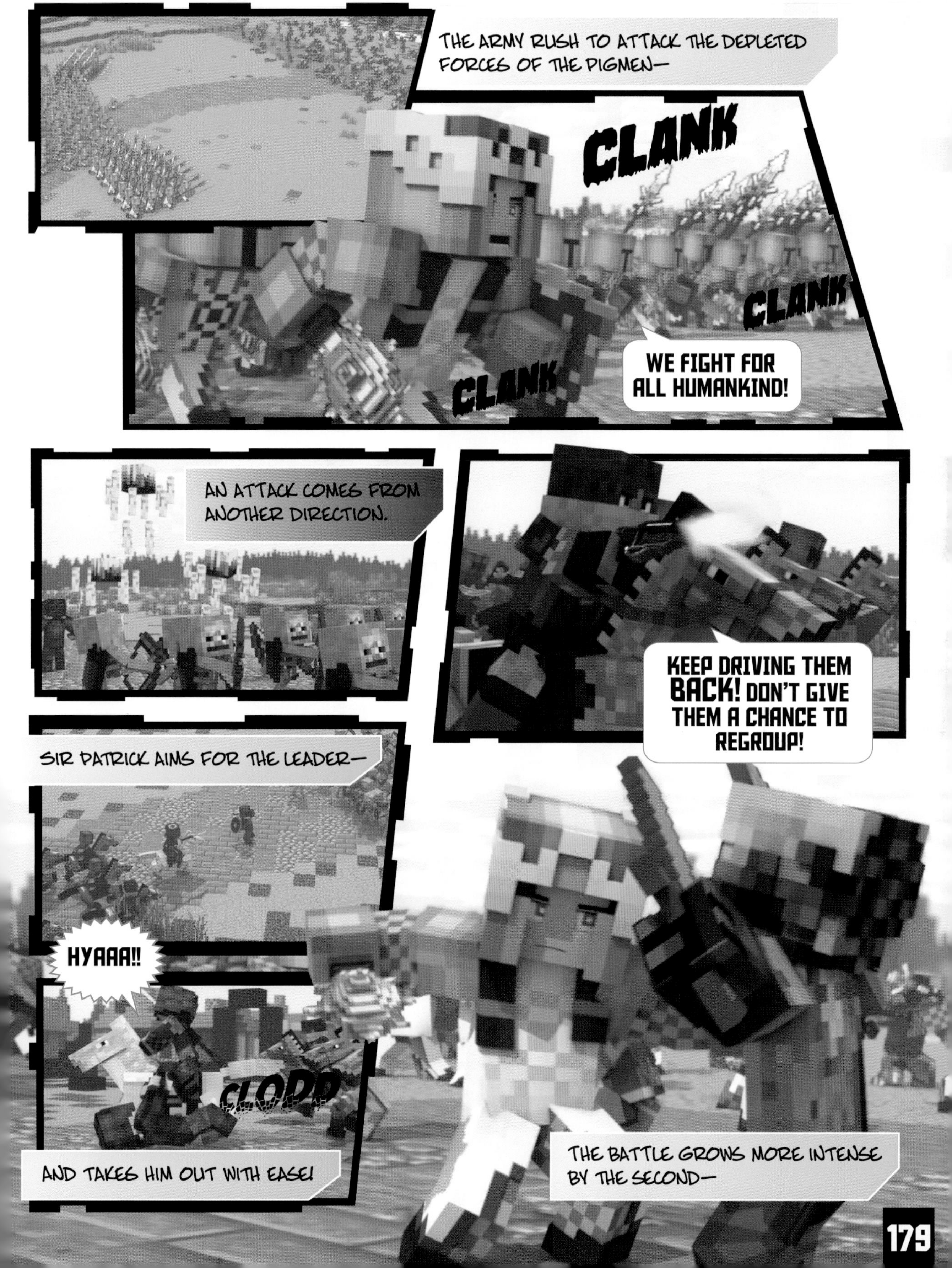
THE ARMY RUSH TO ATTACK THE DEPLETED FORCES OF THE PIGMEN—
CLANK
CLANK
CLANK
WE FIGHT FOR ALL HUMANKIND!
AN ATTACK COMES FROM ANOTHER DIRECTION.
KEEP DRIVING THEM BACK! DON'T GIVE THEM A CHANCE TO REGROUP!
SIR PATRICK AIMS FOR THE LEADER—
HYAAA!!
CLOPP
AND TAKES HIM OUT WITH EASE!
THE BATTLE GROWS MORE INTENSE BY THE SECOND—

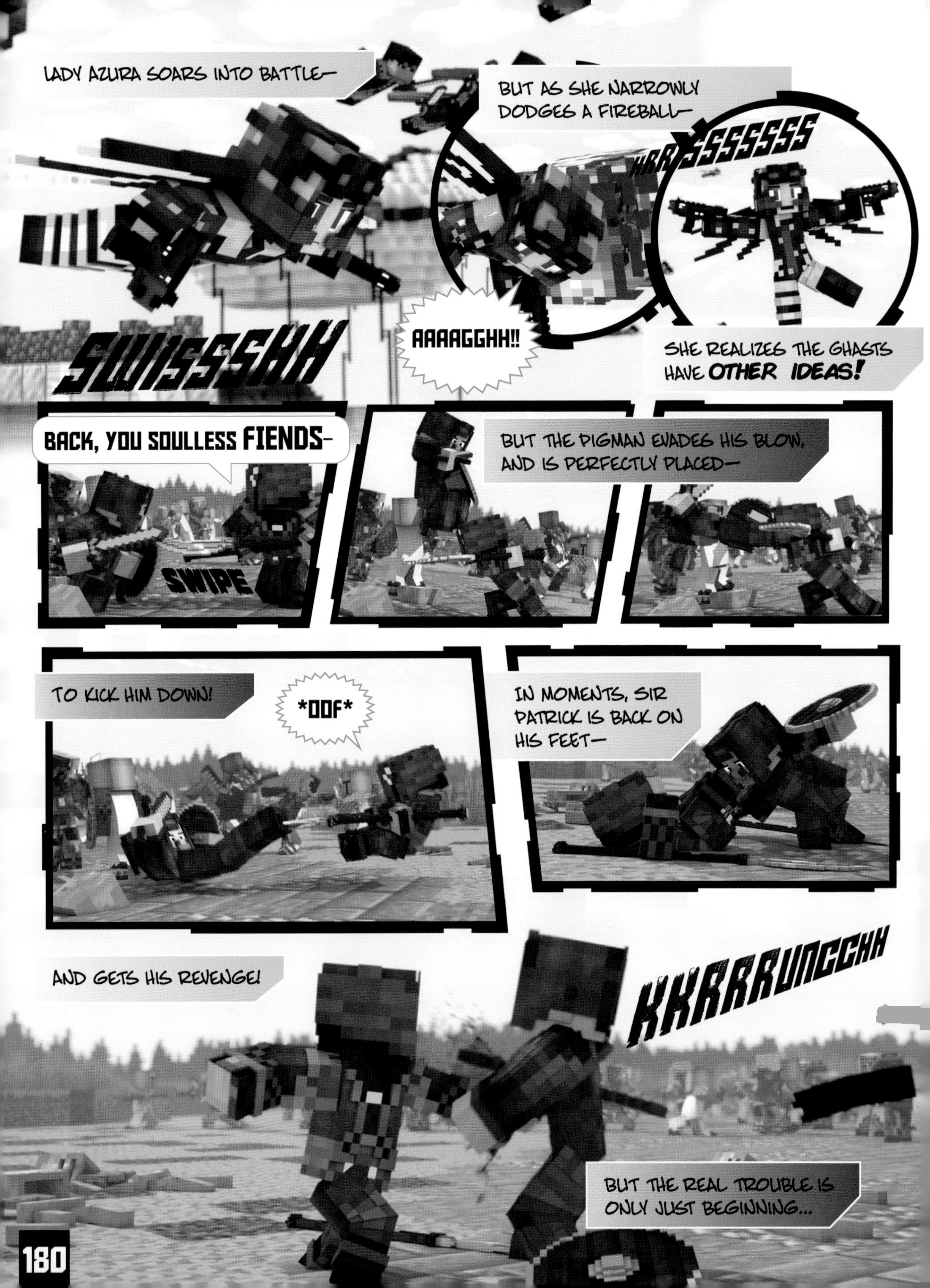

LADY AZURA SOARS INTO BATTLE—
BUT AS SHE NARROWLY DODGES A FIREBALL—
SWISSSHH
AAAAGGHH!!
SHE REALIZES THE GHASTS HAVE OTHER IDEAS!
BACK, YOU SOULLESS FIENDS—
SWIPE
BUT THE PIGMAN EVADES HIS BLOW, AND IS PERFECTLY PLACED—
TO KICK HIM DOWN!
OOF
IN MOMENTS, SIR PATRICK IS BACK ON HIS FEET—
AND GETS HIS REVENGE!
KKRRRUNCCHH
BUT THE REAL TROUBLE IS ONLY JUST BEGINNING...

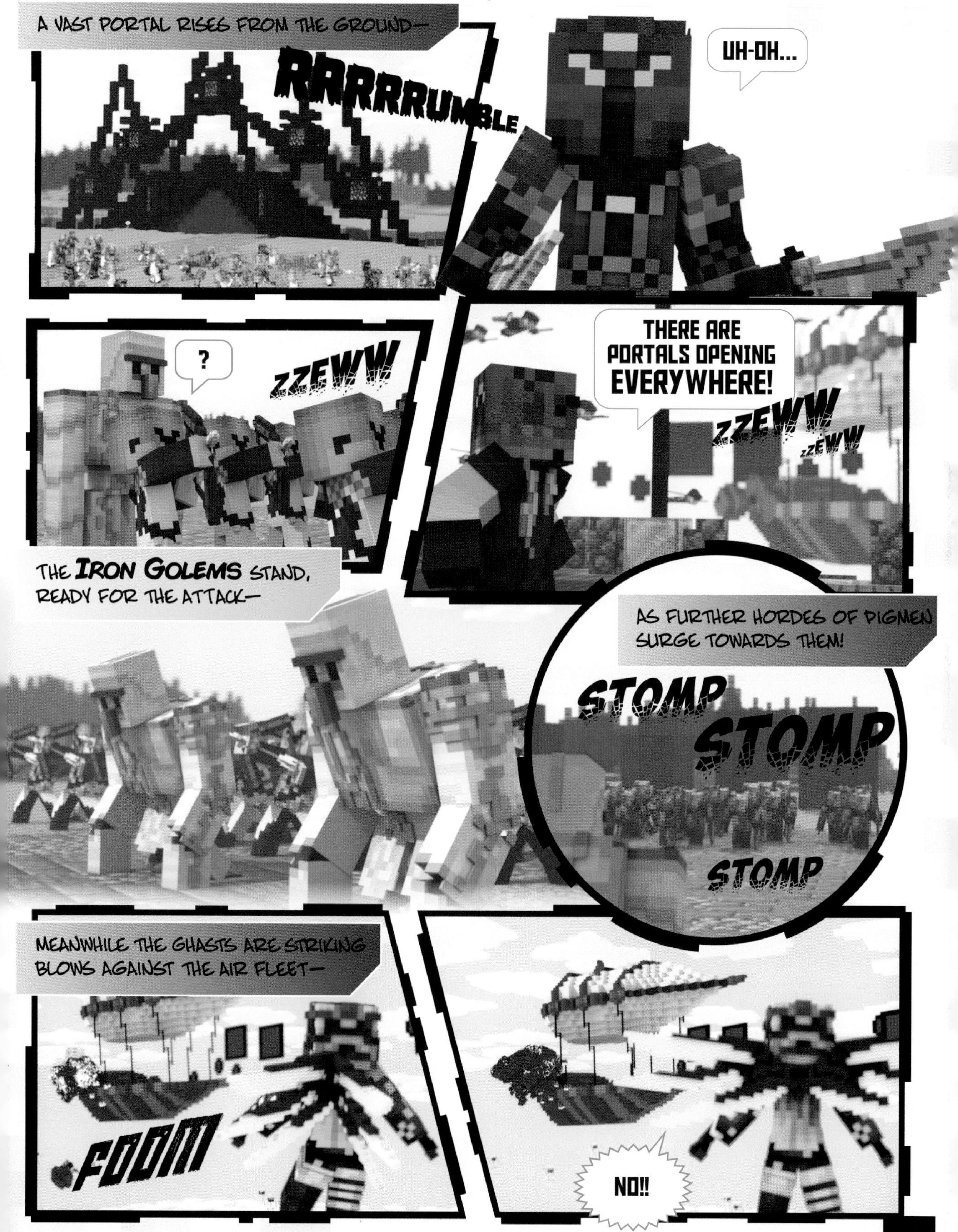
A VAST PORTAL RISES FROM THE GROUND—
RRRRRUMBLE
UH-OH...
?
ZZEWW
THERE ARE PORTALS OPENING EVERYWHERE!
ZZEWW
ZZEWW
THE IRON GOLEMS STAND, READY FOR THE ATTACK—
AS FURTHER HORDES OF PIGMEN SURGE TOWARDS THEM!
STOMP
STOMP
STOMP
MEANWHILE THE GHASTS ARE STRIKING BLOWS AGAINST THE AIR FLEET—
FOOM
NO!!

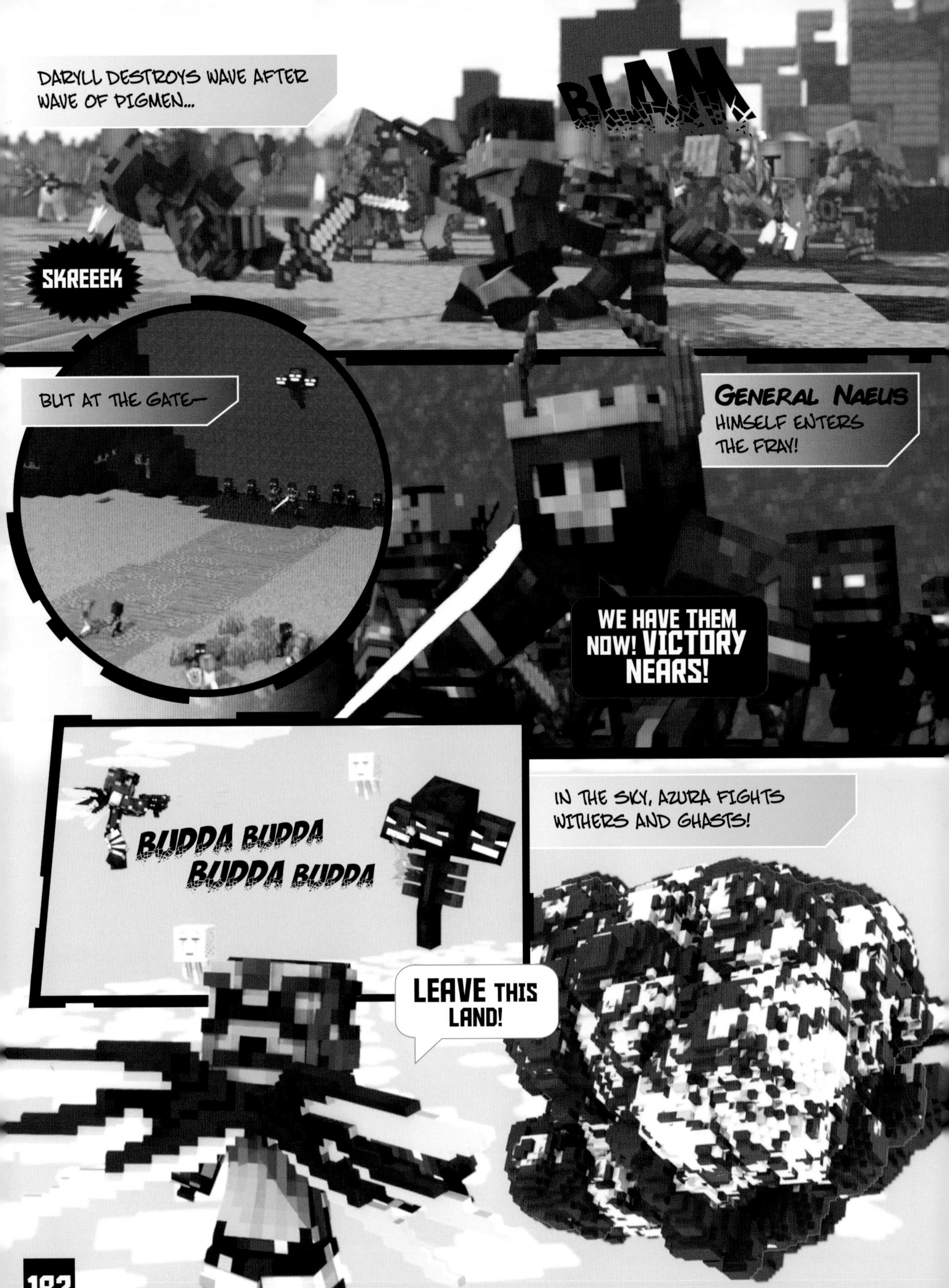
DARYLL DESTROYS WAVE AFTER WAVE OF PIGMEN...
BLAM!
SKREEEK
BUT AT THE GATE—
GENERAL NAEUS HIMSELF ENTERS THE FRAY!
WE HAVE THEM NOW! VICTORY NEARS!
BUDDA BUDDA BUDDA BUDDA
IN THE SKY, AZURA FIGHTS WITHERS AND GHASTS!
LEAVE THIS LAND!

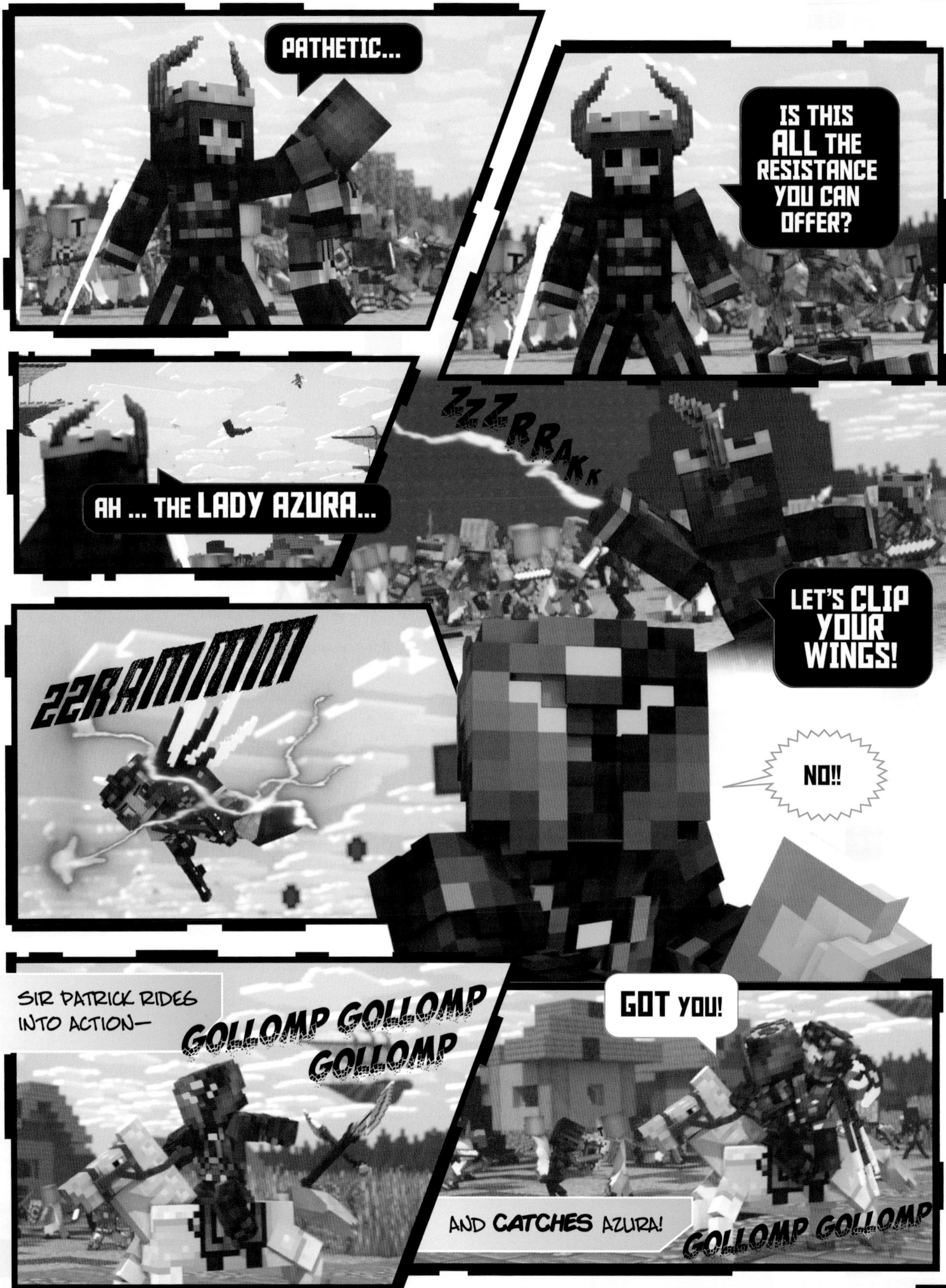
PATHETIC...
IS THIS ALL THE RESISTANCE YOU CAN OFFER?
AH ... THE LADY AZURA...
ZZZRRRAKK
LET'S CLIP YOUR WINGS!
ZZRAMMMM
NO!!
SIR PATRICK RIDES INTO ACTION—
GOLLOMP GOLLOMP GOLLOMP
GOT YOU!
AND CATCHES AZURA!
GOLLOMP GOLLOMP

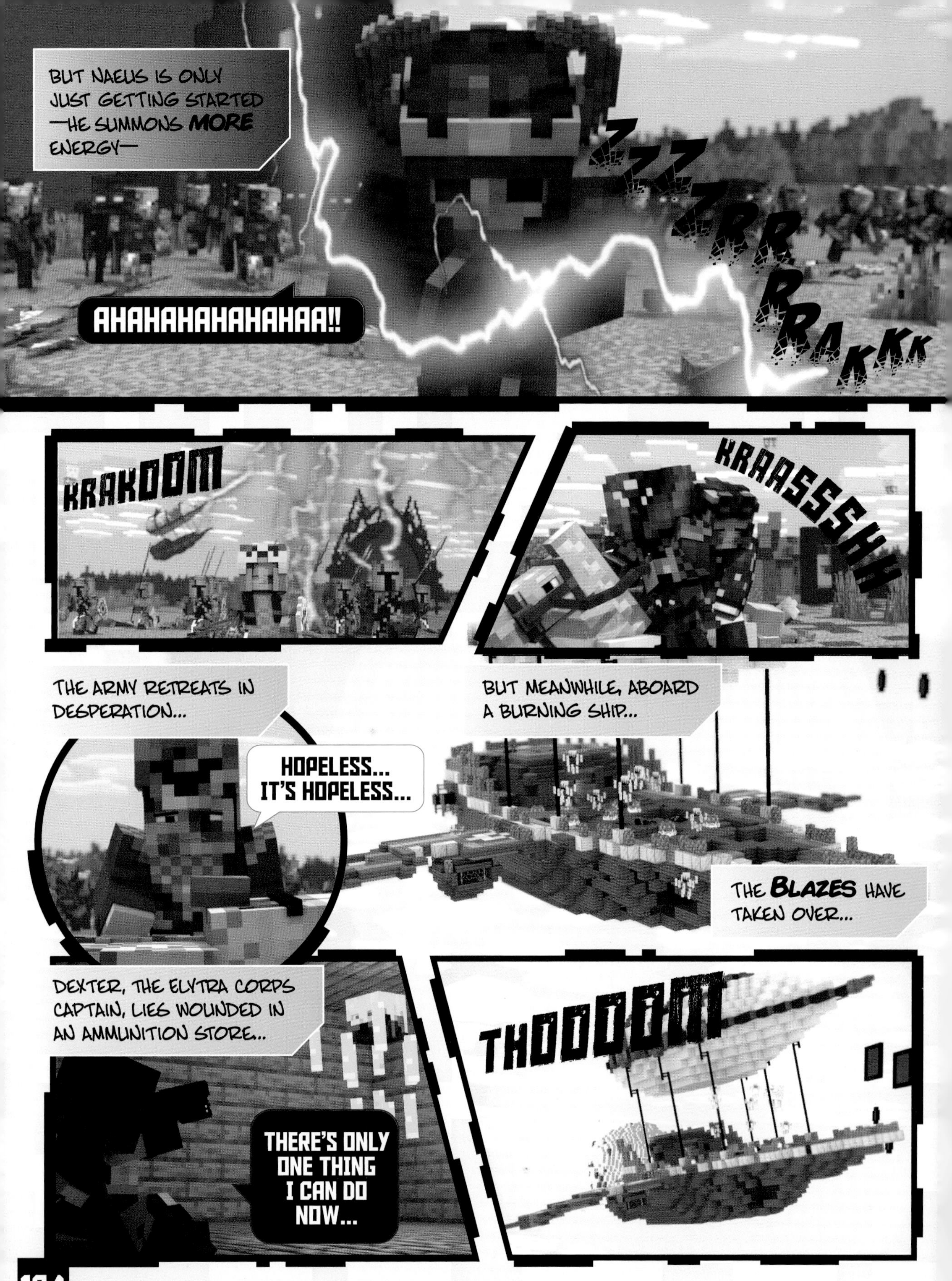
BUT NAEUS IS ONLY JUST GETTING STARTED —HE SUMMONS MORE ENERGY—
ZZZZRRRRRRAKKKK
AHAHAHAHAHAHAA!!
KRAKOOM
KRAASSSHH
THE ARMY RETREATS IN DESPERATION...
HOPELESS... IT'S HOPELESS...
BUT MEANWHILE, ABOARD A BURNING SHIP...
THE BLAZES HAVE TAKEN OVER...
DEXTER, THE ELYTRA CORPS CAPTAIN, LIES WOUNDED IN AN AMMUNITION STORE...
THERE'S ONLY ONE THING I CAN DO NOW...
THOOOOM

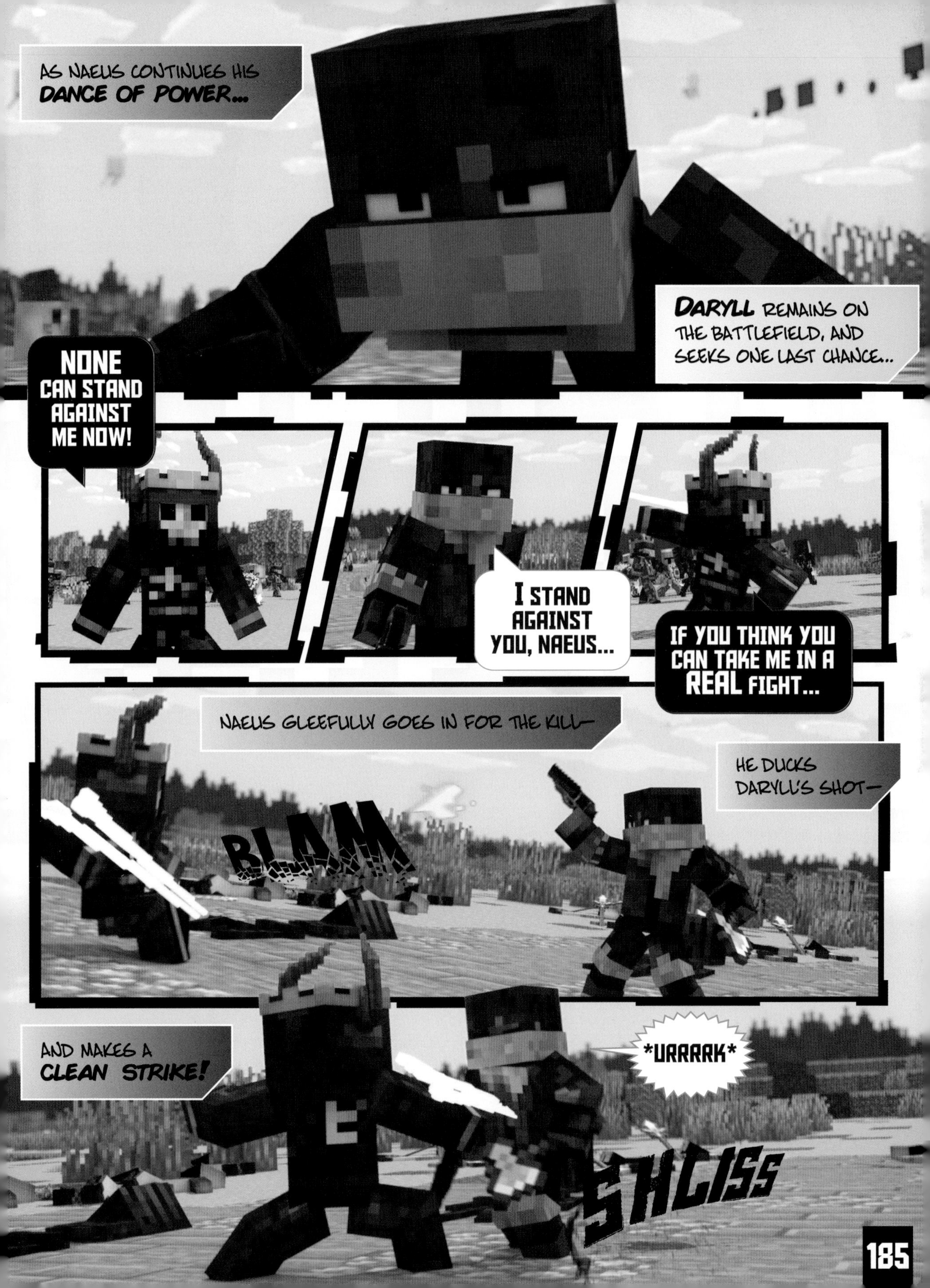

AS NAEUS CONTINUES HIS DANCE OF POWER...
DARYLL REMAINS ON THE BATTLEFIELD, AND SEEKS ONE LAST CHANCE...
NONE CAN STAND AGAINST ME NOW!
I STAND AGAINST YOU, NAEUS...
IF YOU THINK YOU CAN TAKE ME IN A REAL FIGHT...
NAEUS GLEEFULLY GOES IN FOR THE KILL—
HE DUCKS DARYLL'S SHOT—
BLAM
AND MAKES A CLEAN STRIKE!
URRRRK
SHLISS

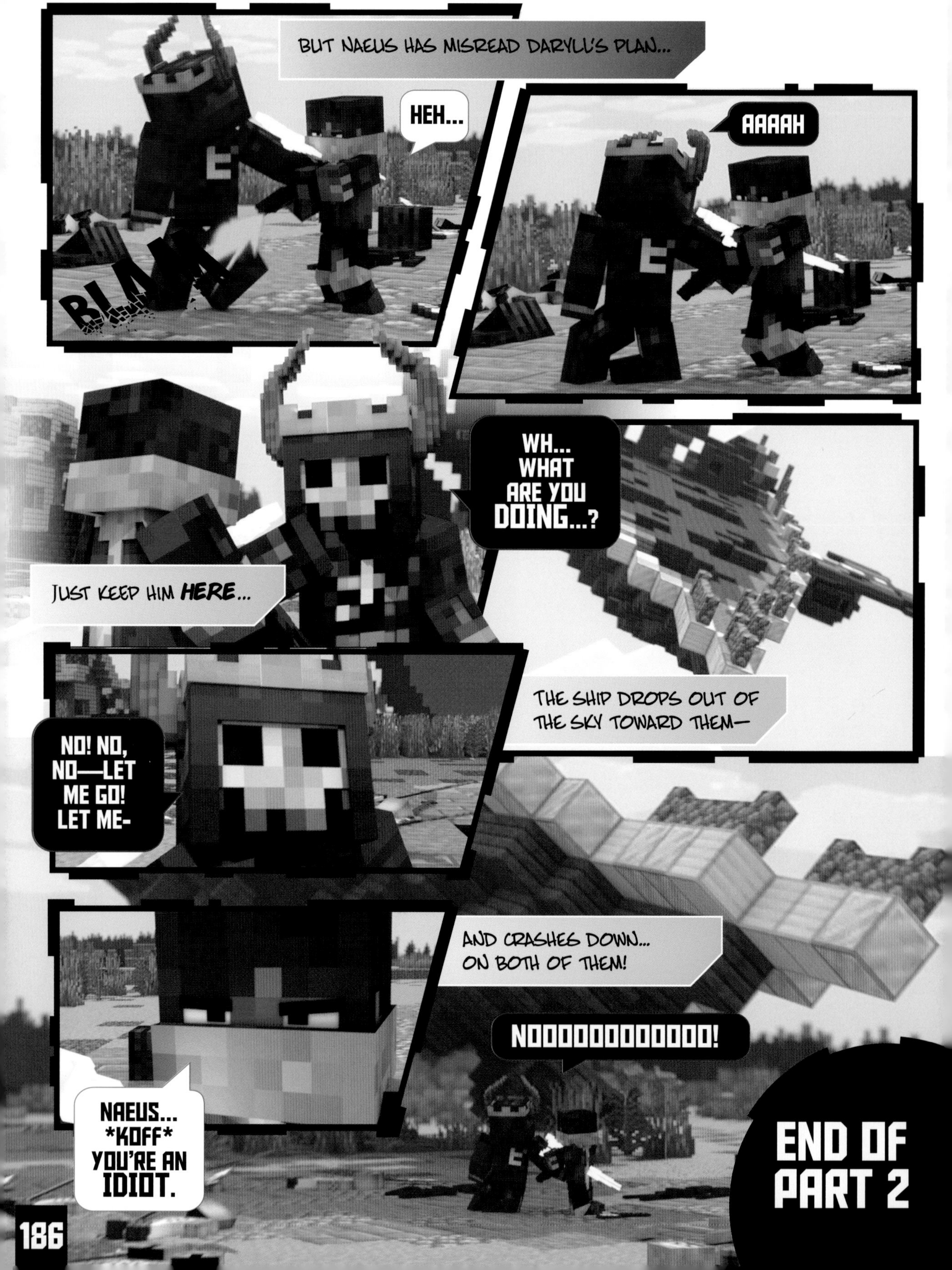
BUT NAEUS HAS MISREAD DARYLL'S PLAN...
HEH...
BLAM
AAAAH
WH... WHAT ARE YOU DOING...?
JUST KEEP HIM HERE...
THE SHIP DROPS OUT OF THE SKY TOWARD THEM—
NO! NO, NO—LET ME GO! LET ME-
AND CRASHES DOWN... ON BOTH OF THEM!
NOOOOOOOOOOOO!
NAEUS... *KOFF* YOU'RE AN IDIOT.
END OF PART 2

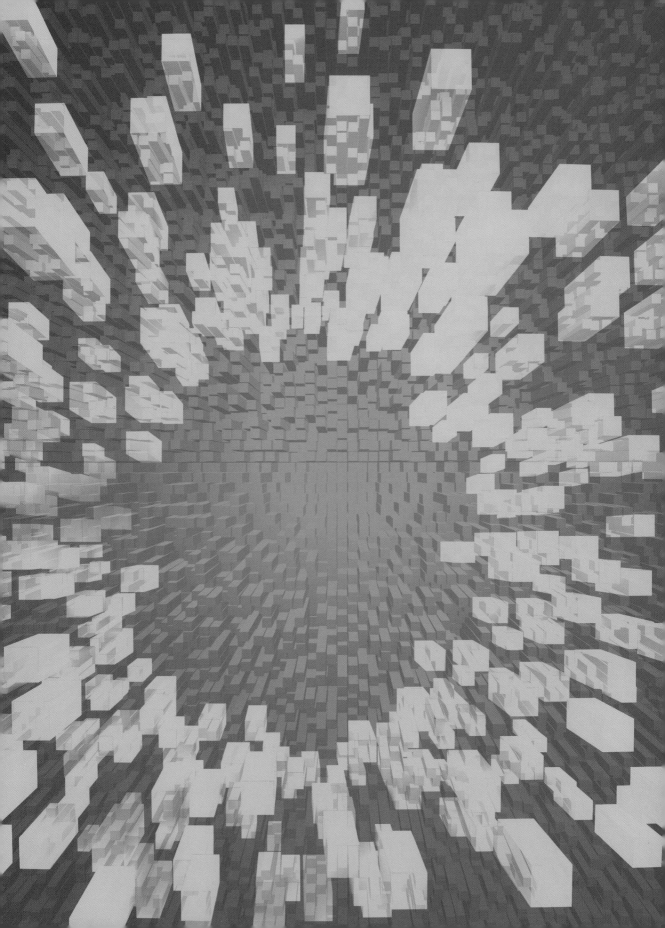

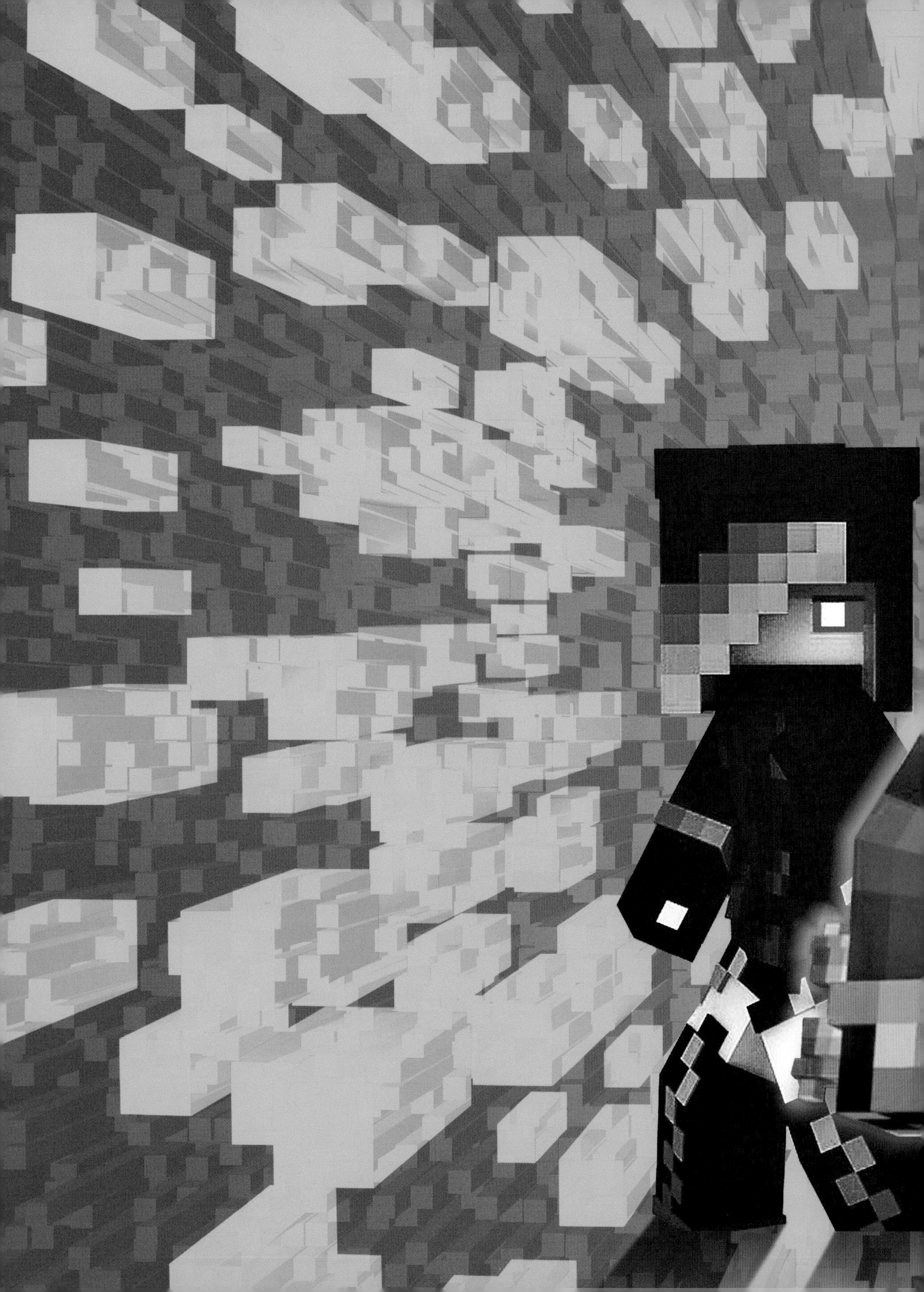

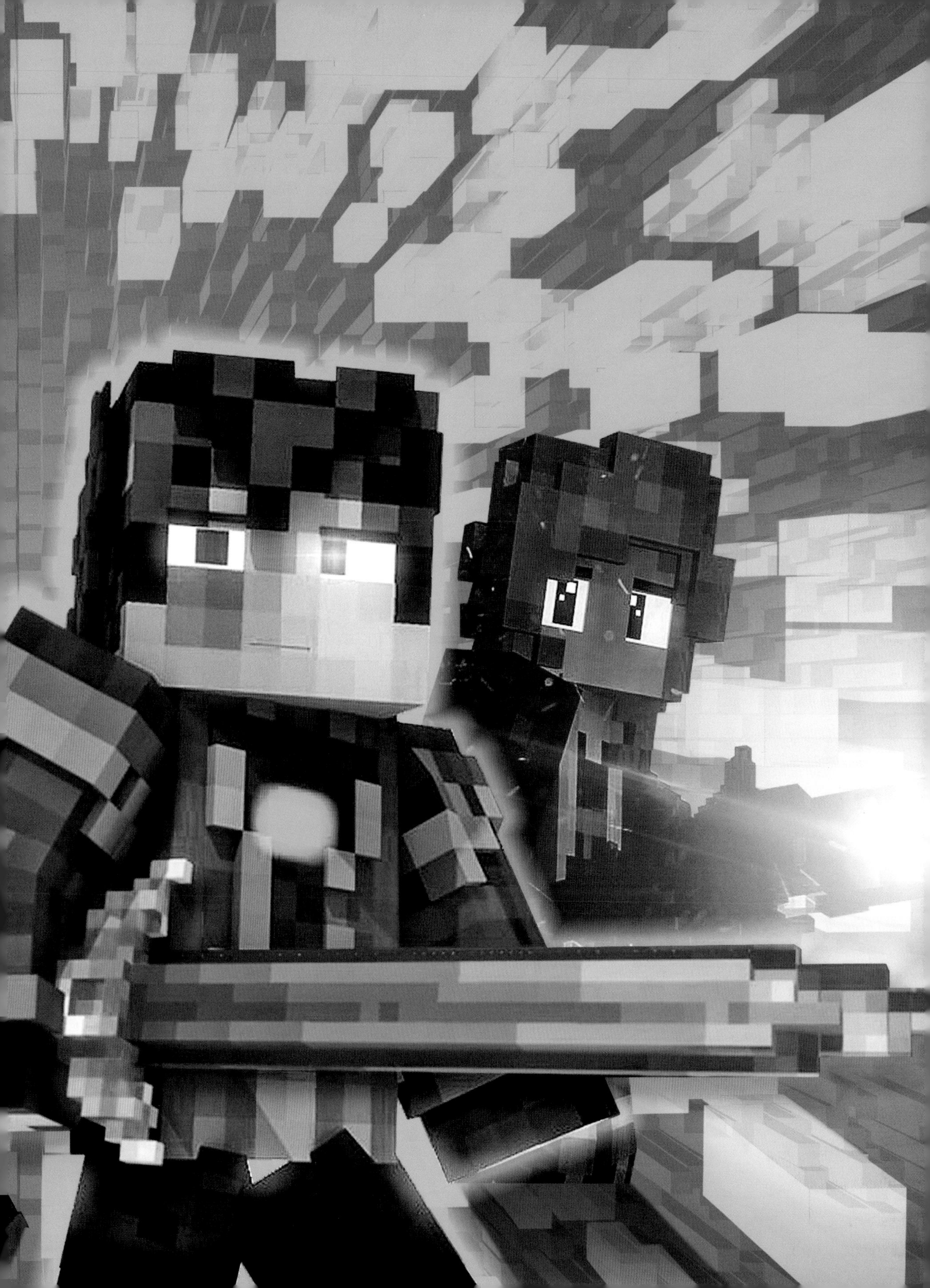

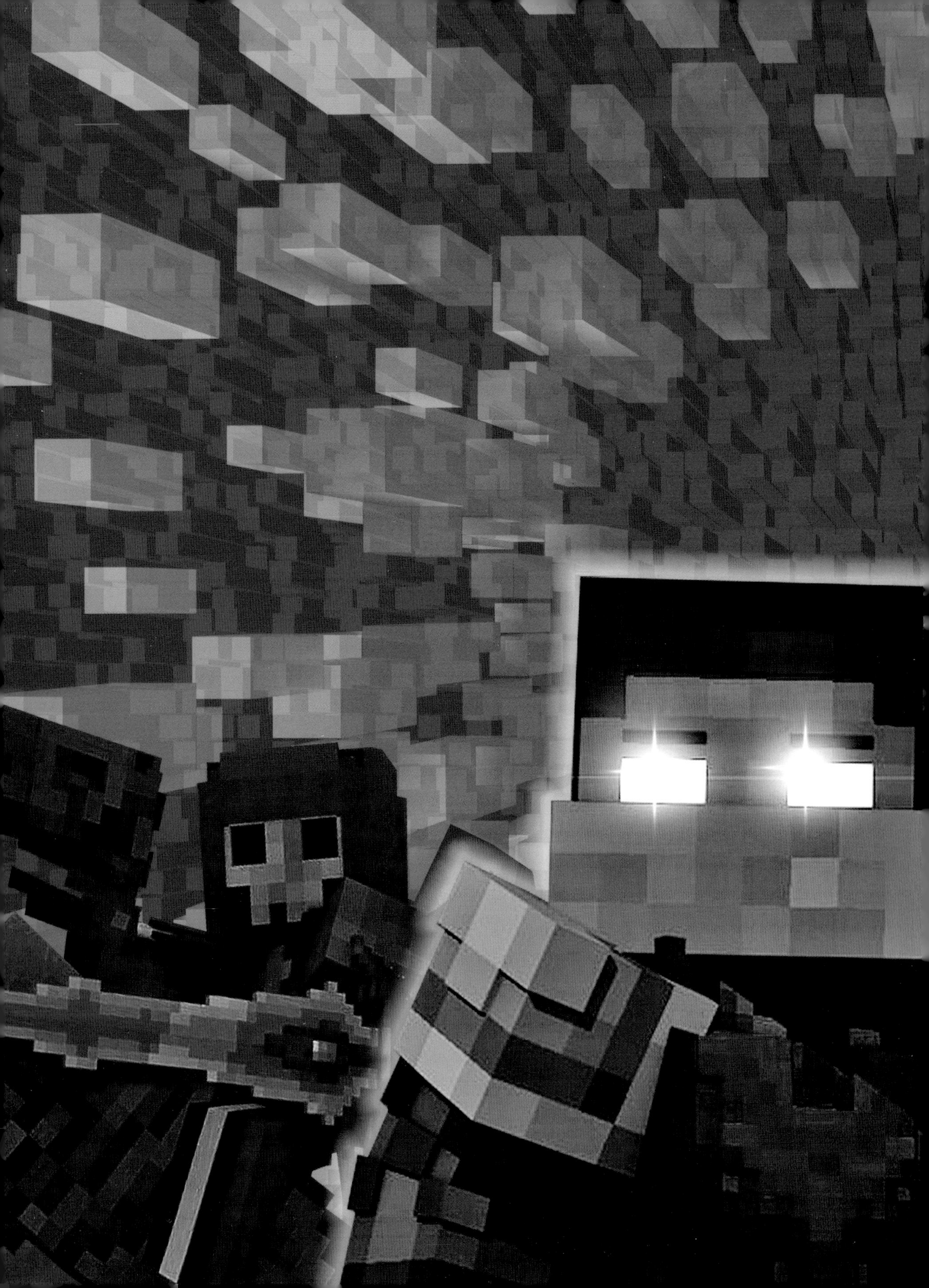